Praise for *Best Friends*

"First novels that track a pair of friends from college days through their subsequent lives aren't exactly uncommon, but Moody's is so freshly observed and gifted with such a palpable sense of the ravages of time that it feels utterly new. . . . The book never loses its edge, at once compassionate and humorous, nor its moving conviction that a strong friendship between women can be one of life's most powerful relationships."   —*Publishers Weekly* (starred review)

"[A] terrific novel . . . You'll definitely see elements of yourself and your girlfriends in this terrific novel. Like many close friends, Clare and Sally sometimes lose touch for months, but they can always depend on each other when times are tough. And isn't that what friendship is all about?"   —*Redbook*

"A valentine to the staying power of women's friendships."
—*The Cleveland Plain Dealer*

"Moody is brilliant at exposing just how emotionally and morally complex a friendship can be. As Clare and Sally survive their own illusions and sometimes desperate accommodations to what fate has in store, they test the limits of loyalty and the latitudes of forgiveness. The course of these paths as they twine and intertwine will enwrap you as well—I guarantee it. This book is a gift. Get it, give it!"
—Diane Vreuls, author of *Are We There Yet?*

"She captures the feel of things, the complexity of human lives, and the ability of time to expose and to heal. . . . Martha Moody's first novel, *Best Friends*, bodes well for the future of this talented novelist."
—Josephine Humphreys, author of *Nowhere Else on Earth*

Praise for *The Office of Desire*

"[Moody] writes with an easy style and a sure eye for the details of people's lives and passions." —*San Francisco Chronicle*

"Moody . . . understands how self-delusion and yearning can hurt. In *The Office of Desire,* she prescribes a remedy: when all seems lost, honesty and generosity can heal the broken heart."

—*The Hartford Courant*

"A bracingly dark comedy . . . Moody, a genuinely original voice, takes an unsentimental approach that never denies life's possibilities. A provocative, intensely moving novel of ideas and opposing philosophies presented by deeply flawed, deeply human characters."

—*Kirkus Reviews* (starred review)

"Sharply observed . . . Moody keeps things moving . . . and gets details right, whether adding up emotional balances, Prozac samples, or a patient's bill." —*Publishers Weekly*

SOMETIMES
MINE

MARTHA MOODY

RIVERHEAD BOOKS
New York

RIVERHEAD BOOKS
Published by the Penguin Group
Penguin Group (USA) Inc.
375 Hudson Street, New York, New York 10014, USA
Penguin Group (Canada), 90 Eglinton Avenue East, Suite 700, Toronto, Ontario M4P 2Y3, Canada
(a division of Pearson Penguin Canada Inc.)
Penguin Books Ltd., 80 Strand, London WC2R 0RL, England
Penguin Group Ireland, 25 St. Stephen's Green, Dublin 2, Ireland (a division of Penguin Books Ltd.)
Penguin Group (Australia), 250 Camberwell Road, Camberwell, Victoria 3124, Australia
(a division of Pearson Australia Group Pty. Ltd.)
Penguin Books India Pvt. Ltd., 11 Community Centre, Panchsheel Park, New Delhi—110 017, India
Penguin Group (NZ), 67 Apollo Drive, Rosedale, North Shore 0632, New Zealand
(a division of Pearson New Zealand Ltd.)
Penguin Books (South Africa) (Pty.) Ltd., 24 Sturdee Avenue, Rosebank, Johannesburg 2196,
South Africa

Penguin Books Ltd., Registered Offices: 80 Strand, London WC2R 0RL, England

First Riverhead hardcover edition: August 2009
First Riverhead trade paperback edition: May 2010
Riverhead trade paperback ISBN: 978-1-59448-468-1

The Library of Congress has catalogued the Riverhead hardcover edition as follows:

Moody, Martha.
Sometimes mine / Martha Moody.
p. cm.
ISBN 978-1-59448-870-2
1. Middle-aged women—Fiction.   2. Care of the sick—Fiction.   3. Friendship—Fiction.
I. Title.
PS3563.O553S66   2009   2009010321
813.'54—dc 22

PRINTED IN THE UNITED STATES OF AMERICA

10   9   8   7   6   5   4   3   2

FOR MART
my always

FOR TWELVE YEARS I loved a man I knew to be somebody's husband. I didn't think of him as a husband. I thought of him as my fated one, my true and perfect heart. His name was Mick Crabbe. If you care about college basketball, you'll already know part of our story. Mick Crabbe was for fifteen years the head men's basketball coach at Turkman State in West Virginia. Under him, the Warriors went from being a conference and community embarrassment to being a cohesive group that made two credible runs, in Mick's final years of coaching, at the NCAA title. Roger Fenster, Keevon Simpkins, Eluard Dickens: these are some of Mick's Turkman State alumni. If you follow pro basketball, you'll recognize these names.

My name is Genie Toledo. This is a name you won't recognize. I'm a cardiologist, divorced with one grown daughter, in private practice in a suburb of Columbus, Ohio. My two most distinguishing characteristics are that I'm short and that I'm driven. My two younger brothers are each eight inches taller than I am, and they are not tall men. "A pint-sized young lady with a gallon-sized brain," my principal said before my valedictory speech in high school. I was the first female to make it through the cardiology fellowship at Columbus General. My original partner in Suburban Heart Associates, Jeremy Greathouse (the two of us brought in Howard later on), went through the same fellowship I did, and according to him, when people heard my heels clicking down the hall someone would almost always say, "Holy torpedo, it's Genie Toledo."

"And then people would smile," Jeremy added.

"Was this affection?" I asked, startled, wondering if my shoes were really that noisy. Probably so. From a young age I've been aware that serious shoes and clothes are key to gaining respect. A short woman has no fashion leeway.

"I think so," Jeremy said, tilting his long head. "Yes, definitely. Because you were kind of a figure." In that moment I could almost see myself as others did: a tiny woman with a big head of dark brown curls, throwing open charts and tossing out questions and barreling through doors.

IT WAS A SATURDAY in early February 2000 when I almost lost a patient in the cardiac angiography suite. No one loses a patient in the cath lab, but I almost did, that day. People may not believe this, but doctors are normal people: they remember their failures and their almost-failures over everything else they do.

"Genie," Raj the pulmonologist said, waiting for me at the door of the hospital's doctors' lounge. "I knew I heard you." He glanced at my shoes and held open the door.

"Tough cath," I said, walking into the lounge, my hand hesitating above the platter of doughnuts at the entrance. Doctors' lounges resemble the lobbies of chain hotels: chairs and sofas in tasteful neutrals, with a burst of color from the TV hanging in the corner. "I wish they'd bring back those pecan rolls," I said. "I love those pecan rolls. Yeah, my lady coded. V-tach."

"Get her back?"

I nodded, and bit down on a frosted doughnut with a creamy filling. "Seven years younger than me too. Forty. It worked out. I got the stent in. It wasn't even a major vessel. The spooky thing was when I was putting in the wire I said, *Maybe we could treat this with pills, but as long as I'm in here I'm going to open it,* and she said, *Good, you get me cured,* and then, kaboom, I inflate the balloon and she's out."

"That's the great thing about bronchoscopies, my patients can't talk." Raj sat down and turned up the volume on the TV, used the remote to run through the channels.

"Her name's Nola. Pretty name, isn't it? She said it means 'little bell.'" I was talking too much, but I did that after a scare. Raj stopped the channel-changing at basketball, and a familiar announcer's voice broke in: ". . . and once again you've got to credit Mick Crabbe for the amazing things he's done and just keeps doing with this . . ."

Mickey? That late already? I checked my watch. 2:05 P.M. That late. "You watching much college basketball this year, Raj?"

"Of course." Raj laughed apologetically. He was even younger than my patient Nola, and had done his fellowship at Duke. "This is a good game here." He nodded at the screen. "Walthrop U is always good, and Turkman went to the Sweet

Sixteen last year, and the question is whether they can do it again. Good coach."

"I think I recognize him," I said. Mick looked ordinary, in a boyish (although he was fifty-one), old jock sort of way. When I first described him to my friend Tessa I was reluctant to use the word "handsome," in case she, seeing him later, would smile at my description. Instead I told her about Mick's ruffled light brown hair (not a hint of baldness, he was vain about this), his pink, almost shapely lips and Paul Newman eyes. He was big next to me—six foot one—but short compared with his players. In the eleven years I'd known him, he was constantly fighting a paunch. "Look at this," he'd say one week, squeezing the fleshy part of his belly between his two hands, "I can do the jiggle dance!"—and a few weeks later he'd be turning himself sideways for me to ooh and ahh over his silhouette.

"His name's Mick Crabbe," Raj told me. "Very smart. He recruits these kids nobody thinks are very good, and then he motivates them somehow, and they get great. No one knows how he does it."

I knew how he did it, sort of. He found kids who didn't think anyone would be looking, who didn't expect to be found, and through discipline and cajoling and belief shaped them into people who felt useful. There were certain kids he simply recognized, understood, after a few moments of watching them, what they yearned for, what they feared. The spark and the dark, Mick called it.

"Oh!" Raj said. "Damn, damn, damn." He turned to me. "Did you see that? Turkman just got the ball to their forward, he was totally open, but he missed the shot and Walthrop got the rebound." Raj had come to the United States when he was in his twenties. I wondered if he'd followed basketball in India.

The forward's name was Tom Kennilworth. He was a married sophomore with a child, and a week ago he'd told Mick he was thinking of leaving his wife for his English tutor. Since then, Mick had been trying to get the tutor changed. Kennilworth was Turkman's only white starter and his tutor was black: a twist in the story, I thought. I would have liked to tell Raj.

Someone on the Walthrop team made a three-pointer, and Raj hit his forehead with his palm. Frederick Flitt, the Turkman point guard, took the ball to Turkman's end of the court and passed it around, finally getting it to their center, Eluard Dickens, just under the basket, but instead of taking a shot Dickens passed it out to Kennilworth, the forward who'd just missed. Kennilworth arced this one through the basket: three points.

"Oh!" Raj said, throwing his arms up and closing his eyes and paddling his feet on the floor. "The unselfishness of that guy!"

"You mean Dickens?" I said. Raj nodded emphatically, and I wished that I could tell him why Eluard Dickens was not a player to be admired. At the same time I felt a pang that was close to jealousy, because if there was one thing that scared me, it wasn't Mick's wife or children or team or even the sport of basketball, it was Mick's affection—his devotion—to a certain type of player, a player whose focus was not personal glory or statistics but the success of the team itself. Mick would not use the word "unselfish" for Eluard Dickens—Eluard was a disappointment—but he used it all the time in that sense for his point guard, Frederick Flitt. I often felt uncomfortable when Mick talked about

Frederick. He might have been going on and on about some woman, making it clearer with each compliment that I, while a good person, was not in the same league.

The game went on. "I should go home," Raj said, not moving.

"I should too," I said, although there was no one for me to go home to. *Unselfish*—I wondered if anyone ever used that word for me. Maybe. Probably. Locally, I was a respected cardiologist. Most nights my heels clicked through the hospital halls until sometime after eight. Some nights I barely slept. I often told my elderly patients, who worried most about my being alone, that any man not married to me was lucky.

At halftime the Turkman State Warriors were leading by two points, and I left Raj to watch the rest of the game by himself. Another one of Raj's new cars—a red Corvette with PULMODOC, for "pulmonary doctor," plates—was parked in the doctors' lot next to my Honda, and I walked sideways to my door so I wouldn't touch it.

At home, I switched on the TV. Claudia had finally moved out, gotten an apartment for her final year of college, although her collection of ceramic frogs still sat on the mantel. Claudia had declared a major in marketing recently, which was a shame, I thought, for a pretty girl with a kind heart. But everything these days was a business. I knew Claudia, who would always prefer hanging out with her friends to studying, would never be a candidate for medical school, but what about nursing or physical therapy? "Why should I do anything in health care?" Claudia had said, her face flushing as it always did when she disagreed with me. "Health care eats you up."

Eluard Dickens had been fouled and was standing at the free-throw line. I wished for the umpteenth time that I understood fouls better. I would get a lot more enjoyment from a game, I thought, if I understood fouling on a deep level. A few times Mick had agreed to watch a game with me in our hotel room so he could explain the arcana, but that had never lasted long.

Eluard missed the first shot. The camera flashed to Mick and I sat up straighter. Mick's mouth was a line and he was looking straight ahead. He'd said on the phone the night before that he might be getting a cold, but why was he just sitting there? The camera peered up at Eluard as he made his second shot. He was a handsome guy, with dark skin, a broad flat face, and eyes that always looked like they were searching for something. This time his shot went through the basket. A Walthrop player took the ball out-of-bounds, and the game was back on.

I stood up until the game ended, there in the family room of my enormous house that backed onto a golf course, try-ing to catch another glimpse of Mick, as if by standing I could look into the TV and see things outside a sitting viewer's range. Mick's cellphone number was programmed into my phone, and the instant this game and the postgame interviews and Mick's obligatory fifteen minutes with his team were finished I'd dial his number. Turkman State won, 74–69, and Mick should look happy, he should have that relaxed face, that thrown-back-shoulders walk, he should hug his players, shake the opposing coach's hand with firm graciousness. He was doing these things, but something was wrong: his step was slower than usual, and his face was caved in on itself like a partially deflated balloon.

It was rare to see Mick unhappy. Once he told me that before he went to sleep each night he ran through a mental list of his players—not in prayer, exactly, but as a way of wishing them well. My name was on that list too. He believed in positive thinking. Missed buses, delayed flights, canceled games—when something unfortunate happened, Mick always said it wasn't the end of the world. "We had extra time to go over the tapes," he'd say, or "The guys played poker in the airport, had a really good time," or "I finally got some sleep"—and then the closing, his mantra: "It all worked out." Always, things worked out for Mick. What other people might take as a setback or failure, Mick took as a step toward working out. "A loss can be your best friend," he often said. I read somewhere that the Chinese think of luck as a character trait, like stubbornness or generosity. It seemed to me that Mick believed so fervently in luck that he brought it on himself. At some point during our years together, I started thinking I was lucky too.

My beeper went off. I always kept my beeper close—clipped to my pocket or waistband, or attached to the strap of my handbag—and set to the vibrate mode, because I hated calling attention to myself with beeping. I looked at the message tickertaping through the window:

JEFFERSON CAROTHERS: NEEDS REFILL

followed by the patient's phone number.

I hated med refill requests. A weekend refill meant two phone calls—one to the patient and one to the pharmacy—and listening to a lot of explaining. I reached for the phone on the coffee table, but before I could pick it up it started ringing. "Hello?" I said, muting the TV, and the abruptness in my voice startled me, made me tell myself to calm down. "Mickey?"

But it wasn't Mickey. Mickey was on TV talking to Elaine Johnson of ESPN, who always, I thought, looked at him a little too intently. "She stares at you like a dog," I complained to him once. "She's not a dog at all," he answered, grinning.

The person on the phone was my manicurist, telling me she was pulling into my driveway for her weekly housecall (four P.M. Saturday). "Just walk in," I said. My beeper buzzed again:

CALL 4-NORTH: ORDERS

Mr. Carothers's sister was visiting from Illinois, and first he didn't think about his pills, then he . . . On the screen in front of me Mick's forehead gave a twitch. *My God, Mick,* I thought, *are you feeling okay?* Every cardiac disease scenario I knew ran through my head. A thought almost made me gasp: *Mick, how could I live without you?* "Wait a minute, wait a minute," Mr. Carothers said. "I've got to find the pharmacy number here. . . ." My beeper went off again.

MAURINE SCOTT: STRANGE THROBBING

I scribbled on my palm the number Mr. Carothers gave me. The beeper buzzed again:

GLENDA ZAHLLER: BLOOD PRESSURE LOW

and I could hear Angela shut the front door behind her, and Elaine Johnson was addressing the camera. Mick was gone and I'd missed what he said and I was swearing at myself for not taping it, and then somehow I had called in Mr. Carothers's prescription and ordered a blood thinner for a patient on 4-North, and I was on the phone again, listening to Mrs. Scott describe her throbbing—which was less in her chest than in her abdomen, and maybe was worse after eating—as Angela unfolded her little table and set out her implements. "On call this weekend, hunh?" Angela whispered, making a sympathetic pout. I gave her my free hand.

THOMAS DINGLE: QUESTION RE MEDS

ANNA WAKOSKI: BP 220/180 AND DIZZY

NICKI LEWIS: NEEDS REFILL

MEGAN WECKSTEIN: POSSIBLE STROKE

3-WEST: PT ALLERGY

"Busy day, hunh?" Angela said, pointing at the number on my palm. She went to my kitchen and came back with a slip of blank paper.

I ended up sending Strange Throbbing to the ER, and also Glenda Zahller, because both of them were my partner Howard's patients and I didn't feel safe making diagnoses on the phone. Howard was a mediocre cardiologist: who knew what pathology he'd missed or discounted? I privately referred to Howard as my unfortunate partner. Calls from his patients were like grenades I had to step elaborately around. The other calls were from my own or Jeremy's patients (I trusted Jeremy, my other partner: we'd known each other since we were med students) and easier to take care of. I made each person promise to call again if what I'd suggested didn't work.

"It wasn't bad until half an hour ago," I told Angela, who had finished her massaging and soaking and cuticle clipping and was now painting my nails their usual In the Pink. Could I call Mick yet? I wondered, glancing at the time on my beeper. "I'm supposed to meet my daughter for dinner at six."

Another buzz as I was talking to Mr. Lewis's pharmacist, and a message from a patient I didn't know:

PHILIP MERCER: SEVERE CHEST PAINS

"Shit," I said to Angela, removing my right hand from under her drying light and carefully reaching for the phone. "I may not get to dinner at all."

B UT AN HOUR LATER I was at dinner, surprisingly, because Philip Mercer, who was Jeremy's patient, actually had inactive heart disease but active lung cancer eroding his ribs, and he was only calling for a cardiologist because his oncologist wasn't answering his page. Mr. Mercer wanted to know if he could up his dose of morphine. I told him yes. "Thanks, doc," he said. "You saved my life."

"At least you haven't had to go back to the hospital," Claudia said at the door of the restaurant. Her round face was rosy from the cold and she was wearing a knit striped hat that made her look like a child, although she was twenty-one years old. She had my curly hair and her father's fairer coloring. When she walked her toes pointed slightly inward, which gave her a wiggly bounce. "Adorable," people always said about her.

"Not yet." I followed Claudia inside, to a dark room where the tables were topped with checkerboard linoleum, and all manner of battered road signs and farm implements hung on the walls. Claudia and I liked the hamburgers at this restaurant. "Shoot," I said, reaching for my beeper, seeing another name I didn't know:

WILMA EDWARDS: CAN'T BREATHE

"It may be nothing," I said. "I just called a severe chest pain and it was nothing." God, I was thinking, I hope it's someone of Jeremy's. I reached into my handbag for my cellphone, careful of my new nails, and pushed my menu to the center of the table. "You order for me."

Wilma Edwards was sick. Wilma Edwards was eighty-four and a diabetic and Howard's (damn it, damn it) patient, and the shortness of breath had hit her while she was watching the home and garden channel. It took a while to get this out of her, because every few words she interrupted herself with a wheeze. She hadn't had chest pain, but a diabetic can have a heart attack without chest pain. I told Wilma Edwards to call 911.

"I may have to leave," I told the waitress. "Can you put a rush on this?"

MATTHEW MONEY: PALPITATIONS

"Here," Claudia said, handing me a bookstore plastic bag. "Before it's too late."

"Oh God," I said. "It's not a Tessa book, is it?" For years my friend Tessa Fletcher Swensen, in an attempt to improve my life, had given me books whose authors she had seen on TV talk shows. Claudia was used to my wisecracks about those books, which had started feminist but lately veered from the psychological to the spiritual—on the shelf where I kept them you could trace the evolution from essay collections blurbed by Gloria Steinem, to how to be an optimist, to the Dalai Lama.

"I hope not," Claudia said as I opened the bag. "It's a relaxation tape. Detra recommended it." Detra was Claudia's oldest friend, the indulged child of two doctors, a girl with a barbed-wire tattoo around her upper arm and what she called a jones for yoga.

Soothing Sounds for Seasons of Serenity was the tape's title. "Great," I said, nodding. "Serenity." As if I'd ever have the time to play it.

CHRISTINE ROUDEBUSH: EAR PAIN, PACEMAKER

"I better catch up on these calls."

Claudia said, "I bought it for you to play in the car. Maybe, you know, Thursdays."

Thursdays were the evenings I drove the interstates to and from Mick. "Claudia," I said, pleased and startled, "that's very, very sweet. Thank you. I will play it."

SIMON JACOBS: OUT OF POTASSIUM

Money, the patient with the palpitations, I took care of with an extra dose of his med. For Jacobs, I called in a refill.

"How's school going?" I asked Claudia.

She shrugged. "Okay."

"How's your apartment?"

"My garbage disposal backed up and I had this disgusting water in the sink. I called the landlord but he . . ."

"Hello, this is Dr. Toledo." Christine Roudebush had answered. I held a finger up to Claudia. She nodded and started in on her hamburger.

"Well, Mrs. Roudebush, I understand you're my partner's patient, but ears really aren't his area," I said. "You need to call your primary care doctor. I wouldn't even know what to give you for an earache. I'd probably prescribe you nose drops or something."

"I don't know how you stand it," Claudia muttered.

"No," I said, "definitely not. An ear infection will not affect your pacemaker."

WILMA EDWARDS: STILL CAN'T BREATHE

"I saw part of Turkman's game today," Claudia said when I hung up.

"You did?" Claudia hardly ever watched Mick's games. This was a new leaf for her, all this attention to me and Mick. "Did you think he looked all right at the end? I was worried about him. I wanted to call him earlier but . . ." I realized that between my manicure and the commotion of my pages I'd forgotten about calling Mick at all. What was wrong with me? I'd been so worried about him! Now it was too late to call him, because he might be home. Of course Mick was all right. He was always all right. He was a man blissfully free—other than some urinary hesitancy, which between us had become a joke—of symptoms and neuroses. I rechecked Wilma Edwards's number on the pager. "I'm sorry, but I'd better call this one right back. It's the same lady I told to call 911."

"Could it be asthma?" Wilma Edwards wheezed. "My grand-daughter has asthma, and I thought . . ."

I told her again, more firmly, through bites of my hamburger, to call 911.

"You'll meet Mick someday," I told Claudia. "You'll like him."

She shifted slightly in her seat, looked toward a rusty license plate hammered to the wall. "I hope so," she said.

I picked at my french fries, cutting each one in three bites so I'd feel satisfied with six. "So did you get your disposal fixed?"

"My neighbor did it."

"A male neighbor?" I asked, as Claudia blushed. "A nice neighbor?"

"I was embarrassed for him to see what was in my sink."

WILMA EDWARDS: REALLY CAN'T BREATHE, 3RD CALL

"Oh, for crying out loud." I reached again for the phone. "Mrs. Edwards," I said, "call 911. Have you heard the expression 'God helps those who help themselves'? You need to help yourself."

She didn't have the air to pronounce a full sentence. "I don't want to . . . wake up . . . husband."

"When 911 comes, let them wake up your husband. Listen to me, you've called three times and the next time you'll be dying and I can't come flying through the phone to resuscitate you. I'm not a magician, okay? I can't come flying through the phone."

Claudia dropped her hamburger and pushed her plate away.

"I'm hanging up right now so you can call," I told Wilma Edwards.

"She'll be okay," I assured Claudia in a milder voice. "She's old and she's scared, and I'll call her back in a minute to be sure she's called for help."

"You were almost yelling at her."

3-WEST, PROTIME RESULTS

"Patients can be like children. Sometimes you have to shout for their attention."

Claudia scratched an eyelid with her thumbnail, gave a short laugh. "I'm glad you never shouted at me like that!"

"Oh, Claudia," I said, and my voice broke with affection. "Remember how Tessa used to lift up the back of your hair?" *Is she a cyborg? Is that why she's a perfect child?* Tessa would ask, checking Claudia's head for a hidden switch. *I wish Giles and Mandy were even half as good.*

That Giles really was bad, I thought bitterly, wishing again I'd stepped in between him and Claudia. Had that brief and unfortunate relationship really ended just over a year before? In a way it felt like something from another life. But maybe not to Claudia.

"I always hated it when Tessa pulled up my hair like that," Claudia said, and maybe I should have pursued her comment, should have said, *You really hated it? Why?* But I had crazy, stubborn Mrs. Edwards to think of, and I already had picked up the phone to call her back. The life squad was coming, she told me, and her husband was awake. "I hope . . . right thing," she fretted on the phone.

DEBBIE FISHER: PAIN DOWN LEFT ARM

"Of course you did the right thing, Mrs. Edwards," I said.
Claudia looked relieved.

AN HOUR LATER I was at the hospital, helping the on-call
nurse, Helen, push Mrs. Edwards on her cot down the
hall from the emergency room to the angiography suite. Mrs.
Edwards was having a massive heart attack, and it was my job
to slip a catheter in her groin and up through the aorta and out
into the heart's major blood vessels, where I hoped to locate
the blockage and open it. "With a little luck, we can reverse
this heart attack," I told Mrs. Edwards. "Your heart will be like
nothing ever happened."

Helen looked tired. She was in her mid-fifties and had been
working in the cath lab for almost twenty years. Jeremy called
her Lady Madonna for her calm. Her children were grown,
and her husband was ill with chronic hepatitis. When she was
on call for the cath lab she wore two pagers, one for hospital
calls and one for calls from him. "You'll be fine," she said to
Mrs. Edwards, who looked frail enough to be smothered by the
weight of a blanket. "Dr. Toledo is our best doctor."

"Thank you, Helen," I said. I used to tell patients *I pay her to
say that,* but then I realized that response was not quite kind.

When I opened Mrs. Edwards's blocked vessel her breathing
went from labored to normal within minutes. "Oh," she said
in surprise, opening her eyes, "I feel better." Modern technology had indeed made possible tiny miracles, and for a moment,
as my eyes met Helen's above her surgical mask, I appreciated

that again. I wished Helen's husband's hepatitis could be wiped out with such a miracle, but the medicine they'd tried hadn't worked, and he was too old for a transplant.

Soon I was standing in the hallway next to Mrs. Edwards's cot, holding down the wad of bandages to keep pressure on the punctured groin artery for the obligatory twenty minutes, using my left hand to click through the messages that had accumulated on my pager during the cath.

> JACK CRAIG: DEFIBRILLATOR WENT OFF
>
> LUCY ZHOU: TOOK 2 PILLS BY ACCIDENT
>
> MARJORIE RHODES: ANGINA AGAIN AND AGAIN

My cellphone didn't work this deep in the building, and as I waited for Helen to bring me a portable phone I looked down the white corridor and thought how this scene was the essence of hospital: an empty corridor that looked like daylight in the night. Where's Mickey now? I thought, imagining him with his feet up on an ottoman, a remote control in his hand, and I saw something like a scarecrow approaching, arms held out from its body and long stiff legs and a bobbing head. I wondered for a second if I was hallucinating.

"Is that your husband?" Helen said, emerging from a side room with my phone, and as Mrs. Edwards turned to look down the hall her face lit up. "Harry!" she called. "Here I am!"

He asked, once he finally reached us, if his wife could have some water.

"Ice chips would be fine," I said, and Helen went away and came back with a plastic cup, from which Mr. Edwards, his quivering hand made still with purpose, spooned pieces of ice into his wife's waiting mouth.

"The ER just called to say Mrs. Fisher's here," Helen whispered. "Her EKG and her enzymes are okay, but she refuses to go home until she talks to you."

I nodded, thinking how Mrs. Fisher was a worrier, but not without reason, and it would be easier for both of us to admit her overnight. "Tell them I'll be down there in ten minutes."

"Umm," Mrs. Edwards said in her wispy voice, "tastes delicious."

"I'm glad you woke me up," her husband told her. My hand was on Mrs. Edwards's thigh and I was making my phone calls maybe eight inches from Mr. Edwards's shoulder, but as far as they were concerned, I could be a thousand miles away.

I wonder if we'll get there, I thought, thinking of Mick and me together in our old age. Not married—I would never marry again—but together every day, in our own place, with our own big bed and kitchen table. We could go out to eat then without fear of being seen. We could see a movie.

"You'd better get to the hospital," I told Marjorie Rhodes over the phone. "I'm here. As soon as you hang up, call 911."

I know not everyone can understand the person I was then. On Thursdays I left my office at the early-for-me time of seven and drove eighty-four miles by interstate to a Marriott hotel in Marietta, Ohio, a mile from the northern bank of the Ohio River. I was eleven years into an affair with a married man I saw for two hours once a week, and I was delighted with those hours. They were enough for me. I wasn't suffering with doubt or angst or anger, although if I read the books Tessa gave me, I

suspect that they would tell me that I was. They weren't judg-
mental books. They wouldn't call what Mick and I were doing
immoral. Their concern would be my happiness and fulfillment.
They'd tell me that I was being *used,* that I shouldn't *settle,* that I
was a *deserving person* in the process of becoming *so much more.*

I *was* more. In Mick's and my hotel room, my serious clothes
and shoes were off, my beeper was in my car, and no one but the
man I loved knew exactly where I was. How could I taint such
peace with pleadings for divorce or separation, or practical plans
for the future? I read somewhere that astronauts, freed from
gravity, find that a small space becomes enormous. In Mick's and
my hotel room, we lost gravity. Not every meeting was perfect,
but most weeks, for at least some minutes, Mick and I were tum-
bling through the air.

THE NEXT THURSDAY it was almost ten when I slipped the keycard into the door and found Mick propped up on pillows on top of the covers, still in his trousers and crewneck sweater (the blue one this week), his feet bare and his reading glasses on, a report from one of his assistant coaches on the clipboard in his hand.

"Hi," I said, "sorry to be late"—and his face lit up, which thrilled me every time.

He didn't "make a smile" for me, no—his face lit up. There's a difference.

"Hi, luscious cupcake." Amazing the nicknames he had for me, every kind of food. He slipped his glasses to the end of his nose as I shed my coat to a hanger. "Is that a new outfit?"

It was, a cranberry suit with a scoop neck, a little more daring than my usual. I twirled around to show it off.

"Very attractive," he said. "Sexy." He pushed himself higher on the pillows and looked down at my feet. "Nice shoes." This was a prompt, of sorts, and I kicked off my right shoe and caught it. "Good hands," he said, and then I was scrambling up the bed toward him like a kid after a toy, and I climbed on top of him and grabbed his glasses and his clipboard and said, "Enough of *those*."

That day he ended up on top. "Thanks for coming," he said, arching up on his arms and grinning down at me. Our old joke.

"My pleasure."

"Oh, my pleasure, I'm sure."

Our room was nothing special, just a rectangular box with a king-sized bed, two night tables, and a low chest of drawers topped by a cabinet containing a TV we never turned on. Two armchairs, backs to the curtained window, flanked a round table. We had remained loyal to this place through two bouts of remodeling; by now the colors were peach and teal.

Eventually, sated, we settled in our usual spots, me snuggled up to Mick with my head on his left shoulder, his arms a circle around me. I had finally talked to Mick on Sunday, the day after the game, but not since then. Our telephone communications had always been erratic, and we never e-mailed, but Thursday night the wires hummed between us. "So how's Eluard?" I said, trying to hide the distaste in my voice. Mick had told me on the phone why he had looked tense talking with Elaine Johnson of ESPN: just before Saturday's game, Tom Kennilworth had come to Mick, hinting that there was something going on with Eluard Dickens's brother. Mick knew that the brother was a bad actor (his history included drug convictions, rape acquittals, and a prison term for armed robbery), so he called his friend Marcus and asked him to look into it. As of Sunday, Mick didn't know if Eluard was okay. Something about stolen goods, Marcus had told him. Something about where Eluard's brother was hoping to stash them, in Eluard's car or maybe Eluard's dorm room.

Marcus Masters was Mick's old college roommate, and it was Marcus whom Mick claimed to be playing poker with each Thursday night. For years I had heard about Marcus. Marcus, who at first had been distressed that Mick, his assigned freshman roommate, was a white guy (there was still a Black Power movement on campus); Marcus, who had moved himself and his extended family (cousins, foster sons, sister, no wife) to Turkman following Mick; Marcus, who owned his own insurance agency and managed all Mick's investments; Marcus, described by Mick as a big sheltering tree; Marcus, whom I had never met. I sat up. An agitation rose in my chest, and I couldn't say if I was jealous, or afraid, or angry. I was something. "But what did Marcus do? Did he go to the police? Did he go to the *campus* police? How does Marcus do these things, exactly?"

Mick broke the circle of his arms around me, used his right hand to rub his eyes. He shifted, looked at me with weary consternation. "Genie. We watch out for our kids. Clean program, remember?" This was something Mick was proud of, a change from the programs of the Turkman coaches before him, who turned blind eyes to players smoking dope and accepting meals and apartments and even cars from Turkman alumni. "We don't do anything illegal or immoral or even fattening. We protect our guys."

"Okay, but *how*?"

From day one I hadn't liked Eluard. Eluard seemed *too* big, *too* tall, and Mick seemed to have more faith in him than Eluard deserved. I resented the way Eluard had acted like such a hotshot

as a freshman, making Mickey believe that with a little more discipline and coaching, Eluard would be a key to a winning team.
This year he was no more than a copy of a key, something that
worked only after shaking and jiggling. Eluard had long arms
and enormous hands, and anyone could picture what a monster
shot-blocker he could be—like a giant windmill guarding the
basket—and yet he was only a mediocre defender. Mick blamed
himself for this, partly (saying that if he understood Eluard better,
Eluard would play better), and partly Eluard's own nature. Eluard
got headaches. He'd spent two weeks out early in the season with
a hurt shoulder undiagnosable by either specialists or MRIs. He
rarely committed fouls—not because he was smart but because
he lacked aggression. "He needs a mean-bone transplant," Mick
once said. Mick and his assistants went over game tapes with Eluard until he could spot his own mistakes. Still, Eluard couldn't
seem to make the connection between the tapes and a real game.
In the heat of the moment, he couldn't stop being precious.

Eluard and Marcus and Mick's wife were our sensitive topics.
Otherwise, Mick told me everything. Normally, our conversations wrapped around us like a worn, cozy scarf.

Mick said, "All I know is that Marcus says Eluard's fine."

"But what did Marcus do to keep him fine? Did he lock him
up somwhere? Did he, I don't know, buy his brother a one-way
bus ticket to Manitoba?"

Mick laughed, his chest shaking in a rhythmic, reassuring
way. "The resident adviser in Eluard's dorm keeps an eye out.
Marcus talks to him."

"Wait till next year when Eluard can move off campus."

"He's not going to move off campus. Marcus will see to that."

A silence, and I bobbed my head to stroke Mick's chest. I loved it when he laughed. Mick said, "You know what Eluard said to me yesterday? *Don't you think I can handle my own brother?*"

"He came to you yesterday? After he didn't have the nerve to talk with you himself last weekend?"

"I guess his brother came by the dorm on Sunday, but Eluard wasn't there and he couldn't get in," Mick said. "Marcus and his people were keeping Eluard busy. You know what else Eluard said? *I guess you feel like you own me now. I guess you've paid for me.*" Beneath my head, I could feel Mick's shoulder stiffen. "I hate that race stuff," Mick said. "Hate it, hate it, hate it."

Mick liked to say he didn't know black from white. Anyone could guess that wasn't completely true, but it was Mick's mantra and he stuck by it. Of course Eluard would throw race in Mick's face, I thought. Would that Eluard could muster such sharp defense on the court! I said, "No good deed goes unpunished."

"Well . . ." Mick's tone turned conceding. "Eluard's trying to look after his family. I got my people to interfere. That makes Eluard feel like I don't think he's a man. And the thing is, he *wanted* me to interfere, and that makes him feel like less of a man to himself."

Of course. I hadn't thought of it that way. Mick was rarely wrong about people. Sometimes I was relieved that he hadn't met Claudia or Tessa. It frightened me to think of what they'd give away.

I propped myself up on my arm to better see Mick's face.

"Eluard could have a future," Mick said, not looking at me but at the blank screen of the TV. "I think Hugh"—the harder-ass of Mick's two assistants—"is finally getting him to act aggressive."

"Aggressive?" I reached across Mick's face and turned his

chin toward me. "Why'd he throw that ball out to Kennilworth the end of the first half on Saturday? He should've taken that shot himself."

Mick laughed. It pleased us both when I noticed some subtlety of the game. "That was a gift for Kennilworth, after Kennilworth's airball."

"So what if Eluard lets his brother keep stolen stereos in his room?" I said, keeping my hand on Mick's face to assure his gaze met mine. "Even if he loses his scholarship, he could go to the NBA. The NBA lets their players commit crimes."

I'd gone too far. Mick's mouth twisted and he closed his eyes. "What the heck was I supposed to do, Genie? Have Eluard ruin his life?" His eyes flew open. "It's his brother! It's family. He's loyal to his family." He pushed my hand away. He shifted in the bed, as if he was trying to find a more comfortable position. He looked at the ceiling, not at me. "That's supposed to be a good thing, loyalty to your family."

I winced a bit at this statement. But Mick's loyalties were broad: he was loyal to me too. I said, "Couldn't you call his parents?"

"Come on, Genie." I remembered the story of Mick's first recruiting phone call to Eluard, when Eluard's mother set down the receiver and wandered off, forgetting to tell Eluard there was someone on the line. But now . . . I hated to think of Mick wasting his time and mental energy on Eluard. Did Mick even need him on the team? There was a junior backup center who Mick put in occasionally, and a couple of slow-moving forwards who could be moved into Eluard's position.

"It's his life," I said. "His life. Maybe you don't even need him."

Mick rolled away from me and spoke into his pillow. "Don't talk like that. I'm trying to be unselfish here. I'm trying to let Eluard make something of himself."

I was looking at Mick's back, freckled at the shoulders, the five moles like a constellation in its middle. I kept an eye on those moles; one of my fellow residents had died ten years before with metastatic melanoma. Almost a compulsion, I thought, that every Thursday I made sure to check those moles. But that was my professional life: my job was to evaluate and worry.

"No one thinks you're selfish," I said, slipping my arms around him from behind, pressing my small breasts into his back. "No one."

M ICK AND I had first met in 1985, at a charity sports banquet I attended as a favor to a patient. It was right after Jeremy and I had opened our practice. The patient who introduced me to Mick Crabbe was an elderly man whom friends called The Big Booster Himself, or Himself for short, and I agreed to go to the banquet with him at his wife's behest, because Himself's wife got tired of sports-sports-sports, and Himself wanted to show his lady doctor off. "I got my doctor here!" he told everyone. "My cardiologist! Isn't she something?" A charity sports banquet, if you've never been to one, features a group of coaches and athletes (and the occasional sportscaster) roped into speaking to raise money for a cause. The coaches and players who are still working use notes and are not that interesting, but the former athletes ramble like guys sitting in a bar. You can imagine them the next day reading their quotes in the paper. "Did I really say that?" A little harrumph and a shrug. "Well, it's true."

The cause for this particular banquet was juvenile diabetes. Mick was then the head coach at a minor college, although Himself—whom everyone at the banquet seemed to know—said Mick had started out coaching high school, and he was a guy on the way up.

"A cardiologist?" Mick said, a flicker of interest crossing his face. "Like, you cut people open and hold their hearts in your hands?" It was a routine mistake to confuse a cardiac surgeon and a cardiologist, so I didn't bother to correct him. *Dumb jock,* I remember thinking, turning away.

We didn't meet again for almost four years. By then Mick had indeed moved up, to his Turkman State position. Himself took me to another banquet, the same situation, although the cause that night was spinal cord injuries and Himself said, "I got my doctor here! The one who saved my life!" and Mick Crabbe was one of the speakers and not a member of the crowd. "We met once," I told him, not sure why I remembered this. "Several years ago. When you were still at Mt. Alliance."

"The lady cardiologist," Himself said. "My heart was almost stopped and she . . ."

Mick's face fell. "Oh, jiminy"—Mick never swore, and his imprecations were ridiculous—"I thought you were like an Aztec. I thought you opened people's chests up and . . ."

I laughed in surprise, touched by his embarrassment. "It's okay. Lots of people don't . . ."

"I did a golf weekend with a cardiologist a couple years ago, he set me right. Wait a minute, I'll make this up to you. You got kids? I'll give you a signed ball. I'll take it back and get the whole team to sign it."

I am always looking up at people, and it's a pleasure to talk with a man who makes an effort to look down. Mick was making that effort. "Thank you for the thought but, honestly, my daughter and I know less about basketball than you know about heart surgery."

"Really." Not a question. His surprisingly lush lips met and he looked at me, eyes narrowing, in an assessing way. I felt myself blushing, which only made me blush more. "Where are you sitting?" Mick asked. Himself pointed to a table respectably close to the front dais.

"Not anymore," Mick said. "I'll get you two seats with me." And he headed off to arrange it.

Himself was beside himself with excitement. "Oh, he's a great coach, a clean coach," he said, spreading his arms like he was illustrating the size of a fish. "Those Turkman coaches before him, they were scalawags."

"What's your biggest strength when you coach?" I asked him during dinner. Mick had squeezed Himself and me on either side of him at the table on the dais; I felt awkward and misplaced, but the men around us seemed perfectly happy to have Himself in their midst, and by extension they accepted me.

Mick said he could see potential. In response, I told him I was stubborn, I didn't give up on my patients.

"Didn't give up on me!" Himself said, reaching for the butter.

"So what's your weakness?" I asked.

Mick puzzled over this awhile. "I'm too loyal, I guess. Some players just don't have it, you know? Or they have some but not enough."

"Her weakness is she's too busy!" Himself said. He was slightly deaf and his comments were perhaps more explosive than he intended. "You can't get in to her!" Mick glanced at me, and we both smiled.

Had I heard of John Wooden, the greatest basketball coach in the history of mankind? Mick chuckled when he said this, added, "Well, it's not a very old game." At any rate, loyalty was the center block of the bottom row of John Wooden's pyramid of success, but loyalty could be tricky—including, as it did, not just loyalty to your family and team but loyalty to yourself as well. Ah, loyalty to yourself, we agreed—that's where things get hard. And I told him about my divorce and how, essentially, my ex-husband had done nothing wrong, but living with him had made me a stranger in my house. "You don't deserve that," Mick said, and I said no, but in a way my ex didn't deserve my divorcing him, either—he was just being his low-key, lazy self—and Mick said that life was peculiar, and both my ex and I might well end up happier apart. "It'll work out," he assured me, and little did I realize that that phrase and its permutations were things I'd hear thousands of times.

We talked more. How we were two professional people with widowed mothers, recently dead, whom we hadn't seen that much of toward the end (and surely there was guilt and some hidden pain there?). How we were both from small towns, mine in Ohio and Mick's in the Maryland panhandle. How it was a risk anytime you brought in a recruit: Mick had stories of new coaches and green freshmen, and Jeremy and I had just hired Howard to help us out in the office. How we both had daughters who made us nervous, girls who were maybe too sweet (Mick's older two were boys, but boys were easy), and how do you protect a girl like that without destroying the sweetness itself? Our conversation felt like a mansion. There might be a beat or two when we were standing

in a hallway, but then one of us would open another door, to a
room even bigger and fuller than the last one, and we hadn't even
started upstairs, much less explored the attic or the basement or
the closets or what lay behind the heavy dark wood door.

I don't remember Mick's speech at all, although I can see him
standing at the podium speaking. I had to keep tearing my eyes
from him to look at my melting sundae, afraid of being caught
staring up at him like a typical adoring female.

He didn't grow up in the happiest family. Alcohol, mostly.
He was never good at school and never popular, but he was athletic, and one day his high school basketball coach, a guy named
Eddie Kean, pulled Mick aside. "What's the story with you and
the team?" Coach Kean asked, and Mick said nothing, really,
he just didn't have a lot in common with them, and maybe he
should try more to fit in.

"You don't want to fit in," Coach Kean said. "You're a leader.
They need to learn to be like you." And that was it, really, Mick
said, because if Coach Kean could, in ten seconds, change a person's life so totally, how could Mick not want to be like him?

I stared. He saved me / I'll save them. I felt suddenly poorly
dressed. My own story, with its petulant rebellion against a well-
meaning, albeit maddening, father (an immigrant's son who'd
divorced himself from his family to marry an Ohio Methodist
and sell appliances), seemed about as appealing as an old pilled
sweater. My father had told everyone, especially me, that I was
brilliant ("despite that dingbat mother of yours," he'd add); my
only battle was to prove he didn't matter. After I went off to college, I never went home, even for Christmas. When my father
died I hadn't seen him for over a year. Who had I been looking
after? Myself, only myself. But Mick Crabbe had been motivated

by something beyond pride, and the gorgeous linearity of his career path pierced me like an arrow between my ribs.

Two hours later the three of us—Mick, Himself, and I—walked together to the parking lot, the banquet program rolled into a tube in Mick's beringed left hand. He hadn't mentioned his wife at all, other than to say they'd gotten married just out of college. Was this an intentional omission, or simply a reflection of the tiny space she took in his life? We reached Himself's car and I stood outside the passenger door, looking toward Mick to say goodbye. There he stood across the hood, his index finger darting in and out of the hole he'd made with his program, staring at me as if he didn't realize he was visible. Talk about Freudian, I thought. Himself was headed around the car to open the door for me when he hesitated beside Mick. For a moment his gaze swiveled between the two of us. "Tell you what, doc," Himself said, "why don't you let coach take you home? You two kids take one car."

Himself was my patient for five more years, until he finally died from heart failure. "How's our friend the coach?" Himself would say each office visit. *Good year this year,* I might answer, or *He's in Delaware recruiting this junior college forward,* or *He's a little tired.* The insider-ness of my comments acknowledged Himself's collusion, and Himself never asked for more. At the funeral home I was stung by the selfishness of my mourning. I would miss Himself, yes, but more than that I'd miss Himself's approval.

WE'VE GOT TO GET NUCLEAR," Howard said at our next partners' meeting. "The three of us can share the profits even-steven. It's the only way to guarantee our income." He meant nuclear cardiology. He meant buying an isotope camera and modifying one of the rooms in the center of our office suite to do cardiac scans after stress tests. He meant one of the three of us taking the course to read the scans ourselves.

Howard McClellan was not much taller than me, with a neat brown mustache and a balding head. He looked like a jolly baker in a TV ad. His patients thought he was sweet; he greeted them with a musical "Why, hell-o-o" and said goodbye with a shuffle-off-to-Buffalo wave. Other doctors told me I was lucky to be in such a balanced group. Behind his pleasant demeanor, Howard was the practice's businessman, the bottom-liner. Jeremy, through his wealthy wife, was our connection to regularly paid bills and the executives who chose their companies' health plans. I roped in women, who over time roped in their husbands. "You guys have everything covered," Raj the pulmonologist said in envy. Raj's previous two partners had quit on him, and his new one, a wunderkind straight out of U of Michigan, wanted to spend all his time doing bronchoscopies and managing ICU patients, leaving the boring office work to Raj.

"What about Lenny Moss?" I said now to Howard. Our offices were in a medical arts building attached to the hospital, and Lenny Moss was the hospital nuclear medicine physician who read the scans we ordered.

Howard said, "I like Lenny as much as the next guy, but we've got to think about us."

Not much loyalty anymore. Everything a business. I thought of Mick at the edge of the court, gesturing at his players, and everything about his job—even a large RA standing menacingly outside Eluard's dorm door—seemed honorable and courageous, not adjectives I associated with medicine anymore at all. My partners and I spent our office meetings talking about insurance payments for EKGs and the price of cloth exam gowns versus disposable.

Jeremy was shaking his head. "I have three kids to get through college," he said. Reedy and pale, Jeremy was not a guy who said much. Sometimes, when I saw his patients for him in the hospital or the office, they asked if they could switch to me. But Jeremy was an excellent cardiologist. When my mother developed atrial fibrillation, one of her many premorbid ailments, I had brought her to the office to see Jeremy.

"Who'd take the training to read the things, Howard?" I asked.

"I'm already signed up." Howard looked pleased. "I should have the accreditation by July."

"But how will you have time to read nuclear?" I asked. "You're already spacing your patients out to six months." I'd just seen an emergency chest pain patient of Howard's who hadn't had an office visit in two years. Office time was wasted time, Howard said; he could bill more for hospital work and caths.

"They're fuzzy-grams, Genie," Howard said of the scans. "They take two seconds."

I massaged my forehead with my hand, reminding myself that Howard was good for something: he was as attached to his Tuesday nights off as I was to my Thursdays, so that when Jeremy hinted about changing our call schedule, Howard and I, voting as a bloc, could keep things as they were. "I see your point, Howard," I said, sighing. And honestly, I did. Reading the scans in our office would mean more income, something I would need not now but in the future, in the vague and golden retirement days I dreamed of for myself and Mick. If I had any questions about Howard's reading of a heart scan, I could always go to Lenny Moss. I pictured myself leaving my private office (walls painted a dappled rose and cream), walking past my exam rooms, through the reception area and lobby, down the long hall to Lenny's office in the hospital, fuzzy-gram in my hand.

T HAT FIRST NIGHT, after Himself had left us, Mick and I drove in Mick's car in an awkward silence. I knew what both of us wanted, but after a few unfortunate postdivorce forays, I hadn't had sex in four years. With my husband, sex had come to seem like no more than an acquiescence, a way to reassure him he still possessed his male power. But his day-to-day actions didn't appeal to me, and when I got home from work, exhausted, I curled up on my right side and closed my eyes, feeling the bed shift as my husband rose up on his elbow to see if I was sleeping. Toward the end I almost wished that he'd have an affair, so that I could ignore him in peace.

Mick was driving, and I was giving him directions to my house. "Here's a park," Mick said suddenly, turning right into a cutoff I'd never noticed. A small parking lot, some children's gym equipment, a tennis court with a dim light at its far end, grass, trees.

We pulled into the corner of the empty parking lot and Mick half opened his window and stopped the car. Silence. He switched the headlights off and darkness sprang up around us. "Okay?" he said, turning toward me.

It didn't hit me until years later that coming into my house that night—or any night—might have seemed too intimate, might have crossed a line that Mick didn't want to cross.

It didn't take us long to move to the back seat. We didn't love each other. How could we? We had met three hours before. But what we did with our lips and hands and bodies was loving, with a sweetness and an intensity I'd never felt before. The bristles on the back of Mick's neck, the dip where his deltoid tendon bit into his arm, the swell of his belly, the musky scent of his chest hairs—everything about him seemed not beautful but *worthy*, as if his body were a special landscape, a secret garden only I had the key to, where every flower and shrub had been waiting years for my footstep, where even the grass was straining in excitement: *she's here she's here she's here.*

The clip of the seat belt was digging at my back and the air through the window was chilly and Mick's lips were on my neck and I was falling, falling and falling, and suddenly there I was caught, stopped and gripped like a baby against someone's chest, enveloped by two strong, warm arms. My parents must have held me like that, sometime. They must have. But I never recalled that sensation until that night with Mick. Falling and falling and then the wondrous rest, the sense of being cherished and protected.

"Thank you," Mick said, and something that I thought was sweat dripped on my chin. Looking up, I was astonished that his eyes were filled with tears. I was his secret garden, I realized, as much as he was mine.

As we struggled to get our clothes back on, we got giddy. "Forget it," Mick said as I struggled with my pantyhose, and he peeled them from my feet and wadded them up and reached over me to toss them out the front window.

"Evidence," I said, giggling.

Mick said, "Let some mother with a stroller explain *that*."

We got back in the front and snapped our seat belts. "Happy?" Mick said, turning to me.

"Happy."

"Again?" His younger son, he'd told me at dinner, had gone through a year of toddlerdom with only two words: "No" and "again."

"*Now?*" I said, shocked.

Mick widened his eyes in comic dismay. "No. Again?"

I hesitated, calculating what he was asking. "Thursdays are good."

Mick closed his eyes and his chest visibly swelled, as if my words were proof of some cosmic plan. "Thursdays are good for me too." He reached out and patted my hand. "You wouldn't mind a bed next time, would you?"

"Oh no. Moving up in the world."

"I'll arrange it. I'll take care of it."

And there it was. Mick turned on the engine and the lights and started backing out, only to stop and jump out of the car and scamper forward. It took me a moment to realize what he was doing. He bent over, scooped up my pantyhose with one hand, straightened, and tossed them with a swivel and jump into a trash can twenty feet away.

"Wow," I said when he got back into the car, "nice bucket."

"Nice bucket?" he said. "Nice *bucket*?" and I felt confused and a little hurt, thinking I'd said what basketball players said, but then Mick had his hand behind my head and was leaning toward me, even with his door still open and the overhead light on, and in his face I saw nothing but astonished delight. "You're delicious," he said, "you're perfect"—which was so far from what I was that I wanted to object, but his lips were on mine, and I couldn't.

He drove me home and pulled into my driveway. It was an unspoken collusion that I didn't ask him in. "Next week?" he said, not cutting the engine, his hands still on the steering wheel. I nodded and smiled. I kissed my fingertips and pressed them briefly to his cheek.

From my house door I looked back at him. Mick's window was down, and he was waving from the car. I can't describe the joy I felt, my heart inside me nudging me like a helium balloon. It crossed my mind as I walked through my door that my head might rise and bump against the top of the door frame.

IN OUR ELEVEN-PLUS YEARS, we'd had our rough spots.
In the middle of our second year, I asked a question: "Does your wife have any idea?"

"Karn's not very curious," Mick said after a pause. "You think that shouldn't matter, but it does. You probably don't remember this, but the night we met you asked if certain players made me feel like they were coaching me. I can't tell you, this electric bolt went through me. Thirty years I've been with my wife and she's never seen this. That moment I thought, I need this woman around to talk to."

"You didn't seem interested in talking at the time."

"Strategic." Mick grinned. "I had to sleep my way into your mind."

I always thought the name Karn sounded threatening— reminding me of carnal, carnival, incarnate—but Mick said it was simply Scandinavian for Karen. In fact, on her birth cer-

tificate her name was spelled K-A-R-E-N, but she had changed
the spelling because people always messed up the pronunciation.
Karn was tall and blond and broad-shouldered, with the sort of
body when she was young that would be featured in beer com-
mercials. She and Mick had met in college when one of Mick's
basketball teammates set him up. Their relationship had been,
Mick told me once, pretty hot and heavy at the get-go. "Blinded
by lust," he said.

Karn was part of a bridge foursome that included the Turkman State president's wife. Beyond those women she didn't have
many friends. She belonged to a garden club and fretted over her
hostas. Her goal in life, Mick said, was to run a nice house and
raise nice children, and she had done that, you couldn't take that
away from her. No one said it was easy to be a coach's wife. It
wasn't as if Mick was often home.

I'd seen some pictures. In the looks department, Karn gave
me nothing to fear. It helped that she had gotten fat. It helped
that she had, in my father's scolding phrase, "let herself go."

The women in Karn's bridge group, Mick told me, spurred
on by the president's wife, were experimenting with liposuction
and eye tucks; Karn wouldn't mind some improvement herself,
but she was scared to death of anesthesia.

"What does she need it for? I told her," Mick said. "She's
fine."

"If she's healthy, plastic surgery is really quite low-risk," I
said, feeling a surprising surge of sympathy for Karn.

"It's not worth her worrying," Mick said. "Believe me, she
can worry."

Still, Mickey and Karn had three children. Two boys and a
girl and thirty years of marriage and a shared bedroom, which, if

you thought about it (and I tried not to), was a remarkable feat for two people Mick described as having separate lives. The "separate lives" comment was something I never repeated, even to myself, because I couldn't quite believe it. There had to be a dozen tiny cords—private jokes, shared memories, pieces of furniture one or the other of them always sat in—that held their lives together. I had my own term for Mick's behavior: loyal. The middle block of the bottom row of John Wooden's pyramid of success . . .

Year six, I wanted him to leave his wife. Not, God forbid, for the two of us to get married—I was still busy growing my practice, and marriage was the last thing on my mind—but for us to have more time together. My daughter's old enough and your kids are old enough, I said. Claudia was then fifteen; Mick's daughter and two sons were fourteen, twenty, and twenty-three. "Are you crazy?" Mick said flatly, and this *made* me crazy, made me start devouring every self-actualization book from Tessa on my shelf, until finally, lying beside him on a Thursday, looking up at a patch of skin under his left jaw that Mick must have missed when he was shaving, I understood what he was saying. By that point, Mick had transformed Turkman State basketball from a dirty to a clean program, and leaving his wife would be, for him, like going the other way. He couldn't stand it for his children to look at him differently. He didn't want his players exchanging secret smiles when he talked about self-control.

"There's something wrong with that marriage if Karn hasn't figured out Mick's Thursday nights by now," Tessa told me once, after Mick and I had been seeing each other for years, and this was a comment I clung to. Tessa was already a settled wife by then, so I trusted her opinion on Mick's marriage.

From the beginning, my daughter Claudia knew I had a

friend named Mick. My mother, before her death, was aware that I and "that basketball coach" shared a relationship, although my mother was fastidious in not mentioning it. Mick had a few male friends who knew, and Lionel and Hugh, Mick's assistant coaches, surely suspected, being within earshot of Mick's phone calls, but all of them admired Mick enough that they accepted, maybe even envied, our affair. Lionel, after his divorce, briefly dated a chiropractor, which I took as a skewed compliment.

Year seven I got tired of our weekly hotel room and made Mick take me to a villa in Hawaii—more complicated and less fun than I had anticipated. It was especially odd to eat with him. At one point he ate a piece of roast pork in a way I can only describe as *shoveling it in*. That I'd noticed this, that I'd thought these words, made me unbelievably sad. I truly was doomed, I remember thinking. I was sabotaging myself, and I couldn't stop it.

Just before I'd left on that trip I'd been seeing a Mrs. Shaw in my office when her husband burst in. "She tell you she wakes up at night and can't breathe?" Mr. Shaw said. "She tell you she's starting to sleep in a chair?"

She had not. "Shoo!" Mrs. Shaw said. "Get out of here, you devil!"

But Mr. Shaw ignored her, regaling me with more useful examples of his wife's worrisome symptoms. "Wow," I told him, "thank you for telling me this."

"Isn't he awful?" Mrs. Shaw said happily from the exam table. "I hate him."

That was the real thing, I'd thought at the time: a happy and functional marriage. In my practice, I glimpsed such relationships with surprising frequency. The wife reaching for her husband's hand as she talked about her palpitations; the rueful exchanged glances as I read aloud someone's cholesterol; a couple with a list of daily weights and urine outputs, laughing over the social inconvenience of that extra water pill. People did it, they created contented married lives for themselves. But it had to require enormous resources of forbearance and time and the bizarre ability to simultaneously change and stay the same. I had no idea what else it required. A lot. My stock answer to my patients about marriage was "I don't have the patience for it." That was true enough, but it underrepresented the depth of my feelings. Thinking about marriage reminded me of watching a Chinese contortionist on TV. She started lying on her side with her head on her hand, and then her legs were intertwined and elevated above her head, and before I'd blinked twice her whole body was in the air, supported by no more than her forearm. It looked so effortless that I tossed myself to the floor in front of the TV and tried it. But it wasn't effortless, it was impossible. I would have had to have agility and nerve and superhuman strength and years of practice to do it. It was, as simple as it had at first looked, an astonishing feat. Why humiliate myself by even attempting it?

"What's wrong?" Mick said during that dinner in Hawaii, noticing me across the table.

"I'll miss you when we get back," I lied.

He didn't say he'd miss me. He didn't say we'd have to find a way to be together all the time. "We'll have our Thursdays," Mick said, not raising his napkin to cover his mouth. "We'll always have our Thursdays."

Year eight I had a fling with a neuroradiologist, but being with someone who expected me to spend evenings with him even when he fell asleep on the sofa wound up being exhausting. Also, talking about medicine was boring. Also, I felt like I was cheating on Mick. Year ten Mick's unwed daughter got pregnant.

The last few years, if anyone had asked us, I'm sure Mick and I would have said our relationship was nothing but sex. That was how we could keep it going. After all, Mick was a married man, and he had vows. As bad a Catholic as he professed to be, he was still a born-and-baptized Catholic, and a marriage in the church was to him forever, no matter how strained and forlorn that marriage had become. To this end, he was pathologically afraid that someone would see us together. When we went to Hawaii, we took separate flights both there and back. We never walked into or out of our hotel together, and we each took our key from the evening's desk clerk (all the clerks recognized us by now) with no more than a comment about the news and weather, never a remark about each other.

As for myself, I was a woman in a man's field, a physician who spent almost all my hours, waking and sleeping, in thrall to my myriad patients. The two hours or so a week I had my beeper and phone off were reserved solely for me and Mick. "I guess he's a release for you," Tessa said at one of our latest dinners. "It's almost good you have him." I wouldn't be surprised if Marcus said the exact same thing to Mick, and I imagined Mick responding just as I did, with a nod and a wise sort of smile, relieved that a friend had found a way to accept us.

But. "Cuddle," Mick might say, flat on his back and stark naked, his arms lifted in a V in front of him, a supine man's version of a touchdown signal, his fingers wiggling in a childish way. I, just out of the shower, fully dressed except for my shoes, would walk across the room and crawl across the bed and let him wrap his arms around me. We'd talk. I'd fiddle with his chest hairs, chuck him under the chin when he got cheeky. He'd put his hand behind my neck and gather up my hair. "You should wear it up," he'd say. "You know, like a librarian. You should only let it down for me."

"Ridiculous sexist fantasy," I'd say. "You wish."

"I do wish," he'd say back, and we would laugh.

Falling and falling and caught, again and again. I remembered his first phone call to me, with the name of the hotel and a time for our meeting, how for two days before I'd been thinking of nothing but "You're delicious, you're perfect," and wondering what I could give him back. I wanted to say something extravagant and blissful—*You changed my life the other night; I love you*—but my doctor's moderation clutched its fingers to my throat, and all I could manage was "I can't wait."

Over the phone, there was a hitch in Mick's breathing and a sigh. I was flooded in gratitude, knowing that he understood.

M R. DICKIE DYLAN was sitting at the end of my exam table, shrunken and puckered as an old zucchini. His deceased wife had been one of my first patients. "I'm an impossible woman," she used to announce from her wheel-chair. When she knocked her pills to the floor, Mr. Dylan crawled around and picked them up. "Married fifty-six years," I'd told Jeremy. "The amazing power of habit."

"Oh, Dr. Toledo . . ." Mr. Dylan looked embarrassed, but pleased. "To your house? I couldn't do that, I'm boring." I'd just invited him for dinner.

"Oh, come on. My daughter will be there. I bought a piece of meat last night that's too big for the two of us."

He agreed, finally, and I wrote out instructions. "Did you really ask that man to dinner?" Lindy, the receptionist, asked me as she headed home. "Aren't you a sweetheart." I mentally replayed Lindy's words, checking for sarcasm, but even in repetition I heard none. Lindy was a thirtysomething divorcée who shared clothes with her teenage daughter and seemed to have a soft spot for Howard. I was never sure about Lindy.

T HAT EVENING, Claudia was tearing up romaine lettuce when she startled me. "I wonder if it's a luxury," she said, "for you and Mick not to have to see each other every day."

"A luxury? I don't think of these days as a luxury," I told Claudia. "I think of these days as just busy."

Where would Mick and I live, in our fantasy years of retirement? We never talked about marriage or sharing a home, but we joked about the days after we both retired in a way that implied we'd be together. "Santa Fe?" he'd say. "Too many people doing yoga." "Sarasota, no way," I might complain. "Half of Ohio retires to Sarasota."

Eleven more years until Mick turned sixty-two. We were halfway there. Not that I had any idea what Mick would do about Karn when that time came. Her actual absence when he retired seemed about as likely as a passenger in his car disappearing in a puff of smoke.

"Detra says it's a luxury," Claudia said. Detra, Claudia's worldly friend. "Detra says she's never going to move in with someone again. She says men like you better if they think they're free from you."

"That may be true at your age. As men get older their needs change. They don't want to run around having sex with everyone. They settle down."

ANITA HARDMAN: WEIGHT UP SEVEN LBS

"Maybe I'm scaring him," Claudia said. "Maybe it would be better if I just"—she made a quick gesture with her hand—"flitted in there and flitted away."

Was I hearing things? "Who?" I said. "Who's him? Is there someone you're interested in?" Other than Giles, Tessa's nightmare offspring, whom Claudia had dated for eight months, Claudia had never had a serious boyfriend. I had not long before asked Tessa how she'd figured out that her own daughter was a lesbian. "You'd know," Tessa had said quickly, reading my mind. "Trust me, Claudia isn't Sapphic, she's shy. Giles says she's almost pathological." *That's interesting,* I wanted to say. *I think Giles is pathological too.* But Tessa was my friend, and I didn't want to hurt her. She had to be much more unhappy about Giles than I was.

"It's a guy from my statistics class," Claudia said. "I could be good for him. I can see it."

"He's not married, is he?"

Claudia made an odd noise. "Mom. Of course not."

"Any children?"

"No! Mom . . ."

I glanced at Claudia, at her dreamy, nestling look, and I could see as clearly as reading a road sign that there was a curve ahead. Claudia and a decent boyfriend! This could be exciting. I reached for my phone as I waited for more details. Anita Hardman had chronic heart failure; she probably needed extra doses of her diuretic.

"His name's Toby Polstra," Claudia said. "Detra says he's every mother's dream."

It turned out Toby was the teaching assistant. He wasn't in her class, he helped teach her class. He had an undergraduate degree in math and a master's in environmental studies, and he was filling

in time while he decided on his career. There was a family hardware store in Indiana, and he was thinking of moving back. On
the other hand, he was thinking of starting his own environmen-
tally friendly business, maybe a consulting service for businesses
that wanted to go green. He'd told Claudia that, for him, living
lightly on earth mattered. Living ethically mattered. They could
be no more than friends so long as Claudia was his student.

"That's reasonable," I said. "A very conscientious young man.
Mr. Perfect." I was surprised at the edge of anger in my voice.
Claudia must have heard it too, because she didn't tell me more
about Toby.

Mr. Dylan didn't show. I called his house at about eight but
there was no answer. I got Claudia to eat, which she did halfheartedly, and I phoned Mr. Dylan again at nine. He'd come
all right, he said, his speech slurred, but nobody was there. It
turned out he'd arrived at five instead of seven, and after a spell
waiting he'd gone home.

"Maybe he thought you were mocking him," Claudia said
when I put down the phone. "Maybe he thought you invited
him knowing you wouldn't be home."

"Claudia," I said, "he knows I'm not an ogre." Claudia nodded, looking unconvinced, and it disturbed me that she imagined someone distrusting me so profoundly. Does *she* think I'm
an ogre? I thought. When Claudia left she almost tripped over a
bouquet of flowers left on the stoop, the green paper twisted and
torn. She had come in through the garage, so we'd both missed
them.

"I feel terrible," I told Mick when he called later. "I wanted
to do something good, and I only hurt him."

"Welcome to the club," Mick said.

. . .

OTHER THAN THE QUICK GLIMPSE when he dropped me off that first night, Mick had never seen my house. I had never seen Mick's house, either, although I'd visited, once, anonymously, the place the Turkman Warriors called "our house," the arena where they played. Mick didn't want me coming there—he had an unreasonable fear that Karn, who came to all his home games, would somehow scan the crowd and sense a threat.

The town of Turkman was tucked into a valley. Roads crept like vines up its hillsides. The university was near the entrance to the valley, in the flattest part of town. I went to a game on a Saturday afternoon in February during Mick's and my second year. I had the day perfectly planned. I'd arrive in the town of Turkman, a three-hour drive, late Saturday morning, walk around downtown to see the people in their maroon-and-gold Turkman State regalia, eat a fast-food lunch in my car, then sneak into the arena early to watch Mick and his team warm up. As it happened, that morning a spring broke in my garage door, and my car and I were stuck inside. By the time I got to the Turkman Arena the game was nearly half over. I had to park in an overflow lot, and my feet scuffed the icy dirt as I walked through a ghost town of cars. The city of Turkman lived for basketball, Mick said, and when I opened the arena door the heat and noise almost knocked me backward.

I had never been in a basketball stadium before. It surprised me to find myself, at ground level, almost halfway up the seats, the court at the bottom of a sloping hole. I walked past concession stands, framed portraits of coaches and players, elderly male ushers spaced along the ground floor walkway. The lights over the crowd were dimmed, but it was clear the place was packed. The attendance that day was almost thirteen thousand—average, I learned later. Hanging from the rafters were banners stitched with the names and years of tournament wins. The usher read my ticket by flashlight and pointed up, and I climbed to the next-to-last row. The arena's roof was an inverted peak, so everyone's view was forced down to the court, brightly lit and golden-shiny, like hot lava.

The Turkman Warriors were playing a team dressed in green. I sat down during a time-out. Mick was at the far side of the court in a cluster of players. I took my place next to a large woman eating popcorn, and reached for the binoculars in my pocket. As I focused on Mick's group I was stunned by the thought that that man—*that man,* his minions bunched around him—was someone whose eyes lit up when I walked through the door. In the binoculars I could just make out the whorl in the crown of his hair. I thought of Mick's eyes, his bitten left thumbnail, the distinctive red-brown color (unlike the color anywhere else) of the hair on his inner thighs—and my knowledge made the cavernous arena seem as intimate as a den.

Turkman State was down by one at halftime, and Mick and his team left the court to frenzied music from the PA system. The lights went up, and I looked at the people around me. The woman to my left was with two large men who had to be her relatives; to my right a group of boisterous young men kept sending off the same guy (the only one with an ID, I suspected) to buy them beers. There were two elderly couples in front of me and a mother with a baby directly behind me and four small children of uncertain parentage climbing on and off the back row of chairs. Lots of people wore maroon and gold, and one man three rows ahead wore a T-shirt emblazoned on its back with Turkman's former, politically insensitive mascot, the Turk, wrapped in a turban and holding a scimitar in his teeth.

There was a halftime show featuring Frisbee-catching dogs, and then the pep band played as the current mascot, a maroon-and-gold eagle unofficially called the Hot Hen, shook its tail. "You're hot, baby!" one of the young guys beside me screamed.

The lights went down and the music stopped and the teams reappeared from their tunnels, and the ball started moving back and forth, back and forth. At some point it struck me that my behavior was no longer independent, that I was one jostling molecule in a pot of boiling water. In the tagged-red-cell nuclear medicine studies, the heart is a hot spot in the center of that body, the place where the red cells get together, the place, it would appear, *where red cells want to be,* and it wouldn't have surprised me if someone outside reported that the Turkman Arena was throbbing. Outside was cold and gray and barren; inside was alive. The boys beside me were starting to fall over, and one of them ended up in my lap. I laughed and propped him up and stood cheering with everyone in that arena (not quite everyone—there was a section of green team fans a few rows down) because one of Mick's boys had stolen the ball and ripped it downcourt and through the net. In the last five minutes, Turkman pulled ahead to win by fifteen points. The crowd, buoyant and contented, started for the exits, scattered shouts and war whoops whizzing above us like bottle rockets.

I made my way down the steps. Mick was standing at the entrance to a tunnel talking with someone who was writing things down. I moved with the crowd along the walkway. Mick headed toward two male radio announcers seated at a table behind one of the baskets, ready for the postgame show. It was a thrill to see Mick looking so comfortable and masterly, an even bigger thrill, perhaps, to know he didn't know I was there. I'd tell him about it later, when we could laugh about his fear that Karn might see me. I'd report to him my theory of the water molecules, my image of the arena as Turkman's heart. I'd say he'd made me feel like busting my buttons; maybe, our next Thursday, I'd show up in my new shirt with the snaps and actually bust them. Then it hit me, what I hadn't yet imagined: how different this arena must be when the Warriors lost, the sullen silence and the shuffling to the doors.

On TV, in the suit and tie he wore for games, Mick looked like a boy who'd been padded and stretched and dressed to look, not totally successfully, like a grown man. His ties were loud and made of shiny fabrics, like my father's ties. By the end of a close game his jacket was off and his rolled-up shirtsleeves flapped around at his wrists. But the rare times I'd seen him in public—the sports banquets where we met, an American Heart Association dinner we'd both attended—it was startling to see the power of his presence. Women sipped their drinks and glanced his way. Men shook his hand and at the same time gripped his arm, as if the contact of a handshake wasn't enough.

Part of Mick's and my attraction, always, was the glamour of each other's competence. I found the things Mick had to deal with—reporters, parents, teenagers, all the complex dynamics of a group of kids and coaches sharing buses and hotels and meals and games—almost frightening; I couldn't imagine being part of, much less enjoying, such an aggressively social enterprise. But until that season, '99–2000, when Eluard's brother found trouble and my daughter found Toby, Mick seemed to clamber like a monkey around the ropes holding people together, finding footholds and pathways I wouldn't recognize were there. "We're a team, that's the main thing," Mick had said several years before in the Turkman paper, when—despite his best rebounder dislocating his shoulder and his center spending a night in jail—the Warriors had come in second in their conference and won the conference tournament. That was what hurt Mick about the '99–2000 season: his team, even when it won games, never had the feeling of a unit.

I had never been part of a team. Howard and Jeremy and I were three cardiologists in group practice, but other than sharing our billing and profits we functioned like individual practitioners. In the square of our office suite we each had our own hallway and our own nurse and our own ways. The three of us passed on necessary information about patients and held a monthly meeting, but beyond that we barely spoke.

To Mick I would always be, despite his disavowals, a woman who held beating hearts in her hands, who accepted a part in the ceremonies of aging, rejuvenation, and death. Mick, although he didn't go to church (his wife and kids did), was a believing man, and he had a great respect for death. When I talked to him about a dying or dead patient he'd fall silent and watch me with his lips tightened, as if I were a tightrope walker whose balance and concentration he'd never threaten with a word. "The things you go through," he'd told me more than once, his lips constricting until their billows became a line.

I know that people like talking about gazing into their loved one's eyes, but it was never exactly Mick's pupils I looked into. The inner canthus is the notch in the eye next to the nose, and there was a dip in the arc from Mick's inner canthus to the top of his eyelid that moved me. No matter how widely Mick smiled, he still had that aching arch. That visible ache made me trust him. Without it, he might have seemed too perfect.

Mick liked my back, what he smilingly called—running a big hand down my spine—my bird bones. He lived in a world of muscled, bruising men, and I was his little woman. There were instants I knew he imagined me small enough to curl up in his palm; there were instants I imagined I could.

We made sense, we told each other: Mick worked in sports and I in medicine, both professions ruled by the body. "You heal me, doc," he used to say. "You teach me, coach," I'd say back.

THAT TIME OF YEAR AGAIN, March, when the doctors' lounge buzzed with talk about betting pools and seeding. "The committee wants Duke to win," one of the surgeons complained. "They gave them the easiest bracket." Raj, a little defensive because of his personal Duke connections, ignored that comment and weighed in about the mid-seed battles in the Midwest, as one of the ENTs piped up with his opinion of Oklahoma and a urologist started talking about rebounding statistics as the best predictor of NCAA tournament success. "You can't forget foul-shooting," Jeremy, my intelligent partner, said. When we first got together I used to run these comments past Mick, learning to my astonishment that some of them made sense.

Turkman State was the number 6 seed in the West—way too high a seeding, Mick said, after the season they'd just had. "What do you think of Turkman?" I asked Jeremy. Somehow they had managed to win their conference tournament.

"You like them, don't you?" Jeremy said. "I remember that from last year. They're a decent team. They have a chance." The sort of studiously neutral statement that maddened his more anxious patients: *This angioplasty could work, yes. I'd say the odds are you'll survive the surgery.*

I asked Raj the same question. "I knocked them out in the first round," he said, referring to his betting-pool sheet. "I didn't want to, because Flitt's a great guard and they've got that big center, but he holds back some"—Raj winced, as if it hurt him to admit this, and I was glad to see he'd gotten some doubts about Eluard—"and Sierra State, who they're up against, Sierra's been looking good." Mick was worried about Sierra State too. He would have preferred for Turkman to be seeded lower, to face almost any other team. "And that's a weird conference placement," Raj added. "Why'd they put them in the West?" I eyed Raj with renewed appreciation. I sent him all my pulmonary referrals. "He's very smart," I always told my patients.

CLAUDIA AND I WERE in a mall department store, Claudia searching for a dress to wear to the wedding of a friend of Toby's. *It's not a date,* Claudia had said, *it's just that he needs a companion*—and I wondered at this convenient hairsplitting, this willful disguising of the fact that Claudia was dating someone who was almost her professor. Eight years older, the survivor of not one but two broken engagements, Toby made me nervous, although we'd never met.

"Do you think you'll ever get a real boyfriend?" Claudia asked, trailing me into the Better Dresses department. "You know, one you could spend a lot of time with?"

Toby rode a bike to work. He had installed a special water-saving device in the toilet in his apartment, and used only expensive energy-saving lightbulbs. He'd persuaded his landlord to let him start a compost heap and garden in his building's back yard. I couldn't understand the antipathy I'd developed for him, other than my sense that for Toby to be so picky about the environment, he must have in him something metallic and vaguely threatening. I thought of him as a sort of industrial juicer, an implement to press the sweetness out of Claudia within seconds. When I finished a cath and looked around at the mass of throwaway sheeting and instruments and supplies, I half wanted Toby to walk in on the sight.

"It's not the amount of time you spend together, it's the intensity of feelings you share," I said, answering Claudia. It hurt that she was questioning me, however indirectly, about Mick. "Remember when you first met Detra?" During a medical staff picnic, Claudia and Detra had sat under a honeysuckle bush for hours. "Compare that to how much time you spent with your Girl Scout leader. Remember all those weekends? Well, is Mrs. Toscadides one of your best friends?"

"It's not the same." Claudia reached deep into the rack and extracted a dress in yellow chiffon. My beeper went off:

M. L. HOPKINS: LOST HER PILLS

"Too bridesmaidy," I said, reaching for my phone. I'd had hundreds of hours with Mick, surely. Thousands of hours. Well, at least one thousand. "You have to admit the time you spend with different people isn't equivalent. For me, every moment with Mick is a peak moment. Every moment I feel alive." Oh boy. Some things are true enough but they shouldn't be said out loud.

"I guess you don't drift off to sleep on his shoulder," Claudia said, turning to another rack. "Waste of time."

"M.L.?" I said into the phone. "What happened?"

M.L. was only thirty-one but had the stretched-out, irritable heart of an old alcoholic. Her heart choked up her lungs with fluid; her heart burst into her sleep, rap-tap-tapping like a demented drill team. In an ideal world I would have her on a blood thinner to prevent a stroke, but I didn't want to risk her taking it. Drunks fall and get hurt. Drunks irritate their stomachs and get GI bleeds.

When M.L. was sober, or at least near-sober, she decorated houses for rich people. She had shown me a photo, her last office visit, of herself with a stately-looking woman in the living room of a villa in Slovenia. In the picture, M.L.—wearing an odd green shift and her usual Buddy Holly glasses, her shock of black hair tipped in pink—was beaming. "I love Europe," she said, and then, in a bizarre accent: "Europe understa-a-ah-nds me." She crossed her eyes and raised her eyebrows, her typical stupid-me gesture. There was a small smoldering fire of self-hatred in M.L. I could see it, but I couldn't stomp it out.

Now M.L. was home in Ohio, and I gathered that she'd had to leave in a hurry wherever it was she'd been staying. I got the number of her pharmacy and a list of her meds. M.L. didn't have insurance, but she found ways to pay me. She was the one who'd painted my private office and arranged the furniture in my home.

"What's gotten into you?" I said, turning toward Claudia. Not exactly the question I wanted to ask, which was *When did you stop being on my side?*

"Oh, Toby and I have been talking. *As friends.*" Claudia hesitated, pointed at a distant mannequin. "What about a suit?"

"A suit would be fine. You didn't tell Toby about me and Mick, did you?"

"Not exactly. I mean, he knows he's a college basketball coach, but he doesn't know where." We were walking down a central aisle toward a mannequin.

"But Claudia!" I heard myself almost sputtering. "Toby's a man!"

Claudia gave me a look. Surely she knew what I was saying. To a man with any interest in college basketball, any few details, however inadvertently spilled, would give Mick away. Mick's record being 20–5; his team having a hot freshman shooter and a big center and an assistant coach who was a graduate of the program; even a mention of Turkman State's opponents. Especially with the NCAA tournament going on, it would be a miracle if Toby didn't figure out Mick's identity.

"I talk with Toby, okay? We're getting to know each other. You talk about life with someone, information bleeds out." We had reached the suits.

MORGAN KINSOLVER: "NOT RIGHT," HEART
PATIENT DEBRA STEIN: SWELLING IN GROIN

Damn. Morgan Kinsolver was a patient of Jeremy's who was on the heart-transplant list and in and out of the hospital almost weekly. Debra Stein was a recent angiogram patient of mine who could have a problem at her puncture site. These calls couldn't wait. "But I'm not talking with Toby, Claudia. There's no reason you have to bleed my information."

"You can't rule me anymore, okay?" Claudia snatched two outfits off the circular rack.

"How about the blue?" I said. "You look wonderful in blue."

ROGER COOPER: CHEST HURTS, CAN'T BREATHE

"Claudia!" I called. "Try on the blue at least." But Claudia was already disappearing into the dressing room, carrying the black suit and the beige. I reached into my handbag for the phone.

V IA MY SATELLITE DISH, I could pick up the West Virginia and Maryland TV stations that followed Mickey's team. They wouldn't carry all of his remarks from the pre-NCAA news conference, but I could count on them to run a quote or two on their evening sports. I used to have to choose between the two stations' news programs, but then I got a second VCR and attached it to my bedroom TV. Now I could record the evening and bedtime news shows from both stations, and lately I'd been recording Mick's games. I watched the tape of the evening news when I first got home at about eight-thirty. I watched the bedtime news shows in the morning when I first woke up. Technology was a wonderful thing.

It was Wednesday evening. Mick's team would be playing their first NCAA tournament game the following afternoon. The next night, no matter what happened, would be a Thursday Mick and I spent apart. "In terms of the NCAA, I don't see the benefit of winning the conference championship," Mick said on TV. A blue curtain with the tournament logo hung behind him. "Did it get us a better seed? No. A better first-game placement? No. A better first-game time? No. They've got us playing two time zones away on the tournament's first day." There was a forced hardness in his voice; his chin jutted out in a pugilistic, hopeless way. A sick feeling came over me. "Come on, Mick," I said to the screen. "Buck up, babe. It'll work out."

Later that day, he phoned me from the tournament. "It's a crummy practice gym too," he said.

"The whole thing's just shitty," I said, rolling onto my bed and taking pleasure in the word.

Mick had his battery of oaths—shoot, gosh, freakin'—but not even "damn" or "God" crossed his lips. "I'm not against it," Mick said about cursing. "I just can't do it. It sounds like some alien is inside me." When he was growing up, his family had all sworn. He told me his sisters swore and drank and were generally chips off the block. Mick had never even tasted any alcohol. "I'm afraid I might like it," he said.

"Don't you agree?" I asked him. "Shitty."

But he would not say it. That day I found his persnicketiness embarrassing. He was trying too hard, I thought. He wasn't sounding real.

I HATE MARCH MADNESS," Tessa said. It was a Friday night at our favorite restaurant, a Chinese-Thai place. "I hate it when Herbie takes over the big TV." At one time it hurt me when Tessa expressed such disdain for basketball. I used to think that if Tessa had a long-term relationship with a conductor, I would at least pretend to like music. But Tessa was married, her second marriage, and this marriage was working. Ultimately, despite our friendship, Tessa's primary allegiance was with The Wife.

She had realized after her divorce that the power in the world lay with the coupled, that there was a brutal reality in the expression "odd man out." She thought that was one reason Mick stayed married. He was clearly a team player, and what was society but a team of couples? Also, staying married was itself an accomplishment, one Tessa routinely associated, oddly (but possibly not, her husband was a dentist), with good dental hygiene. "Herbie sees some oldster with all his teeth, he knows they've done something right." Staying married, in Tessa's mind, was much like keeping your teeth. A compliment a day was simply flossing.

"How many colleges do they start with again?" Tessa asked now. "It's a bunch."

"Sixty-four. Sixteen teams in each of the four arms. By the time this weekend's over they'll be down to sixteen. And after next weekend they'll be down to four, and the next weekend they weed it down to two, and those two play Monday Night." Monday Night, the college national championship game, was huge. Every college coach and player dreamed of Monday Night.

"Herbie bets on it, I know. He's always talking Valparadise and Gonzalo and colleges I've never heard of. Like Turkman State, honestly." Tessa shook her head, which had the effect of shaking her long brown hair. Tessa was the only middle-aged woman I knew who could pull off having hair past her shoulders. She spent a huge amount of time on it, puffing and smoothing. She liked to say Herbie loved her hair more than he loved her. Seeing it draped over his exam chair had been the start of their romance. The next step was Herbie bending over to examine his patient and having the transgressive thought (Herbie loved this story) that he'd much rather kiss those lips than stretch them out to check the healthiness of the gums.

Valparaiso. Gonzaga. I wondered if Tessa was misnaming these on purpose. Probably not. There was nothing calculated about Tessa. "Did he have Turkman going far?" I asked.

"Genie. I worry about you."

"Of course you do. It's entertaining." Once, I went with Tessa to her Classics and Future Classics book club. The book was *Anna Karenina*, and the book club ladies attacked Anna for her affair with Vronsky so ferociously that I left the meeting feeling flayed. "She deserved to die, basically," one of the women had said. I told Tessa I wasn't going back. "Too much on your plate," Tessa had said, wrinkling her nose in understanding.

But we had been friends forever, since I was a cardiology fellow and Tessa, already divorced from a man she never talked about, lived in the apartment next door with her two young children. No one could have been more angrily supportive when I tired of my spouse. At that point Tessa was working as a personnel manager for an accounting firm, and she had been dumped by a lawyer who told her that with twenty pounds off she'd be attractive. This was before Dr. Herbie Swensen noticed her hair and lips.

Through the years, Tessa recommended me to any friend or acquaintance who needed a cardiologist. She once referred to me a woman she met in a supermarket line. There had been times in my career when every patient in the waiting room knew Tessa. But for years my life itself had been letting Tessa down. I could almost hear her: "She's really smart and intuitive with patients, but her personal life . . ."

Tessa lit a cigarette, blew the smoke defiantly outward. If she quit she wouldn't live longer, she said, it would just seem longer. I wondered about the effect of cigarettes on her teeth, but this was an argument I'd let Herbie make to her. "So the Claud's rebelling," Tessa observed, returning to our earlier topic of conversation. "Good for her. I'm glad Giles didn't leave her as a puddle. Listen, rebelling is a child's life. You think you were going to get off easy?"

In a way, I already had. Until now—and Giles—Claudia had left her decisions up to me. Did she need to pack a sweater for band camp? Should she sign up for honors or regular algebra? Should she keep playing soccer? Well, why not? I said. Soccer was good exercise and maybe it would toughen her, make her less dangerously herself. But before I knew it Claudia was staggering off the field, her face as twisted as her arm, her sullen teammates (those girls were monsters) rolling their eyes. She didn't reproach me. In the emergency room she told the doctor she'd slipped on wet grass.

In contrast, Giles, Tessa's son, before and after he broke Claudia's heart, had required—was still requiring, although he was holding a sandwich shop job now—rehab and antidepressants; Tessa's daughter, now a social worker with a tidy house and a bossy female partner and two adopted daughters, had once pierced her own labia. At times I envied the willfulness of Tessa's children. One night when Giles came to pick up Claudia she asked me which movie they should see. "You and Giles decide," I told her, but Giles already had.

"She's not coming home smelling like pot yet, is she?" Tessa asked.

"Giles didn't have that much influence," I said, smiling tightly and not looking Tessa's way. I hadn't really smiled since the day before, not since Mick's team was tossed out of the tournament in the first round. Raj was right. Beaten by seventeen points, although Eluard Dickens had had a career-high day of scoring.

"Frederick did what I asked him to," Mick had said wearily on the phone. "He got the ball to Eluard even though he didn't want to. I probably won't call again till Sunday. Love you, babe."

"You're a very dominant figure," Tessa said. "Remember what that shrink told me: How would you like to be your child?"

B ut she's Hank's child too, I thought as I undressed that night. I wasn't sure what this told me, what precautionary bells it should ring. I clipped my beeper to my nightgown, then remembered this wasn't my weekend on call. Claudia's father and I met in college. Hank liked to play the piano in the dorm lobby, and once I complimented him on "Rhapsody in Blue." We got married just before I started med school. My father was not alive to give me away. "He grows on you," I remembered reassuring my mother about Hank, "like a fungus."

He did become quite fungus-like. By the end of my cardiology fellowship, I was getting home at nine at night to find no supper fixed and an unmade bed with Claudia conked out on it, Hank having spent his day talking sports with the Super Duper Dads group, whose children ran amok in the indoor playgrounds of fast-food restaurants. I was in the hospital, some weeks, up to 150 hours. After a while I started commiserating with the other cardiology fellows, particularly with Judd, the elegant Kentuckian whose wife offered him the choice of Grape-Nuts or Cocoa Puffs for dinner.

"What do you mean I don't do anything?" Hank said. "I'm doing the most important job in the world!"

My lawyer was worried we'd be assigned a female judge who'd deny me custody, but in the end we got the perfect judge for my purposes, an older man whose daughter was in med

school. Hank's and my custody arrangement was highly traditional: I had Claudia all the time and Hank got her every other
weekend. At first it was terrible—"You don't know me!" Claudia wailed; "Daddy knows all of me!"—but eventually I found a
good live-in sitter and things settled down. Hank remarried and
had two more children, diverting much of his attention from
Claudia. I actually came to like Hank's new wife, a teacher's aide
who wouldn't think of Hank as not working. Hank taught piano
lessons now at a music shop. He had come, I often thought, full
circle: he was what he was, and nothing more. Soft.

I'm not soft, I thought. I'm a grown-up, I'm dutiful, I see
things clearly, and I'm capable of change.

My phone rang—Mick's number on the display—and I scam-
pered to it.

MICK HAD LEFT the door cracked open with a section of
newspaper and was lying on the bed fully clothed in
a pullover sweater and trousers, looking at nothing. "I don't
know, muffin. Sometimes you've got no choice but let them go
out there and suffer." There were more NCAA games on TV
tonight, but the TV wasn't on. Mick snapped his fingers. "Boy,
we were out of there fast. A week ago today and it was over. Did
I tell you Maguire was crying in the locker room?" Maguire
was one of the seniors. "I felt like crying with him."

I tilted my head in sympathy, sat down on the edge of the
bed, and stroked Mick's hand. He said, "You see Art Quinlivan's
column in the paper Sunday?"

Occasionally, if Mick's team had won a really big game, I did
go online to look up articles in the Turkman city paper, but I

hadn't done that for weeks. Next year. Next year would be better for everybody. I shook my head. "What'd Quinlivan say?"

Mick nodded at a folded newspaper on the nightstand, and I moved it to my lap to read. At first I thought the column must have made Mick happy. There were quotes from Mick's recent interviews, comments he'd made about haphazard play and players who seemed to be sleepwalking. One of Mick Crabbe's classic strengths, Quinlivan went on, one of the things every fan had to admire about him, was his enthusiasm for coaching. "In the past, talking with Crabbe, you knew that he loved working with his team. But these days he seems tired of his team." Haphazardness, sleepwalking: didn't Crabbe's players, Quinlivan asked, deserve some credit for a winning season? "You get the feeling the Warriors can't win even if they win," he wrote. "Every career has a burnout point. Every coach, like every player, has a shelf life. Maybe, for the sake of his beloved Warriors, Coach Crabbe should make room for new leadership. Maybe the Warriors are crying out for something positive. Maybe the Warriors need a coach who'll say he loves them—even if they win."

"Who put rocks in his socks?" I cried, setting the paper down.

"I went insane when I saw it," Mick said. "I almost broke my foot on the kitchen door."

"You didn't," I said, trying to chuckle, but the sound stuck in my throat.

"I did. You've never seen me really mad. I'm not a nice fellow when I'm mad."

Sunday morning. I wondered if Mick had read it sitting in his kitchen with a cup of coffee, Karn at the counter fiddling with the toaster oven. "I know where Quinlivan has brunch every Sunday," Mick said. "I almost went there."

I raised my eyebrows and looked at Mick askance. "I hope someone talked you out of *that*."

Mick's mouth gave a bitter twitch. "You think I'm kidding! I'm not kidding. How do you think a column like that makes me feel? I have my pride."

"What does it matter what Quinlivan thinks? You don't even like him. You thought what he said about Morgan was baloney." Mick liked his player Corey Morgan, but he had laughed out loud when Quinlivan, early in the season, had referred to him as the Warrior's new soul.

"I've never thought of quitting! We had a winning season! We went to the NCAA for the second straight year! I don't know where he gets the nerve."

I thought, *It's Quinlivan's business to have nerve.* I thought, *Isn't that just like a commentator, cutting people down to make themselves look important?* Mick was already negotiating a new contract with Turkman, to replace one that would expire this summer: Quinlivan, I thought bitterly, must know about the contract too. I thought, *Maybe if what Quinlivan said upsets Mick that much, it's because Mick is scared it's true.* I didn't say anything. I felt an inner agitation that reminded me of certain patients' descriptions of the way they felt before a heart attack, and this frightened me, not for myself (I was fit, I was female, I was premenopausal and had an enviable cholesterol) but for Mick, because my inner feelings might well be his feelings too.

"I don't know," he said, sighing. "Who am I kidding? I'm not going to be a legend. I'm no John Wooden." He shook his head. "I thought we'd have a great team this year, my center and my point guard together at last. And all I got from Eluard was anger." He fell silent a moment. "It was arrogance, thinking

I could take it to another level." Beneath his frown, his eyes searched out mine. "I'm not a kid anymore, okay? I'm not *promising*. By this point in my career, I should be delivering."

In all our years together, I had never heard Mick sound hopeless. I was silent a moment, waiting for him to burst out with his mantra. *It'll work out.* Mick's eyebrows were looking bushy, and at that moment—wildly, inappropriately—I pictured getting out scissors and a tiny brush and grooming them.

Aren't you going to say it? I felt like asking.

"People love you!" I said, looking around as if there were a hundred fans surrounding us. "Your players love you—well, except for Eluard. The president of Turkman State loves you. So what if your players aren't happy every year? Is it your job to make them happy? You're not some counselor at a summer camp, you're a coach. You're trying to make positive changes. So what if you get knocked out early in the NCAA? You've got Roger Fenster calling you for advice" (Fenster had gone to the NBA); "you've got Darren Collingwood telling you you turned him around" (Darren's brother was in prison). "You found Korshak a job!" (Korshak was a former assistant coach whom the Turkman athletic director had seen fit to fire without consulting Mick.)

"Okay," Mick said, his eyes shifting away from me. "It's nothing to sneeze at. But a coach sets the team's atmosphere, and this year, this year . . . Of course I'm happy when we win! Does Quinlivan think I'd rather lose?"

"Oh, Mickey." I stroked his arm. Above his inner wrist his veins protruded; I pressed on one with my finger, felt the sweet tube give way. In everyone, I loved a healthy vein—its rubbery toughness, its resilience—but Mickey's veins I loved with special fervor. "What am I? I'm nothing special. I'm not the best doctor in the country or the state or even the county. I'm just a ho-hum cardiologist."

He smiled slightly, and his breathing got calmer.

"Come on," I said. "You're Mick Crabbe. It'll work out."

He rolled on his side toward me, and I faced him lying down. The blue of his eyes got a little paler each year, as his aching arch got redder and slightly rheumy. Ah, aging. "There are always personalities on a team," he said, "but you hate to see dissension."

"How many coaches would use the word 'dissension'? See? I knew you were a cut above."

"I don't know what I can do with Eluard next year. He just looks right past me."

"Don't worry about next year." I took a finger and traced his right ear. "Don't think about next year."

"You should see Eluard and Kennilworth now." Mick pressed his thumb and his forefinger together. "Big buds." Kennilworth was still angry about Mick's attempt—ultimately unsuccessful—to change his tutor. Mick shook his head. "Sometimes I think the only players I'm losing are the ones I like. Except for Flitt. And Frederick Flitt's not doing himself any favors sticking up for me."

"It'll work out," I said, watching his face, but he showed no recognition that I'd said anything significant. "It always does. You're tired. You need some stress relief." This was more talking before sex than usual; I wouldn't say I felt impatient, but I could feel Mick's warmth through our clothes, and that warmth always pulled me to it. I pushed up Mick's sweater, untucked his polo shirt, moved my fingers through the bald spot on his belly down to the thicker, coarser hair. He was already starting to rise; I was already starting to vibrate.

"Ho-hum," Mick said, smiling.

W HY DON'T YOU TAKE the nuclear cardiology course with Howard?" Jeremy said. "Keep him in line."

"I don't want to do that stuff." I wrinkled my nose. "I'm a cardiologist, not a heart merchant."

"Someone's going to get the income. Why not us? It's not just the reading fees, the technical fees are what pay. Plus, it's a trail of crumbs leading Howard out of the cath lab." That did make me look up: between Jeremy and me, Howard's frailties in the cath lab were an open secret. "Tangential liability," Jeremy whispered at appropriate times. I thought of Howard's CV, its listing of awards back into grade school. Still, we'd hired him. And neither of us wanted to go back to being on call every other weekend.

"Oh, let him read them," I said. "They're probably not as easy as he thinks."

. . .

I DON'T SEE THE PROBLEM," Claudia said in my living room that weekend, sitting in the leather chair she always sat in. It was two weeks from May, but the weather was gray as November, clouds blanketing our bit of earth. "I can always go back. My credits aren't going to disappear." In her final month of her final semester of college, Claudia had quit school and gotten a job at a bed-and-bath store.

In one way I felt like picking her up and shaking her. In another way I was relieved she was making her own decisions. But maybe it wasn't her decision. "Is it because of that professor?" I said. "That . . . Toby?"

"Mom, he's wonderful to me."

"He's been engaged two times, you told me."

Claudia shifted in her seat. "You can't judge him, Mom. You said yourself he was a nice young man."

I had met the two of them at the Columbus Zoo. Toby's looks surprised me. I'd pictured him as someone wispy, but he looked like a rugby player. He was almost a foot taller than either Claudia or me, and his neck looked almost as big around as Claudia's waist. Hard to imagine a body that size poking around in my daughter's. Of course, people could say the same thing about me and Mick.

Toby didn't talk much, and insisted on calling me Dr. Toledo. I noticed, as we walked around visiting Claudia's favorite animals (koalas, monkeys, penguins), that he had extremely small teeth.

"I'm not judging him, no. Him I do not judge. What I'm

judging are your actions, your quitting school. I hope you're not quitting school for a man."

"Mom," Claudia said.

"That would be very old-fashioned, you know. Very 1950s. Don't forget, I was the first female cardiology fellow at Columbus General!"

NESSIE LOCKHART: CAN'T SEE RIGHT EYE

"I'm not on call," I said in irritation. "Why are they paging me? Can't I get a rest for one minute?"

"Mom, you should turn off your beeper."

"I fought for you, Claudia. Women of my generation, we opened things up for you. It's almost"—I struggled to find the right word—"a betrayal for you to plan your life around a man."

Claudia looked away. "You don't understand, Mom."

I was worried about Nessie Lockhart. She had an irregular heartbeat: could she have thrown a blood clot to her head? "I'm not even on call," I said again, picking up the phone.

H I, SWEET POTATO." Mick opened the door just as I inserted my keycard; once again he'd beaten me to our room. "How was your weekend?"

I shrugged and moved past him, shedding my handbag and jacket onto the TV cabinet. It was almost nine but just now getting dark. On the drive down, with each hill I crested, I'd tried to work up some joy over the green haze spreading through the trees. "Oh, Sunday I alienated Claudia," I said, and Mick's face fell (*I can tell the second you walk in how your day's been*). "Saturday I had a date."

Mick's face lost its sympathy. "A date? What do you mean, a date? You mean a date date, like dinner and a movie?"

"Actually, dinner and a play." I was tired. I should have kept my mouth shut. I had kept my mouth shut about dates before.

"How could you do that to me? How could you betray me like that?" The corner of his left eye was twitching.

"For crying out loud, Mick. It was a social obligation. Sukie set me up." Sukie was Jeremy's wife. I explained the situation—an old high school classmate of hers, newly divorced; two spare tickets to a play; Jeremy on call. Maybe once a year Sukie set me up like this. She and a couple of my elderly female patients fretted relentlessly about my being single. "And besides, Mick," I ended, "I'm not married to you. In fact, you're already married. In fact, every time you leave me you go straight home for a date with your . . ."

"That's the whole point!" he burst out. "You and I are better than married. We're united by desire."

There, I thought, delighted. My date had been a handsome guy, better-looking, in his chiseled way, than Mick, but he had been too smooth and scripted, while Mick could still pop up with things that surprised me.

"Did you screw the guy?" Mick said. "Did he touch your nipples?"

"Mickey!" I tried to laugh. "Don't be a Neanderthal."

"How would you like it if I went on a date with Courtney from the athletic director's office? Would you like that? Would you want to hear about that? She'd go out with me, you know. Courtney. In a flash."

"Don't flatter yourself." Courtney was probably Claudia's age. Men. I shook my head. I placed myself in front of Mick, blocking his movement, then reached between his legs, meaning to tease him.

"You think my dick is on a string? You think it should hop up to your service when you tug on it?"

I stayed, but it was the worst evening we ever spent together, ending with a peck and a hard-shut door. Outside it was cold again, despite the promise of the day, and I turned the heat on full blast in the car. This isn't even worth it, I thought as I drove home. Why couldn't I tell Mick about one date, when for years on any given Thursday he was allowed to talk about his wife? I put on the "soothing" tape Claudia had given me, but the music was droning and tuneless, something you'd hear in an incense-and-candle shop. I thought serenity had structure.

WELL, CONSIDER," Tessa said that Sunday during dinner out. "He clearly has a fragile ego. Genie, I know he fills a need for you, but when are you going to open yourself up to a real relationship? One that takes up, I don't know, *ten* hours a week."

This was belittling to both me and Mickey (I was thinking of him lately as Mickey, not Mick, and perhaps that in itself meant something?) and I hated Tessa's bossy tone. I didn't need someone else beside Claudia trying to correct my life. "Will you ask Herbie something for me?" I said. "Is there any sort of syndrome where a person has very small teeth? That Toby has teeth half the size of my teeth, and he's a good foot . . ."

"I'll ask Herbie," Tessa said. "Now, stop trying to avoid the subject."

"Mick's had a rough year," I said, wishing I'd never mentioned any problem with Mick to Tessa.

Tessa said, "Let's have some perspective. He loses games, you lose patients."

BILLY JAMES: SKIPPED BEATS AGAIN

M. L. HOPKINS: GOING ON TRIP, NEEDS PILLS

I shifted in my seat and waved impatiently at the beeper, thinking how Tessa's words might be close to how Mick saw me. "I heard this author on the radio yesterday," Tessa said. "She's religious but not too . . ."

Billy James was highly nervous, with a benign arrythmia he'd require sedation to not feel. M. L. Hopkins must have another decorating job in Europe. "Tessa, no offense, but I've got to get these pages." Tessa did look slightly offended. "In a way," I said, punching in Billy James's number on my phone, "Mick cares more about his job than I do about mine." I didn't realize this was true until I said it.

Tessa drew back and arched her eyebrows. "This is Genie? This is Dr. Genie I-Make-House-Calls Toledo speaking?"

I did make house calls. But not that often, and only for good reasons. And I couldn't see myself as better than Mick—professionally, morally, intellectually, in any way, really—or that would doom us both. And Mick had to be the better parent to his daughter. She adored him. She still lived, with her baby, in his home.

"It's boom boom BOOM, boom boom BOOM," Billy James said. "It's like Ringo Starr is in my chest."

Since the Sunday we had argued, Claudia had disappeared. Every call on my cell now was Mick calling to talk about quitting, saying he couldn't read people anymore, that the team had gotten away from him this year. His voice on the telephone wobbled and swerved, dangerously close to bathos.

"Did you take your Xanax this morning?" I asked, and Billy James launched into one of his endless stories.

"I just want to hold you," I imagined saying to Mick. "I want you to hold me." Something tender to calm us both down. I thought of Claudia's my-favorite-person paper from third grade, her homemade Mother's Day cards, the kiss she had tossed from the stage after *Alice in Wonderland*. I wondered if in one moment those things could indeed be wiped out.

Tessa was writing something on her napkin. She held it up: *Knitting Toward God,* by Wendy Weaver. I put my hand over the receiver and whispered, "I don't knit."

"It's spiritual," she whispered back. "It's not really . . ."

"I'm sure your mother doesn't hate your cupcakes," I said to Billy James. "She was probably still full from lunch. Listen, try one more Xanax and walk around your complex, and if you're not better in an hour call me back." I hung up and dialed M.L. "I don't even sew," I whispered to Tessa as M.L.'s phone rang. "I'm worthless with my hands."

KNOCK-KNOCK-KNOCK. I JUMPED UP to the door, and there he was. "Mickey. I got worried. I thought you were standing me up."

"Muffin. I finally made it." That crushing embrace, the door latching shut behind him. It was after ten.

He almost carried me to the bed. He laid me on my back and undressed me—no, that's inaccurate, he opened my clothes and his fly—and plunged into me with a desperation that for a moment, just a moment, before my own circuits started firing, made me feel less like a partner than a receptacle. I thought fleetingly of my ex-husband.

Mick lay heavily on top of me, his shoulders slumped forward, as if he were trying to imprint me on the bed. It was an uncomfortable position. "Thank you," he mumbled. If I didn't know him better I'd have thought he was drunk.

"Honey." I patted his flank and he rolled off me. He pulled off his shirt and pants and I my clothes and we settled into our usual position.

"I'm sorry I was hateful," Mick said. "Last time. That wasn't fair."

"It's okay. You didn't mean it."

I was too tired to argue. I'd spent half of Tuesday night at the hospital fussing with a malfunctioning pacemaker, and Wednesday I'd had a woman go bad in the CCU, pushing several hours of office time into today, and then this morning I'd had to cath two patients with acute myocardial infarctions. Mick's chest was warm on my cheek and I must have drifted off. The next thing I knew Mick was dressed again, sitting on the end of the bed.

"Tired, hunh?" Mick smiled, pulling on a sock. "You don't know what I went through. I had to pay cash. That's why I was late. I had to drive around and find an ATM machine. At least it's nice out."

I thought that I must still be sleeping. "What did you say?"

I asked him. He repeated his words, exactly, and for an instant
I thought I'd had a stroke, because what he said made no sense.
"What are you talking about?" I asked, struggling to push
myself up.

He grinned. "For our pleasure palace here. I left my new
expense account card at home."

"Expense account?" I pulled the sheet over my breasts. "You
put this room on an expense account?" I could move all four
extremities. I could speak.

"Sure. I get a credit card from the school. Always have. Pays
all travel."

It took me a moment to grasp this. "Doesn't someone look
over the receipts?" I said.

"Who, the AD's secretary? They don't care. They like me,
Genie. They really like me."

He had just signed a new contract. He was making serious
money, much more money than I made, and no one paid for my
hotel rooms.

The hairs on my arms stood on end. "But your name's on the
card. The hotel people know it's you."

"And? Are they my mother?"

He was different. No, I was different. No, the way I was seeing him was different, as if I'd taken a step back from him and
were watching a stranger across a room. *Pleasure palace. And?*
The cynicism in those words was frightening. This was Mick?
He edged around the bed and put his hands on the bed on either
side of me, bent over my face. "Umm," I said, my lips darting past his "I really like you too"—but this sounded so fake
I was mortified I'd said it, and it was troubling when he laid
his hand on my cheek and stroked it, then kissed me on the

forehead so tenderly the mark almost burned. What is going on here? I thought. What is *with* him?

Of course he'd use his credit card from the college, I thought, as I drove home. Why shouldn't he? That's what people did, stretched the limits, financial or otherwise, of whatever they'd been given, took out of things whatever they knew they could. The most trivial offense imaginable, one that ninety percent of the population would say was no offense at all. I was lucky I had a cardiologist's income and only myself and (partly) Claudia to support. Who could say what advantages I'd take if I were poorer?

But wasn't Mick cheating Turkman? Of course he was, but what had he been doing with me for the last eleven years? Cheating, cheating, cheating. And it had cost him literally nothing. The gas for his miles of driving to meet me—I suddenly knew this—was covered by his expense account too. I felt almost dizzy, as if I'd found myself on the edge of a canyon, the pebbles I dislodged with my feet echoing on the ledges below.

It was supposed to get cold tonight, one of those late-spring freezes. The tulip beds of my neighbors were covered with beige cloths.

Stop thinking like this, I told myself as I crawled into my own bed. Forget it. Put it away.

A FEW DAYS LATER there was an evening knock at my front door. I thought for a frantic second that it was Mr. Dylan, months late and confused again, but when I opened the door it was a gnome-like older man I didn't recognize, although he identified himself immediately as a neighbor and pointed at his

house down the street. He had a clipboard in his hand. "I'm collecting signatures from people who won't feed the cats," he said.

"What?"

"The wild cats," he said, his mouth twitching, "the feral
cats"—and as he said this I realized that, yes, sometimes driving
home I did see, illumined by my headlights, cats running across
the road or disappearing somewhere, although I'd never really
thought about their lives.

"Are they a problem?" I said, wondering which neighbors fed
them.

My gnome neighbor screwed up his face in distaste. "They
reproduce indiscriminately," he said, "and they are a terror to
the birds."

It was probably their indiscriminate reproduction that made
me sympathetic. I refused to sign the gnome's petition, although
from the looks of it many of my neighbors had. He glowered and
shook his head as he walked away.

WHEN WE FINALLY got together again, four weeks later,
after my week in Florida at an echocardiogram update
course and Mick's recruiting trip and yearly family cruise, Mick
told me to come to a new place, a Hilton. It was early June and
unseasonably warm and sticky, and through the hazy windows
that faced the hotel parking lot I could see vacationing kids and
parents in the indoor pool. Mick was waiting for me in the lobby,
and in the elevator up he pinned me to the wall and kissed me.

"Oh my, look at this," I said when we entered our room.
There was a wallpapered dado, and Chippendale chairs upholstered in green and red stripes. "Bed frame and all," I said,

pointing. Our usual bed (even on Mick's expense account, ha!) consisted of a mattress on top of a box spring with an ersatz headboard built into the wall, but this was a proper bed, with a dark wooden headboard and a footboard with decorative posts topped by carved pineapples. It touched me to see a place this elaborate: Mick was worried.

"I thought you deserved it." Mick looked pleased. He had phoned me twice a day from his cruise, almost making a nuisance of himself. A phone call during a cardiac cath is never welcome. Not a lot of joy for him lately, I thought, and I tried to play up my pleasure.

"It's beautiful, Mick," I said. I did my shoe trick and hopped upright onto the bed, jumping like a child.

"Be careful, sweetie," Mick said. "I don't want you falling and breaking your noodle."

We had a great time, as if we really were making up for all our missed sessions. Afterward I felt so frisky I stood up on the bed again and put my left foot on the footboard and bounced, shaking the bed. "Get down, you crazy woman," Mick said from the pillow behind me, and I looked back at him over my shoulder and made a face. I lifted my leg off the footboard and held it in the air, showing off a pose from my new tai chi tape (I'd always wanted to learn tai chi), but the bed wobbled and I tipped forward. I had to twist myself around to avoid hurtling over the footboard and I ended up sitting on the bedpost pineapple.

"Oh my God." I pushed myself up and off the bedpost. The pain was tremendous. I ran toward the bathroom, blood coursing down my legs. Like every cardiologist I knew, I took a daily aspirin as a blood thinner.

"I'm not hurt!" I shouted as I slammed the bathroom door. "It's the aspirin." I could hear my voice trembling.

But maybe I was hurt. The floor was white and the towel was white and the bathroom looked like a massacre.

"Open up!" Mick banged. "Open up or I'm calling the front desk! I'm not letting you bleed to death in there!"

I remembered the axiom from my med school days—*Bleeding always stops*—and pressed the towel harder between my legs. I got in the bathtub to keep from dripping on the floor.

I ended up opening the door for Mick and letting him do a sort of gynecological exam as I lay in the bathtub. He was pale and his hands were shaking. "God," he said, getting me another towel. "You're torn up."

I poked around my lower abdomen, relieved to find no pain where I pressed down. I was only cut, not perforated. "It's just a laceration," I said, wishing I had a mirror. After the initial blow the pain had faded.

"But the cut goes right up your, up your . . ." He couldn't say it.

"Vagina?"

His face was quivering and deformed. "We have to get you to the hospital."

"No way." I imagined myself on a stretcher in some emergency room hall. "I'm applying pressure and waiting. Give me another towel."

"I coach basketball!" he burst out. "You don't think I know when a vagina needs stitches?"

The grandmotherly desk clerk couldn't have been nicer, and the nearest hospital was only minutes away. "Female trouble," Mick said, as I waved and smiled and leaned on Mick's arm, hoping this sweet lady wouldn't think I'd been beat up. It was dark out now, and cooler, but still there was a sweet green smell. It wasn't until we got in Mick's car—me lying on the back seat with my knees curled up, fully dressed but for my stockings and panties, a towel between my legs—that the full hilarity of our situation hit us.

"You coach basketball?" I said. "You know when a vagina needs stitches?"

"What are we going to tell them?" Mick said, speeding along.

"Perineal laceration while on aspirin," I said to the admitting clerk at the ER, adding for both protection and explanation: "I'm a doctor." They hustled me to a stretcher, then put me into a room behind a curtain right away. The nurse winced when the injury was exposed, and no one asked many questions. "Last week we had a lady with a vibrator stuck up her butt," the young female transporter said brightly. The male doctor who did the stitching gave Mick a puzzled glance, but maybe he thought Mick looked familiar. Soon the doctor, like everyone else, was calling him Mr. Toledo. "Could be worse," the doctor said. "This is nice and superficial." The doctor let Mick stay in the room as he worked on me, Mick beside me on a stool, clutching my hand. We grinned at each other like two kids who'd gotten away with something.

"I'll call home," Mick said. "I'll make up some excuse. I'm not leaving you alone tonight."

"I'll send the ER flowers," Mick said as we drove back to the hotel. "From Mr. Toledo."

I couldn't tell Claudia. What could I possibly say? What would she think of me? "Mother!" I imagined her saying. "That's disgusting! What were you doing bouncing around on a bed?"

For a few days, I moved a little slowly at the hospital, but it was surprising how quickly I healed.

Two weeks later, rushing up a hospital back stairwell to see two patients on the third floor before my office hours, I passed my gynecologist, a pleasant, gentle man who was always impeccably dressed. "Hi!" I said, hurrying by him, although I could tell by the slyly curious way he looked at me that he'd received my ER records. When I was almost to the third-floor door I heard his voice behind me. "Are you okay now?" I turned to see him stopped on the steps, waving his hand in the general vicinity of his crotch.

"I'm fine." He looked at me expectantly. My patients on 3-West were both talkers, and I was plotting how I could most quickly get into and out of their rooms. "It was a pineapple," I said.

The gynecologist's eyes widened, and he started talking so quickly—"nothing to fret about . . . the wonderful perineal blood supply . . . your own business"—he couldn't possibly hear my explanation, and within seconds he'd skittered off and I gave up.

For crying out loud, I thought, my hand on the third-floor doorknob. On top of avoiding Lenny Moss (who'd read our heart scans before Howard took them over), now I'd have to avoid my gynecologist too.

"DID YOU DO GRIFFITHS TODAY?" I stuck my head into Howard's office. "She worries me." Early July, our group's first month of nuclear scanning.

"Griffiths?" Howard frowned. "God, Genie, let me think.

This is a madhouse without Jeremy." Jeremy was on his usual monthlong vacation at his wife's family's cottage in Michigan. "She's your lady, right? In her fifties, little woman, looks like you?"

Leora Griffiths looked like me? She was petite, yes, but prematurely gray and wrinkled, and I wondered if Howard knew the comparison was insulting. "Leora Griffiths," I repeated. "You did her treadmill and scan."

"Oh, Leora!" Howard said. "She did fine. Her scan looked great."

"It did? She has a good story. It's not typical chest pain but it's suggestive. She gets it with exercise."

"Sorry I can't help you. Scan looked perfect. Heart of an eighteen-year-old."

"Dr. Toledo?" LeeAnn the nurse was behind me. "Mr. Konrad's daughter insists she has to speak to you. Here's his chart."

"Can we fit Mrs. Tuckitt in somewhere?" Lindy the receptionist appeared. "She's Dr. Greathouse's patient and her heart is palpitating."

"I can't see her!" Howard threw up his hands. "I'm drowning!"

"I'll add her on," I said, grabbing Mr. Konrad's chart. I glared at Howard but he didn't notice. "Is she palpitating right this instant?"

S O WHAT DID MICK AND I talk about that night, me on my back with my legs parted, a plastic bag of ice between my thighs? Death.

I wasn't sure how we'd gotten through eleven years without discussing it, especially when scores of my patients had died during that time, not to mention Mick's former boss, Coach Neely. But this was the first time I remembered our really delving into it.

He didn't believe in heaven, not really, but there must be some kind of energy that carried on.

Most people didn't fear death, I said, from what I'd seen. Most people were ready. Of course, everybody wanted to go quickly—good for the person but harder for the family.

"I made my father quit smoking three weeks before he died," Mick said. "I took his last carton of cigarettes and tossed them in the Dumpster. He couldn't get out and he begged me to buy him more, but I wouldn't. I shouldn't have done that."

He talked about his former player Dashona Lykins's mother standing outside the room at a hospice as Dashona lay dying of lymphoma, listing the sins of Dashona's brothers, saying, "It shouldn't be Dashona. It's not right that it's Dashona."

I told him about my most recent patient death, Phyllis Landers, who'd refused to sign the Do Not Resuscitate form despite being eighty-nine years old, and how, as I was running from the hall into Mrs. Landers's room after she'd coded, I was greeted with two loud snaps—her ribs cracking from the arrest team's chest compressions.

Mick shook his head. "Oh, pie-face."

"Well. I hope I do more good than harm."

"If I die, I want to die with you."

"Thank you. I'll put that in your file."

Mick had seen hell on earth once, when he was a boy. The hired man who lived in a trailer at the edge of his Uncle Tad's farm, who sat on the toilet with the bathroom door open, screaming to little Mickey to get him help so he could shit, as his wife sat outside in a deck chair drinking beer, ignoring them both. "Bowel cancer," Mick said. "He died about a month later." I shook my head, understanding. I'd seen cases like that too. "How lucky we are," Mick said, tightening his grip on my shoulder.

Before we fell asleep we planned our future. Actually planned it, decided on a place that we both liked. Mick had been hearing good things about San Antonio; I had liked it when I visited there. Mick said, "It'll work out. We'll get our years in."

When I woke up the curtains were cracked and light like a slab of butter poured into the room. Mick was dressed and sitting in the chair. "How do you feel?" he said.

I squinted. "Okay. Better." The bag between my legs was now a lukewarm sac; I lifted it out delicately and laid it on the bedside table. Almost miraculous to see Mick in the morning. We ordered a room service breakfast. My office hours were canceled for a stomach virus and Mick's wife thought he was with Marcus, who Mick said had had a concussion in a minor car crash and needed watching. "God," I said, "I don't have makeup."

"You look beautiful."

"I don't even have a toothbrush."

Mick grinned and held up a plastic bag. "Toiletry kit from the front desk. This is a classy hotel."

I sank my head back into the pillow, as Mick wiped off the pineapple with a damp washcloth. "Bad pineapple," he said, "naughty pineapple," light glinting on his big round watch face and the pale hairs of his arm.

"I almost love that pineapple," I said.

A WOUND IN THE GROIN!" Tessa said. "That's classic. That's mythic. Like Joseph Campbell on PBS. Remember that show?"

I did not. For years, I hadn't watched any TV other than basketball. "So what's the wound supposed to lead to?" I asked.

"I don't know. Wisdom? Transformation? Something good. Oh, and I finally remembered to ask Herbie: there are some syndromes with small teeth, but they have other abnormalities, and probably someone with a syndrome wouldn't look completely normal. Does Toby look normal?"

I nodded.

"Then Herbie says don't worry. Some people just have smaller teeth. Like noses. Respect the human variety, he said."

There's always Viagra, I thought as I drove toward Mick in late July, thinking of our previous few Thursdays. He didn't want to hurt me, he said, and each time as he tried to angle into me he'd gone soft. Before last month, this had happened maybe two or three times in all our years together, not enough to worry about or mention. But when I reached our room—our old comfortable room, not the site of my injury—I knew it would be an insult to mention Viagra to Mickey. He was in the middle of his basketball camps for kids, mired in eager kids, ambitious parents, and the needs of what the Turkman athletic director referred to as "fan development." *Respect the human variety*, I thought. I told Mick about the wound in the groin, how it resulted, invariably, in greater happiness and wisdom.

"But the wound was in *your* groin," Mick said. "You're not saying it's infectious, are you?"

"In a way. Because you're worried about me. But you don't need to be. See?" I leapt out of the bed and danced on the carpet. I felt like an idiot.

"Stop that!" Mick snapped. "You'll hurt yourself." I did stop. I sat down on the edge of the bed, stroked Mick's cheek, and told him I was healed.

"You never know how you'll react to something," Mick said later as we lay in our usual position, skin to skin, his heart throbbing in my right ear. "When I saw that blood running down your leg, oh my gosh. I can't tell you how much I've thought about you these last few weeks. I got up at four a couple mornings last week and just walked around our back yard." I wished he hadn't told me this; the image was almost piercingly forlorn.

"It must have worried your wife," I said, picturing a woman reaching toward an absence in the bed.

"Karn? She sleeps like a dead man." She must, I thought, thinking of Mick's and my years together. I hoped Karn kept sleeping. "I would have called you but I didn't want to get you up."

"You could have called me. I get woken up all the time. If it's serious, sometimes I have to go in. Who knows? I could have been in the cath lab while you were out pacing."

There was a hitch in his breathing, as if the reality of my life had just hit him. "You do get woken up, don't you?" he said. "I guess you do." I wished I hadn't mentioned my cath lab nights, because the image of the both of us awake in the dark and apart made me feel terribly alone. The night we'd spent together had changed things: it showed us what we were missing.

Y OU KNOW HE KILLS THEM," my neighbor with the blond hair and three grade-school sons said when we met one evening at our mailboxes. "Poison. My husband found the big gray one stiff in our kitchen window well. I think she was a mother too. I was always seeing her with that yellow striped kitten. Have you seen that kitten? Oh my God, she looks like something on a calendar. I haven't seen her for a couple days, though." She gave me a worried look. "I hope he didn't . . ."

"What's his story, anyway?" I asked. "I didn't recognize him."

"Oh, he never comes out. The wife doesn't either. They have bird feeders out back, by the seventh fairway, and they sit inside and watch them. My oldest sold them popcorn for Cub Scouts, but when he went back to deliver they wouldn't pay."

The neighbor and I looked at each other. I didn't tell her that I'd been putting out milk and tuna on my deck for the last month, ever since the gnome man told me not to. I didn't tell her that I'd been concerned about the disappearance of the big gray cat, that the black cat and the calico and the tabby were also missing, that I'd seen the yellow striped kitten before I left for the hospital at six that morning. I could have told her all these things, she would have liked me for them, but my neighbor was a cheerful, robust woman, implacable in the face of boys sling-shotting each other with walnuts or riding their bikes down the slide in her back yard, and I didn't want to sound like a solitary woman who worries about cats. I didn't want her, I suppose, to see the ache in me.

M ICK'S NEW CONTRACT, signed in April, brought him a little more than half a million a year. In August, the head of Turkman State's English Department was offered a dean's posi-tion in Iowa, and he made it known that without a salary boost commensurate with his experience, he had no choice but to leave. Turkman State's president said—not publicly, but in a luncheon comment overheard by a reporter for the student paper—that, to bottom-line it, English was worth two cents to every basketball dollar. That a college president who wore bowties and professed to love both baseball and Yeats with equal fervor should speak so crassly about their department added salt to the English Depart-ment's wounds. Soon word leaked from somewhere that Coach Crabbe had no respect for his athletes' education, that he had in fact tried to have the English Department's most effective tutor, who happened to be the one who had started something up with Tom Kennilworth, fired. The student paper, in its late-August edition, reported this allegation. By the time the fall semes-ter started, members of the English and Romance Languages

Departments were circulating petitions outside the humanities building, and a Rally for the Humanities was planned for the Saturday after Labor Day.

Mick's salary was complicated, a base salary topped by various bonuses and annuities, but the English Department chair's salary was quite simple. "That's it?" I said. We weren't even undressed yet. The only thing Mick had removed was his shoes.

"I'm not blaming him for being unhappy," Mick said. "But his salary is completely independent from mine."

"But your president linked them," I pointed out. "And the contrast is stunning. And compare and contrast is a good rhetorical device, and all those English professors probably were on their debate teams in high school, and . . ." I trailed off at Mick's comically horrified face.

"Whose side are you on? If the English Department gets some of our money, they get some of our power, and power's something you don't just want to hand over. It's a turnover. We may be up by forty points, but I'm going to be out there yelling if the other guys steal our ball."

I looked at him, and suddenly the air between us seemed to thicken with a viscous substance that might be greed. "Well . . ." I shrugged. "Forty points . . ." This is what impotence does, I thought. It makes money matter. I thought of the thick gold chain Howard wore around his right wrist. God knows what he did on Tuesdays. I glanced at Mickey's profile, then looked guiltily away.

"We just stole nuclear cardiology from the doctor who'd been doing it for years," I heard myself say, as if this confession would even some score. "We've been doing the scans in our office the last couple months."

"Who'd you steal it from? Were they happy?"

Was Lenny Moss happy? Of course he wasn't, but I hadn't asked him. In fact, I'd gone to some pains to avoid him. I tried to explain the situation to Mick, realizing as I spoke that Howard and Jeremy and I were the strong robbing the weak, that I would never have a friendly chat with Lenny Moss again. I had planned to have him check over Howard's difficult scans; in truth, I'd been so busy I hadn't glanced at Howard's scans myself. I hoped Howard was reliable. He was probably reliable.

"I didn't steal anything from English!" Mick said. "I only wanted Kennilworth's tutor reassigned, not fired! God, I hate the press," he muttered. "Why does the press have to stick its big runny nose into everything?"

He had started out coaching because Coach Kean had cared, because Coach Kean had said he was a leader. *He saved me / I'll save them.* It almost made me cry to think of the purity of that starting impulse, and how it had brought Mick to this.

A FTER A VIRTUOUS DINNER, Tessa ordered a piece of cheese-cake. "Thank God for nightgowns," Tessa said when her plate arrived. "Oh, come on," she said, noticing my puzzled face. "Aren't you thanking God for nightgowns at our age?" She popped a bite of cheesecake into her mouth and leaned forward confidingly. "Herbie hasn't seen me naked in ten years."

Mick sees me naked all the time, I thought, but that thought led to me seeing him naked, his consternated look and flaccid penis. Naked and impotent, you couldn't get more naked than that. "That's a shame, Tessa," I said. "You'd look like Lady Godiva."

Her face changed. "Do you really think so?"

"With your hair? Of course you would. You'd look gorgeous. You should surprise Herb one night and walk out of the bathroom naked. You know, *present* yourself to him."

Tessa frowned and leaned forward, tapped her bent index finger on the table. She sat up straight and smiled, gave a little flick to her hair. "I'll have a couple drinks first," she said.

S EPTEMBER CAME. The rally proceeded as planned. I watched the West Virginia news via satellite dish and video recording.

TWO CENTS, FOUR CENTS, WE DESERVE A DOLLAR!
SET OUR TUTORS FREE
CRABBE'S CASH MAKES US CRABBY

A thin man with a beard and a knitted vest, almost a cartoon version of an English professor, said, "We're faintly ridiculous, but we have a point."

"Coach Crabbe refuses to comment," the reporter said, and there was Mick, striding toward a building, shoulders hunched, square-jawed, looking almost like a football coach, looking—my heart sank to see this—faintly ridiculous himself.

"You do something all-American like make a lot of money and what happens?" he said to me over the phone.

I opened a mail subscription to the Turkman city paper. I thought in reading it I might glean something useful in protecting Mick.

"I'm just tired of it, you know?" he said that Thursday. "I spoke at a Rotary Club yesterday, and the guys there seemed to think I was all right."

"How're the players taking it?" He couldn't get them together as a team until the middle of October, an NCAA rule, but he could meet with them individually. Mick sighed. "Eluard can't write. Two of my incomings can't read. You think the people in English are going to cut them any slack? And that tutor's back with Kennilworth. If his marriage splits up, so be it. I wash my hands of it."

For the first time I saw the irony of Mick's being upset over Kennilworth's affair. I wondered if he recognized it. "Mick . . ." I started, then stopped myself. But he'd caught my point.

"We're different," he said, giving me a sideways glance. "Don't ask me how, but we are."

"We're grown-ups," I said.

"That's right. We know what we're doing."

"We're friends."

Mickey nodded. "Of course we're friends. Platonic."

I didn't know how to respond to this. I pretended to laugh and started talking about my patient M.L., off decorating a hotel complex in Costa Rica.

YOUR LEORA GRIFFITHS came in Saturday," Howard said, pulling up a chair beside me at the nurses' station. I glanced up from the progress note I was writing. "Big anterior wall MI." Myocardial infarction: the anterior wall ones were usually the biggest ones. "She was already in heart failure," Howard went on. "I took her to the cath lab but she died on me. Bad, bad scene. V-tach, flash pulmonary edema, hypotension . . ." Howard shook his head. "Not much I could cure there."

"Leora Griffiths? *My* Leora Griffiths? The one you said looked like me?"

He nodded. "I mean, far be it from me to criticize, but that lady'd been having chest pain forever. I'm surprised you didn't cath her months ago."

My God, I was thinking, why didn't I? But then the memory rebuilt itself, like squares of patchwork filling in a quilt. Leora Griffiths's chest pain was worrisome but atypical, her heart scan had been normal, and Leora herself had wanted a trial of meds before agreeing to a cath. Still, the thought of missing that much pathology in someone was unbearable. And I had liked Leora—her wry little mouth, her peculiar bursts of speech. I concentrated now on slowing down my own breathing. "I ordered a scan on her," I said. "You did it. You read it as normal."

"I reviewed that scan this weekend." Howard nodded in a serious way. "I reviewed it." Something in those words made me leery. "Someone could argue with my reading, I admit," Howard went on, "but it's just as likely they'd call it breast artifact like I did." Sometimes, on a heart scan, the shadow of a large breast could obscure the image of the heart.

"She's five feet tall and weighs ninety pounds," I said. "She has no breasts."

"Had."

I stared. In all my years of practice at this hospital, there had been a death in the cath lab only once: an elderly male whose cardiologist soon quit and moved to Canada. "You supervised her stress test!" I said to Howard. "You said she looked like me. Look at me: do I have breasts?"

His eyes darted to my chest.

"Excuse me." It was the ward clerk, holding out a chart for Howard. "Is this supposed to say 'Chemistry profile'?"

"You got my report," Howard said to me. "It was your responsibility to read it." And to the nurse, "Yes, that's what it says. Doesn't anybody read anymore? Excuse me"—he straightened his white coat on this shoulders—"I have rounds to make."

T ESSA LEFT A MESSAGE on my answering machine, and her voice was almost musical. "I just wanted to tell you: L.G. was a hit, a huge hit. I think L.G.'s going to be visiting again soon."

I thought at first that Tessa was making a joke about Leora Griffiths. How could she? How could Tessa of all people be so cruel? Then I remembered Lady Godiva.

M Y PARTNER IS AN ASSHOLE," I told Mick when I walked into the room.

"Howard? That's no surprise." He was lying on the bed on his back with his eyes closed, fully dressed down to his shoes.

"I guess not." I bit the inside of my cheek. I had called Leora Griffiths's sister, the closest relative she had. "It's all right," the sister said. "She loved you as a doctor. And she always wanted to go fast."

"I think I'm going crazy," I said to Mick.

That did make his eyes open. "You?" he said. "You?" He patted the bed beside him. "Come here and let me calm you down."

Things worked. I was glad I'd never popped out of the bathroom naked or mentioned the Viagra to Mick. He positioned me on top of him and held my hipbones as he entered. Tenderer, I thought, gentler. As if our formerly hectic lovemaking had slipped gratefully into middle age.

"When you walked in and said you were going crazy, was that a panic attack?" Mick said later as we rested. "Like, you can't breathe and your brain feels scrambled?"

I frowned, wondering why he'd ever associate panic attacks with me. "No, I just . . ."

"Karn has panic attacks," Mick said. Karn, his wife.

C LAUDIA SMILED COYLY across the table. We were in our usual burger place, and for the first time I noticed the wicked-looking scythe hanging on the wall behind her. What kind of decoration was that? There was nothing cheerful about it. "Are you ready for some news?"

"You're getting married. You didn't even talk to me about it and you and Toby . . ." I wanted, suddenly, for us to find a new restaurant for our burgers: I didn't want to ever again see that horrid thing behind my daughter. "Tell me, have you ever wondered about his . . ."

Thank God, a familiar buzz stopped me:

M. L. HOPKINS: SWOLLEN ANKLES

because I had been precariously close to asking Claudia if she'd noticed Toby's teeth.

"Shit," I said, reading the message. "I bet she's drinking again."

Claudia stared. "You do it every time. It's amazing—you do it every, every time."

"What?" I said, confused. Could Claudia be pregnant?

"You don't listen to me! I try to tell you something important and all you pay attention to is your beeper." A moment before, Claudia had looked normal—lovely, luminous, in that pink square-necked shirt that flattered her light brown hair and rosy face—and now she was almost in tears.

"Claudia," I said. I felt like crying. "Honey, I'm sorry. I didn't mean to sound all worked up. I knew you and Toby were serious, I understand if you . . ."

"Just listen for once! Listen! No, I'm not getting married, no, you don't have me off your hands. My news is I found a new job."

WHAT DO YOU THINK?" I asked Lenny Moss, using my hand to cover the date on the corner of Leora Griffiths's films. "Could that be breast artifact?"

"No way." Lenny chuckled. "Sorry, Genie, this is one you've got to cath."

MICK WAS SPOOKILY CHEERFUL on the phone, despite the continuing fuss over his salary. "Now we're getting phone calls. I changed our number at home to unlisted. It's too hard on Karn." What did it mean that Mick was mentioning her so often? "People love you a lot, they hate you a lot," he said. "They still want me for that leadership seminar in Baltimore, though. And get this, guess who's saying now I'm worth every penny? Art Quinlivan, of all people. Not that he likes me. He just wants Turkman looking big-time." Mick laughed, and the sound went on and on, as if nothing in the world could ever bother him at all.

Now that the Turkman paper was appearing in my mailbox, I had read Art Quinlivan's column. I thought he was more ambivalent about Mick than Mick took him to be, but Quinlivan was certainly optimistic about this season's team.

What's wrong with me? I thought. Why do I notice Art Quinlivan's *but*s and *somewhat*s? Why can't I snap out of things like Mick does?

This isn't a good time, I thought. Life's like that, I reminded myself. There are always bad days.

Claudia's new job was a secretarial one at her old college, in a building two buildings from Toby's office. The benefits were minimal, her office was a cubicle, her coworkers were entrenched and unfriendly, and the only advantage of the job, so far as I could see, was its proximity to Toby.

We'd made a date, two Sundays away, on a weekend I was not wearing my beeper, for Claudia and Toby to come to my house for dinner. They were serious, clearly. Claudia wanted me to know him better. I wanted to know him better.

I ran through my tai chi tape every night, but my chi seemed to be ebbing. At the drugstore to buy lipstick I picked up a kickboxing tape instead. Maybe I'm secretly angry, I thought, remembering Claudia's red face. The manicurist on her weekly house call rued the state of my nails.

But Mick and I were having sex again. That helped. That helped us both.

Zucchini and red peppers and portobello mushrooms on the grill. The sky was a beautiful autumn blue, the tips of the leaves yellow and red. I should notice the world more, I thought. Whole years circled around and I hardly saw them. I'd just run into one of my patients in the grocery. "You got old on me!" I felt like saying, shocked by his stooped posture and shuffling gait. Then I realized he'd been my patient for sixteen years, time enough to age us both. Funny I hadn't noticed that in the confines of my exam rooms.

"Have you been a vegetarian long?" I asked Toby. I hadn't known he was one until Claudia warned me as I planned this dinner.

Claudia, fork in the air, looked at Toby like an adoring mother in an advertisement for macaroni and cheese. Toby met my eyes warily, rubbed his hand over his burr of hair. Hard to imagine that body fueled by nothing but vegetables.

"I don't like meat politics," Toby said.

We had already talked about Toby's graduate school days, his teaching schedule, his family, his hobbies (besides his vegetable garden, he coached coed soccer to elementary students), and I was desperate for any topic of conversation. "What do you mean?" I said.

Toby looked at me unblinkingly. "Everything's political."

"You mean . . . everything's susceptible to the influence of position and power?" Ridiculous the sprightly way I said this, as if I were talking to a three-year-old. But I was pleased to have landed a definition so quickly.

Toby stopped chewing. "I personally would like to grow my own meat."

"You mean have chickens?"

"Rabbits."

I glanced toward Claudia. The thought of my daughter involved with the slaughter and cooking of rabbits was incomprehensible. Claudia never even used the word "rabbit." She said "bunny."

Claudia looked at me and smiled.

A ND SHE'S AN INTELLIGENT GIRL," I told Mick. "She's not a fuzzy thinker."

"I wouldn't think so. Not with you as a mom." Mick lifted his arm from behind my head and shook it out.

An edge in his voice, as if he meant some criticism. Maybe I was imagining it. Maybe not. What stupid thing had I said when I arrived? *How's my half-million-dollar man?* I should be more politic myself.

I sat up. "He's older, she looks up to him. He's feeding her all kinds of vegetable ideas."

"Oh, I'm sure he is." Mick scratched the back of his head. "But you have to be careful. Being mad at you could be the glue holding them together. Look on the nightstand. Page two." I opened the *Turkman Tattler*—the Turkman State student newspaper—

and saw a headline, "Athletics Blend Diverse Lives." There were photos. Two tennis players, a gay male and a straight woman; a Serb and a Bosnian both on the soccer team; a black guy and a white guy, "best friends," who played basketball together. The last pair was Eluard Dickens and Tom Kennilworth. *The friends have been even closer since last season, when reported differences between the pair and Coach Mick Crabbe led to . . .*

"I hear B.C. put the paper up to it," Mick said, reading over my shoulder. B.C. was the Turkman athletic director. Mick couldn't stand him. His initials were appropriate, Mick said. The guy was a cockroach; he came from a land before time.

I looked at Mick inquiringly.

"Jealousy," Mick said. "B.C. makes a lot less than I do. But Karn says the trustees are on my side."

"Karn? How does Karn know?"

"The president's wife."

I felt as if I'd walked into a spiderweb. I set down the paper and flicked at my face as if brushing something off.

"I hear Eluard is really looking hot in pickup games," Mick said, propping himself up on his elbows. "I hear all he wants is the ball." He smiled. "He stayed all summer with this guy who'd played in the NBA, and this guy took Eluard to his gym and ran him and played him one-on-one, and Flitt says this guy told Eluard he was too soft, no NBA team would ever want him, and if I was telling him different I was lying. Eluard's bigger now— twenty-three pounds of muscle—and he's mad. Flitt says he's becoming a motherfucker." I was startled at the word, then realized Mick was quoting.

"And that's a good thing," I said, half questioning. I knew

what it meant: a fierce competitor, someone who'd be in there with his knees and elbows, intimidating, pushing, doing anything to win.

"You bet."

"But he's insulting you by saying you didn't try to make him tough."

"What do I care? He gets a couple more rebounds, a couple more shots each game—he can hate me all the way to Timbuktu. He looks at me now." Mick gave a twisted sort of smile. "He glares. He looks at me like *I've got your number, sucker.* Listen, why should everybody like me? Some folks might be better off to hate me."

For Mick, even before it started, this was already a better season than the last one. I wished I could be happy with him. I wondered what was wrong with me that I wasn't. I thought about the yellow striped cat. Another night of frost and I might be able to lure her inside. She had lost her baby look but she was delicate, with slim paws and big blue eyes. Plenty of room on my big bed for her, if I could get her in.

THE MIDDLE OF THE NIGHT on my next Tuesday call night: the phone was ringing and someone was asking me questions. "You want the usual heparin? Five thousand units followed by an eight-hundred-unit drip?"

"What about Lovenox?" The newer, safer blood thinner.

"His chart says he's allergic to it. But he says he took heparin okay."

Dickie Dylan. Chest pain. So long since I'd ordered heparin. I had a glimpse of my mind like a disembodied hand groping for something on the night table.

"Fifteen-thousand-unit bolus," I said. The hand—disturbingly—had turned into Toby's hand. What did he and Claudia *do,* exactly, since he was so damn moral?

"Fifteen thousand?" the voice said sharply, making me doubt myself. Wasn't it fifteen thousand? I used to order this all the time. The hand was moving between books and picture frames, threatening to knock things over. I remembered the gynecologist's face when I said *a pineapple.*

"No, twenty-five thousand," I said. "I'm sure. Twenty-five thousand, then keep him on the eight hundred." I was asleep before I hung up the phone.

In the morning I walked into Mr. Dylan's room and there was blood in his bag of urine, blood oozing around his IV site, streaks of blood where he'd spat out toothpaste in the sink.

I flung open his chart to the orders section, wondering if it was actually possible I'd ordered—as I suddenly remembered—a 25,000-unit bolus of heparin. Sweat erupted on my forehead. Mad. Insane. A mistake a competent doctor could not imagine making. Take two hundred aspirins and call me in the morning.

But Mr. Dylan was fine. He was sitting in his bed looking at me, saying, "And how are you today, Dr. Toledo?" A concerned look changed his face. He gagged, and bloody vomit splashed his gown.

HE'S ALIVE," I said to Mick over my cellphone. I was sitting in my parked car in my dark garage, too tired to open the car door and make my way inside. "I mean he's fine, really. He's in intensive care and his blood's unthinned and his GI bleed seems to have stopped and he's not having any more chest pain. His chest pain probably wasn't even cardiac. His EKGs and enzymes are fine, and when the GI guy looked into his esophagus it was all tore up."

"Did you tell him what you did?"

"Yeah. You know what he said? *I don't need this information! I don't want this information!* I tried to report myself, I went to the chief of staff, and he said it's a systems problem and they should have had dosages already on the order sheets and the nurse might have written down my order incorrectly and basically I shouldn't worry. But how can I not worry? I mean, there are things that I should *know*."

"Oh, honey."

"I should be . . . I should be . . . I should be able to do it in my sleep!"

"You work too hard, honey."

It took a moment to realize the mewling sound I heard was coming from me; I thought at first that the yellow-striped cat was trapped under one of my tires, and this vision sent me into a panic because I usually spotted her when my car pulled into the drive. "I know I work hard, I always work hard, but then I think that this is a message to me, if I weren't spending all my time running around with you and worried about Claudia, I . . ."

I kept a flashlight beside the door from the garage into the kitchen. I got out of my car and stumbled toward it.

"Listen, if you weren't worried about Claudia, you'd be worried about your taxes. If you weren't running around with me, you'd be running around with Tessa. It's always going to be something. It's life."

I snorted gratefully, turned the flashlight on, headed outside through the garage door.

"You should take it easy, babe," Mick said. A hesitation. "You want to skip tomorrow?"

"No. God no. But I won't get there till late. I had to reschedule all my morning office patients for tomorrow. And I'm on this weekend." I knelt on the ground and shone my flashlight under the deck. Where was my kitty? Her usual sleeping spot was empty. A little bowl of ground with nothing in it.

"They never let you rest, do they?" Mick said softly. "The games are on the schedule. The fans are in the stands."

I jerked the flashlight beam around with increasing franticness, thinking of my gnome-like neighbor. *There.* Thank God. The cat was under a new corner of the deck, sound asleep. Ginger, I'd taken to calling her. "You know, Mick," I said, my eyes filling with tears. "You know."

S TRANGE, but two weeks later my life was again normal: I saw my patients, did my angiograms, shopped with Claudia, saw Mick and his well-functioning parts on consecutive Thursdays. One of these Thursdays was the day after my birthday, and Mick gave me a pair of sea-glass earrings.

It was a Friday and I was sitting in my office going through charts when a hand with blue-polished nails slapped a slip of paper on my desk. "Can you maybe call this guy pronto?" Lindy said. "He's been bothering us since we turned on the phones. Says you're a"—her voice took on a whine—"personal friend. Coach Crabbe. Coach Crabby, in my opinion."

I frowned at the paper, with its notations of Mick's cellphone number, his pager number, his office number, the number of his phone at home. The home phone number I didn't recognize. "Urgent" was scrawled across the top of the paper, with a listing of the times Mick had called. "Why didn't you page me?" I asked Lindy, reaching for the phone.

"He's not a patient! Not even related to a patient. Listen, this guy is a case and a half. *Coach* Crabbe, *Coach* Crabbe. What's he a coach for, roller hockey?"

"Mick?" I waved Lindy away, beckoning her to close the door behind her. "Are you okay?"

His daughter, Jessica, twenty-two years old, was having chest pain. Had been having it off and on for weeks. She couldn't push a stroller up a hill without getting short of breath and hurting. Mick's wife was the one who first noticed it. "Karn said Jessica got white and beads of sweat popped out all over her forehead. Karn was afraid she'd die on her right there."

"Did she go to the emergency room? Call her doctor?"

"She doesn't have a doctor except for her OB. She's scared of doctors, see? Always has been, probably gets that from me." Mick moved over those last words so quickly I barely registered them until later. "So I talked to her for like an hour last night and she finally agreed to see you. Because there's a connection. Because I told her she can trust you."

I was speechless. Mick's daughter! I could think of a thousand reasons I didn't want to have Mick's daughter as a patient.

Mick said, "I told her you were Marcus's girlfriend."

I made a laugh that sounded like a honk. What was happening to me? Why was I making these bizarre noises? "But my office is a long way from your house, Mick," I said. "If she needs to be hospitalized or a procedure done—not that that's likely, not at her age—are you sure you want to do it here?"

"We go where my friends are," Mick said. "Friends help out."

.   .   .

I WAS UP HALF the nights all that weekend. What if Karn insisted on driving her daughter to see me, on sitting in the waiting room until I emerged with my opinion, or—this was the worst—marching herself right into my exam room? But Jessica was an adult; she surely would be coming on her own. Or perhaps not, since she still lived in her parents' home. She had a job at a children's clothing store owned by a Turkman State alum (friends help out). I suspected, although I hadn't asked about this explicitly, that Mick paid for all the diapers and toys that Jessica needed for her baby.

"Your new patient's here," LeeAnn said Monday, tapping the chart in the container outside the exam room door.

"Miss Crabbe?" I said, peeking around the door, and there was—thank God!—only one person in the room, a pretty young woman with straight light brown hair.

"Dr. Toledo?" she said from her perch at the end of the exam table, holding out her hand. Mick around her eyes, I noticed. A friendly face, a lap that was a little abundant. A good diet-and-exercise person, I thought, relieved. Someone who'd be grateful for some lifestyle advice. "Thanks for seeing me," the young woman said. "I don't like doctors, no offense, but how could I not like a friend of Marcus's?"

I can't tell you how relieved I was, how proud I was of Mick for having this polite and pleasant daughter. All my thoughts of the day before (scared of doctors, eh? well, she was probably hysterical, had that panic attack chest pain that always required multiple negative tests and countless office visits to allay) popped like a balloon. I could see that Jessica was not a person to make up chest pain. Jessica would have something wrong. It would be something minor—esophagitis or a prolapsed heart valve—and I'd find it and treat it and everyone would be happy.

"Oh, no problem," I said. "I'm glad to see you." I wish Mick could meet Claudia, I thought. He'd like Claudia.

I sat and we settled down to business. I asked questions and listened, inspecting the form Jessica had filled out in the waiting room, wondering what Claudia would think of Mick, how she would behave toward him (I hoped she wouldn't clam up and stare), and within minutes I was filled with such anxiety I didn't trust myself to speak, because Jessica's story sounded exactly like angina, the classic symptom of a blocked artery in the heart, and a blocked artery was something I wanted to suspect only in an older person, not in a young woman like Jessica.

". . . and I sat myself and the stroller on the edge of the road for about five minutes," Jessica was saying, "and then I could go on."

Difficult to picture Jessica as a mother. Like Claudia, she looked dewy as a child herself, barely older than a junior high school student, and her lips were puffed and rounded like her father's, and the thought of slipping a catheter into her groin, of running its tip up through her abdomen into her chest and her cardiac vessels, of possibly finding a blockage, of opening that blockage with a balloon, was impossible. I didn't often think of what I did as an invasion, but of course it was. *I can't handle this*, I thought. *I can't do this.* "Any recent stress?" I asked, the next question on my list.

"Have you ever met my mom?" Jessica said. She laughed in an exasperated way, and I hurriedly shook my head, startled at the mention of Karn. "I live at my parents'. That can be a little stressful."

I was careful to keep my face neutral. "Is your chest pain ever triggered by stress?"

"See"—Jessica tapped her head with her index finger—"I'm figuring her out. I finally realized that she's the above-the-title star of our household, and if you treat her that way, if you think of everything you do as supporting her performance, then things can go pretty well. But if you make her look bad, or if you want a breakout role for yourself, well . . ." She laughed a shade too heartily. "That's when the shit hits the fan."

She swore. Mick's daughter swore. And his wife was a witch. Why would a normal man put up with the sort of drama-queen spouse that Jessica was describing? I had trusted, I realized, that Mick's wife was a pleasant, harmless person, a woman he stayed with out of loyalty and guilt, not out of some crazy need. I felt like I'd been thrust under murky water, and I was watching my opinion of Mick sink like a stone.

"You need a stress test," I finally said. "You're way too young and healthy to have coronary artery disease, but sometimes strange things happen. You could even have a congenital narrowing in an artery. I know you drove a long way to get here. Let's see if I can arrange something right now." I wandered out to the front desk, where Howard, chattering away with a patient at the window, was massaging Lindy's shoulders. I'm not handing her over to *him,* I thought, thinking of his reading of Mrs. Griffiths's scan. I walked back to my office and closed the door.

"Of course!" Lenny the nuclear-medicine doc said over the phone, the eagerness in his voice making me queasy. "Send her over and we'll do her right away."

I see what's coming, I thought, sitting at my desk and chewing on my right thumbnail. The scan will be abnormal and I'll have to cath her. When I took my thumb from my mouth there were dents in the polish of my nail.

M Y WHOLE FAMILY CAME," Jessica said, smiling from her hospital bed the next morning. And indeed there they were, lined up on chairs against the wall of her room like a panel of judges: Mick, Karn, the sons Bobby and Eric, Eric's wife Delilah. A toddler was standing pressing buttons on the control panel that moved Jessica's bed, and when he tilted his head to gaze at me he looked startled.

"You're not used to a grown-up my size," I said, and he frowned with something like suspicion before he looked away.

"Dr. Toledo," Karn said, rising, and then both she and Mick were in front of me.

I had never realized Mick was quite so tall. He was huge, he was a mountain, and Karn was almost as big as he was. They looked to me like a pair of giants. They looked to me as if they fit together.

"I'm Jessica's mother, Karn Crabbe." Karn gripped my hand and held it. "You'll take good care of her?" Up close Karn had pale eyebrows and eyelashes clumped with mascara, as well as crow's-feet and vertical lines around her mouth. Too much sun, I thought, painfully aware of my fingers being jammed together. *Pool rats,* my father used to call the tanned country club members, although he smiled and preened in their presence. "Marcus speaks so highly of you," Karn said.

"I'll do my best," I said, wondering if I'd ever meet Marcus.

Now that I was confronted with Mick's whole family, it seemed impossible I'd ever met Mick. Our hotel room seemed like a phantasm, or a remembered room in an exotic place—Helsinki, say, or Madagascar—I'd probably never get back to and could scarcely believe I'd been to.

"Thank you for seeing her," Mick said. "Thank you for finding the problem." He extended his hand as Karn finally let go. "I'm Mick, by the way. I'm Jessica's dad."

I could barely touch him. "Pleased to meet you." A perfunctory handshake, and I couldn't meet his eyes. "I'm not sure what the problem is, really, but the cath should let us know. Your echocardiogram, by the way"—I aimed my words at Jessica— "the heart ultrasound was fine."

Jessica's bed was moving higher and higher, to the delight of the toddler at the controls. "Oh, no!" Jessica said as the boy giggled. "Don't make me hit the ceiling!"

I met the sons. Bobby, a carpet installation supervisor, was shaggy and overfriendly, like a pound dog desperate for a home. Eric was more composed; he wore a shirt and tie and had lacquered, pharmaceutical rep hair, and his darkly exotic wife clung to him like an accessory. I knew that she was Muslim, and that their marriage was a family crisis. Karn had converted to Catholicism when she married Mick, and she didn't understand why Delilah didn't do the same. Eric managed the dining room at a country club. He looked more like Mick than his brother did, although both of them had Mick's blue eyes, and Bobby— this disturbed me, as if he'd stolen something—had his father's aching arch.

"And here's Grandma's cupcake!" Karn said, scooping up the toddler from behind, and for an instant a flash of terror transformed the boy's face. She calls people by food names just like Mickey does, I thought. "Oooh," Karn said, squishing the side of her face into her grandson's, and I realized her eyes were as blue as Mickey's, that someone could say her sons had her eyes too.

"How's the patient?" I asked, approaching Jessica's bedside, now almost at the level of my shoulders. "How's the reason everyone is here?"

A FTER LENNY CALLED ME with Jessica's scan report, I'd stayed after office hours talking with Jeremy, then gone online at home with a cardiology chat group. Jeremy had had a twenty-year-old male with three-vessel disease who'd gone to bypass, but he had been from one of those bad-cholesterol families, and his father had died at forty-one. None of the docs online had seen coronary artery disease like this in a twenty-two-year-old female, but each of them knew someone who had, and the consensus opinion was to treat it just like coronary artery disease in someone older (the usual angioplasty and stent, or the occasional laser, or referral to bypass for severe disease). Of course, they all admitted, treating someone that young made you nervous. No one envied me.

I almost crawled under my deck that night reaching for Ginger, but she moved herself to a more distant spot and lay down.

Jessica was my second and final cath that Tuesday. After I'd finished with my first patient's family in the waiting room, I went to the sinks to rescrub and gown up. A trainee nurse was observing my procedures. "No high cholesterol?" the trainee was saying to Jessica as I passed. "No diabetes?" The naïve believe in pure causation; they don't think of bad luck.

"Boy, she's a young one," Helen, the head nurse with the sick husband, said in a low voice, and I wasn't sure if she was referring to Jessica or the trainee.

Jessica had been medicated before her stretcher was rolled into the angio suite; she was in the perfect state for a cath, awake but relaxed, floating. The cath lab's assistant nurse scrubbed Jessica's right groin, letting the trainee make a swipe or two, and once Jessica was draped I inserted the needle through which I'd pass the guidewire and then the catheter that would snake up Jessica's aorta to her heart.

"Little bee bite!" the student nurse said. Across from me, behind the trainee's back, I could see Helen under her mask mimicking those words. She noticed me and winked.

"You okay, hon?" I asked, glancing at Jessica's face, and Jessica nodded. Hon, darlin': the cath lab brought out the small-town in me.

Unusual in this place to see such a young leg, firm-fleshed and unveined and hairless. At the end of the table, poking out past the sheeting, was a big toe with a purple polished nail.

I expected to find something, yes, but what I found was worse than I expected: a blockage a full half-inch long at the head of the heart's main artery, the left anterior descending. It was so narrow the dye, on the viewing screen above the angiogram table, wafted down the artery like a spanning thread of spider's silk. The rest of Jessica's vessels looked fine. I didn't know what to do. If the blockage were farther downstream in any of her vessels, or if the blockage were less narrow, Jessica would be an ideal candidate for an angioplasty followed by a stent. I could slip a guidewire through the narrowed artery, pass and expand a tiny balloon over the wire to smush the clot and plaque against the vessel wall, and follow this, once the artery was opened, with the insertion of a minute mesh tube—a stent—designed to keep the vessel clear. It could be so easy. But with a narrowing this severe, the guidewire, the first thing I'd need to insert, might block the blood flow totally, and then I wouldn't know where I was. Worse, blocking off with a balloon—even temporarily—a vessel this close to its origin was to run the risk of killing off a tremendous amount of heart tissue. It would be like damming the Mississippi at Minneapolis. Block flow farther down at Memphis or New Orleans, and there would be less territory deprived of flow. "You have a narrowing," I imagined saying to Jessica. "It's in a bad spot and to be safe I think you'll need a bypass." Bypass: her young chest sliced and held open, a vessel from beneath her rib prised out, the beep of her heart on the monitor disappearing, the whirring chug of the heart-lung machine kicking in. "I hate to say this, but you're going to need a bypass." I opened my mouth to say these words but something different came out.

"You've got a very tight blockage in a major heart vessel called the left anterior descending," I said. "I'm going to try to open it."

Jessica nodded.

I was aware, across the table, of Helen's unusual stillness. I ignored it. I edged the wire forward down the artery, had Helen inject a bolus of dye. I lifted my eyes to the viewing screen. Nothing. The wire had indeed occluded the artery.

I fiddled with the wire, reinjected: was I imagining it, or did this time a strand of dye go through? "Good," I said, to no one in particular. "I can open this."

"You're doing it?" Helen asked, a hint of sharpness in her tone. "It's an awfully high . . ." But Helen stopped because it wasn't her place to question, and besides, it was too late. I was doing it.

Jessica moaned. "Start the IV nitro," I said.

"Jesus," Helen murmured, glancing at the monitor, and whatever had driven me into this—self-assurance, or hubris, or the urge to impress Mick (my God, not that!)—I would have to live now with the repercussions: the monitor showed a huge heart attack—a temporary one, I hoped—caused by my inflated balloon, the rising ST segments extending to the far reaches of the heart's front wall. If I let the balloon down now the artery might not be ready for the stent; if I kept up the balloon too long, a very big chunk of Jessica's heart muscle would die. I was too committed now for second-guessing, too far in to turn around. For the glory or the agony, for better or for worse, I was committed.

I glanced at Jessica's pale and beaded face. No question, this must hurt. "Let's go with some morphine," I said to Helen. The trainee's eyes were wide behind her mask, as if this was the most exciting thing she'd seen.

It was almost like sex, I thought later, as I wadded up my gown and mask to toss into the wastebasket: in the middle of a procedure, the rest of the world fell away. Lists of chores, anxieties about Howard, the sound of my pulse in my ears, Claudia, Mick, Karn—all this disappeared. There was only the tree of vessels on the viewing screen, and my fingers, and my equipment, and my brain. I still felt half in a reverie as I walked into the waiting room to talk with Jessica's family, and that was why it was such a surprise, after I said my few words, to see Karn moving toward me with her arms out, her bobbing breasts coming at me at eye level. "Mickey, get off the damn phone!" Karn was saying. "Mickey, Dr. Toledo has wonderful news!"

The news was not completely wonderful. Their daughter had heart disease—this was news. Their daughter had squeaked through a challenging procedure with no evidence of lasting heart damage—this was news too. But all Karn heard, all anyone seemed to hear, were these two sentences: "We got a really good result. The vessel's open."

Later, Karn wouldn't let go of my hand. "How can we thank you?" she asked. "How can we ever, ever thank you?" She turned to Mick. "We should take Dr. Toledo and Marcus out to dinner."

Under other circumstances, I would have laughed at Mick's startled face. "Sure," he said. "Sure. That'd be nice."

"Just not very practical," I said quickly. "I work, like, all the time."

THREE MINUTES WITHOUT OXYGEN," I told Jessica twenty minutes later in the recovery room. "That's about the maximum the heart will forgive." I hesitated. "We took you to the max."

Jessica smiled brightly from her gurney, a plastic cup filled with water and ice on the bed tray beside her, and I wondered how much she—how much any of them—understood.

"You're totally open," I said. "I just hope you won't make me do it again."

"Oh, no!" Jessica was radiant in her innocence, the whites of her eyes and her teeth so bright they reminded me of touched-up senior pictures back in high school. *I almost killed her,* I thought, and I wondered, not for the last time, why I'd gone through with it, why I hadn't simply said to Helen, Get the surgeons on the line. I patted Jessica's foot and headed for my office and the moment the staff (I know this for a fact, they have told me) still talk about: when Dr. Toledo stood in the back hallway crying and shaking, and it took LeeAnn almost half an hour to calm her down.

"So she's fine?" LeeAnn said. "It worked out?"

"It was too risky. I should never have tried it."

"You saved her a bypass."

"I don't do that sort of thing," I said. "I'm not a cowboy." The ER docs who split people's chests were cowboys, as were the pulmonary docs who stuck needles in their patients' chests without using an ultrasound for guidance.

"When's your next angiogram?" LeeAnn asked. "You've got Cotter and Perkins both scheduled for tomorrow, right? You okay with that? Of course you're okay with that. You're going to get back on that horse, Dr. Toledo. Tomorrow you get on that horse."

"You opened her?" Jeremy said. "Your baby patient had an LAD lesion that proximal and you opened her? Holy torpedo, it's Genie Toledo." And it was not exactly admiration, I knew, that led to his next words: "Nerves of steel, baby. Nerves of steel."

"Don't you try it!" Jeremy would tell Howard at our next group meeting. "This stunt should only be attempted by paid professionals!"

Tessa said, "An angel on your shoulder."

I said, "An angel on Jessica's shoulder."

Two days later I walked into our room. "Mickey, what the hell? I come out of the cath lab to tell you about your daughter and you're on the phone? *On the phone?*"

Mick gave a heh-heh-heh sort of laugh. "I was talking to Hugh," he said. "I wanted you to see I wasn't worried."

"Jesus, Mick, you should have worried." I sat on the edge of the bed. "I almost killed her."

"But you didn't, and even if you had you wouldn't have meant to," Mick said imperturbably.

"Mick, come on," I mumbled, startled. "I think that's a little too much faith."

"I knew you could make her well." He opened his arms and beamed. "And to think you do things like that every day. Wow, wow, wow."

Jessica had left the hospital the previous morning, blowing me a kiss as she walked with her brother Eric and his wife down the hall. "Thanks a lot," her brother Bobby said, lagging behind them. "I don't usually like doctors, but you're great." Their mother thought so too, Bobby said. She wanted to come upstairs and say goodbye herself, but they were parked illegally and someone had to stay in the car.

The flowers Karn and Mick sent me on Monday barely fit through my office door. Enough blossoms to cover a casket, I thought.

THE NEXT THURSDAY, when I got up to shower, Mick pulled on his boxers and trousers and followed me into the bathroom, still talking about the physical he'd just had. "And listen to this, my cholesterol was up—230, with a bad cholesterol of 142." Jessica was great, he said. Jessica was cured.

"So take a pill," I said, turning on the shower. "No big deal." I wasn't in the best mood. Tessa had wondered if I'd feel differently about Mick now that I had met his wife. "Oh, I don't think so," I'd said. But I did. Together, Mick and Karn had looked well suited and substantial. My body must seem crushable compared with Karn's. My legs must look bony and coltish. My nearly nonexistent breasts must feel like pillows with stuffing missing. During sex I couldn't stop thinking about Mick and Karn towering over me. I hadn't come.

"But why's it up?" Mick asked. "It was only 182 a year ago."

I've always thought cholesterol was boring, but when you

work with hearts, the questions never end. "Maybe it's stress," I said. "Stress can elevate cholesterol. Have you changed your diet? Are you getting enough exercise? Are you getting the blood test repeated?"

I let the water run over me as he answered. It turned out that during a preathletic physical in college, Mick had had a bad experience getting his blood drawn. It wasn't the needle going in, he said, but glancing down to see his blood going out, filling a huge syringe. What if the nurse kept taking his blood, filling syringe after syringe, draining him dry? At this thought he passed out. When he woke up, the nurse and a doctor both over him, the first thing he did was check his arm to be sure that the needle was removed.

His worry about taking future blood tests complicated his decision about taking a pill for his cholesterol. He got through blood draws, when he absolutely had to, by fixing his gaze on the ceiling. Not very manly.

Also, it turned out his "physical" had been nothing but blood tests.

"Have you thought of getting a real physical?" I called from inside the shower. "Have a doctor examine you?"

He said, "But you examine me."

When I got out of the shower he was leaning against the sink looking worried, and the simple fact of his trust in me stopped, for an instant, my breathing. He had handed over his daughter to me, truly, and in saving her I'd gone very close to making her a sacrifice. Mick wasn't that far off the mark when he'd likened me to an Aztec. "Take the pill," I said, thinking of primary prevention, thinking of long-term survival, of his daughter who had heart disease. "Ask your doctor to give you the pill." I stood

on my tiptoes to kiss him. "And tell him not to let Vampira draw
your blood." His high cholesterol was nothing, a minor flaw that
was eminently treatable. Would that all our problems were that
trivial.

Mick said, "Listen, I've been thinking, why don't I get a
vasectomy?"

Startled, I laughed. "Why now?" I'd complained to Mick the
last few months about a low-level headache I was blaming on the
pill, and he had suggested I stop it. Almost hubris to be thinking
of fertility at my age (forty-eight) but, still, if I stopped the pill,
conception would be possible. I'd figured we could just use con-
doms. I'd wondered if Mick would buy them furtively, or with
a sort of pride.

"It's not a bad surgery. I talked to Marcus about it."

"You did?" I could hardly believe it. "Would you tell Karn?"

"She had a hysterectomy in 'eighty-five for bleeding."

"Oh. I guess not. But why now?"

Mick raised his eyebrows consideringly. "You've done so
much for me. It doesn't seem fair that you have to take a pill for
my sake."

I nodded. "That's thoughtful of you, Mick."

He smiled, dropped his chin, and stole a look in my direction. "You can stop your pill, then?"

Good grief, I thought. As if there'd ever be someone else.
"Yes, absolutely," I said. "I can stop my pill and be a hundred
percent safe."

"Good." Mick's face cracked into a beam. "Just what I wanted
to hear."

I snickered in spite of myself. "You should be shot," I said,
poking a finger in his belly.

. . .

W E'RE NOT GOING TO SUE YOU," Mr. Dylan's daughter said
from her chair in my office, as Mr. Dylan's son bit his lip.
"But we thought that you should know that we considered it."

Fair enough, I thought, nodding. Admirable that they had
the nerve to speak about it directly with me.

"But we're going to switch from you as his heart doctor. Daddy
doesn't want to but we've got to have someone we trust. And you
probably don't remember but you stood him up for dinner."

"I do remember," I said. "Actually, he . . ."

Mr. Dylan's daughter cut me off. "We want him to see Dr.
Howard McClellan. Right here in this office. We hear he's
superb. Very friendly and he always has time for his patients."

Howard? I thought. A laugh-or-cry situation. Earlier that
morning I'd overheard him in Jeremy's office. "I'm reading the
scans better now!" he'd said. "There's a learning curve!"

Not that I couldn't make mistakes. I saw Mr. Dylan in the
hospital bed, his smile dissolving as blood erupted from his
mouth. I saw Leora Griffiths making a face about her neighbor
who blew snow into her yard. I saw the wide and trusting eyes of
Mickey's daughter. I had, at that moment in my waiting room,
maybe six patients I had helped, but the only patients I could
think of were the ones to whom I'd done, or almost done, harm.
"Dr. McClellan would be fine," I said.

C LAUDIA AND TOBY ANNNOUNCED their engagement, and at
the same time told me that at the end of October Claudia
would break her lease on her apartment to move herself into

Toby's apartment. "Because we have a committed relationship," Toby said. "It's not like we're just living together." No, I thought, it never was.

Claudia and Toby's wedding would be in the spring at Toby's family's church in Indiana, where everyone in Toby's family had been married. Claudia was having Hank walk her down the aisle. She knew I would think that maybe I should walk with her, but Claudia wanted her dad.

"That's fine," I said, disturbed by her view of me. "It should be the father who . . ." I'd always been civil to Hank. I thought he was weak and foolish, yes, but denying our years together would be a form of self-hatred. Besides, we saw each other so rarely he hardly mattered.

"I mean, like Toby said, you didn't exactly raise me," Claudia went on. She smiled, softening the blow. "You birthed me and you called up your troops."

But that was absurd. I saw what Toby was steering her toward, some poor-little-rich-girl view of her past. "Claudia. You know what your life was like. Don't let someone else tell you what you went through."

Claudia's eyes shifted away.

Yes, I had hired a live-in nanny; yes, Claudia hadn't seen her father often (whose choice was that?); yes, I had worked, and worked hard. But so much of my attention and hope had gone into my daughter. Ask my patients. Every one of them had heard about Claudia, seen the drawings and the photos on the walls. I had read to her and tucked her in almost every evening, even if that meant keeping a patient waiting in the ER.

"I know what I went through," Claudia said, and she started her litany, one so disappointingly predictable I almost cried.

The truth, I thought, must be somewhere in the tangled space between us: perhaps invisible, certainly unreachable. I remembered my own almost desperate attempt to be a good—a conventional—mom. I had taken vacation days for school field trips, sitting alone on buses as mothers around me sat in gaggles and talked about working mothers with disgust. Now Claudia was holding up, like an amulet to ward off danger, a different version of her past. That had to be Toby speaking, I thought, Toby the oversimplifier. Meat was political. There was no other place to be married than a small-town church in Indiana. Claudia had been deprived. The idea that Claudia could have come up with these ideas herself was more than I could bear.

"Nothing's that simple," I said, unwilling to enter this argument. I missed your soccer game because . . . My workday started at six, that's why I didn't know your favorite cereal. "I'm sure I did things to hurt you, but I never meant to. And sometimes life just hurts."

Claudia looked confused, as if she'd just thrown herself against a door to break it and found that it was rubber and not wood. I glanced at my watch. But why? It was Sunday afternoon, and I had nothing on that evening. "You want to see a movie or something?" I said. "You want to order pizza?"

We ended up renting *Doctor Zhivago* and eating meatball subs, sitting together on my sofa. "Don't tell Toby," Claudia said, giggling and pointing at her sandwich. It felt, for that night at least, as if Claudia was happy to be hanging out with me.

I walked into the exam room for Jessica's two-week office visit. "No more chest pain? You're getting up the hill with the stroller?" Stroller! Shocking to associate that vehicle with a stent patient. Usually I was asking about walkers and grocery carts.

"I'm fine." A quick, eager smile.

"You're taking your pills every morning? No shortness of breath? No palpitations? No swelling?"

Jessica shook her head. "I do have some stress, though. Could you maybe talk to my mother?"

Her mother wouldn't give her any privacy. Jessica couldn't lift up a cup of coffee without her mother hovering. And then her mother was always on the phone with her friends: Oh my poor daughter, oh poor me, how can I stop worrying? That kind of shit. But Jessica was the one with the clogged-up artery, right? Jessica was the one who'd have to be on medicines forever.

Jessica was speaking very loudly. I glanced at the walls, trying to signal that the patients in the adjoining exam rooms might hear her. Poor Karn, I thought, and what surprised me was that this was not a pang, this was a whole wave of sympathy that lifted my feet off the sand and knocked me over. I couldn't talk for a moment, and when I did it came out in a splutter, as if I were shaking my wet head. "Your artery's not clogged up now. And I'm sure your mother does worry, any mother worries. You'll worry about your son when he's fifty."

There might have been—was I imagining this?—a shadow of embarrassment on Jessica's face, and her anger vanished like a magician's dove. Her voice now was very small. "I know, but I still wish you'd talk to her."

"Why don't you talk to her?"

"She'd listen to you."

"How about to your dad?"

Jessica sighed. "Dad's great and all, but once his season starts we're not much competition. I always thought I was lucky to have a birthday in the summer. My brothers were born in January and February. They wrestled. My dad never made it to a whole match." She gave me a rueful smile.

I said, "Tell your mother I said you're fine." But I was stuck on Jessica's characterization of Mick as a father. Not one whole match? I hoped that wasn't true. I wondered if talking about how little Mick did with his family was one of Karn's cherished themes.

Jessica's brow knit. She asked if she could come back and see me in two weeks, instead of waiting four weeks for an office visit after her stress test.

I called Mick from my office after hours. There was gym noise in the background over the phone. "I told her we'd do a stress test at six weeks," I said, "but she's not having any symptoms. She says her mom's really worried, though."

"Karn?" A shout in the background, and a thump. "Jesus, you should see Eluard rebound. His brother's in rehab, I tell you that? Ninety days clean."

"Get this," I said, "Jessica asked me to talk to Karn."

I waited for a moment for Mick's response. When he said nothing, I continued more nervously. "Mick, you can imagine, if there's any way for me not to do that I'd . . ."

"Karn worries," Mick said. "We call her the designated worrier." The phone went silent for a moment, and I could hear Mick shouting something I couldn't make out. "Oh, man"— Mick said, returning to me—"Eluard has a confidence this year, an intelligence . . . He's coaching me."

"Mick, listen to me. This is important. I told Jessica to tell Karn she was okay."

"He even found his own job. Eluard's brother."

"Well, that's just super." I made no attempt to hide my sarcasm.

"Genie, can you call her? If you don't mind. I told you, Jessica's fine. But Karn . . . I know it's awkward, but she really liked you. You could put her mind at ease like nobody. And that would put my mind at ease."

"Mickey, I . . ."

"As Jessica's doctor. As a professional. You don't have to say a word about anything but Jessica." His voice dropped. "You're my friend, right?"

"That's mean, Mickey."

"Well, aren't you? You think Karn's going to listen to me?"

He had a point. I hung up. Just do it, I thought, sitting staring at the phone. It can't be that bad.

I am insane, I thought as I dialed. I have a God complex. Only I Can Set Things Right! I thought of Howard and his Short Man Complex. Mine might be worse.

Give her five minutes, I thought as the phone rang. Not much payback for the hours I'd had with Mick.

But forty minutes later I was still paying, and I felt, the phone at my ear with the mouthpiece pointed toward the ceiling, as if I were in a theater with my eyes propped open, forced to watch every moment of a rambling monologue whose performer had forgotten she had an audience at all. I was hoping to be beeped. I was hoping I could say, *Mrs. Crabbe, excuse me, but I have to call the ER*. Could she be drunk? But then Karn said she and Mick never drank at all, Mick's folks had had a problem, so she and Mick decided early on not to . . . I swiveled the phone down and made one of the grunts I'd made a hundred times. Was she

a nutcase? Probably a mild one, but nothing she said hinted at a
loss of reality. I had written responses to all today's patient calls
in the charts piled on my desk, I had counted my patient visits and procedures from the week before, and now I was sorting through the drawers of my desk. What a bunch of junk:
old Tampax with dirty wrappers, handouts from ancient conferences, drug-rep giveaways, a pair of running shoes splotched
with mildew. Thieves of time, I called particular patients, and
if Karn weren't Mick's wife I would have figured out a way to
cut her off. *Splat:* the shoes went into my wastebasket. *Clunk:* a
heavy plastic paperweight that encased a suspended aorta. *Clink:*
a mug painted with a dark purple heart whose vessels turned red
when the cup was filled with hot water. *Don't you ever stop talking?* part of me was thinking. But part of me was happy Karn was
prattling, because in her stories, in her leaps of topic and choice
of words, she was sketching for me a portrait of her marriage.

She didn't talk a lot about Mick. She didn't talk a lot about
Jessica, either, once we'd gotten past my reassurances that Jessica
was really, truly okay. She talked about their friends, who were
always Mick's friends, often other coaches. She talked about restaurants. She mentioned handbags, gourmet coffees, particular
beautiful and well-appointed cruise ships, and any number of
games—football games, baseball games, tennis matches—to
which other people offered Mick and his family tickets. At one
point Karn said she'd talked over Jessica's sickness (that was the
word she used) with a priest. "At your church?" I asked, to say
something. "Oh, not him," Karn said, her voice dropping and
the pace of her words quickening. "I have a Jesuit friend."

A Jesuit friend? I knew what Karn was doing: elevating herself
with an intellectual priest, a priest who wasn't even her parish

priest, but a friend. I wasn't unaware of status—I lived in a house with granite countertops and bought special-event clothing at a shop for petites where the owner made a point of "knowing" my taste—but Karn's status consciousness seemed almost global in its reach, a vast ordering impulse that extended into schools, patio furniture, moisturizers, the fabric used in T-shirts. Peruvian cotton. A new baby formula with added brain-enhancing nutrients. Special-order chocolates from Belgium. "And we looked you up," Karn said at one point, "and you're on the list of Best Doctors in America. Of course we knew you *would* be."

TOMAS QUESADA: MEDICATION QUESTION

"Mrs. Crabbe?" I said. "I'm sorry but I just got a page." In my hand was a wooden plaque I'd gotten fifteen years before honoring my service to med students. I no longer had the time to teach med students. When I dropped the plaque into the wastebasket it split the mug with the picture of the heart on it in two. "You broke my heart," I whispered into the basket, my hand over the receiver of the phone.

"You go right ahead," Karn said. "Don't let me keep you."

Karn wasn't miserable, I realized as I hung up, and she wasn't helpless: in a way she was bustling with power and perfectly content. She had made for herself a world where Mick's salary and standing and connections were payments for his lack of interest and time. It wasn't clear to me—it might never be clear to me—who had given up on what inside that marriage, but however the estrangement had started, it had evolved into a system of assigned compensations for damages, an unspoken contract as intricate and exhaustive as one written by a Philadelphia lawyer. It was a minor revelation when Karn talked about watching Mick's cholesterol: she used a butcher, she said ("used" was her word), who could trim the fat off sirloins and make them as lean as chicken, and these steaks were what she gave Mick for dinner, because she and Jessica could eat chicken breasts forever, but Mick, well, he was a real man. In those words I heard (imagined?) a place for me in her life: if what Mick said was true and his and Karn's marriage was indeed sexless, a real man might be expected, even encouraged, to seek a partner outside. Okay, you can have your little plaything, I imagined Karn saying, but don't expect to get away with it for nothing. Another diamond, a balcony for all their cruise rooms, money to help Eric open his own sports bar. She would drive a hard bargain, yes, but she *would* bargain, and a divorce, done on Karn's terms, might be quite workable. Didn't Mick see this? Didn't he realize how beautifully simple getting rid of her could be? I could hear her cackling now, to some unseen friend: You only got the house? I got the house, the cars, the club memberships, the alimony; I got everything!

Still, there was something sad about all this, a loss I had to hope that Karn didn't recognize. There she was, protected and ensheathed in Lexus and Coach and Hanro of Switzerland, when all she really needed was skin-to-skin.

I PHONED MR. QUESADA and his pharmacy right away, so I would have, once those calls were done, a quiet space to think about what I'd heard. I turned off my desk lamp and leaned back in my swivel chair until it hit the wall, watching the reflections of streetlights in my window. It started to rain.

Slowly it dawned on me what disturbed me about my conversation with Karn. It was her staggering ordinariness. I had thought when I met her at the hospital that there must be something I was missing—some passion or intelligence or wit submerged under the worry about her daughter. But now I saw that Mick's wife had no depths at all.

Of course Mick was loyal to Karn—loyalty was, after all, the main supporting piece of John Wooden's pyramid of success—but what about Mick's loyalty to himself? What did he and Karn talk about, Caribbean itineraries and Ralph Lauren shirts? I had always half believed, I realized, that Karn had mysterious assets—kindness, patience, a talent for mothering—that I simply didn't have. But what if she didn't? Why would an exceptional man, a leader, stay with a woman like Karn? Out of some guilt about their children? As a bizarre atonement for seeing me? Maybe Mick was deficient in some way I hadn't fathomed. Beneath these thoughts lurked another, sickening realization: That's my competition and I'm *losing*?

Twenty-four-hour ambulatory heart rhythm monitoring," Howard said, twirling his reflex hammer. "That's got to be our next push. We've got three monitors and they're way underused. We could be doing eighteen a week. Medicare'll pay if there's any indication of heart disease, and you know the common thread in all our patients . . ."

"*Any* heart disease and they'll pay?" Jeremy asked.

Howard ran through the acceptable diagnoses—a wide range, to be sure. "There's no reason every patient of ours shouldn't walk around for one day every year toting our little squeeze-box," Howard said. "Ordering ambulatory monitoring should be like this"—and Howard used his little hammer to jerk his knee.

T HAT THURSDAY, Mick thanked me for calling Karn. That Thursday, we had brisk and impersonal sex, as if Mick had slotted time for an exercise session and I was a new machine designed to isolate pelvic thrusting.

"Kennilworth moved in with that tutor," Mick said afterward, as he sat on the side of the bed tying his shoes. "His wife's filing for divorce."

"What do the other guys think?"

"Oh, I don't know. Personal life. Our practices are going great. I cut back the drills and we're doing a lot of five-on-fives, because they've got the fundamentals. Frederick thinks of everything this year. I'm half tempted to sit back and let him and Eluard take over."

"You seem confident."

Mick raised his eyebrows. "We've sure got talent. Don't worry, I'll be going insane soon. Jeepers, I hope no one gets hurt. That's the only thing I worry about."

Dad's great and all, Jessica had said, *but once his season starts we're not much competition.*

A BELL TINKLED as we opened the door to the store, and a floral scent hit my nostrils. "Rosalie?" Claudia said. "I brought my mother to look at the dress. Could you just bring it out? We don't have time for me to put it on."

The clerk smiled and disappeared, reemerging with a white concoction displayed with such timid deference I knew the thing must cost the moon.

Awful dress. Pearls, lace, satin panels, tulle sleeves. Almost a female impersonator's wedding dress. "Isn't it gorgeous?" Claudia said.

"You really like ruffles," I said, although, looking closely, ruffles were the one ornamentation this dress didn't actually have. "I like something simpler, something . . ."

"Can't you just say *You like ruffles,* period? Why do you have to say *You like ruffles, I* . . . and then start in on what you like?" Claudia brought a hand to her mouth and bit at her index finger. "It's a wedding dress, Mom. It's supposed to be feminine. I want a traditional wedding, Mom. I want a marriage that lasts forever." Rosalie had vanished during this speech, leaving the gown hanging on a display hook; I was sure she'd heard many outbursts like Claudia's, but that didn't make me any happier. "I'm getting married for keeps, Mom. I'm not you."

Wait a minute, I thought. You really think I should have stayed married to your father? I remembered Rosalie, listening in from somewhere. "How much is it?" I asked, keeping my voice calm.

An impossible amount, more than a small car. "Look, the pearls are sewn on by hand," Claudia said, pointing, "and the lace is from . . ."

Rosalie reappeared to unlock a display case of crowns. "It's a premium dress, of course," she said. "We have lots more affordable pieces that . . ."

I was watching Claudia's hand as she traced the embroidered pearls. There were toothmarks on her finger.

"We want it," I said, resting my hand on Claudia's back. "We definitely want it."

MICK TOLD ME, the next Thursday, that he had run into Kennilworth and his former tutor at a pizza place when Mick was picking up his order. Kennilworth barely acknowledged him, but his girlfriend introduced herself and shook Mick's hand.

"She was very pleasant," Mick said in surprise.

"See?" I said, pushing myself up on an arm to look at him. "You shouldn't vilify the Other Woman."

Mick snorted and shook his head. "You should see her," he said. "Is she *stacked*."

A month before, I would have hit him with my pillow. I would have hit him with my pillow and he'd have grabbed and tickled me and we would have ended in a writhing, happy ball. But since I'd seen and talked to Karn, things were different. This month my voice was sharp: "Not like me, I guess."

"You have adorable breasts," Mick said cheerfully, blithely unaware of my tone. "You have breasts like little potatoes."

Potatoes. I laid my head back down and wondered what else he really thought of me.

"Remember that work I was going to get done?" he asked later, getting dressed, and it took me a moment to realize he was talking about his body and not his actual job. "I see the urologist Tuesday to get things started."

"Great!" I said. The vasectomy. I shouldn't be mad at him, I thought. That he was having the procedure done now, of all times, when he was starting with his team, must be a special gift for me. I left first that evening, and as I opened the door to the hall Mick wagged his finger. "If I suffer terribly, it's your fault."

For some reason that wagging finger irked me. "Ha ha ha," I said as I walked down the hall. "Ha ha ha ha ha." I almost kicked the elevator door.

M OM'S A TON BETTER," Jessica said at her four-week office visit. "You really helped her. Daddy says once the season's over we'll do another cruise."

"How nice," I said. How had I ever gotten into this mess? How could I get out?

"But Mom's got to follow our cruise rules! We wrote out a whole list. She's not allowed to utter the words 'the waste.' She can't ask Bobby if the dancers make him hot-hot-hot. And especially, especially, she has to let Dad take care of the tipping."

"Well, Jessica, you're doing great," I said, closing her chart. "Wait right here and LeeAnn will be in to schedule your stress test."

"Oh, Mom's such a bleeding heart," Jessica said, seeming not to have heard me. "She can't believe a waiter can be surly. She thinks he has a sick kid in Tobago or a brother who died or something. One time Mom and the guys and me were heading off the ship from our deembarkation breakfast and Mom slips this grouch-pot waiter an envelope with extra cash. Anyway, he opens it and thinks that's all the tip there is, he doesn't realize my Dad's still sitting at the table with the . . ."

My hand was on the doorknob. "Complicated," I said, to say something, but Jessica was still talking.

". . . and he's chasing us, he's saying she's a fat American who eats two desserts, and Mom . . ."

I tried to turn the doorknob but my hand was sweaty.

". . . and she wouldn't tell the cruise people because she didn't want to get him into trouble, and she wouldn't tell Dad because she didn't want him to . . ."

What had Mr. Dylan said? *I don't want this information! I don't need this information!*—and in fact, in Karn's well-intended but disastrous foray with the waiter there was an echo of my asking Mr. Dylan to dinner. "I hope your mother follows the rules this time," I said, turning the knob and pushing on the door, surprised to hear my voice sound jovial. "For everybody's sake."

"You're so competent," Mick said to me once. "I don't have to worry about you at all." No, I wasn't wholly competent. If I were wholly competent I'd have a husband and a happy marriage and a daughter who looked forward to my taking her shopping for a wedding dress. If I were wholly competent I wouldn't be with Mick at all. He must know that. Perhaps his words were not the compliment I'd taken them as. Perhaps he'd meant simply that I was a competent mistress. Good to fuck, he'd say, if he had the guts to use the proper word.

A bleeding heart, Jessica said about her mother, and that dismayed me. I wanted to see Karn as a status-conscious harridan, the sort of woman that couldn't be described without using the word "clutches." I didn't want Mick's wife to be at all tender, to have any weakness that would make it hard for Mick to leave.

C*ARAMBA!*" I'D SAY. "Look at that gorgeous cholesterol!"
Or: "Trust me, the palpitations you can live with."
Or: "This new medicine is working fabulously. That and all your exercise."

Or: "Women's angina can be very atypical. You don't need to feel guilty about worrying."

It was still beautiful to advise, to cajole, to reassure, but sometimes my patients' swollen ankles and throbbing neck veins hit me like a personal reproach. Sometimes their labs made me angry. For years I had misjudged myself. In truth I was needy, not caring; nosy, not curious; smarmy instead of kind. I had always thought of myself as flying from exam room to exam room, but now my flights felt less like hurrying and more like fleeing.

"Do you want a twenty-four-hour monitor on this patient, Dr. Toledo?" Lindy asked, over and over.

"Not this time!" I kept saying back.

"Forget the Marriott," Mick said Thursday morning on the phone. "Tonight I'm taking you out to dinner."

"Dinner? Why?"

"Because I want to, that's why. Something different."

I don't want different! The trees were bare and the air was cold and the doctors' parking lot was carpeted with broken leaves. That evening I drove my hour and ten minutes downhill through darkness and arrived at the restaurant dazed and filled with foreboding, as if Mickey might send in his place another man. I was relieved the restaurant was dim and almost empty; it was nearly nine.

"Screw it," Mick said, grasping my upper arm and leading me to a table. "I have dinner with every coach in the state, I can have dinner with you."

The waiter brought wine for me and root beer for Mick, and we perused the menus, discussed the food, and placed our orders. The waiter brought a basket of rolls, and we found ourselves looking at each other across a vacancy, as if the table itself were a silence to be filled.

"Are you okay?" I asked, but he didn't answer. "I'm taking Claudia to get her wedding gown fitted this weekend," I told him, to say something. He's getting rid of me, I thought. The threat of a vasectomy made him think, *Why do I need this?* The athletic director fired him, I thought. Eluard's brother came forward squawking that Mick had had an RA beat him up. Karn figured out where Mick really spent his Thursday evenings. Or something wildly different, something happy: Mick had had enough of cheating. He'd gone to Karn and asked for a divorce.

"I have cancer," Mick said.

A sound started in my head, a noise that wasn't really a noise, a static obscuring every other sound in the world.

"What kind?"

"Prostate."

"Are you sure?"

"I get the biopsy tomorrow, but the doctor's sure."

"But if you haven't had the biopsy . . ."

"He says ninety-nine percent sure. He can feel it."

"Well, what he thinks is well and good, but without a tissue diagnosis you can't really . . ."

"Don't argue with me!" Mick snapped, his voice a glimpse through a speeding train window of a vast and desolate landscape, a wasteland you would never want to stop in. I dropped my head and closed my eyes. I felt like he had just slapped me.

"How did they find it?" I asked after a pause.

"I went to the urologist Tuesday—I told you I was going—and he said fine, he'd do the vasectomy, but he needed to examine me first. And everything was fine up front, but then he got behind and checked my prostate. I knew when he was doing it things weren't right. He took forever, and he didn't talk, and all of a sudden he's asking me these questions. Am I urinating okay, did I see blood, did anyone in my family have cancer? And you know what really got me worried?" Mick leaned forward. "He seemed *interested*."

I swallowed. I was sure that there were patients I'd tipped off in the same manner. "He's the one doing the biopsy?"

Mick nodded. "Dr. Leakey. How's that for a name?"

But the name didn't sink in until later. "You trust him?"

"He's who Marcus went to for his kidney stones. Nice older guy. He says a young doc might not tell me right away what they found, but he wants to be honest with people. And he's felt over ten thousand prostates." Mick frowned, toyed with a packet of sugar. "My blood test was up some too. My PSA." Prostate-specific antigen, a blood test, an indicator of prostatic cancer or other prostate problem.

"Oh, Mick." I shook my head. I imagined him with his arm out getting his blood drawn, eyes rolled toward the ceiling. "Mickey." Certainly, I'd seen cancer of the prostate, but only in a peripheral way—male patients who had it, or reports from female patients about their husbands. I wished I knew more about it. In old men it was often no big deal. They'd die of their heart disease, of my disease, before they'd die of cancer. But in a younger man it could be different. Mick was fifty-one. Local spread, spread into the bones, a grading scale (the Berle scale? the Gleason scale?—some old-time comedian's name). Choosing treatment, especially in a younger man, could be complicated—surgery or radiation or chemo, and the chemo was usually hormonal and made men impotent. Estrogen shots,

I dimly remembered from my residency, which made men's ankles swell and their penises shrivel. But no, they didn't give estrogen anymore. They gave other shots, testosterone blockers. Suddenly I was hearing Mr. Pelmaster, a patient of mine who'd died two years before: "A beautiful woman can walk past me and she might as well be a Mack truck." That had been a relief to him, I recalled. Less strain on the ticker.

"Did you ever . . ." Mick winced. "Feel anything down there?"

It broke my heart. "You didn't want a rectal exam, did you?"

We smiled a moment. "Geez," he said, rubbing his face with his hand.

"The prostate's not my area."

A pause, and Mick gazed past the edge of the table toward the floor. "Well, everybody and his brother has prostate cancer. It's nothing new."

"People will be great to you," I said. "You'll get so much support from the fans and . . ." I trailed off at his obvious agitation.

"I'm not going to be a poster child," he said. "I'm not going to be out there doing PSAs for PSAs."

"I'll get on the Internet," I said. "I'll talk to people. I'll get you info." Something concrete I could do, and there was knowledge more up-to-date than textbooks on the Internet.

Mick's mouth opened slightly. He hesitated. "Uh. Karn's been doing that. Karn and the kids."

As if I were being loaded into an isolation capsule. The white noise was already in my ears, and now cotton was being stuffed into my mouth, and soon I wouldn't be able to see or smell or move, and what did a measly dinner out matter if Karn and the kids were taking over Mickey's life?

"I'll get you information from the doctor sites," I said. "The latest studies. The major centers. Maybe you should go somewhere else for treatment."

"I'm not leaving," Mick said. "I'm absolutely not leaving. Listen, I've got my center and my point guard this year, and I am going to ride this horse."

"But you'll have to get therapy. Surgery or radiation or . . ."

"Listen to me. I'm not going to miss this year. Not one game."

I thought he was being melodramatic; I thought his staying on without missing a game would never really come to pass. "But you'll have to miss some of it, you've got cancer, you . . ."

"You know what Frederick says? He says he can read my mind. And Eluard? Did anyone else recruit him? Anyone? His high school coach said I was making a mistake. But I saw something, Genie. I saw it."

"Well, you won't have to miss a lot of games, but . . ."

"This is my team, okay? I picked it, I recruited it. And I'm not going to let it run the races without me."

"What about your treatment?"

"It won't change things," Mick was saying, and I realized we were gripping hands across the table, "it won't change things between us."

The waiter put down our salads.

A desperate grip, as if one of us were about to disappear over the edge of something.

I realized I hadn't said I was sorry about his disease. "I'm sorry, Mick. Look, I'll do anything. I'll go away, I'll move you in with me, I'll get a house in West Virginia if you want me to. You tell me, Mickey. You tell me what you need."

But as we walked to the parking lot later, we'd decided nothing. Everything was different, as if the landscape had been suddenly tilted. It used to be easy to get from this to that, but now it seemed impossible. It used to be unthinkable to go from Mick to despair, but now I rolled there like a marble.

"Maybe the biopsy will be negative," I said. "Maybe your doctor's famous finger is wrong."

He glanced right over me, as if he were looking beyond me for a sensible adult.

"I'll be able to see you, right?" I said. "I'll be able to be with you? We'll still have our Thursdays?"

"Sure," Mick said, turning to me, but his hands on my shoulders might be pushing me away. "Of course," he said an instant later, gripping me to his chest. The scent from the smoke in the restaurant clung to him, obscuring his usual smell.

"Aren't we going to the hotel?" I said, digging my nose into his sweater, trying to muffle the tremor in my voice. "Can't we just get a few minutes at the hotel?"

"I can't, babe," Mick said. "Tonight I've got to go home."

ART QUINLIVAN ON SPORT:
REFLECTED RADIANCE

If you're a longtime Turkman basketball fan, you will surely remember this player: a lanky young man with mahogany skin and a gap-toothed smile; a leader whose passion for defense inspired his team to hold their opponents to an average 38 points for the season; a point guard who ended his final Turkman game with a career-high 25 points and the flourish of a double-double (14 assists, 11 rebounds). You will surely remember Dashona Lykins.

"Dashona was radiance," his mother, Esther Lykins, recalls. "I have four boys, and they're all good people, but everybody loved Dashona."

Including Dashona's coach, Mick Crabbe, who in 1987 arrived at Turkman to helm the freshly monikered Warriors. In the young Lykins, then a junior, Crabbe quickly recognized the speed, the native intelligence, and the quick hands of a master point guard. That's why it was such a letdown when, in the Eastern Mountain Conference tournament final, Dashona stumbled around the court like a drunken sailor and scored only 4 the first half. "I really lit into him in the locker room,"

Crabbe recalls. "I told him he was letting his team down, letting himself down, letting me down. He went back out second half and hit two 3-pointers, boom, boom. And that was just the beginning."

Little did Coach Crabbe know that this triumph would be his player's swan song. Little did he realize what Dashona—with his weight loss, his sweats at night that soaked through his sheets, his fevers—surely suspected: that the player was a desperately ill young man. Three weeks later Dashona was diagnosed with leukemia; eleven months later, despite chemotherapy, radiation, blood transfusions, even surgery, the young star went to his heavenly reward.

Dashona's passing had consequences for Turkman's head coach, who is perhaps more sensitive than his often implacable visage reveals. Coach Crabbe calls the day he heard Dashona's diagnosis the worst day of his life. In Dashona's last months, the coach visited his former player almost every other day. Later, perhaps out of a subconscious fear, Crabbe ignored the position of point guard. Crabbe slotted players to the position after Dashona, but he failed to give them the direction and guidance they needed. "I let them flail," he admits now. This is an irony, because Coach Crabbe himself played point guard at tiny Spooler University in Virginia. Although Crabbe claims he played the position "not very well," a quick phone call verifies that he still holds Spooler's record (28) for single-game assists.

That is why, for long-term Turkman fans, it's a joy and relief to see Crabbe on the sidelines conferring with Turkman's current point guard, Frederick Flitt. Flitt is now a junior, like Dashona. He is shorter than his predecessor (5'10" to Dashona's 6'2") but just as fast, just as nimble with the ball. The point guard is the player who dribbles the ball down the court, who calls plays and gets the ball to shooters (sometimes himself) and figures out how to block. His job is to make his team look good, and Flitt does. Last year Flitt racked up more assists (11.4) and played more minutes per game (34) than any Turkman player, at the same time rarely fouling and never fouling out. "He senses everything," Crabbe says. "You could blindfold him and he could still play."

Admittedly, Frederick Flitt does not have the crowd appeal of Dashona. He lives off campus in his own apartment, and his teammates are more likely to call him "Intelligence" than "Radiance."

Frederick's major is a demanding one, mechanical engineering. While other players put on T-shirts or jerseys after games, Frederick dresses in pleated trousers and open-weave buttoned shirts. He finds ironing relaxing; sometimes, before a big game, he sets up an ironing board in the locker room and presses everyone's clothes. "He doesn't talk," says Tom Kennilworth, the forward who receives many of Flitt's laser-swift passes. "He's action, not words."

Flitt acknowledges that Coach Crabbe has talked to him about Dashona. "He sounds like he was something," Flitt says. Then the laconic Georgian turns away, leaving the listener to ponder the perfect crease in his pants.

Which is not to say Flitt doesn't appreciate Dashona's legacy. Any good point guard understands the game. And understanding the game means knowing its history. This season may be a great one for the Warriors. This season, the team has passion and experience and talent to burn. And Frederick Flitt must know he will be carrying the ball not just for himself, not just for his coach and his teammates, but on behalf of a radiant ghost named Dashona Lykins.

There were the usual inaccuracies: Mick attended Spooler College, not Spooler University; Dashona had a lymphoma, not leukemia. Plus, the article was written in sportswriter hokey, which is hokier than anything else in the paper, including the women's section. Still, I knew the piece would make Mick happy.

"Glad to see Quinlivan's back on the booster wagon," I said over the phone.

"What? Who? I didn't read anything."

"Like hell you didn't," I said, and we both laughed.

"Are you sore today?" I said. "Can you sit down?" Mick had had his needle biopsies that morning.

"I sat down to read Art Quinlivan. Less of a pain in the butt than the biopsies, that's for sure."

"Call me as soon as you hear anything, okay? The second you know."

Now, about Frederick Flitt. Flitt had pale, almost yellow skin and the hooded eyes and prominent cheekbones of an El Greco saint, and there was no way in hell he was carrying the ball for Dashona. The spark and the dark—that was what Mick thought about in his players. Frederick's spark was pride. Several times his freshman year he stomped away during practices when he felt he was being insulted. Mick realized early on that he would have to lie to him. *Say something simple,* Mick liked to say, *even if it's not true.*

Mick told Frederick that he was the best player he'd ever coached. He told Frederick that in Mick's mind he referred to him as "my secret weapon" or "my buddy" or, rarely, "God." Frederick lived up to these expectations. Mick called him the engine of the team.

"Positive," Mick said on the phone Monday.

I swallowed. *Positive:* I'd never again think of that word as a happy one. "How positive? How many of the samples? Did they give you the Gleason score?"

Frederick's dark was fear of chaos, which was not, Mick pointed out, the same as fear of disorder. If Frederick were afraid of disorder—and lots of players were—he'd be tentative, cautious, rattled when the ball came unexpectedly whizzing toward him or when a fellow player broke out of formation. But Frederick was daring, not cautious. He craved dropped balls, missed layups, errant passes; those teetering moments drove him to make things right. Mick could always see a cloud of thought, like a cartoon bubble, over Frederick's head. Other players might have chicken scratches in their bubbles, but Frederick had a whole flowchart, dividing and branching. He played by thought, not instinct. Mick had never seen a player think so fast. Sometimes Mick didn't see what Flitt would do until he'd done it.

"All I know is positive. I've got to go to Leakey's for details."

Other coaches understood Frederick's importance, but many of the fans didn't. They were more excited about Corey Morgan, the sophomore shooting guard who was becoming a leading scorer, and some of them still pinned their hopes on Eluard.

"You'll be cured," I said. "It's no big deal. It'll work out." *Say something simple. Even if . . .*

By that Thursday, Mick had his final biopsy report. "I'll fax it to you," he told me that night in our hotel room. "I didn't want to bring it here." The Thursday after, a week before Thanksgiving, he had a plan. He decided not to tell his players or his assistants or the Turkman athletic director. He did tell the university president, in a meeting made peculiar by the president's own confession: he was on antidepressants, had been for years; he knew what it was like to have to hide things.

"He had a rope and a ladder and everything," Mick told me that Thursday night. The president and Mick had spent more time discussing the president's health than Mick's health. Mick was delaying his surgery to remove his prostate until the spring. Mick would get through his season with monthly hormone shots to shrink the tumor. Both Mick's urologist, Dr. Leakey, and his oncologist, Dr. Simon, would have preferred surgery sooner, but Mick had the final say.

"Did she argue with you?" I asked. "She": Mick had chosen a female oncologist, one he said patients called "Dr. Leslie."

"A little. Obligatory stuff. I'm not saying she accepts it, but she understands it. She understands it more than Leakey, that's for sure. I'm done with him. I'm getting a new urologist. I don't want that nerd cutting on me." Nerd: a new insult from Mick, and I was startled at the anger in the word. *I was a nerd,* I thought, thinking of high school.

The last two weeks I'd been mentally running through my patients who had refused therapy, who argued with me, who put things off. Some did fine, even beautifully—Mr. Vikartovsky, who kept smoking through two bypasses and three angioplasties, was still alive—but most of them had had progressive heart or vascular disease and died.

"If it's my last year, it could be my best year," Mickey said.

"Your last year coaching? You'd retire?"

There might have been, inadvertently, some excitement in my voice, because he gave me a reproachful look. "My last year."

I said, "It's not your last year." But his words chilled me, because Mick's cancer was Gleason Grade 8 out of 10 (one pathologist of the three that reviewed Mick's specimens called it a 9), a very aggressive tumor, and although his bone and CT scans had been negative, Dr. Leslie was concerned enough that she wanted them repeated in three months instead of the customary six, as well as a bimonthly PSA.

Fatalism, stubbornness, the belief that they knew better: those were traits my noncompliant patients shared. And sometimes fear.

"I don't understand why I don't feel bad," Mickey kept saying, as if his body were a no-longer-reliable instrument, something he needed to whack against a wall to get restarted.

"Karn's a problem," Mick said. "Karn's a huge problem." She had tracked down a prostate cancer specialist from Johns

Hopkins, who telephoned Mick in the middle of a practice; she kept renting movies starring people like Chevy Chase and Rodney Dangerfield, films she expected Mick to laugh his way through, because, she told Mick, attitude was everything. Each morning Karn set out a handful of pills (vitamins, soy, saw palmetto) and hovered until she saw Mick swallow each one.

"She's worried about you," I said, stroking the hairs on Mick's chest. I wondered if Karn, by her pestering, was proving she loved Mick more than I did. I seemed to be doing nothing.

"I told her to watch the movies. I can't stand it."

We were in bed. There was no question of sex, because of the testosterone-blocking injection he'd had. Still, it calmed me to be lying next to him, to have his odor in my nostrils. At the same time I could picture us as we must look from the ceiling, huddled like two frightened animals.

I F I TELL YOU SOMETHING, can you promise not to tell anyone, not even Toby?"

Claudia's eyes narrowed but she quieted, as if she'd just heard, in the distance, someone calling her name. She set down her hamburger. "It's Mick, right?"

"You won't tell anyone?"

Claudia shook her head. I told her. "I guess this probably seems to you like punishment, right?" I said.

Claudia said nothing. Her eyes were full of a tragic awareness, as if she were seven years old again, cradling her dead hamster. She stood up and walked around the table and wrapped her arms around my shoulders. I felt my face crumple. The old man at the table across from ours looked away. "I'm sorry," Claudia said.

"Thank you, sweetheart," I told her, patting her arm. Sweetheart—that name fit her. It was cruel of me to think she would wish Mick ill. I closed my eyes, thinking of something I'd noticed with my patients: sometimes illness brought people together.

It got cold and Ginger moved into the house. It took surprisingly little to coax her—a can of cat food in the kitchen two mornings in a row—but once she was inside I rarely saw her.

Turkman had two home games on TV in November, "confidence builders," preseason games against easy teams. I taped them, as I would every televised game that season. The whole Crabbe clan was at each one, seated two rows behind Mickey and his team, visible as the camera swept up and down the court or isolated Mick in a moment of frustration or elation. At first, I had to tear my eyes from them to look at Mick. I took to rewinding the videotapes and watching the family footage several times, concentrating on different people. I felt like a CIA agent in the days of the USSR, reviewing images from Moscow for signs of intent. Did the way Karn sat with her back half toward Delilah make a statement? Was it at all significant that Bobby and not Eric had Jessica's son on his lap? Later, my conjectures about the Crabbes started to feel like a sickness. I knew that anyone seeing me sitting in front of the TV with my remote, playing and rewinding, stopping the action to catch key expressions (often blurred ones— the Crabbes were only wallpaper in these shots), would find me as pathetic as a stalker. I thought of calling the appliance store to ask if there was a device to block out background on the TV. But of course there wouldn't be, and I'd feel even stupider for asking.

The lines Karn had from the side of her nose to her mouth seemed to have deepened. She looked like a young girl in a play who'd been made up to look old. At Turkman's second TV game, she showed up in a maroon-and-gold-striped shirt so appalling I got angry at Jessica for letting her wear it. Claudia would never let me go out like that. Claudia, for all her kindness, was honest in her assessment of my looks. She'd told me once that green was not my color.

The first home game there was a glimpse of Karn with her fist in the air and her mouth open, an image I couldn't erase from my mind. She looked less like a fan or a coach's wife than an objector at a protest rally. "She's stressed," Mick said over the phone. With Thanksgiving, we were missing our Thursday. "She had this thing: she never wanted to be a widow."

Me either. I felt as if I were fording a flooded stream, scanning the water ahead for my next rock. I almost said, *We won't be,* but I caught myself and said, "She won't be."

"No?" Mickey said. "Good." Then he changed the subject. Had I noticed the big sloppy-looking official? Mick couldn't stand that official. He had missed three obvious fouls, and never mind that two of them were Turkman's. "He umped a game in Ohio last night and one in Pennsylvania two days before that one. He's working too much," Mick said. "He doesn't see things."

T HE DAY AFTER THANKSGIVING I finished my office hours, went home and fed Ginger, then got into my Honda and drove to Chicago, where my little brother lived and where my middle brother was visiting from Racine. Every year I did this, although this was the first year I went without Claudia, who was spending the holiday with Toby's family. My brothers always did their Thanksgiving dinner on Saturday so we could all be together. Doing this took the pressure off Christmas. Over Christmas, my partner Howard always went somewhere warm, Jeremy had obligations with Sukie's family, and I took our group's calls. In exchange for this I was off both Thanksgiving weekend and New Year's.

My blond neighbor said she'd come to my house twice a day to feed the cat, saying her boys were excited to play with Ginger. I didn't tell her that Ginger would almost certainly be hiding. I'd underestimated the time needed to tame her; it was possible she'd never be tamed at all. She emerged only at the sound of the electric can opener. Her favorite spots were under Claudia's old bed and behind my family room sofa.

My middle brother, Rick, was a psychiatrist, and my little brother, Dean, a lawyer who specialized in personal injury and medical malpractice. Between the two of them they had five children ages five to fifteen, all but one of them girls. Thanksgiving was always at Dean's house, his corporate lawyer wife cooking with her usual resentful zeal. I brought a shrimp tray from Columbus—a minor contribution, but I always hosted a restaurant brunch on Sunday before I took off.

After dinner all the kids but the youngest went swimming in Dean's indoor pool. Dean's younger daughter sat at the kitchen table with her crayons drawing pictures of butterflies, and I sat talking with my brothers as Dean's wife, having refused all offers of help, cleaned up with a maximum of clattering and banging.

"I got a cat," I said. "She was a stray, but I lured her in with food."

Dean said, "What's going on with you, are you turning human?"

"Make him stop," I said to Rick.

"It's insecurity," Rick said. He glanced under the table and said to Dean, "You've always had very small feet."

"At least my dick's not in my head like yours is," Dean snapped, glancing at his daughter, but she was coloring a wing and seemed not to have heard him.

There was a moment's silence, then Dean said, "Not to get into your area, Rick, but I've been thinking how we're all over-achievers. And as overachievers, I'm sorry, we're making up for something. And I think Mom and Dad, God rest their souls, I think Mom and Dad didn't give us enough attention." Dean's full name was Constantine, which was never used. Too much like an immigrant, my father said. Rick's full name was Richard. Eugenia and Constantine: those are the clues that there's Greek blood in our background. People don't believe it, but my father never talked about his parents. He told Dean once that Toledo was not exactly his parents' name.

"Are you kidding?" I said. "They never gave us a free minute." I'd played piano, Rick violin, Dean bass. For years we were all on the swim team, in Scouts, in the church youth group. None of us ever missed an honor roll. The one time one of us brought home a B (Rick, social studies, ninth grade) our father took the grade card outside, set it on fire, then jumped up and down on the ashes, a story that had become Rick's cocktail party version of Why I Became a Psychiatrist. "All our children excel," my father used to say. We kids were like steps in a stair-case that would someday deliver him, he hoped, to the elevated wooden deck he took to be the heart of America. But he died too soon to see us reach the goals he'd dreamed for us. I was twenty, my brothers were in their teens. Yes, my father died of a heart attack. Yes, he knew I was planning on medicine. No, I hadn't until then decided on cardiology.

"Sure, we got attention," Dean admitted. "But affection? It was like they had a tiny jeweler's bag of it, and we each had to fight for our share."

"I don't want to judge them," I said. "They loved us as well as they could. And look at us. We're normal, we're successful."

Dean got a gleam in his eye. "Normal, okay. But are we happy?" Dean was always up for an argument. "It's fun," he used to say about picking a quarrel.

"I'm happy," I said, standing up and looking out a window. The grass in Dean's yard was zoysia, which turned a sickly yellow in the fall. "Do you have an extra suit here? Maybe I'll swim. Rick, do you want to swim?" But Rick was gazing at our niece and her picture and didn't seem to hear me.

"How's Claudia?" Dean said.

I winced. Thank God Dean was a malpractice lawyer in Illinois, not Ohio. "She's fine," I said. "Planning for her wedding. You've got the date free, right? The second Saturday in April?"

"Sure, I'll manage it. She didn't go back to school?"

"Not yet. She's working in an office."

"How's your love life?"

I breathed in sharply. "I have a friend, actually." I had never told my brothers about Mick.

"A male friend?"

"Yup."

"He a doctor?"

"He's a urologist." *Oh, Mick, forgive me*—but the lie had just popped out.

"A 3-P doc, hunh? Pee, penis, and prostate, that's what my golf buddy tells me. What's his name?"

"Peter," I said, looking over at Dean, and I saw that Rick was smiling to himself. I knew Rick would recognize that I was lying. He and I had been relieved when Dean decided against med school. "Stick him with the lawyers," Rick had said. "He'll fit in."

"Look at this!" Dean snatched up his daughter's picture. "She's got talent, doesn't she? We got her signed up for pen-and-ink class." Rick and I exchanged glances. I should call Rick more, I thought.

B EFORE I KNEW IT, it was the Thursday after Thanksgiving, and we were propelled—always a fast time of year—into December. Mick pushed his fingers through my hair, pressed at my scalp. He said, "Part of me wants us to get on a plane and just fly south. Fly to some island where no one knows us and live out our lives." A throb in his voice. I opened my mouth to reassure him, but he went on. "How did this happen, Genie? I feel like an old man."

There was a second's hesitation, then he went on in a new tone, as if he'd gotten off one train and hopped onto a new, sleeker model. "On the plus side, we're in great shape for Satur-day. Eluard's a machine. They can double-team him and it won't matter. Frederick's got our defense cooking too. And these injections they're giving me are nothing. Nothing. Other than poky Oscar here"—he nodded—"I don't feel sick at all."

Later, I couldn't make myself move from the bed, but Mick was ready to leave. "Hang in there, kiddo," he said, sitting down beside me to say goodbye. He had on his soft blue sweater, and I wouldn't stop rubbing the roughness of the ribbing at his wrist. Finally, Mick lifted my hand off his sleeve and laid it across my tummy. "Better days ahead, okay?" he said, bending over me. "You've got to let me go."

The door made its little click as he left for the hall. I moved over in the bed to the warm spot where he'd been sitting and fell asleep, and it wasn't that the floodgates opened. It was that they were imperfect, leaking and seeping, until I woke up to find myself cold and adrift on what seemed to be an endless expanse. No shore anywhere, no distinguishing landmarks, no land to mark at all. Mick could die, I thought. It takes cancer for my daughter to not be scared of me. Even my cat doesn't like me. How odd to find myself alone and floating, in landlocked and sensible Ohio. I felt overwhelmingly tired, as if my limbs were melding into the bed. I don't have the will to fight this, I thought, and I recognized how much of my life, for years, had depended on will: the will to pack Claudia her lunches, to add on a fourth cath, to finish my dictations in the car on the way to meeting Mickey. The simple will to push myself out of bed each morning at five. How had I done it? Why had I done it? What had I been fleeing?

All our children excel. And why? Because the resources were scarce. Because we had to.

It hit me that the very thing that kept me going—my own will—was what had brought me down. I'd never enjoyed the moment as it happened, I'd always been preparing for the next thing. Even with Mick: all my Thursdays lying next to him,

I dreamed of the days we'd be together all the time. Now I doubted we'd ever be together. The best lay behind us, not ahead. As if Mick and I had been driving up a mountain, chatting about nothing, looking forward to the summit view, and then we rounded a curve and the road was gone. Brakes slamming, the two of us hopped out. The forest ranger shook his head. Sorry, there's been a landslide. No one's getting anywhere today. And Mick and I stood there, wondering. What had we passed so far? Had we even noticed it?

I could hope for no more now than another evening together, another whole night together, perhaps, once his season and his surgery were completed. But he'd be impotent. I'd never again feel his semen leaking out of me. Or his hips banging my thighs with something like desperation. I'd never again hold him inside me and rock my pelvis like a cradle. Women didn't miss it, people said. Women said that. I already missed it. Without sex, our need had no fulfillment. Without sex, our touching seemed like clutching.

I realized it was the dawn and not some neon sign that was coloring the chink between the curtains, and I had to get up, I had to rush home and shower and change and feed Ginger and make it to the hospital for my angiograms, I had to move, and instead I was lying gazing at the hotel window and light fixture and wall. The scene itself seemed to be wavering, as if the glue behind it were weak and bubbling, as if with a tug I could peel off the real world.

A T LEAST MY PATIENTS were happy.

"I'm doing great since that last stent."

"My ankles hardly swell except for sauerkraut."

Treadmills, caths, hospital rounds, office visits. Treadmills, caths, hospital rounds, office visits. You heard too little about how work was healing. You heard about work wearing people down, deathbed confessions that careers had been too consuming. You didn't hear about the comforts of a busy day.

Mick and I had discovered e-mail. Before, the thought of this had made Mick nervous, his secrets exposed. Even though he used his Turkman account, there was still the chance that Karn or his children could get into his file. But now that fear had been made trivial by the Big Fear, the fear Mickey didn't want to say existed. Mick wrote, I'm sitting here writeing and B.C. is right in front of me. Do I love you or what????

B.C., the athletic director Mick couldn't stand.

I typed, I'm sitting here and Howard is right in front of me. Is he oblivious or what???

Mick: B.C. at least can read.

I loved getting e-mail from Mick. When I pressed send I saw my message stream into the air, one strand of a series of criss-crossing ligatures, a house of our own we were building line by line.

"Your stress test looks great," I said, riffling through the papers. "And the thallium was perfect." Both reports were clipped to the front of Jessica's chart, and I wondered if Lindy had noticed that Jessica's stress test had again been done in the hospital and not our office. Better think up an explanation, I thought, anticipating Lindy telling Howard.

"Do you think I need a heart monitor?" Jessica asked. "The lady at the front desk said . . ."

"Ignore her. She flunked out of med school."

"Good, because I feel fine." Jessica was perched at the end of the exam table, dandling her son. "Except my dad has cancer."

I heard, I almost said, but I stopped myself. No one was supposed to know. "Cancer?" I said, and it was a relief to say that word out loud. "What kind?"

"Prostate. My mom's going crazy. He's getting shots, but Mom thinks he needs surgery, like, yesterday. She found this doctor at Johns Hopkins who agrees with her." Jessica explained about Mick's team, his plans for surgery at the end of the season. She looked at me face-on. "What do you think?"

"I . . ." There was urgency in Jessica's eyes. "From what I've heard," I said, "prostate cancer is very treatable."

She frowned as if I'd disappointed her. "His cancer's got some high score. I know Marcus is worried."

Marcus! I'd forgotten I was supposed to be Marcus's girlfriend. "Well . . ." I stammered, "Marcus did tell me. But I didn't know if he was supposed to."

"It's okay," Jessica said, reaching across the space between us to take a swipe at patting my arm. "My brothers and I wanted you to know. You being a doctor, you could help us. You know Mom." She looked at the ceiling. "She makes him watch the Three Stooges. He hates the Three Stooges. She says, 'This'll be one hell of a Christmas.'" Jessica's voice cracked. "You think you could call her again?"

I couldn't believe she was asking me this. I was her cardiologist, not her buddy. Was it my supposed connection to Marcus? Did she just not know better? Or was it the entitlement of a coach's daughter who was used to having her family's seats saved and their meals paid for? "I'm not a cancer specialist, I wouldn't know . . ." I wondered about the doctor at Johns Hopkins. Did he know things I didn't? (Of course.) Was he reasonable? I'd visited websites and reviewed textbooks and talked to the urologist in the office down the hall. Mick did have a chance, but the high Gleason score was worrisome, and his putting off full treatment was risky. I was standing at the exam room counter finishing Jessica's note, trying to correct my handwriting's steady downhill slant.

"My mom always wants to direct things," Jessica said almost dreamily. "She made lists of boys I was allowed to like." I turned, puzzled by what I was hearing. "Starting in eighth grade. She used to talk to the school secretaries to get information. It didn't work, though." Jessica nodded toward her toddler. "His dad wasn't on the list. She did it for my brothers too. In my opinion, that's how Eric ended up with Delilah."

Lists? Lists of boys Jessica was *allowed* to like? How in the world could a parent control the affections of her offspring? I don't want to know about this family, I thought. I don't need to be dragged into this craziness. I turned my back to Jessica and faced the exam room counter as I installed the results of her stress test into her chart.

"Dr. Toledo?" Jessica said. "Would you call her?"

At least she had the decency to ask this in a timid voice. But the repeat request stunned me.

I swiveled to face her, hitting her chart with my elbow. "What about your father?" Out of the corner of my eye, I saw the chart career across the counter and stop at the edge of the sink. "Where's your father in all this?" Did Mick know about Karn's lists of acceptable suitors? Did he approve of such tactics? "Why doesn't he tell your mother he hates the Three Stooges?"

The words were a little too loud, they emerged with too much pressure behind them. An outburst, someone might say. The silence that followed was loud. The toddler on Jessica's lap took the pacifier from his mouth and extended it in my direction.

"She trusts you," Jessica said, ignoring her son's gesture. "That's why I asked. I thought because of you and Marcus . . . I thought you might do her a favor." She slid off the exam table and brought the child to her shoulder. "Am I done?" A hint of suspicion and anger in her face, as if she wondered now what Marcus saw in me.

"You're done." I filled out Jessica's billing form, scrawled "Back 3 months" with a particular flourish, and handed the chart to Jessica with what I hoped was a stalwart grin. She was a good head taller than I was, and in that moment I felt the difference. Jessica smiled back, but her eyes slipped from my face to a spot between the window and the floor.

O N December 12, a Tuesday, Mick's forward Tom Kennilworth was arrested for aggravated menacing at a party. He had been brandishing a gun, telling another attendee to stay away from the infamous English tutor/girlfriend. Kennilworth's lawyer was angling for a deal with the prosecutors, but in the meantime Kennilworth was off the team. Mick and I had been over and over it on the phone. Privately, the Turkman State president had said the possibility and the timing of Kennilworth's reinstatement would be up to Mick, but Mick should remember that the faculty was still upset about the English chair's resignation (he had indeed moved to Iowa). It might be better, under the circumstances, to err on the severe side and keep Kennilworth off the team unless the charge was dropped to a misdemeanor. The president hinted at Kennilworth's convenient whiteness. The Students of Color League, he said, would not be making a statement.

Mick was bursting with advice he had given his players.

"Whatever happened to a good old fistfight?"

"I tell them all the time, nothing good ever happens after ten P.M.!"

"No one cares if it's not loaded."

I could imagine Mick's players rolling their eyes at these statements. Each one made Mick sound old.

When I got to our room Thursday Mick was by the window, slumped in a chair as if it had been pulled out from beneath him. He was wearing his nubbly brown sweater. His eyes rolled toward mine as he spoke. "I'm beat," he said.

Immediately, I thought about the trouble with Kennilworth. The Warriors were 6 and 1. The partisan TV commentators were sounding almost giddy. "What are you talking about?" I said. "You can't be your players' babysitter. You can't be their conscience, sit on their shoulders like Tinker Bell all night long."

He didn't smile. He looked to his right, away from me, and worried his upper lip with his lower teeth. "I don't feel like much of a coach."

"You've got Eluard."

"Eluard's a kid."

Kid. The word itself seemed to burst with the plosive truth of it. I sat down on the edge of the bed.

"I have Frederick, sure," Mick said, "but Frederick can't do everything."

I traced the stitching in the bedspread with my finger. "And Chiswick," I said, "and Morgan, and your freshmen."

Mick said, "I don't know if I have the energy for this."

I looked at him, thinking of Mick's life that was secret from his team, the cancer and the antitestosterone shots and the expectation of surgery. I wished that I'd had cancer myself, because I couldn't really know what Mick was experiencing. Sometimes I thought the same thing with my patients. What did chest pain really feel like? What sensation let people know that they were about to die? You could see, sometimes, the understanding fill their faces, but its source was as mysterious as starlight. It was possible Mick couldn't be the coach he was the year before. "Are you tired?" I asked, and it hit me that "tired" was a word as rough and rudimentary as a caveman's hammer.

"I don't have the endurance." Mick pushed himself upright in the chair and turned toward me, and the deliberate way he did this made me think of Himself before he died. "It gets frustrating." In his last office visit, recalling the effort of walking from a stadium to his car, Himself had almost cried.

"Sit down here beside me," I said, patting the bed, and when he did I removed his nubbly sweater and the shirt beneath it. I moved my hands over his back, circling each mole, then over his chest and down his shoulders, all the time wishing that my hands, my doctor's hands, were capable of healing.

"How about my cholesterol?" Mick asked later as we lay in our usual position. "Can I just forget about my cholesterol?"

I unwrapped my legs from his and sat up quickly. "Oh no! You can't stop the medicine. That's long-term."

HE'S ALWAYS TIRED," I told Claudia when she brought over her invitations. "It's come down to talk and sleeping."

Claudia's eyes widened, her right hand flew to the base of her neck and touched the hollow there, a gesture that struck me as vaguely religious. "That's all we can do together now," I said. "Talk and sleep."

"Oh, Mommy," Claudia said.

I hadn't realized the power of simple kindness.

CHURNING. I lay in bed and my toes were hot, my right hip hurt, my eyes under my closed lids wouldn't stop moving. I flipped on the light and sat up. 1:42. I'd be up for good in less than four hours.

A list of boys Karn's daughter could like. Madness. Yet wouldn't I have made a list for Claudia—at least a mental list—if I'd ever gotten the idea? That was what a parent did: worry about her offspring and her choices. If I'd had the opportunity, I might have pumped a school secretary for information. In fact, I'd never met a school secretary. I was always working, and I never had the time.

I plodded to the bathroom, thinking of Toby. Pleasant enough, I supposed, and God knows he made a point of being wholesome. Intelligent? Who knew. At least he wasn't threatening to stay home and look after his and Claudia's future children. At least he was nice to Claudia. At least he wasn't Giles.

"You could do better," my mother had said when I got married. She was right, yet it was wrong of her to tell me. A person had to learn things for herself. Look at Jessica. A guy on Karn's list might at least pay child support.

In the bathroom mirror my face sagged like an old donkey's. "Oh God, go away," I said, waving at my image, and with relief I flicked the switch that made me disappear.

IN THE MEANTIME, Mick and I kept e-mailing.
  How's my dozey-bear? Planning to rest up Wednesday night?

You wait. Next time I'll tie you down and nibble you up.

Sickening, yes. We were like kids again. We were playing make-believe.

T HREE MONTHS AGO, *they were saying Coach Mick Crabbe was paid too much. . . . Well, tonight they're saying he's priceless.* The Saturday bedtime West Virginia news. I watched it at least five times.

Eluard backing into a crowd of opposing players. Eluard dodging and shooting. *And the Warriors take it, 75 to 60.*

Eluard Dickens and Corey Morgan were vying for the points-per-game title. One game Eluard got more, another game Corey.

Mick was on camera. "He can get in there and play with the best of them. But I'll tell you, it was a team effort. We had the rebounds, the steals, we had the defensive plays."

"What about Tom Kennilworth?" The player awaiting his charges.

"He's working on his problems and we hope to get him back, but that's in the court system now. Todd Jackson's stepping in just fine."

"Congratulations on what has to be a satisfying victory."

A brown hand—Eluard's?—appeared on Mick's left shoulder. "Thanks," Mick said, looking away from the reporter, and his face was radiant. I pushed the pause button. No one would ever dream that man was ill. I wished there was a way to make a photo from the image on the screen.

The next evening, I told Mick on the phone about my oldest patient, Beatrice Lampry, age ninety-seven. Her son said that whenever Bea heard about the death of a celebrity younger than her, Bea grinned and chortled, "Beat 'em."

"See?" Mick said. "Even old ladies want to win."

"You looked great on Channel Eight," I said. "Who put their hand on your shoulder?"

"Oh, that was Leon Chiswick. Was he stoked. Did you see his three-pointers?"

"They didn't run the whole game."

"They didn't put Chiswick on highlights?"

"The highlights were all Eluard." I was standing in my kitchen. Ginger appeared from the family room, stopped and looked at me, then trotted toward the steps upstairs.

"No Chiswick? No Frederick? Idiots. Well. Everybody likes a star."

"You're my star," I said, pressing the phone more firmly between my chin and my shoulder, as if he could feel the squeeze.

The next day, the Monday a week before Christmas, Lindy staggered into my office holding a huge bouquet of flowers. I knew the sender before I opened the card. There was something troubling about Karn's excessive generosity. "I am not worthy," the flowers seemed to say. "Jessica is cured!" the note read.

"Thank you for giving us our life back. Merry Christmas! Love, Mick and Karn."

Not even a last name, I thought, flicking the card with my fingernail. My God, I am in deep.

"She sent you flowers?" Mick said on the phone. "Nice ones?"

"Maybe Jessica should get a cardiologist in West Virginia," I said, blinking back tears that sprang more from confusion than pain. I was glad that Mick couldn't see my face. E-mail was for flirting, our hotel rooms were for comfort, and the phone alone was left for things that mattered.

"Why?" Mick sounded hurt. "If you had a son in college, I'd want him here with me."

DECEMBER 21, A THURSDAY, and Mick was still talking about the damn flowers. "Karn has this thing: she loves to find the right gifts for people." I didn't tell him that within two days the petals of the white roses had been curling. Mick peeled off his socks. There were bits of navy lint stuck between his toes. So much about Karn had slipped out of him in the three months since I'd met her, when for the years before, Mick had barely mentioned her. *Karn has this thing . . .* As if now that I'd met her he had the right to bring her into our conversation. There are reasons he's stayed with her, I thought, and I swallowed as if the thought were something nasty I was hurrying through my mouth.

I draped my skirt over the chair. "She seems like a very decent person." This Christmas was working out for us. Some Christmases were interruptions, falling on Thursdays or Fridays.

"That's the problem." Mick rolled his eyes significantly, pulled his blue sweater over his head, struggling for a moment with the neck. "She could be my mother."

But the mother he'd described to me had been, except when she got angry with the drinks in her, passive and beleaguered, a woman who forgot the clothes in the washer until they were stiff and dried. His mother sounded nothing like Karn. "She's been your wife a long time," I said. I was in my panties and bra, perched on the side of the bed. "You shouldn't compare her to your mother."

Mick looked at me in surprise. "Whose side are you on?"

"I'm on your side, Mickey." As if there had to be a side. Turkman had lost their most recent game; maybe that was Mick's problem.

Mick's eyes shifted warily, then sparked. "Show me," he said.

That Thursday we stayed awake. That Thursday Mick let me fondle him and kiss him, but that was where it ended, as if there were nothing he could do for me. As if he didn't have fingers and lips and arms; as if, since he was unexcitable, there was no reason to excite me. *Why are you so selfish?* I thought, lifting my head from the pillow. If he died, I'd have nothing to show for him, not even the souvenir basketball he'd tried to give me when we first met. Karn was the star of the family, Jessica had said, and that I could accept. But the flowers suggested Karn was something more. She was the family's ambassador, the giver. She might well be—as unimpressive as she'd been over the phone to me—the family's heart.

"Merry Christmas," Mick said later, nodding at a bag on the chair. Chocolates. "You like those, don't you?" he asked, a trace of anxiety in his voice. His gifts were typically something I suspected he'd picked up driving to meet me—a handbag, a scarf—and I'd always accepted them as the sweet and awkward gifts of a busy man. But getting chocolates that day—and not even good ones, drugstore chocolates—hurt my feelings.

"I like them too much," I said. "I'm trying not to eat sweets." This sounded harsh, and I added, "But for you I'll make an exception." I removed my gift for him from my handbag: a watch with an engraved face and a copper and silver band. "It's a real work of art," the clerk had said as she wrapped it. He might not show it at home, but Mick could wear my watch at work.

I took time with my gifts for him, always. Time and thought and, yes, expense. And look what I got back.

Good sex is a sort of thrilling confusion from which you emerge dazed and content, convinced the world is a good home after all. Bad sex is transactional. I'll make you come if you make me come. What, no blow job for a lobster dinner? I'll do it now if you won't bother me tomorrow. Mick and I had rarely had bad sex. But now we were having bad no-sex, and I thought fleetingly that I'd just as soon we'd never met than see our love turn into this. I started crying, something I never did. *Take it and fake it,* that was my motto. "Do you even like me?" I said, wincing inside as I heard the words.

How could I say that? He loved me, he loved me. He felt terrible about the chocolates; he'd been too busy, he should have gotten me something I deserved. He held me and he stroked my hair. I let myself be comforted, I tried my hardest to believe each thing he said, because who could say how many Thursdays we had left? And after all these years I owed him something.

. . .

ARE YOU LISTENING TO YOURSELF?" Tessa said when we met Saturday for a late lunch. In fact, looking back on it, I wasn't sure what I'd just said to her. I was zapped. Thursday night I'd been up for hours wondering what I was doing with Mick, and Friday night I'd spent at the hospital with a recurrently coding patient. The patient had made it, barely, and it felt like a dream to be sitting in a busy restaurant, surrounded by conversations and the smell of food. There was jangly Christmas music playing, and our waitress wore a Santa Claus hat. "*The time we have left,* you say. But Mickey's getting treatment, in the spring he'll get surgery, and . . ."

"It's just this feeling I have," I said, feeling agitated and resentful, as if I were being forced to defend something that should never be attacked, like charity or goodness.

KENDRA O'DELL: FUNNY IN HEAD

"You have to be more positive, Genie. If there's one common thread in every book I read, it's . . ."

"Oh, God." I covered my face with my hands. Before Mick's diagnosis we had had some reasonable chance, in any given week, of joy. Now we seemed to have no chance—not now, not in the future. I slid my hands down, sagging my eyes. "It's like he's withdrawing from everything but basketball."

The waitress slapped down our bill. "You two have a great holiday."

M. L. HOPKINS: QUESTION FOR DOCTOR ONLY

"It's his season!" Tessa said, and I thought how much she sounded like I might have in another year. "He has a lot on his mind. And the fact is that the man looks perfectly healthy, and you always said he wasn't mentally all there for you during his season, and prostate cancer is a treatable disease, and . . ."

At that moment I hated her. Tessa had made herself more than a person. She was a mess of barbed wire impossible to roll up, a gigantic pill I was being asked to swallow. *This must be how Claudia feels,* I thought, *sitting across the table from me.*

I drove straight from lunch with Tessa to Claudia's apartment, answering my calls on the way. M.L. wanted to know why she couldn't have two drinks a day. "I could handle that. And if I had, like, one drink today, I could maybe have three tomorrow."

"It doesn't work like that," I said. "You're an alcoholic."

"I don't think you understand me," M.L. said. "I've got that artistic temperament. Every day's not easy for me."

Claudia and Toby lived on the third floor of a nondescript brick apartment building with cream-painted cinderblock halls. Claudia, in a green flannel shirt decorated with a brooch in the shape of a poinsettia, looked startled to see me at her door. "It hit me that I don't always listen to what you want," I said from the hall. "The things I say must make you feel attacked."

How quickly her face softened, as if I were a pan too hot for butter to resist. "Come in, come in." Their apartment was crowded with Claudia's ceramic frogs and Toby's furniture and *People* and gardening magazines. Toby wasn't there. I sat down on the sofa.

"Mom, are you okay?"

"I'm too old for this. I used to be able to get by without sleeping."

"You work too hard. You could work less hard and still be a good person."

Good person, good person . . . "I'm going to collapse now, honey."

"You sleep right here. I'll get you a blanket."

"Wake me up so I can get home for my manicure."

"I will, Mommy. Sleep tight."

She woke me up, we talked. We made plans for Christmas Eve dinner there, at her and Toby's place.

Things I imagined: I would leave an exam room and there was Karn. "How could you?" she would scream, breaking away from the front desk and chasing me down the hall. Behind her, Lindy our receptionist, enjoying every yelp, would be running on her tiptoes and trying not to grin.

Or:

"It's Karn"—Mick's voice over the phone—"she took all her pills. She's on life support right now, but . . . Genie, she knows. She's *known*."

Or:

"You're sleeping with my father? You're sleeping with my *father*?" Jessica clutched at her chest.

What a delightful life I'd made for myself. An over-the-top melodrama, complete with speeches and tears and threats of death. The disturbing thing was, I couldn't stop picturing these scenarios. The thought of Mick being torn from me by such circumstances was perversely exciting. What if I couldn't see him? What if our meetings were no longer weekly sleep-ins but dangerous and stealthy assignations? We'd have our zip back, I

thought; we'd have our passion. Much more satisfying to imagine this than the alternative, a life deflating like a punctured
tire.

I should have wished for boring Thursdays forever. I should
have fantasized about Mick's PSA dropping to undetectable
levels, his urologist with the experienced finger saying, "Mr.
Crabbe, I don't feel a thing."

Mick had not changed his urologist. His remark about Leakey
being a nerd had been no more than a moment's outburst.

T HE WEEK AFTER CHRISTMAS, the Turkman Warriors lost
their third game in a row, their longest losing streak in four
years. There had been other years (particularly five years before,
when the team had been especially eager and star-crossed) when
a loss would make Mick visibly ache, put him in the mood for
obliterating, angry sex, but this year Mick met each loss with
spooky equanimity. At one point after an official's inauspicious
call he was described by Stan Furman, a veteran radio announcer
who wasn't used much, as "sitting on the sidelines looking Zen."
(I read the quote later in the *Turkman Telegraph*; I lived too far
away to get Mick's team on the radio.) Each missed block or
errant free throw, Mick told Art Quinlivan, was an "educational
opportunity"; each game was preparation for the bigger games
later on. "Why should I go crazy?" he wrote me on e-mail. "I
don't need crazy"—a reference I thought must apply to his situation at home as well.

Mick scared me. I'd seen any number of people who'd had
heart attacks triggered by traumatic events—a sister's funeral, a
wife's disappearance, a gambling son who'd shown up needing

money. Surely the growth of a cancer could be accelerated by such things. Mick's whole season looked to me like a dangerous road he was heading down alone. All I could do was stand beside it watching for thieves or snipers, ready to scream out a warning if I saw a movement in the bushes or on a roof.

Not that he'd listen. Not that he'd care.

The next Thursday, four nights before the new year of 2001, I told Mick I was sorry about his losing streak. "It's conference play," he said, shrugging. "They've seen our tapes. They're reading us. Our guys have been getting lazy. Things'll be different soon. Frederick has an idea." A furtive smile crossed Mick's face, as if he were about to reveal some sexual secret.

"I screamed at them," Mick said. "I absolutely screamed. I didn't think I had the oomph to do that anymore, but it really felt good. I said, 'If you guys want to stay alive, you can't go out there and lie down!' I said it a bunch, and then I went through each guy one by one and said exactly how he'd laid down and died, and when I finished everybody was quiet, I mean spooky quiet, have-I-gone-too-far quiet, and then Frederick—and I wasn't easy on Frederick, believe me—Frederick raises his hand and says, 'Coach, why don't we think of the ball as a creature that wants to go through the net?' And I said, 'What?' and Corey Morgan sort of laughed and Frederick repeated it.

"You get it?" Mick said, turning his face to me.

"Kind of," I said, not sure if I did.

"They got it," Mick said. "They got it right off. I saw everybody looking at each other, and Lionel got this light in his eyes and Hugh started laughing and the next thing you know we're planning. We can't wait for the next game. Some of the guys went out in the practice gym and started shooting."

I didn't understand it, really. I flopped onto my back and looked at the ceiling. "It changed everything," Mick said. "One comment. It gave us hope, okay? It gave us freedom." Mick hesitated, turned and propped himself up on an elbow. I felt him studying my face. "It's hard to defend against freedom," he said.

I looked up at him. "You mean you'll use fewer set offensive plays."

"That's part of it. We're going to be more spontaneous. We're going to be ready for whatever the ball wants." He grinned. "*The ball is a creature that wants to be put through the net.* What a concept."

"Are you planning to tell Art Quinlivan about this?"

"You've got to be kidding. This is private. This is between me and the guys. And you." He placed a hand on either side of me and lowered his face down until we were nose to nose. "We're going to win," he said in a whisper. "Don't tell anyone, but we're going to win all year long." I looked into his eyes and saw he believed this. A shiver went through me, as if Mick were risking everything with those words.

"Karn's got some group from St. Catherine's praying for my health," he said a few moments later, once he had flopped onto his back.

"For you? They know?"

"Sworn to secrecy," Mick said, raising a finger to his lips. "I guess they've prayed for all sorts of people. I've got my own psalm."

"Which one?" Not that I knew any.

"Psalm Twenty. It's got something about hanging banners for me. I like that."

Mick seemed like a child at that moment, and I felt a gush of indulgent love. "Very sporting," I said. "Who picked it?" I sat up to look at him.

"I guess Karn did."

"Oh." I lay back down.

We were silent for a while. "Kennilworth was back at practice this afternoon," he said.

In surprise, I lifted my head. "What about the felony charge?"

"They dropped it to a misdemeanor. There're a couple of alums in the prosecutor's office."

"You didn't call them, did you?"

"Not I."

Marcus called the alumni, I thought, laying my head on Mick's shoulder. Everyone even remotely involved with Turkman State seemed to know Marcus.

Politics, I thought. All power and politics. Toby Polstra's face—square, righteous, antimeat—appeared in my mind and I was seized with a ferocious weariness, as if I'd been called upon to defend and explain Mick's life, which was by extension my life, and the mustering of excuses was more than I could bear. We're adulterers but we're not bad people. We work hard, we care. But we really did care. I thought of a particular glance that passed between Frederick Flitt and Mick after a successful play: a quick half-smile that was half triumph, half collusion. I thought of myself earlier that day, sitting in one of my exam rooms sorting through dead Mr. Kegler's bottles of medicines as Mrs. Kegler and her daughter watched, all of us wanting his pills passed on to another patient.

We lay there silently. I could hear Mick's steady heart. The body brought you back to the important things, to the simple fact of life itself. "I've been thinking," Mick said, his finger bumping over the vertebrae in my back. "You think you'd want a vacation house somewhere? I could buy you something. You know. Some haven you can go to if I'm not around."

What was he saying? What did he mean by "not around"? I pictured our condo in San Antonio, with painted tiles in the kitchen and vines around the door. "Mickey!" I'd call. "You want an over-easy egg for breakfast?" But the kitchen table was empty, and he wasn't in the bathroom or on the porch. I looked everywhere, and still he wasn't there.

"Don't talk that way," I said, my mouth gone dry.

"You should let me," he said. "You're a doctor, and I can't talk that way at home."

"I can't let you," I said, my head pressing harder into his chest. We lay that way for ages, his chest hairs leaving a swirling impression on my cheek when I sat up. It was wrong, I thought driving home, it was a waste: Mick was still in every way alive, but during our time together all I thought of was his absence.

Next time would be different. My New Year's resolution.

I got home, I did step aerobics, and when I got in bed I had a revelation. When you love someone, it can take years to fully plumb their oddness. "That's just them," you say, and it seems normal, even if, objectively, their thoughts and behavior are at the far end of some human bell curve. Mick, for example. He had a potentially fatal disease, a disease for which the window of cure might now be open, and yet he was ignoring that window. He ignored it not to retire and spend more time with his family or with me, not because he was paranoid about medical treatments, but because he had something better to think about. He wanted to be a coach. He wanted around him all the glory of his team. And therefore it was clearly true, despite his protestations, that there was something he loved more than me.

This thought gave me great comfort. Any truth does, once you see it.

N EW YEAR'S EVE I watched the Lifetime network, switched to Times Square close to midnight, then dialed Claudia's cellphone at 12:03. Claudia answered on the fifth or sixth ring. "Uh, Mom," Claudia said, and there was a rustling in the background. Sheets? "This isn't a good time for me, okay?"

"Oh," I said, startled, "maybe it's a very good time! Happy New Year!" I hung up. At first I was nothing but pleased, but then I got lonely.

Ginger was asleep under Claudia's old bed.

I did two tapes that night, Intermediate Pilates and Power Yoga. Ridiculous to talk about exercise tapes saving my sanity, but there it was. I almost wished I was on call. A massive MI with complications would have been a fine distraction.

May he grant you your heart's desire, and fulfill all your plans!
May we shout for joy over your salvation, and in the name of our
God set up our banners! May the Lord fulfill all your petitions!

And there was more. I left the Bible open on my bedside table. I tried to read Mickey's psalm each morning and night.

T HE NEXT THURSDAY Mick was standing grinning, fully dressed, inside the door of our hotel room. "Don't take your coat off," he said, putting his hands on my shoulders. "Turn around."

Seize the moment, I thought. Live the day. How perfect—
unsurprising, really—that our minds were going in the same
direction. "What's this about?" I said in the elevator. "You're
going to take me out in public?"

"You can only hope," Mick said. The previous Sunday his
team had romped over their archrival, West Virginia. Tuesday night his team had won in overtime when Corey Morgan's
three-pointer rolled around the rim and went in. At the end
of each game the court took minutes to empty, Mick's players hugging one another and jumping around. He's a genius, I
had thought, staring at my TV. "We're going with the ball,"
Mick had said over the phone. "We're putting it where it
needs to be."

We walked through the parking lot, our feet leaving black
spots in the skim of snow. I looked for Mick's yellow Corvette
but didn't see it; instead we were headed for a light blue Jaguar.
"You got a new car?"

He opened up his hand to reveal a set of keys. "It's your car.
Merry New Year's." I'd told Mick once that of all the luxury
cars, I only liked Jaguars, although the women who drove them
always seemed to be smokers who looked worried. "You can't
start smoking, though," Mick said, turning his palm to drop the
keys in my hand. "That's not the point."

I was stunned. "Did you buy it?" I said. "With your own
money?"—wondering for a moment if this was some Turkman
benefit Mick was passing on to me.

Mick snorted and gave a nod. "Of course I bought it. With
my very own money." He added, reading my mind: "They don't
like me *that* much."

I knew it was the most extravagant thing Mick had ever

done. Raj will be jealous, I thought. Raj will want to know how much I paid.

"I guess I don't get the vacation house, then," I said, thinking wildly that a second house would at least be something I could hide.

He laughed. "I'll get you the house. I'll get you anything."

"I don't want anything," I said. "I mean, I only want you. Chocolates are fine, Mick, chocolates . . ." A car. A Jaguar! It was a preposterous gift, after years of earrings and scented lotions. And a car like this would be fussy, need special parts, confuse the mechanics at Maaco. But it was Mick's dream that I love it, so I did.

"Thank you, Mick. It's unbelievable. It's gorgeous." And all I could think, looking up at him, was *Get well for me*. We didn't touch. I felt as if he knew my thoughts, as if he were answering with his eyes *I'll try*.

He stepped in front of me and opened the driver's door. "I bought it in Ohio," he said. "I'll meet you somewhere next week and we'll transfer the registration."

I sat down behind the wheel and he got in beside me. The car had a padded leather dashboard and a wonderful smell. "Let's blow this scene," Mick said, but it took some time until I felt calm enough to drive.

Toby's teaching position was part-time and didn't offer health insurance, and since he and Claudia wanted her to get pregnant soon after the wedding, for several months Toby had been looking for a new job. The two of them were attending a church that ran a recycling program in their parking lot, and one of the parishioners there, a man who owned a chain of nursing homes, offered Toby a job as the ordering clerk in his main office.

"It's not really Toby's thing, but this guy wanted someone he could trust," Claudia said from her leather chair. "I think the minister talked him into hiring Toby." We were in my living room. She was knitting Toby a sweater for his birthday, a project that had taken weeks, although looking at the pieces I wondered if the sleeves would accommodate the girth of Toby's arms. Even Claudia's ball of yarn had not enticed out my ghost cat.

I smiled. "Like Toby said, everything's politics!"

"Yeah." Claudia laughed, but then she stopped abruptly, and an unease close to fear entered her face. "Don't tell Toby I said that."

"Claudia. It's an innocent comment."

"I know it is, but he might not . . ." Claudia hesitated, laid down her knitting needles. "I want to be good enough for him."

I made a face. "Of course you're good enough for him! You're good enough for any man in the world!"

Claudia shook her head and buried her fingers in the knitting on her lap. "I'm not perfect."

"Who's perfect? Is Toby perfect?"

Claudia shook her head again, twisted her arms over each other, and intertwined her fingers. "No."

"Claudia." I pushed myself to the edge of my seat and leaned forward. "If there's anything you want to tell . . ."

"It's complicated," Claudia said, cutting me off. She glanced at her watch. "I need to get to the grocery before four." A few minutes later, she gathered up her knitting and left. I heard her opening the front closet for her coat and then she was out the front door. "Bye, honey!" I called, wondering if I should have followed her to the door, and it seemed like an age before I heard her thin "Bye, Mom" in return.

NOTHING I SAY to her is right. I try to be kind, I try to be loving, and still . . . The things I say to you are okay, why can't I say the right things to her?"

I'd never talked this frankly about Claudia to Mick. For years, I'd hidden things from him—not consciously, exactly, but in an attempt to make his view of me more pleasant, the way when the doorbell rings a person closes the door on a messy room. I felt chilled and homely and totally naked, but we were in our hotel room fully dressed with our coats on, sitting in our armchairs at the round table. We'd arrived in our room at the exact same time, and these chairs were where we'd ended up.

"Maybe she can't hear the right things. You say them, but she doesn't hear them. Bobby can be like that."

I nodded. "I never meant to hurt her, never. I used to take days off to go on field trips . . ."

"Maybe it was the divorce."

"I was working fourteen hours a day. I'd get home and there were dirty socks on the kitchen counter and ground-up crayons in the carpet and . . ." I was leaning forward into the table and holding Mick's eyes with mine and a startled look—an alarmed recognition—came over his face and his eyes slipped way. He went through the same thing, I realized. But he stayed married.

"You don't know what it's like being home with the kids," Mick said. "That's what Karn always said."

I slumped back in my chair. "You think I did the wrong thing getting divorced."

"Did I say that? Did I?"

"You thought it."

"How do you know what I thought? Don't tell me I have thoughts I don't have!"

I closed my eyes. This is like me and Claudia, I thought. The simplest words turned into accusations. I wondered if my worst arguments were really disagreements with myself. I stood up, passed around the table, and took a seat on Mickey's lap. What was this? Giving up or triumphing. The cheapest trick or the

finest tool. I ran my fingers down Mick's stubbly cheek and onto
the smooth skin of his neck, slipped my index finger under his
collar and swirled the hair on his chest. I undid buttons. He
unzipped. Neither of us said a word. Touch was what we used to
take things back.

That winter, we had some sweet times. One evening I got to
our room early and made us hot cocoa, using the coffeemaker
in the bathroom, and we propped ourselves up on our pillows
to drink it. Another night when I arrived Mick was on his side
under the covers with the blanket pulled up to his nose. "I can't
move," he said. "I feel like a caterpillar in a cocoon."

"Let me slip in with you," I said, stripping down in front of
him and sliding myself under the covers.

"Ooh, what a nice warm twig," he said. Then we both fell
asleep.

IT HIT ME that Claudia had experienced something that
changed her, an event I'd somehow missed. One morning I
was rinsing my breakfast dishes when I figured out the date: a little over two years before, the Christmas season when she'd been
so quiet, when her gift to me wasn't a blouse or a nightgown but
a charitable contribution to a family in Haiti. I remembered the
livestock pictures on the card. "That's lovely," I said. "Three
chickens will make a feast."

"They're for laying eggs!" Claudia said. "Nobody's going to
kill them!"

At the time I thought the gift itself was a comment on my
being rich; it was only now I saw it could have been her atonement for something. Shortly after New Year's Claudia had started

looking for her own apartment; the next Christmas she gave me her usual sort of gift, a patterned bag for makeup.

I flashed to a toilet seat left up ("Did you vomit? Are you sick?"), a Sunday brunch after Thanksgiving when Claudia had eaten only fruit. She was pregnant, I realized. She was carrying my grand-child. This was around the time Giles split up with her but before he totaled his car and got arrested and phoned her for help. Claudia had arrived at the jail to bail him out and found him already free and entangled with a girl Claudia had once babysat, his hand under the girl's shirt. The baby would have been Tessa's grandchild too.

That same morning a letter arrived in the mail and onto my desk in the office.

Jan. 10, 2001
Dear Dr. Toledo,
    I understand you are busy but I need to talk to you in per-son right away. This should not wait. Call me during the day to arrange a time and meeting place.
    Sincerely, Karn Crabbe

It struck me that I didn't have to answer it. It struck me that the U.S. Postal Service wasn't perfect. All I wanted to think about—all I could think about—was Claudia. That whole week-end, Karn Crabbe didn't cross my mind at all.

Sunday afternoon Claudia and I were alone in our—no, my—living room, Toby off at a woodworking exhibition with his father. Claudia was in her leather chair, a heel digging into the cushion. Toby's sweater was complete, but Claudia's hands were moving as if they yearned for knitting.

"I had things taken care of," Claudia said.

"Oh, Claudia. I wish you'd come to me."

"I couldn't tell you. I was ashamed, and . . ."

"I'm a doctor," I said. "I could at least have helped you through the medical system."

"You were busy, remember? Mick's daughter was pregnant." I blanched: Jessica and Claudia had been pregnant at the same time. For a while, Mick had called me two or three times an evening. The irony of it stopped my breathing, and when I tried to explain my tongue stuck to the roof of my mouth. "One night I was going to tell you," Claudia said, "and I was sitting in this chair, sitting and sitting and you kept talking on the phone, and finally I thought I can't stand it, and I got up and went for a drive. You were in bed when I got back." She hesitated, looked down at her anxious hands. "I had it on a Thursday. I knew I could spend the rest of the day in bed and you wouldn't notice."

A Thursday. "Oh, Claudia."

She never thought of telling Giles. When he crashed the car she knew he was back to drinking, and if she'd told him about the baby he would probably have started up with coke again, and Claudia would have blamed herself.

"God," I said, "I hate that guy, I hate him, the way he made you . . ."

"Mom," Claudia said, "he's lost. You should pray for him, not hate him."

There wasn't much I could say to that. "I should have been there for you," I said. "I'm sorry."

Claudia shrugged. I stood and went to her chair and embraced her, and I realized her scent hadn't changed since childhood; she still smelled like a Strawberry Shortcake doll. "Have you told Toby?" I asked, one hand on her hair.

She stiffened. "I will."

"It's not my business, I know. But you two are getting married, and I thought . . ."

"Mom, just stop. No offense, Mom, but you're not exactly a marriage expert."

No, I wasn't, I thought as I lay in bed that night, curled up so tight I felt like I could slip through a pore in my sheet.

Maybe Claudia shouldn't listen to me. Maybe Claudia would end up with a happier life than mine.

MONDAY A PINK SLIP of paper appeared in my office with a note in pencil in Lindy's handwriting. *Call Connie Crabbe, personal,* followed by a telephone number. I saw five patients before I approached that note again; there was a three in the number, and, bending over my desk, glancing toward the door, I changed the three to an eight.

At the end of office hours, I wandered out to the front desk, Lindy's note in my hand. "I tried, but this number isn't right. And are you sure it's Connie? I know a Karn, but not a Connie. At any rate, I'll leave this here, and if she calls back tell her I'm sorry."

My nurse, LeeAnn, appeared from around the corner, picked up the paper, and studied it. "Is that Jessica's mother?"

"She didn't say anything about Jessica," Lindy answered. "I hate it when they call and won't say why."

"Throw their number in the trash!" Howard, on the way out, called.

"Only your number." Lindy stood to shake a finger at Howard's departing back. "Only your number goes in the garbage."

Anyone would do what I'm doing, I thought as I walked back to my office. I have enough to worry about. I'm not a bad person.

Tuesday the pink slip reappeared, with the name Connie changed to Karn and the number crossed out and the original number below it. "Did you see that paper?" LeeAnn asked as I headed in to Mr. Trelburg. "I remembered Jessica lived with her parents so I looked it up in her chart, and sure enough, Lindy wrote down the wrong number." She rolled her eyes toward the front desk.

"You're too efficient," I said. "Thank you."

LeeAnn blushed. "I called Mrs. Crabbe earlier," she said. "I told her it wasn't your fault. I told her you'd phone right after office hours, and she seemed very pleased."

Later, when I tried to dictate him, only one of Mr. Trelburg's myriad complaints stuck in my mind. "It's like the air's gone heavy," he'd said. "I take a breath and it sticks inside me."

I did call, after work. LeeAnn had promised.

The line was busy. Hallelujah! I exhaled, sat up straight. A line from one of my exercise videos came to me. *Pull those ribs in!* No call waiting, no dedicated modem phone line, just a plain, old-fashioned busy signal. Maybe Karn wasn't that bad.

No need to try again for days. I was a busy doctor, Karn had left no message, I had tried.

When I talked to Mick on the phone that evening I didn't mention it. He'd seemed tired the previous Thursday, although his team had won four straight. I wanted him to stay happy. I wanted him to keep listening to the ball.

. . .

W E HAVE TO CHANGE the wedding date," Claudia said. Toby had a cousin in Fort Wayne who already had a wedding on their date in April, and the cousin had booked hotel suites and a K of C Hall and a band, all with unrefundable deposits. On the phone, the cousin had been hysterical—but that was how she was, Toby said. In fact, the timing of Toby and Claudia's wedding, with its dinner reception at the church social hall, was fairly easy to change. "We thought March twenty-fourth," Claudia said. "It's a Saturday. I already talked to the invitation people."

That was the second of three NCAA tournament weekends. It was possible that Mick's team would still be in competition. I imagined the TV above the bar at the Friday night rehearsal dinner, the group of men escaped from the Saturday reception to huddle around the radio in the minister's office. Not that weekend, I thought. But how could I say this to Claudia?

It wasn't at all certain, in any case, that Turkman State would get that far. Yes, they looked great—they hadn't had a loss since their three in December, and by the second week of February they would be ranked 22nd in the nation, but rankings, Mick liked to say (although he voted on them), weren't reality, and then he'd launch into the usual stockbrokers' caveat about future earnings and past performance. Besides, Mick had never taken a team deep into an NCAA tournament. His Sweet Sixteen team had been astonishing enough, and it promptly lost by twenty-one points. Mick might really be—my face twitched as I thought this—a ho-hum coach.

May he grant you your heart's desire, and fulfill all your plans!

"That's fine," I said to Claudia. "It's good of you and Toby to accommodate his cousin."

"Oh, Toby always accommodates his family," Claudia said.

That Thursday, as I drove to Marietta, the music sounded noisy and I turned the radio off. Mick's car was in the corner of the front lot, farther from the door than he usually parked. I parked my new and pristine car so it straddled two spaces. The front desk clerk, helping a male customer, waved and slipped me the keycard. Mick's lost some of his machismo, I thought as the elevator rose. A little of his swagger and confidence really had vanished with the testosterone-blocking shots. It wasn't that I loved him less, but both of us had to struggle with the loss. The door to the hall was shut, and I wondered if Mick was again asleep. "My big fuzzy caterpillar," I'd say. "Mickey?" I whispered, pushing open the door.

There was a light on at the far side of the room, beside one of the armchairs flanking the round table. In the nimbus, sitting in the chair with her legs crossed, was a person who was definitely not Mick. Face your Maker, I thought. And even though this thought was ridiculous, the words popped into my mind as if they fit there. "Mrs. Crabbe," I said, "what are you doing here?"

N o SOUND. No birds, no cars, no garbage trucks, no voices. I lay on my bed Friday morning and couldn't move, daylight seeping through my blinds.

The phone rang. It took me a moment to understand the sound, and then I had to locate the receiver.

"God, I'm glad you answered." It was Helen in the cath lab. "We've had your first patient here since six-thirty and now your next one's here too."

"You woke me up," I said. "I was up all night vomiting and I must have finally fallen asleep. I can't come in today." I wasn't on call until next weekend. My two caths for today were old people with minor changes on their nuclear stress tests, nothing that couldn't be put off. And the office could limp on without me.

"Jeez, Dr. Toledo, you take care. It must be a bad bug if you're sick."

"Can you call LeeAnn in my office?" I asked. "I'm going back to sleep."

After a while I made myself pull on my robe and walk downstairs. One of those shiny, frigid days, a day that leaps up to betray you when you take a step outside. The sun was bright upon the sofa; the floorboards gleamed; the jars and cans and boxes in the kitchen cupboard were lined up in military rows. The elliptical trainer in the family (family!) room, the throw pillows on the sofa, the juicer on the kitchen counter: everything around me bespoke an orderly, health-conscious life, a life of exercise and healthy snacks and tasteful, low-key furnishings. This is hell, I thought, emptying a box of low-fat crackers into the sink. Why should I stay alive for this? "I hate my life!" I screamed out loud, and the echo of this was startling and almost comical. But it wasn't comical, and the next thing I knew I was standing behind the sofa, tears streaming down my face.

Mick's PSA was up. "You're aware that he has cancer of the prostate," Karn said from her chair on the other side of the table, meeting my eyes with startling hate. "I guess that's something he'd have to tell you, to explain his recent"—she glanced at the bed in front of us—"performance."

"How high is the PSA?"

"Ninety-six."

Two months before, Mick's PSA had been five point two. "Nine point six?" I said, incredulous, hopeful, and Karn's scathing look back was the only answer I needed.

His urologist was calling for surgery, and right this minute. Karn wished his oncologist had been blunter, but she was gaga over Mick, you know how women are. Mick said he had to finish out his season. Karn couldn't talk sense into him, and their boys couldn't, either. He wouldn't even listen to Jessica, and Karn had thought Jessica was a secret weapon.

Karn looked like an old house in a storm, flashes of lightning exposing broken windows and slipped shingles.

"Maybe he shouldn't be operated on at this point," I said, wondering what Dr. Leslie really thought. "Maybe, at this point, he should go for alternative therapy."

"Alternative therapy? Are you an expert on the prostate now too?"

I bit the inside of my cheek. "Advanced prostate cancer is treated with hormones and radiation and chemo, and maybe at this point it's late for curative surgery."

"He's on the hormones already," Karn snapped, and this was an important point, this was something I had forgotten. How? The hormones had ruined our sex life. Karn shifted her head like a dog picking up a scent. "What do you mean, 'advanced'? What do you mean 'curative'?"

A radiation doctor might have an opinion, I suggested.

"We have doctors!" Karn said. "He doesn't want to see more doctors!" She sank into her chair, put her elbow on the table between us, and talked into the air. She didn't know what his doctors told him, exactly. He wouldn't let her come in for his office visits. The urologist only told Karn about Mick's PSA so Karn couldn't sue him if Mick got worse. The urologist had told Karn about twenty times that it was Mick's own decision not to pursue treatment.

"It was Frederick at first, then Eluard. But now it's everybody, even Chiswick, now he thinks he has a real team. I told him they could go on fine without him. I told him fighting cancer would fire his team up too. But no-o-o-o. He's got that egotist thing, can't see anyone doing things without him. You let yourself get sick and we'll be doing everything without you, I said. You keep letting that thing grow and I'm a widow and my grandson doesn't have a grandpa and I'm alone. That's how I found out about this setup. I've always done the bills. You ask him, Mick hardly writes a check. But I never went through his Turkman U. receipts. Never had to. Then I thought, Well, maybe I should. I wasn't being nosy. I was trying to take a load off him, not make him be responsible. And there it was, week after week: a hundred twenty-nine dollars to the Marietta Marriott. It took me a while to figure out it was Thursdays. I thought he played poker on Thursdays. I thought he spent four hours in Marcus's basement. So I followed him a couple weeks ago. I sat in the parking lot, and twenty minutes later you get out of your car and walk in. I couldn't believe it. I kept telling myself it was a co-inky-dink, and then I saw the two of you come out."

Co-inky-dink. When I was a child, women of Karn's size and age wore girdles. They had a smooth, hard surface to their formidable heft. They were matrons, women of substance, holier-than-thou-ers. *She came into the store like a Sherman tank,* my father used to say. But Karn was pitiably unsheathed. Her loose knit shirt hung over loose knit pants, and, whatever its origin and expense, the outfit made her bulk a weakness, not a threat. At that moment keeping any secret from her seemed impossibly cruel. "Mick just bought me a car," I blurted, feeling that, in some way, it would be a kindness to tell all. And maybe he had put it on a credit card, and Karn already knew.

"A car? I drive a Lexus SUV. What do you drive?"

"Blue Jaguar."

"What model?" she said, and when I told her her face went

white. "Why'd he do that?" she said, her voice curling like a child's. "Didn't you already have a nice car?"

And later: "What do you talk about? Are you a fan?"

And: "It's really been twelve years?"

She guessed she could understand it, she said, up until the time I met Jessica. Mick was an attractive man, and he was powerful, which was an aphrodisiac, and maybe she hadn't always been the best wife. "There hasn't always been a lot of"—she hesitated— "stuff we did. I mean little things, talking in the dark, taking a ride. I saw this friend of mine, she was putting on her coat and she had trouble with the sleeve and then her husband ran up and he *helped* her. That got me. And I thought, Well, Mick was never home anyway. And then, you know, you're alone with your kids, and you and them make your own life. I guess I never thought Mick would . . . I thought basketball was his mistress."

There was nowhere to look. There was Karn and there was the bed, and both of them seemed to be growing, as if they were trying to push me from the room. "Sex just isn't a big thing for me. I tried the hormones but they gave me headaches," Karn went on. "And then they have this cream but it's messy, and I don't like to, to . . .

"What about the Oath of Hippocrates?" she said suddenly, interrupting herself. The physicians' oath, traditionally recited at medical school graduations. Karn had looked it up on the Internet. The day that Jessica walked into my office, Karn said, the day I took Jessica on, that day I should have said to Mick, *No way, we are done.* "I can understand if you're not moral in your personal life, but shouldn't you follow the codes of your profession? He'll never leave us, we're family." Karn's voice rose.

"Don't worry, I don't want publicity. You know what they do to coaches these days. I can't give them an excuse to fire him."

There was a moment of silence, as if the room itself were taking a deep breath. I was sure the oath of Hippocrates made no mention of marriage or affairs. "Didn't you like us?" Karn asked. "Didn't you see we were decent people? We liked you."

I had no idea what to say. Karn went on.

"I've thought and thought about it. Did we say something to you when Jessica was in the hospital, were we ever not nice? I think we were very nice. Weren't we nice? We sent you those flowers. We had trouble on a cruise once, I think this waiter hated us, but he was from poverty and he had children, and there we were at his table, these big wealthy Americans asking for more rolls. I mean, I could see it. But you . . ." Karn shook her head. "You I can't see."

Too odd. I leapt from the chair, ran to the bathroom, and hurled open the door, expecting to see someone—Marcus, Mick, a hired technician—behind the door twitching with suppressed laughter. But there was nobody. The bathtub was empty, the sink wiped clean, two upside-down glasses in fluted caps beside it.

"I'm not going to divorce him," Karn said. "If you care about him at all, you'll leave him alone. You're wearing him out. Even he says he needs rest now."

"You can't speak for Mick," I said finally. "I can't agree to anything if I don't talk to Mick."

Then Karn said the words that sent the colors streaking by— the peach of the hall, the bronze of the elevator, the cream keycard sliding across the brown counter, the distant flash of my blue car. I stood breathless in the parking lot, my coat open, and it was only the people walking past with scarves across their lower faces that made me realize it was cold. "Why do you think Mick let me come here," Karn asked, "if he didn't agree with me?"

F RIDAY NIGHT I CALLED RICK, my psychiatrist brother. I told him everything, I didn't make excuses.

"Wow," he said. "She was lying in wait in your hotel room? That took balls."

"Rick," I said, "his PSA is up. He's worse. I don't know how long he'll be around." I don't remember much more of the conversation. I do remember several of Rick's phrases: "natural consequences"; "respecting your loved one's choices"; "crisis as a window for change."

Believe it or not, Rick had a female social worker who was a huge Turkman fan. Her brother had gone there. Would it be okay if Rick told her I knew Mick?

I spent the weekend watching the *Godfather* movies and doing exercise tapes; I went so far, at two A.M. Sunday, as to get out some old Jane Fonda. My goal was to drive myself to physical exhaustion, then wake up hours later and without thinking start moving again.

"I won't need you this Thursday," I told Howard on Monday. "I can take my own calls."

"But what about Tuesday? Can you still cover . . . ?"

"Sure," I said. "No sweat"—vowing never to be as obvious as he was, never to let my neediness show.

Later, waiting as Lindy bent over from her chair and rum-maged in the cupboards, I spotted Jessica Crabbe's chart. She'd

never be back to see me. No more big bouquets. I wondered if
Karn had told her. I wondered if Jessica liked me enough to see
her father's side. How could Karn, all these years, not suspect
Mick had a lover? It hit me then that Karn's innocence—like any
innocence carried deep into adulthood—had a willful, almost
petulant quality. "Here you go," Lindy said, swiveling up, a
fresh prescription pad in her hand, and I'll always associate that
gesture with my next, unbidden thought: that my trust in Mick's
and my shared future had been an act of petulance itself.

O N E-MAIL, which I finally checked at home Monday
evening, I had twenty-four messages from mcrabbe@
turkmanst.edu. Their titles ranged from contrition to noncha-
lance to desperation. *Genie! Answer me!* That last title made me
smile. The hell with you, I thought. Go ahead and die. I didn't
open one e-mail. I highlighted each one and deleted the lot in
one stroke. My crawling days were over. Now Mick would have
to crawl to me.

T UESDAY, I took Claudia and Toby to an Indian place where
we all could eat vegetarian. After we'd ordered our main
dishes Toby cleared his throat. "We wanted to talk with you
about our vision of married life."

Now? Their vision? I hadn't told Claudia about Karn's hotel
room visit, and I doubted I ever would. The man I loved was
dying and I'd thrown away his e-mails. Hard to imagine telling my sweet daughter that. "Okay," I said, glancing toward
Claudia.

Their vision was traditional, of husband and wife in the roles they had taken for thousands of years. The wife had her duties—children, order, the nurturing that led to survival—and the husband had his duties of leadership and protection. The husband was the head of the household the way a bull elk was the head of a herd, because without a head a herd would not survive.

"Wait a minute," I said. "Doesn't a bull elk have a *lot* of wives?"

"Well . . ." Toby said, and his grin made me almost forgive him for this whole concept. A bull elk, he admitted, actually wasn't a good example. Maybe a male brown bear. But the animal itself wasn't really the point. The point was to lay out a philosophy of marriage ahead of time, so neither of them would ever be surprised.

"If you look at the natural world," Toby said, "the females are geared to caring for their young and living longer. The males put themselves at risk, being out there protecting and providing."

I said, "You agree with all this, Claudia?"

Toby's new job was a burden to him, Claudia had told me. Every day, he ordered something new that disturbed him: throwaway silverware or adult paper diapers or cleaning supplies bubbling with questionable chemicals. When he asked if this or that was really needed, his boss simply laughed. The term "Toby the tree-hugger" had already taken root in the office. But the people he worked with were good-hearted, changing minds was not an overnight business, and his salary and health insurance coverage were stellar.

Our food arrived. The rice and curries were steaming, but none of us made a move to eat.

"I don't really have a vision of marriage from you and Daddy," Claudia said. "I don't remember it. But from what you've told me about Grandma and your father, I'm not sure their marriage was a great one. Did he respect her? Did he do everything he could to make life good for her?"

"He did not," I said, startled. He had made her life worse daily, criticizing her cooking, her taste in pictures, the thinness of her hair.

Claudia said, "Toby sees me as . . . his mate." She smiled. "It's instinctual. It's like he's a cardinal and he knows. And I know back."

"So cardinals mate for life?" I said, reaching for a spoon. "They're the state bird of Ohio, did you know that?" I felt too bruised to argue. At that moment, I would have liked to have a natural mate to protect and nurture me.

"Do your parents have one of these cardinal marriages?" I asked Toby later in the meal.

"Not really," he said, hiding a smile and glancing at Claudia. "My father spends a lot of time in the basement."

Maybe that's life, I thought driving home: each generation reacting against the mistakes of the one before it, and no one ever, except by serendipity, getting it right.

It crossed my mind that Toby's new job was a sort of sacrifice, that he was serious about his duties as a provider. He has gnawing teeth, I thought suddenly, the vision of his smile flashing in my mind. He could work on his boss over months and years and who knew how the ordering would change? In the nature shows, it was always staggering how big a tree could be felled by one or two beavers.

That evening, I made plans over the phone with Tessa. "You want to meet Thursday?" Tessa said, startled. "Does Mick have a game that night?"

"I'll explain when I see you," I said.

"His wife was impossible," I told Tessa when we met. "She was all over the map. She said 'co-inky-dink.'"

"Whatever happened to girdles?" I said to Tessa. "I could have stood up to her if she was wearing a girdle."

"Has Mick called you?" Tessa asked. "Has he said, *Ignore this woman behind the curtain?*"

"He's e-mailing me all the time. He's frantic."

Tessa nodded.

"He wants to lay low for a week or two, let things settle down. With his season, he's awfully busy, and . . ." In truth, Mick's e-mails had stopped arriving, and I regretted in every cell having deleted his earlier ones unopened.

"I feel bad for you, Genie. I know you had such hopes." My eyes teared up. I thought I should tell Tessa the truth about Mick's letting Karn come to our hotel, but before I had a chance Tessa went on: "Herbie can't believe this year's team. He says they wear down their opponents for three quarters and beat them in the fourth. He heard they had a new conditioning coach."

"Conditioning may be part of it," I said. "A tiny part." Mick had worked for years to recruit and train this bunch. He knew their hamstrings, their sisters, the dominant sides of their brains. "Mick hired the conditioning guy," I added.

"Oh, we know Mick's good. But he hasn't had a team like . . ."

"Tessa, his PSA is up. I'm sure his cancer's spread."

I told her all I knew. I gave her PSA values and medical opinions and a brief lecture on the natural history of prostate cancer. Before I was done she interrupted. "Girlfriend, this is no-choice time. You have got to leave that man alone."

Why was Tessa talking like a black woman half her age? The threat of it, I realized. The swaggering bravado of it. I was gripping the edge of the table, holding on. "But what if I could talk him into treatment?" I said. "What if he'd agree to treatment for me?"

I GOT HOLD OF HIM by phone the next afternoon. "I have to see you," I said. All these years, I'd never had to say that.

"Genie." The gratitude in his voice was heartbreaking. He was in the gym, shouts and dribbling balls in the background. There was a moment's hesitation, then he went on in a softer voice. "I can't do it this weekend."

"Monday?"

"What took you so long? What's wrong with you?"

"Monday?"

"I can't get away then. Hold on." A rush of air, and Mick's muffled shout. *Morgan, move out there! Do I have to get you a golf cart?* Then: "I'm back."

"Tuesday?"

"January thirtieth? I can get an hour free, seven to eight. But that's not enough time to . . ."

"I'll drive to you," I said. "I'll get off early and I'll come all the way there." Mick and I made plans to meet at an Applebee's in Turkman just off the highway. I could ask Jeremy to take calls for me until eleven, and cover for him on a symphony night in return. "Don't worry," I said. "I didn't read your e-mails."

Mick's voice dropped. "Drive something anonymous." I could picture him with his hand cupped over the receiver. "Not the Jag. And Genie . . ."

I couldn't swear, later, that it had been a conscious move, but I clicked my cellphone off before he had a chance to finish. A little trick to guarantee our meeting.

Y OU CUT ME OFF," he'd say. "Why'd you cut me off?" Or worse, he'd look at me sadly, drop the corners of his mouth, and look away. I'd get to Applebee's on Tuesday and he wouldn't be there. Karn would be there. Maybe Marcus would be there, his large frame blocking the restaurant door. "Coach Crabbe wants you to know you won't be needed. Coach Crabbe's releasing you, Dr. Toledo."

I was on call that weekend, which helped, but all the chest pain and atrial fibrillation and inverted T waves in the world couldn't fill my mind. The facts were suddenly around me, beach balls bobbing to the surface, crowding the pool so there was barely room for me. Mick had cancer. His PSA had skyrocketed. He wouldn't have surgery. Did he need surgery? His wife said I'd betrayed their entire family. I cut him off.

I pictured Mick as a juggler on a stage. He had said he'd juggle anything, but tonight he didn't have his timing, and the audience, hungry for blood, was taunting him with bowling balls and chain saws. I showed up in the wings. *What took you so long?* his look asked. *What's wrong with you? I'm dying here, sweetheart.*

MICK WAS JUST INSIDE the restaurant's outer door. "Not now," he said, pushing past me when I tried to embrace him, and then he gripped my elbow and steered me back outside. "Where's your car?" I'd driven my Honda, and he walked me to it. "Can we just drive somewhere?" he said. "You're not hungry, are you?"

"Six Lines Your Man Likes to Hear," the women's magazine in my office lobby promised, and number 3 was *I'm hungry, hungry for you.*

"Not hungry," I said now. Then I did something that surprised me: I handed Mick the keys to my car.

He took them without comment, and I walked to the passenger's side and got in. We sat in separate bucket seats, and I yearned for him to turn and hug me, but instead he put the key in the ignition and said, "Where're we going?"

"It's your town."

"We'll drive around."

Mick headed right, away from the highway and into the town. Even in the darkness, it wasn't a well-groomed city. There were frame houses crouched on hillsides, porches lit by hanging lightbulbs and cluttered with packing boxes. "How're your practices?" I asked.

He told me at some length, citing jokes and lines—how Leon Chiswick draped towels over the balls each night to keep them warm, how Corey Morgan would work on his free throws only with cooperative balls. "Not that ball," he'd say. "That ball has an *attitude*." "We're having a great time," Mick said, smiling. He seemed pleased to have this topic for me, like a child holding up a drawing.

"Good for you," I said. "How are you feeling?"

"Not bad. Tired, but that's the time of year."

"How are things at home?"

"Not bad."

"That wasn't good that Thursday." I swallowed, looked out the right window. "When I walked in and it wasn't you."

He said nothing, and I stole a look in his direction and found his profile set and frowning.

"It was worse than not good," I said, "it was horrible, when I opened the door and . . ."

"You hung up on me," Mick cut in. "Last week. You hung up."

"Did I? I didn't mean to."

"How can you not mean to? We made the date and you cut right off. How do you think that makes me feel? And then all those e-mails you said you threw out."

"I didn't read them. I was mad."

"So how could I apologize if you didn't read your e-mails? What was I doing, sending my apologies to air?"

"You could have phoned me."

"You'd see my number on your cell and not answer! And I wouldn't know if you weren't answering or if you were in the middle of some doctor stuff."

"Let's not fight. We hardly see each other, let's not spend our time together fighting."

"And if you're not going to read them, couldn't you at least e-mail me that you're not reading them?"

"I was wrong, you're right. I should have told you."

Mick glanced at me bitterly and returned his gaze to the road. He said nothing, and I said nothing, and we drove. I have a hundred more reasons to be angry than you do, I thought. I clamped my lips between my teeth so I wouldn't say something I was sorry about later.

Then I remembered Mick's cancer and resting my head on his shoulder and all our Thursdays and I got myself calmed down.

"What do you dream of these days?" I said after a while. A risk, a question from the article in my lobby.

"What do you mean?"

"Fantazize about. What would be the best thing that could happen to you?"

Mick snorted, and I saw a smile play upon his lips. In my relief I started grinning. "I dream we play Monday Night and win. I dream you get an apartment here—I know just the complex, five minutes from the school—and every time I get there you're at home."

My grin faded. My patients, my house, Claudia's wedding,

my partners—my life was too complex: there was no escaping it. "That's impossible."

"Yeah, well." Mick cleared his throat. "That's the thing with dreams."

"I dream you take a leave from coaching," I said, "get your surgery if that's what you need, get radiation, and then five years from now I dream of us living in San Antonio. I can see you right now, bending over trimming the hedges."

He jammed on the brakes and I looked up, saw there was indeed a red light. "What more do you want of me? You want another pound of flesh? I'm working twenty hours a day, I can't have sex, I don't pee right, I'm tired, and you want to put me through more? What are you, a sadist?"

It must have been my mentioning radiation that had angered him. "Mickey," I said, my voice as free of pleading as I could make it, "that's not fair to me. I want you to live."

"What am I doing now?" He lifted his hands off the steering wheel, waved them in the air. "Do these hands look alive?"

"You know what I mean." Those graceful hands. I saw him leafing through pages of statistics, his palm flashing up with each page.

"I didn't let Karn talk to you so she could insinuate her ideas into you."

"Why did you let her talk to me, exactly? Why did you let her put herself in *our space*?"

Silence.

"Our space, Mickey. Our room. It's ruined now, it's gone."

When Mick finally spoke, his voice was mournful. "She found out, Genie. She found out and every day she's screaming, talking about you like you're, you're . . . like you're a whore, I guess. Like you're a sex organ with legs. And I thought, I don't know, I thought if I let her see you and talk to you, then maybe she'd remember how you were with Jessica, maybe she'd see you were a real person, she wouldn't hate you as much. I couldn't stand her hating you. Because I'm married to her, Genie. I'm married to her and I've got this thing now and . . . It's just too much. I've got a team to run, I can't come home to World War Three every evening."

I said nothing. He was ranking us, I saw: basketball, Karn, me.

Mick said, "Karn said she'd tried to get hold of you and you wouldn't answer."

Again, nothing.

"You could do better than me, Genie."

I closed my eyes—on all that, I suppose. "She told me about your PSA, Mickey."

"It's not your business." I opened my eyes and the light was green, and Mick eased the car forward. Then he shrugged his eyebrows, already relenting. "Oh, it's your business. But it's ninety percent my business, and that's what I keep telling Karn."

"That's crazy, it's ninety percent you. You don't think your family gets a say in this? Your team? Me?"

I saw Mick's jaw square. He took a hard right into a street with a lighted stone entryway on each side. *Winding Trail Estates,* an etched stone in each wall read. This was clearly a better part of town, a neighborhood of brick driveways and big homes set back from the street.

"In a way, I was glad to talk to her," I said. "You didn't tell me what was going on."

"Great, now you can deal with her. I'm sick of dealing with her."

"You married her." I was talking at my window.

"We were different people."

"You stayed with her."

I heard a tapping; I turned to see Mick flicking his index finger repeatedly against the steering wheel. "We've been through a lot," he said. "She's not a bad woman. She doesn't usually cut on people."

"I'm the enemy, to her."

He shook his head quickly. "You're nobody's enemy. I'm your enemy. This would be the perfect time for you to forget me. Just cut me off. I wouldn't care. I mean, I would care but it's something I'd accept. You could have a normal life. You could get married."

"Who would I marry? In the last twelve years the only man I've ever thought of marrying is you."

There was a silence, and my face felt swollen, almost sunburned. But I'd told him the truth.

"That's not going to happen now," he said, his voice so soft I had to strain to hear it. "You wouldn't want me."

"How do you know what I'd want? I'd want you anytime."

Mick's face, in the dark and in profile, looked caved in, as if his teeth had been removed. "God, Genie," he said. "I've got tough games tomorrow and Sunday. I can't deal with this now."

Around us, big lighted houses loomed like ships at sea. "Think what's happening in your body!" I said. "Don't you think that matters more than two lousy games? What you're willing to deal with? Isn't that being selfish, hoarding your cancer for yourself?"

"Listen, Genie." His tone lost its roughness. He pulled the car to the side of the road, put it in park. "My life is giving people advice, giving them direction. And I pretty much know what to say. Well, a lot of times I don't know what to say, but when the moment comes, I say it. But this stuff, this sickness . . . I don't have a clue.

"I have these expressions, you've heard them. *Steady forward pressure. Think harder. Listen to the ball.* And I try them on myself and they're not right. They're not enough. They don't take into account the complications." Mick gave me a bitter smile. "What good am I, hunh? God." He pulled his left hand over his face and bunched up his mouth like a paper bag, glanced out into the empty street, eased the car forward on the road.

"That's our house," he said, nodding out my window, and I turned my head to look. *Our.* Karn and Mick's house was a big rectangular two-story, a copy of a frame colonial, not at all modern like mine. The lanterns on either side of the garage were designed to look like candles. Karn must go for an antique look.

"Look, first I've got to finish out this year." Mick turned left up a hill; the car kicked into a grind. "Even if it ends badly. Even if we don't make the NCAA. It's just this . . . thing. It's my destiny to be here with this team and these players, for better or worse, and the cancer can't stand in the way. Because if I let it, if I took time off to get surgery or therapy or travel to Johns Hopkins or something, well, then the cancer would be winning. And I can't let it win." We burst over the top of the hill, headed down. To our left a wicker reindeer lay on its side between two trash cans.

"But that's crazy," I said. "You're letting it win by not fighting."

"Am I? I think I'd be letting it win to have it rule my life."

Part of me understood this, exactly—part of me even agreed—and yet at the same time I saw that Mick was avoiding the issue, that he was experiencing what even a nursing student would recognize as denial. It gave me a sinking feeling to see him so predictable, and this was associated with the realization that I was indeed shrinking, my torso edging down toward my pelvis. I sat up straighter—all those exercise videos had to be worth something—and made my voice teacherish and firm. "I can't let you do that," I said. "I can't watch you kill yourself."

"Good," he snapped, a coldness in his voice I'd never heard before. "You don't have to." He shot me a glance, and even in the dark I could recognize, beneath its weary skepticism, a glint that could be anger and, yes, triumph. "After all, you don't live here," Mick said. "You don't have that little apartment I could come home to"—making moot my tears, my imprecations, my threats to collude with Karn, abolishing, in one stroke, my entire arma- mentarium, leaving me to flail for another twenty minutes, until Mick pulled my car up beside his own and stuck out his hand. A handshake? The cruelty of that gesture stunned me, made me picture, for a second, a slap across his face, but then he grunted a joyless laugh and hugged me—that is, he put his arms around me, giving me what to an observer would appear to be a hug—and when I turned my face toward his he responded with a quick and sparkless, an obligatory, kiss. I prayed that there'd be booze on his breath, but of course there wasn't. What had I done to him? Why did he hate me? "Goodbye," he said, almost cheerfully, dropping his hands from my back and turning to unlatch his door. I tried to remember if ever before at our parting he had used only that particular word. I sat still for a moment, thinking he might circle around the car to open my door, but by the time I got my wits together he was out of my car and into his own, pulling away.

I'M A COMPLICATION. I could understand it, really: the cutting of the lines, the smooth sail of the boat over black water. From the middle of the lake the shore looked glimmery and insubstantial. The water underneath was deep and real and cold. In the middle of the lake there was no noise. How could I deny Mick this peace?

I would work. I would work and work and work. I'd add late office hours on Thursdays. On my drive back from West Virginia I stopped at a Wal-Mart Supercenter just off the highway and bought 110 pounds of weights—almost my own weight— and a bench I could use for lifting.

"Now, you be careful," the salesman said. "I don't sell too many of these to women. Especially women your size."

No one in the world seemed to see that I was hurting. "Dr. Toledo," one of my elderly female patients said the next day, lifting her upturned hand from my waist to my head, "what's your secret?" In the restroom I stared at my ravaged self in the mirror and couldn't understand it. Terrifying to realize the pain a human face can hide. You walk through the world and think, *What am I missing in other people? What are they missing in me?*

At noon, Claudia phoned me about accompanying her to pick flowers for the wedding. "You go yourself and decide," I said. "Take my credit card. I'll never get out of the hospital tonight."

"Do you have your dress yet?" she asked. I had told her Mick and I had had a "flare-up" (my word).

"I'll shop for my dress Sunday. Don't you worry. I'll be fine."

Shopping Sunday would give me something to do during one of Mick's games.

"Mick's doing great," Claudia said, surprising me. "I always look for his scores in the paper and he's always won."

"Good teams find a way to win," I said, quoting Mick.

"The guy on TV said this was the best Turkman team he'd ever seen. Mick must be thrilled." Claudia had never followed Mick's team in the past. That she was doing so now touched me, made me feel, for a moment, that I hadn't been an awful mother. Claudia's voice dropped. "Anything new between you two?"

"High-level negotiations," I said in a hearty way. "But he's not thinking about me much these days. You know what they say: winning isn't everything, it's the . . ."

H E SHOWED ME his house, I thought as I lay in bed Wednesday night. Maybe he meant for me to go there.

It seemed crazy, counterintuitive, to think this after the angry way we'd parted, but still: Mick had, after twelve years of acting as if he didn't have a house, pointed out to me where he lived. He'd asked me to come to his town; he'd acquiesced when I handed him my car keys, already thinking where he'd drive me; he had taken me down his own street. I tried to recall the timing of the house sighting during our drive. He'd mentioned the apartment he dreamed of my renting; he'd told me I should break up with him now; he drove up the hill past his house; he told me his PSA wasn't my business, I told him he was wrong, and then there was the whole explosion. *He showed me his house.* When I'd already said no to the apartment.

The spring of my sophomore year of high school my parents

took an anniversary trip away. My brothers stayed with friends, but I was farmed out to my mother's sister—who didn't have much use for our family, normally—and put up in a chilly bedroom over her garage. Several boys from my high school lived in my aunt's part of town, and when my aunt took me with her to the grocery after school (she didn't trust me home alone) the boys would leave their game of catch and hover by the curb as we passed. One evening I was in my garage bedroom studying when I heard, from somewhere toward the back yard, a peculiar snapping sound. I lifted my head, frowned, sniffed at the air. Another snap, then a whole symphony of snapping. Soon I would open the back window, whisper to the boys below, even attempt, halfheartedly, to climb out on the downspouting, but it was at that moment that I understood, that I recognized the splatter of the pebbles and their import, that my heart became so large and light I felt as if my body nudged the ceiling. I was wanted, I was wanted. The boys were calling me.

THE NEXT NIGHT, I drove my Jaguar and not my Honda to West Virginia. If Mick were to catch a glimpse of me driving away, it would be in the car he'd bought me as a gift. I parked several doors from Mick and Karn's house, hiding my car behind the arms of a huge fir. The first day of February, a little after nine. The night before, Turkman had had their tenth consecutive win, an away game that wasn't on TV. Today I'd told Howard, ignoring his smirk and waggling eyebrows, that I was back on my Thursday-off schedule. In the morning before I went to work I'd picked up stones from a driveway at the golf course. A cold front had followed rain the night before, and the stones clung to each other as if they hated to let go.

It was colder than I'd anticipated, and the wind on my legs was brutal. Still, I was happy the ground was frozen. My heels left no imprint as I scurried up the rise of Mick's front yard, his house to my right across the driveway.

I crept around the garage to the back of the house, imagining an alarm going off, Karn screaming, myself pinned in the lights of a police car: a woman in a black wool coat and pumps and blue Italian leather gloves, clutching a plastic cup full of stones. "You're a lot stranger than I realized," Mick told me once when I imitated Howard doing a cath.

I'm strange, I'd say to the police. I almost laughed out loud thinking this, because absurdity was part of the excitement: that a middle-aged woman, a doctor, would go to such lengths! That a woman of my stature (so to speak) would risk such embarrassment! And I was risking, certainly. The risk was what I wanted Mick to see, that and my trust and my insane hopefulness, so that when he looked out the window, when he spotted me in the bushes, it would make him want to cry.

I knew his schedule of practices, generally, and that he didn't have another game till Sunday afternoon. The odds were high that Mick would be at home and resting. I couldn't say where Karn would be, but I suspected Mick and Karn didn't spend much waking time in the same room. By this time Jessica should be putting her son to bed upstairs. I had a moment of terror when I spotted the fence and wooden door, but the knob turned and the door pulled open easily, not creaking at all, and then I was in the back yard.

Yard? No bushes or landscaping in the back, not what I'd imagined. There was no grass for twenty feet from the house, just an apron of brick, and beyond that a flat vacancy that extended a hundred feet to a wood slat fence, almost six feet high, which wrapped around the entire space. The place looked like a plain, windswept and devoid of footprints, with a few clumps of residual snow near the side wall of the garage. Like the stockade of a fort, I thought wildly, and it seemed impossible to infringe upon it: security lights might come on, a dog appear, shots ring out. Worse, a bright family room, surrounded by windows, jutted out from the back wall of the house, and in a floral-upholstered chair with his back to me Mick sat reading the paper (I recognized the top of his head) and across from him, facing into the house, her plump arm and the curve of her upper back irrefutable, Karn was sitting in her own chair, watching TV.

This is nuts, I thought; get me out of here. All the tittering thrill I'd felt a moment before evaporated. I turned hurriedly back to the door in the fence and reached for the knob. It was locked.

Jessica's son, I realized. Safety features. Childproof doors. I searched frantically up and down the door, sure there was a release catch somewhere. Nothing. The door must simply require a key from inside. I bent over and tried, in the light thrown from the family room, to make out a keyhole in the knob. Couldn't see. I set down my cup of stones, took off a glove, and felt for it. Yes.

I felt along the horizontal board at the top of the fence, felt on top of a metal box (the electric meter?) on the back of the garage, picked up the stray bricks beside the garage's door to the outside. If there's a lock there must be a key. If there's a lock there must . . . Tried a windowsill. Tried another windowsill several steps closer to the family room. Looked around desperately. Tried again the board at the top of the . . .

If I had something a foot or two high to stand on, I could push myself up and over the fence. My arms were getting stronger with all my exercise, and God knows what boosting power I'd get from adrenaline. I swept my eyes over the yard looking for something, anything, that would give me some height. Nothing.

But there was a whole area on the other side of the family room I couldn't see, and I edged myself left along the fence to where it turned. In front of me as I moved toward the back fence was a wide rectangle devoid of grass—the plot for Karn's garden, I realized—and I wished immediately that I hadn't seen so naked and barren a thing of Karn's. I lifted my eyes to the house.

They didn't move, Mick and Karn, they sat there not quite like statues but like people who had no energy to care what the other one thought, who each felt alone and—in the dreariest, most ordinary way—at home. Mick folded his paper and reached for a new section; Karn didn't budge. Is that all there is? I thought, a cry not just for Mick but for the both of them, Mick and Karn together, and then my mind played the music from that lugubrious song, which diminished, somehow, the acuteness of my feeling. That was all there was for them, I realized, a familiarity that had settled itself into sheer durability, a life it would require an effort, like rising from one of their indented chairs, to leave. I'd believed in my selfish way that, for Mick, a life of intensity and desire would trump a life of comfort. Maybe that wasn't true. Maybe comfort was what Mick wanted over all. At least now.

I followed the border of the yard to the far side of the family room, where a child's plastic picnic table was sitting near the fence. I was looking straight at Mick in his chair as I climbed on. He shook the paper in front of him and folded it horizontally, extending his arm to make out the print. His lips started moving, as if he were reading aloud. Karn said something. Mick dropped the paper and said something. Karn reached out and patted Mick's calf.

She patted his calf.

My arms went weak. I couldn't imagine boosting myself over the fence, and I thought I might be stuck in that yard forever. Any moment they'd look out the window and start talking together about me. I started praying, I guess, and then I started crying, and somehow I got my waist draped over the fence, and then a leg, and I rolled over and fell in a bed of ivy on the other side.

I made quite a thud, and for a moment I lost a shoe, but I tested myself by moving all my extremities and I knew I was okay. The shoe was several feet away, and I crawled to it. Later I discovered I'd torn my pantyhose and scraped the side of my knee. I didn't feel it then. I stood up and walked as nonchalantly as I could past Mick and Karn's front door, then down the sidewalk to the driveway and straight to the street. In retrospect, I'm not sure how I pulled this off. But there were no cars driving the street and the front windows of the neighbors' houses were dark. This was a neighborhood, I realized, of back-of-the-house, secret, favorite rooms.

When I reached my car, my fingers were numb and I could hardly bend them around the padded steering wheel. The side of my knee had started hurting. Still, I told myself, I was glad I'd seen this. This was something Mick could never leave willingly. This was home.

I'M LUCKY THAT I made it safely back to my house. I had never been so angry with myself. As if I didn't know that Mick was married! Marriage was all over him, from the ring on his left hand to the predictability of our schedule to his argyle socks. My continuing to see him despite this showed the same disregard of facts that drove me nuts in certain patients. I remembered when Will Sterling came in with his inevitable huge MI, his ruptured heart valve on his echo flopping like a tiny hand waving good-bye. "I told him he needed a bypass!" I said to the ER doctor. "I told him ten thousand times!"

The ER doc said, "Are you calling the cardiac surgeons now, or should I?"

"I will," I said, and despite my righteous anger the surgeons tried to save him, but they couldn't.

It wasn't that I didn't mourn Will Sterling. There were things I'd liked about him—the way he talked about his daughter, his smile. But part of me hated him for his willful obtuseness—and that same part of me hated myself now. Why shouldn't I pay a price for being stupid? What made me immune to natural consequence? My own brother had tried to warn me. I rolled over in my bed like I was turning my back for lashes—ready, even relieved, to get what I deserved.

In the morning, during my shower, I decided to take up running—for the pain of it, for the time of it. The runners among my patients said they went into an autohypnosis that made the minutes and miles pass. A run every day, coupled with one of my longer exercise tapes and a weight routine, would eat up a good two hours. I had a patient in his seventies with coronary arteries as ragged as used pipe cleaners who nonetheless ran marathons and trained for hours each week. It was clear to me that his training was an obsession, that it was not quite right, and yet who was I to judge him? He lived on.

"Have you done the flowers yet?" I asked Claudia on the phone from work. She had. We made plans to have another meal

out together with Toby. "He's really starting to like you," Claudia said.

My runner had been married for ages—he had several children he liked to talk about, explaining how each one resembled
him—and yet try as I might I couldn't picture, despite all the
postcath family conferences we'd had together, his wife. The
runner rarely mentioned her. I realized I saw the two of them
as he might picture them himself: a crude drawing of a colorful
giant with a tiny, pallid woman at his side.

Mick and Karn, I thought. Mick and me.

"Any news from Coach?" Claudia said over the phone.

"I realized something," I said. "He has a wife."

A silence. "Did you see them together?"

"I saw them talking last night," I said.

"At a game?"

"No."

Claudia didn't ask more.

At lunch, I went to the doctors' lounge and ate a turkey sandwich. All that day I looked at the male doctors around me—Raj,
Jeremy, Howard, Kenneth Lundstrom, Andrew Everly—and
tried to imagine them as lovers or loved ones. To me, they were
the most ordinary of men, pleasant, not bad-looking, educated,
but it was true (I'd heard stories) that for periods in their lives
they'd been transformed into veritable tornadoes of confusion
and desire. Kenneth, years before, had fathered two sons born
less than a month apart. Raj had left an arranged marriage for a
patient. To someone other than me, Mick would look as ordinary as these doctors. To someone other than me, my behavior
around Mick would seem like a bizarre bewitchment.

I felt that I'd developed, finally, a clear and adult vision, that I was seeing life for what it was. I envisioned myself sitting on a park bench smoking a cigarette (years before, I'd smoked), eyes narrowed as I watched the world. Now I could ignore my e-mails, my phone, everything but the work-related messages on my beeper; now I could do *whatever* on a Thursday evening. I could act the way I used to act, before Mick, liberated from every sporting season.

I wasn't on call that weekend, which was disappointing, but after I left the office I went by the video store and picked up two Almodóvar movies, both of which had been recommended by an orthopedics doc, Frannie Juergans, who thrived in a medical environment even more male than mine. I was meeting Tessa and her husband for dinner the next evening. Tessa would be relieved to hear that Mick and I were through; she probably would pop up with someone else for me, maybe a dentist friend of Herbie's. Sunday I planned to do an Internet Continuing Med Ed activity and read the paper and run one or two miles if there wasn't too much snow. I had gotten through my weight routine and was doing an aerobics tape at about eight-thirty Friday evening when I heard the doorbell. I thought it was FedEx, because there was a Pilates ring I'd ordered, but when I opened the front door it was Mick. There were snowflakes on the shoulders of his overcoat. He had a suitcase on the stoop beside him and a white plastic cup in his right hand. "I think you left these," he said, rattling the cup's stones.

I HAD TOLD HIM, at some point, about the high schoolers' stones hitting my window. So when he took out the garbage late Thursday, coming out the back door of the garage instead of the front because the opener was sticking, he knew when he spotted the cup that I'd been inside his back yard. He realized, using his key to unlock the gate, what must have happened, and the picnic table pushed against the fence on the other side of the yard confirmed it. "I almost got teary," he said, "thinking about you in my yard like that." He dropped his chin and looked down at me, and there was something in his face of a father announcing a surprise at Christmas. "Hugh and Lionel can cover for me Saturday," he said. "Till Sunday morning I'm totally free."

He hadn't eaten, so I fixed him a cheese and mushroom omelet as he gave himself a tour of my house. "Nice big bed," he said approvingly, inquisitively, as he arrived back in the kitchen.

I saw Ginger emerge from the family room, make her way along the wall.

"My father always said you could tell someone had made it if they had a big bed," I said, sliding his omelet onto a plate. This was true, although I hadn't thought of it for years.

"And you're a small person," Mick said.

"I toss." I handed him the plate. He didn't say thank you.

Eating supper, he was as calm and easy as if we ate together every night, as if my house were his own. He talked about Morgan's flamboyance, Frederick's amazing passes through traffic, Kennilworth's possible getting-of-religion (a minister had appeared with him in the locker room before the last two games). There were certain rebounding drills, Mick said, that really were paying off. Or maybe it was less the drills than the players' sense of boldness, the guys mentally expecting to get the ball and with their bodies demanding it. I tried to get a sense behind his words of what Mick was really saying, where he planned to spend his nights beyond tomorrow. I was too frightened, after what I'd seen between him and Karn, to ask him directly about his plans.

He'd realized he didn't have to like his players. It wasn't liking them that helped them, but *seeing* them. Every one of them was a person to Mick, every one different. It was Mick's noticing and commenting on their small triumphs and little worries that kept them with the program. *You spotted that hole in the defense when it was one thread wide. . . . Your squats are looking balanced. . . . I can tell you're worried about your brother. . . .* Not having to like him removed from Mick some of the burden of Eluard. Mick could shrug when Eluard yawned in his face. "I figure I'm lucky he's still mad at me," Mick said. "It's the hot coal that keeps the furnace burning. Never underestimate the power of pride."

Simple human recognition. I thought of what I'd seen, Mick and Karn together in their family room.

"And now that they're winning . . ." Mick set down his fork and opened his hands in a what-do-you-expect gesture. "Winners win more." He nodded at his plate. "That was delicious. Just what the doctor ordered."

"Do you want to watch a movie?" I said, rising to pluck away his dishes as Mick leaned back in his chair. I wondered if Karn buttered his morning toast and made his coffee.

We sat on the sofa together. I rested my head on Mick's shoulder, and he sat with one leg extended and the other ankle on his knee. I can't recall what movie we were watching, but suddenly Ginger was on the sofa beside him. "You have a cat?" Mick said, surprised.

It turned out Mick liked cats, although Karn had almost a phobia.

"Were we home when you were prowling in our yard?" he asked me at some point, Ginger asleep at his side.

"Nobody was there," I said. "I was disappointed."

He shook his head and smiled, then glanced down at me. "Funny to see you with your clothes on."

And soon we were upstairs and my clothes were not on, although there was only cuddling, and Mick fell asleep on his back with his hand on the bottom curve of my belly, almost as if he were claiming it. Ginger jumped up and settled herself between Mick's legs and mine. I felt, for the first time, that my big bed was too small. I lifted Mick's hand and rolled away and he gave a little moan, turned to his side, and gripped me from behind across my shoulders. Ginger resettled herself on Mick's other side. It was at that point that I simply gave in, let my head

sink into the pillow and my mind go a blank yellow-gray, knowing that for all the things Mick saw in his players, there were
things he wasn't seeing in me.

"What are your plans after tomorrow?" I said in the morning
over coffee and bagels. ("Put some cream cheese on it for me,
honey. Not too thick.") "What are you thinking?" It was sunny
and the snow on the ground sharpened the light. I should call
Tessa and cancel, I thought, thinking of this evening.

"I've been thinking about that boldness, that going after the
rebound. You know I don't have much of a marriage. Haven't for
a long time. You know I'm not going to live forever. If Eggleston
can hear the ball calling and go after it"—Buddy Eggleston was
his shortest player, a reserve guard who didn't get much playing
time—"if Eggleston can butt himself in there, why can't I?"

He hadn't yet shaved, and the sunlit glints on his chin reminded
me of baby grass. Ginger was suddenly in his lap. "Look at this!"
he said, delighted. "Does she jump on you like this?"

I shook my head in irritation. I had told him last night that
she ignored me. "You mean stay here," I said. My coffee mug
made a clunk as I set it down.

Mick lying on my sofa. Mick saying, "Are you always this late?
What's for dinner? Can you make me your famous omelet?"

Mick said, "You have a big bed."

"It's a three-hour commute."

"I may not stay here every night. I can get a hotel room near
home."

I imagined the urologist down the hall poking his nose into
my office. "I've got to know today, is he getting his shot here or
in West Virginia? And what about the radiation, he doing it here
like he said?"

"I don't want to be an escape hatch for you."

Mick looked momentarily baffled. "You're not an escape hatch. You're a rebound. You're the ball." He sipped his coffee, smiled. "You going to take me to meet Claudia?"

I saw a hospital bed set up in my family room. Visiting nurses. Karn ringing my doorbell, demanding to see him. Basketball players trooping in.

There are moments when your life can change, when with one word or look or gesture you can transform it. That was my moment.

"You want to meet Claudia today?" I said.

"Why not today? I've been hearing about her for years."

"But today's different, today's . . . you and me." It was absurd, it was selfish and silly and I didn't know what else, but I didn't want Mick to meet Claudia. There would be spillage between them. Colors would bleed and mix; it would be a mess and I wouldn't be able to control it. Claudia would judge him, would judge me. Or: Claudia would like him as much as Ginger did. Claudia and Mick would sit together on my sofa, planning my life. "She's getting married," I said. "She doesn't need anything confusing."

"Genie, are you listening? I'm done with confusing. Karn knows my life is going to change. And she can accept that, Genie. I'm not that big in her life now. I'm just the guy who pays the bills."

But Karn pays the bills, I thought. At least, she wrote the checks. "God, she's purring so loud," I said. And Ginger was: the noise was louder than a dishwasher, than a microwave, than an overhead plane.

"She likes me," Mick said.

"I can see she likes you. She hates me. I fucking saved her and she hates me."

Mick chuckled.

I said, "Why'd you get so whiny about being stuck in the West?"

Mick's face twisted in puzzlement.

"Last year, before the NCAA tournament started, why did you go on TV and complain about your placement?"

"Oh. That was stupid. I got overcome, I don't know. It's embarrassing, really." And he did look embarrassed, but only for an instant, and then his face changed. "What in the world made you think of that?"

I had no idea; I'd been as startled by my question as he was. "I just did," I said. "I remember looking at you on TV and thinking, He's losing it. He's not going to win."

"And I didn't win. Great. You were right." He set his coffee mug down. The cat was making her engine noise. "You don't want me to meet Claudia."

"Yes, I do, of course I do. But not . . . now."

"What about Toby, are you ashamed of Toby?"

"No, no, you can meet Toby. If you meet Claudia, you meet Toby."

"What about Tessa? Why don't you call up Tessa, ask her to lunch with us?"

I made a helpless gesture. What was I doing? But I couldn't stop myself.

"How about Jeremy? Jeremy and Sukie too? I saw him at the hospital when we were there for Jessica's cath. He came out and talked to someone in the waiting room."

"Jeremy and I aren't friends, Mick. We're partners, but we don't talk about anything but business."

"Well, who are your friends? Why won't you introduce me to your people? You've met mine." He pushed his mug away.

"I haven't met Marcus." I stood up, went into the kitchen, untopped a bowl of sugar. "I haven't met any of your players." He didn't answer, and I poured milk into my coffee and added a spoonful of sugar, not the way I usually drank it, and then I stirred with a gesture that would have to be called ferocious. *You made me meet your family*, I thought, remembering the lineup in Jessica's hospital room. *I didn't ask to meet them.*

"Let me ask you one thing," I said, walking back to the table. "Would you leave Karn if I weren't around, if you didn't know me?"

An uncomfortable comprehension filled Mick's face. The purring had stopped. I glanced in Mick's lap: Ginger was conked out. "Maybe not."

"Then I'm an escape hatch."

He didn't look at me. "What's wrong with doing what I want most for the time I have left?"

Ah, the ill card. How convenient to play it with me, when with Karn he pretended he didn't hold it. "You have an obligation to your family," I said firmly, looking not at his eyes or lips but at his forehead. My voice rose. "There were years that you weren't there for them."

"Of course I was there for them, I . . ." But Mick wavered, seemed to understand he was pursuing the wrong argument. He said, "I don't have an obligation to you, then." Our eyes met.

"Not in the same way." Dropping my gaze.

"You mean you don't want me. You mean I'd disrupt your"—he glanced behind him toward my living room—"perfect life."

Since he'd arrived the silence in my house had become animated, vaguely threatening, like an animal stalking. When he was gone, I realized, the quiet might attack. I'd call Claudia and ask her lots of wedding questions, tell her to describe the flowers. By afternoon the snow would be melting and I could run. I'd have a steak and a couple of drinks during dinner out with Tessa and Herbie.

"You'd disrupt my life, yes, sure, but that's not why I don't want you here." The words puzzled me slightly, like a teleprompter script I was reading but not thinking. "I don't want you here because you've got a wife and kids and a grandson who . . ." *I saw you in your family room. I saw your married life.*

"I see what I am to you. I'm a sugar daddy who buys you things like cars."

"Mick," I said. "Mick, no."

"And then I'm worthless anyway, because I can't screw you."

"That's not . . . I don't care about that."

"Of course you care. I should just die, right? Maybe I'll leave you something in my will."

"You never went to a whole wrestling match!"

Startled, Mick pushed Ginger from his lap to the floor. "Who told you that? Did Karn tell you that? That's not even true."

"It is true! Jessica told me."

"How can I go to a wrestling match in February? Do you know how long those matches are? Did it ever strike you as strange my sons picked wrestling? That's all I heard about, wrestling. Don't you think it hurt my feelings when they didn't play basketball?" It had hurt him, I could see that; it had hurt him tremendously. What was I *doing?* I sat on my hands so I wouldn't reach for him across the table. He turned away, setting his lips and swallowing. Ginger had moved to a spot in the sunlight and was cleaning a front paw. "All right," Mick said quietly, getting up from the chair. "I understand." And he headed for his suitcase upstairs.

Wait, I could have said. *Wait*—and then I could have set things right.

I GOT THROUGH the rest of the day just as I'd planned, I talked with Claudia and ran and exercised and went grocery shopping, and Tessa and Herbie actually agreed to something spontaneous, a movie following our dinner together (I didn't mention Mick's visit), but then I was home and lying in my gigantic bed and there was the smell of Mick. On my pillows, on my sheets, on the blue towel in my bathroom, and when I pulled down the sheets I found several reddish hairs. I had sent him home. Why? Because I didn't want to be his waitress? To prove to myself I didn't need him? To test, in some perverse way, how fully he was under my control? Because Ginger liked him? Because I felt sorry for Karn? Some kind of madness had come over me, I thought. What obligation did I have to Karn that I should send Mick home?

And Mick—why had he left? Wasn't I worth battling for? Wouldn't resisting me at that moment have been a true declaration of love?

Himself—I suddenly remembered, between the Tae Bo tape and a stint on my elliptical trainer—Himself after his wife died had a Filipino woman who gave him massages and sometimes, as he sickened, drove him to his office visits and sat in the exam room. When I changed his medicines Himself looked to the woman to be sure she'd understood. "Susie cares about me," he said once, and even "I hate to be this bad for Susie." His children, I remembered dimly, had been upset. I did not remember Susie at the funeral home.

Or Laura Ewing with the odd, slight man—Collier—who was always sitting by her bed, who was waiting in her hospital room at six A.M. when I stopped by before her cath. Mr. Ewing was large and dithery. "Can you talk to Collier, explain it to him?" Mr. Ewing asked. "Is Collier a relative?" I asked. "Well, he's her oldest friend," the husband said. "See, they grew up together. And he's not one to marry. So he's kind of always around Laura."

Or Dr. Kelly with the young male aide who'd moved in with him, who called me after Dr. Kelly's death asking for a loan. Or married Etta Fishbein with her hearty pal Mona, laughing at the intestinal gas that always plagued Etta on their camping trips.

What were these relationships? I wasn't sure. I suspected they were bonds involving complicated, possibly sexual, tenderness. You could call such relations all sorts of things, but they were not nothing, just as Mick and I weren't nothing. A decade-plus affair. A loyal mistress. A very special friendship. The phrases cheapened both of us, but the phrases were all we had.

Marriage was cement, marriage was the mortar of the social order. Every marriage, no matter how faulty, was sanctioned and sanctified, given its name, recorded by law. Why should society have that much power? Why should society tell us who and how to love? I wished Mick and I were the ages of our children, or as old as two nursing home patients, extremes when there was laxity allowed. I saw us as two birds captured and shut up in separate cages, beating our wings against the bars. But this was, perhaps, a glamorized view. After all, it was Mick's choice to stay married. After all, I had started the argument that sent him home.

I had started the argument. That was the heart of the matter, as much as I wanted to blame the world. I was probably more censorious about Mick and me than even my bird-loving neighbor would be. At the end of the movie *The Year of Living Dangerously,* Mel Gibson runs up the steps of the plane that will transport him out of revolution-torn Indonesia, and his lover, Sigourney Weaver, emerges through the aircraft door to wrap, with breathtaking tenderness, her arms around his shoulders. I should have greeted Mick in the same way. How brutal that the weekend he had launched with such hope (rattling his cup on my stoop) had ended with my outburst at the breakfast table. I had met my Mel Gibson at the door and pushed him backward down the stairs.

He deserved to hate me. I deserved to hate myself, the gaping hole of *I want* that was me. I wanted to do my exercises, I wanted to not do dishes, I wanted my king-sized bed all to myself. Worse, I wanted people to think I was perfect. A hotel room for two hours a week was about right for me—I deserved no more love than that. I couldn't give love, so why should I expect it back? No wonder I hadn't lasted at marriage. No wonder Claudia was scared of me and Mr. Dylan left me and Tessa rolled her eyes.

The scent of Mick in my bedroom would dissipate, I'd have to wash my sheets and towels, the hotel where we'd met for years would be torn down. And I would have nothing, just nothing, to show for my years with Mick. Some newspaper clippings, a few second-rate photographs from our Hawaii trip years before, and . . . *Yes, Genie, this is just what you deserve.*

The next thing I knew I was on my knees on the bedroom floor with my nose pressed into the mattress. I was making a dreadful noise, like women in other countries who are allowed, even encouraged, to wail over their dead.

I GOT OUT OF THE OFFICE early that Friday and, after asking my blond neighbor to take care of Ginger, threw a couple of outfits in my suitcase, and the Jag and I were gone. It wasn't a planned trip, more like a calling—frozen puddles cracked beside the road, the grass a yellow-brown, the clouds a hulking gray. Not an attractive time of year. About five I passed a white frame church in a town consisting of ten or twelve houses. The parking lot of the church was jammed, and more parked cars lined the road. PAINFUL MOMENTS TRUST GOD read a signboard in front of the church. A week ago I'd still been at work, unaware that Mick would be arriving at my house that evening.

It was dark when I reached my hometown. I passed the former hospital, now a county office building, where I'd been born, on a summer day so hot my father had forsaken the fathers' waiting room and stood under a tree outside. I wondered which tree. I drove by my elementary school, the city park with my favorite swing sets, the doughnut shop (now a video store), the hairdresser's (now also a tanning salon), the library. I drove along the street by my old house, around the block and down the alley past the back of it, and I imagined my father watching me from the front as if in a movie, with a typed identification running across the bottom of the screen: Eugenia (Genie) Toledo, age 48, Cardiologist. How pleased my father would be, and not simply with the fact of my returning to our old home. My car, my clothes, my slimness, my career—everything about me would please him. I would appear to have become just what he'd hoped for.

I thought of eating at a restaurant but I didn't want to see anyone I might know. I had a headache, despite being off the pill, and it took some nerve to even enter a drugstore for ibuprofen, but the aisles, like the parking lot, were empty. The clerk had probably not been born when I left this town for college.

Left forever, I'd arranged that. I had known from the back seat of my father's car that I wouldn't be working here summers, or staying for weeks at Christmas, or returning under any circumstances to help out. There had been in my mother's eyes—in her "You'll love it!" and "What a lucky girl you are!"—an avid collusion. Until my father's death, my mother herself would never get away.

I stayed in a hotel on the town square, a place that in my childhood had seemed glamorous, with inside hallways and its own restaurant and lounge. My room was hot and the heater made a racket. The linoleum under the room's round table was sticky, and I ate my fast-food salad seated on the bed.

My mother would be appalled if she saw me here. One glimpse of me in this room, in this town, and she would know that something was wrong.

There was supposed to be cable, but all I could get clearly were adult movies. I hadn't figured out the morning yet—when I'd wake up, where I'd eat, if I'd drive around town again or simply leave. I felt anxious and jittery, so I opened out my bedspread wrong side up on the floor and did what I could remember of my yoga tape. I thought of walking around downtown but decided that might not be safe. Finally, in desperation, I went downstairs to the lounge.

"Scotch on the rocks with a splash of soda," I said to the young bartender, taking the drink and seating myself at a two-top. The only other person in the room was a tall man at the bar hunched over a beer. I took a sip of scotch and studied the grain of my tabletop, old enough to be actual wood. Tried to enjoy the smoky smell of my drink, the soft clink of the ice.

"Eugenia?" a man's voice said. "Is that you?"

The guy at the bar. He stood, and it wasn't his face but his rangy walk and sloping shoulders that I recognized. "Jim?" My God. I had slept with only two guys in my high school, and Jim was the embarrassing one, the farmer's son I'd gotten drunk with—secretly, and more than once—not my official boyfriend, who was now a lawyer in Seattle.

"What are you doing here?" he said. "You've missed every reunion." He gestured at the chair across from me. "Mind if I . . . ?"

He sat down, and I launched into a long, vague explanation of my trip, aware that he was peeking at my left hand.

"Middle-aged crisis, hunh?" he said.

In high school, Jim's mind had baffled me. I couldn't understand how a boy who constructed a chicken coop complete with balconies and a cupola was unable to write a simple verb-containing sentence. I checked his left hand—no ring. Of course my father hadn't worn one.

"That's probably why I'm here too," Jim said. He was still attractive, although his face was weather-beaten and his hair thinned at the temples. "But I'm married. I have to get out sometimes. Cardiologist, hunh?" He seemed totally comfortable with me, his legs stretched out, his arms looped over the back of his chair. "That makes sense."

"Another round?" the bartender called, and Jim held up two fingers.

"You still building things?"

He was. He'd built his house and a pool house and a gazebo. His occupation was fixing heavy equipment.

I asked him about the sign at the church and he shrugged. Maybe kids on one of those country roads, you know. Maybe a heart attack. He hadn't heard of any murders, and you would one county over. Of course, a suicide was always possible, and that wouldn't make the paper.

"Not something you're thinking of, is it?" he said.

In high school, he wanted to walk me from English to Science and I wouldn't let him. First off, I had a real boyfriend, and second, Jim embarrassed me. He wore jeans that were too short and got excited about B-pluses.

Although I wasn't horrible to him always. Although he'd been a real country-boy lover, whooping and romping. Once we'd done it in the haymow of his father's barn.

"I'm not that extreme," I said, and then the whole story came spooling out, as if Jim had pulled a thread on a bobbin. "Would I know this guy?" he asked at one point, and I said "maybe," and told him Mick's name and team. "Figures," Jim said, giving me a bemused smile.

I was on my third drink by the time I finished. By then we were both hunched over the table.

"Pretty knotty life there, Genie," Jim said, watching me until

I nodded. "You're kind of a loner, aren't you? And you're used to it. I've been married almost twenty-nine years. It's awful, in a way. There's nothing I do surprises her one jot. In another way, it's great. I'm comfortable with her, and you get to a certain age, most days that's all you want."

I said, "That has to be how Mickey feels with his wife."

Jim straightened, leaned back in his chair again, flashed me his radiant smile. "I don't suppose you want to take me upstairs with you," he said.

"Not really."

"I'm not bad." He waggled his eyebrows. "I take my time a little more these days. Not so quick on the trigger."

I laughed. "Thanks but no thanks," I said, belatedly thinking he really wasn't asking.

But he was gallant. "I'm not offended. I know you're saving me from myself." He tapped the face of his watch with his index finger. "And you used to like my wife."

His wife, it turned out, was a girl with whom I'd snuck cigarettes during high school lunch periods. "You can't cheat on Denise!" I said.

"I don't try too often." Jim reached for the saltshaker at the side of the table, lifted it from its wire basket, and centered it on the table. "I'm sure your coach is crazy about you. Why wouldn't he be? And part of his whole thing with you—it's a guy thing, I'm telling you—is possession." He lifted up the pepper shaker, clicked it against the salt. "But you don't want to be possessed."

"No," I said, surprised at the word "possession" applied to something other than a ball, surprised to hear a truth—and it was a truth, I recognized—enunciated so matter-of-factly.

"You'd probably like his wife," Jim said, setting the salt and pepper back in their container, "if you'd met her in a normal way."

I smiled. "I probably would." Co-inky-dink. *I thought basketball was his mistress.* The sort of exuberant guilelessness the years usually knock out of a person.

"I should go," Jim said. He retrieved his jacket from the bar stool, then took a seat at the edge of his chair across from me. "You okay?" he said.

I nodded. "Fine." *Don't go, don't go, don't go,* Jim had said, his face squinched up, bits of straw sticking out of his hair. But I had to; I had choir practice later.

"You'll survive," Jim said, standing up.

I nodded, feeling clearheaded but unconsoled. That was never my issue, survival.

"See you later," Jim said, "maybe"—giving, as he passed me (I didn't imagine this, I could feel the sensation days later), a quick stroke to the back of my hair.

WITH MY PHONE SILENT, with my Thursday evenings empty, with my computer mailbox devoid of anything important, all I had of Mick was his team on the TV. I never realized how much space in my life he took. I kept up my watching and taping, and I spent my extra time replaying entire games. I knew that I would say, years from now, if anyone ever asked me (and why would they?), that it was during this February that I started to understand basketball. I could see the anticipation that preceded certain rebounds. I saw the many ways that Frederick controlled a game. I knew which shots were stupid, which were lucky, which were opportunities well seized. I recognized when a player was scared to make free throws, which fouls were careless or angry and which were planned. I could identify the moment that a team gave up its fight.

Mick's team was beautiful. The players twisted and ducked and nudged in a way that the commentators called aggressive but that to me looked like pure larkiness. Morgan arced the ball so gracefully that it appeared, truly, as if the ball were using him. Kennilworth had a way of protecting Eluard that was almost provocative, as if he were saying, *Go ahead, I dare you to come after him.* And while those two were distracting everyone with their drama, Frederick Flitt would maneuver the ball to Chiswick or Morgan, and another shot would sail through the net. There were moments when the team seemed less like individuals than an amorphous creature—a hyperactive amoeba, perhaps—reshaping and moving on the court.

Mick moved less than in his prior years. He moved hardly at all, but to think he was relaxed would be a total misreading. I had never seen Mick more intense. True, he sat on a folding chair leaning over with his elbows on his thighs and his hands clasped, and all that moved was his head following the ball. But his eyes and his shoulders gave him away. I understood that he was willing plays and passes and fouls and blocks. I knew that he believed that by thinking hard enough, he could influence the path of the ball.

In years before, when Mick had leapt up or shouted or banged his hands on the floor, often his teams had hardly glanced his way. Sometimes they'd looked at one another in amused tolerance; sometimes, for a moment, they'd hopped around angrily too. But there had always been a gap between Mick's actions and the team's actions, always a sense that the team understood that Mick's actions were more a show for other people—fans, the officials, the media—than for them. But now that Mick's reactions were almost imperceptible, his players took every opportunity to glance his way. He might blink quickly over something that distressed him, or make a quick downward motion with his mouth.

If he was pleased, his mouth would relax and open slightly; if he was very pleased—as he was when Eluard's hard foul left a show-boating opposition player rubbing his arm—his right hand would half turn upward and his thumb lift, a minimalist thumbs-up. When he was thrilled, when his team amazed him, his eyes widened and a quick half-smile cracked his face. That smile went mostly to Flitt, although Morgan and Chiswick got it too.

Smile for Eluard Dickens, I thought. He wants it. He craves it. I don't know how I knew this—I was dependent on TV coverage for all my visual information, and there weren't many shots of either Mick or Eluard close-up—but I did. I knew that Eluard felt about Frederick the way my little brothers had once thought about me: *Why does that child get all the attention? I'm good too!* It bothered me enough that I thought of sending Mickey an anonymous letter: *Smile for Eluard.*

But I didn't. Mick, as much as he understood people, had to know that Eluard yearned for his approval. He had to be holding back for a reason, maybe to make Eluard work more. When Turkman beat Merriweather by sixteen points and Eluard made an icing-on-the-cake two free throws, Mick turned from the court and shook his head with almost rueful pride, as if he were saying, "Sure, I'm good, but do I deserve this much?"

Each home game the Turkman fans cheered so loudly the other coaches had to cup their hands around their mouths and bellow. The Turkman fans were cheering for something bigger than themselves—for youth, for intelligence, for beauty. The Turkman fans were cheering against death. At least, that's how I took it.

I thought often of going to a game, of sitting in a high-up row, but that would be placing myself in the same enormous room as Mick, and all I could imagine myself doing there was crying.

Karn didn't know what she was watching. At one point Chiswick was fouled beyond the perimeter while he was shooting, and when the official deemed it a nonshooting foul and called for two free throws instead of three, the camera caught Karn looking around blankly amid the uproar, turning to Jessica to ask her what had happened. The moment was almost too personal to witness; when I watched the game again, I fast-forwarded through it. "She's not very smart," Mick had said years before, and this was surely part of what he meant. I felt bad for both of them. I was almost relieved when my phone didn't ring. It might be cruel to Mick to think this, but sending Mick back home had come to seem exactly right.

I SAT IN TOBY'S PARENTS' LIVING ROOM in Indiana, surrounded by his sisters and female cousins and aunts. The drive to Indiana in the back seat of Toby's car had been depressing, flat and gray, but being here was worse. The decor was aggressively cozy, with chintz sofa covers and wall light fixtures etched with flowers, and the heat was turned up so high that I'd noticed Toby wince in dismay and peel off his sweatshirt when we'd come in through the kitchen door. There were too many pillows on the furniture, and some of them had been scrunched against armrests or pushed onto the floor.

"You still eating those bean sprouts, Toby?" one of the aunts asked as Toby appeared in the living room, a plate of cheese and crackers in his hand. Toby said he was. The aunt went on: "I had a ribs-and-chicken last night, what do you think of that?"

"Go to it." Toby smiled and excused himself as the women scooted their chairs to open a path to the basement door. The men were downstairs watching an NBA game, which was good, because I couldn't have torn myself away if Mick's team had been playing.

"I don't know where he got those notions," the grandmother said. "They're like hippie notions."

"Don't worry, Meemaw, he's young. He'll get over it."

"We're really a big, happy, friendly family," said one of the aunts suddenly, turning toward me, "except for Alice."

Everyone agreed that Alice was a problem.

"Where does she live?" I asked, imagining Chicago or Columbus, maybe even New York City, the way Toby's mother raised her eyebrows and dropped her shoulders, as if to show how good Alice thought she was.

Toby's grandmother stood and walked to the side window, pulled back the striped curtain, and pointed. "See that yellow house? That's Alice."

"She married a *dentist*," Toby's mother said, plucking a pillow from the floor and handing it with a glare to another sister sitting beside her.

The grandmother sat heavily down. "Alice made her choices."

"My best friend's married to a dentist," I said. "I like dentists."

The room fell silent. "You don't know *this* dentist," a middle-aged woman with dangling teddy bear earrings finally said.

Claudia was sitting very erect in a high-backed dining room chair, smiling as if Toby's family were just lovely. I felt a wave of fury. "Is Alice coming to the wedding?" I asked, turning to Toby's mother. "She's your sister, right? I hope you're inviting her to the wedding."

Toby's mother winced and didn't answer.

"It'll be a challenge," I said to Claudia later, "keeping your independence in that family."

"We're not moving there," Claudia said quickly. "Toby doesn't want the hardware store." Had she told me about the new thing at his job? Using graphs and numbers—cold, hard facts, she said—Toby had persuaded his boss to stock his nursing homes with washable plastic cups instead of throwaways. Next step: the abolition of foam cups. "He's really happy now," Claudia said, her radiant face showing that she was happy too. "He has a purpose."

I SLEPT RESTLESSLY, and then I dreamed that Mick was beside me, talking about sports. We were in a stand somewhere, but a football, not a basketball, stand, and somehow we were able to lie down. "I don't usually look at things from a fan's viewpoint," Mick said in my dream, "but I actually enjoyed that game. I felt bad that somebody had to win.

"When a team wins really big," he said, "sometimes you don't remember the opponent. But after a great game you can name both sides."

"Shhh, honey," I said to Mickey in my dream. "Go to sleep now. Get your rest."

LINDY STOOD at the door to my office. "There's someone on the phone insists she has to talk to you. Karn Crabbe."

Was Mick worse? Had something happened to Jessica? I picked up the phone in alarm. It never crossed my mind to say I wouldn't talk with her. "That car"—Karn started in without a greeting—"how did he give you that car?"

The Jaguar was in the doctors' parking lot, maybe three hundred feet from me through walls, but I had no idea why Karn was asking about it. Her voice was like a shove into my chest. When I watched Mick on TV there was a distance between us, as if he were a rock star and I a besotted fan. Hearing Karn's voice made him real. She had seen him this morning. She knew which sweater he was wearing.

"Is everyone okay?" I said.

"We're fine. Was it a surprise or did you shop for it together?"

Like being stalked, I thought. I squinched my eyes closed. *Leave me alone, you bitch. I'm leaving your husband alone.* "A surprise," I said, not sure why I was answering. "Mick gave me the keys and we went out to the parking lot and there it was."

"At your hotel?"

"Yes." I should just hang up. Or scream into the phone: *Stop bothering me, you crazy woman!*

"How'd he know you'd like it? Did you two shop together for a car?"

"No. I don't know. One day I said I liked Jaguars. We never shopped. And he knew I liked blue." What was the point of this? Was she angling at some legal stratagem to get the car ownership transferred to her?

"Had you told him you wanted that specific model?"

I glanced at the clock on my desk, the list of patients I had yet to see. How dare she steal my time? "No. Not at all."

There was a silence, then a sigh. "He must have really liked you."

I was startled. "I think so," I said, standing up and shutting my office door. "I hope so."

"We went to this jewelry store in Italy once. On our cruise through the Mediterranean. We got off the boat to go to some ruins, and on the way our bus stopped at this jewelry store. They do that, you know. It's kind of a racket. Beautiful store. They had armed guards. And I was looking in this display case and there was this incredible ring, tanzanite surrounded by diamonds—do you know tanzanite? This purple-blue stone from Africa, gorgeous. And the boys and Jessica ran to get their father and he came back and looked, and the salesman took the ring out and I had it on and the salesman had his little calculator and he kept bringing down the price, and the kids were beside themselves and Mick was looking, looking, and I was trying not to get excited and then we left. It could have been a great moment, but it wasn't. Mick said he wasn't that much of a sport."

I didn't know what to say. Ungenerous. A great moment that wasn't. I had my car, and Karn didn't have her ring. She continued.

"Things had gone on. High school wasn't easy for the boys— they both quit wrestling, and Eric got into this ratty crowd and Bobby was like a hermit, he went to his bedroom after supper and never came out till the morning. We thought he was better off than Eric till we found out about the drugs. And Mick, well, Mick was setting things up at Turkman, and I handled it. We got through it. Then right away Eric goes off to college and I end up with emergency gallbladder surgery and my mom gets sick and I clean out her house in Pennsylvania and move her into a nursing home near us and check on her every day until she passes. I don't know, it would have been a good time for that ring. I thought Mick might hop off the bus and go back for it. We got to the ruins and I thought he might take a taxi to the store. And then

I realized, *This is Italy. Mick doesn't speak the language.* But I tried to stay upbeat because, you know, it was a cruise. We never had much time as a family."

"How long ago was this?" I dimly remembered Mick's mother-in-law dying.

"Let's see, the boys were both in college. Ten years ago, maybe." Karn's voice wavered. "You were probably seeing him then."

Nice lady, Mick had said about his mother-in-law. A good old-fashioned cook. "He should have bought you that ring, Karn," I said. I was leaning over in my chair now, my head on my hand, oblivious to my charts or to the time.

Mick learned from Karn, I thought. He learned from his wife to give to me. I could have told Karn this but what good would telling her accomplish? I didn't want Karn and myself to turn into that odious stereotype, two women with their heads together complaining about men. Mick didn't deserve that. I saw him slumped in the hotel room chair, looking at me with those weary eyes. But he could be ungenerous, yes. Almost comforting to hear it was the same with Karn.

"What could I do?" Karn said. "For better or worse. That was worse."

I got angry. Why toss in a crack like that? Pounding on the table with the Bible of her marriage. "You stayed together, though," I said, not hiding the sarcasm in my tone. "Good for you." Because of course this phone call was tactical, because by telling me about her own disappointment Karn could taint my pleasure in the gift Mick had given me. I'm sorry, I thought, but I'm not going to be tainted. I'm sorry, but in his heart Mick belongs to me.

But by that afternoon I wasn't sure who Mick's heart belonged to. It was possible Karn's phone call wasn't tactical, but even if it wasn't, it had worked. When I faced, that evening, the gleaming and pristine blue surface of my new car in the parking lot, I fought an urge to key the door myself.

Now TOBY'S PARENTS SAY they're selling the store and retiring to Ohio. Near us."

I was sitting with Toby and Claudia at the kitchen table of their apartment, having just had a dinner of artichoke quiche and spinach salad. Claudia had become quite a cook. I looked from Claudia to Toby. "What about your sisters?" The sisters were in Indiana.

"They're all pretty busy. Mom doesn't see them that much."

"What about you?"

"I don't want them here."

"Have you told them?"

"I'm working on it."

"Maybe you should just elope," I said, envisioning Toby's mother at her church fussing over bows at the end of each pew.

"No," Toby said. His face got firm. "We're throwing them a sop."

"Grrr. Natural man gets angry!" I said, making sure my voice was light, knowing this comment was a risk.

Toby's eyes flicked my way. He smiled. This marriage might work, I thought.

TURKMAN STATE PLOWED through their conference matches. By the middle of February they had locked their conference title.

Their TV games always got basic game coverage, with two or three cameras and invisible commentators and no trickery. I yearned for trickery for Mick. I wanted his team to get far enough for freeze-frames and slow-motion replays and ten-second biographies of key players. I could see why these tricks were effective—because they reproduced, in an odd way, what happened in a person's mind watching a game. The herky-jerkiness of attention, the brief ruminations, the glossing over of inessential minutes—of whole periods—and the end-less replays of key seconds. It was like someone sitting behind you shouting, *Did you see that? Did you see that?* and you had to shake yourself to think just what you had seen.

Eluard was changing. Even on the bench, he looked different. He sat upright with his eyes and chin alert, a ruler surveying his troops. The commentators were running out of superlatives. At times they almost sputtered:

"Dickens and Flitt, it sounds like a Victorian law firm."

"Those two lay down the law, all right."

Mick midwived that, I thought. Mick permitted it. When Mick's image appeared on the TV, I kissed my fingers and touched them to the screen.

I WAS PAYING for the rehearsal dinner, but Toby's mother had chosen the restaurant and planned the menu. She wanted steak for everyone but Toby and Claudia. She also suggested ice cream nutballs for dessert, although they were an extra-charge item.

"That's really okay with you?" I said to Claudia and Toby. "I didn't think you'd want to sit there smelling meat."

"We don't," Toby said. "But it's political."

"Political?" I said. "Everything's political"—and the three of us broke into wide, colluding grins.

I WAS AT THE FRONT DESK dropping off a sample of pills for a patient when I noticed Lindy writing "dec." in orange marker on one of the charts. "Who died?" I said.

"One of Dr. McClellan's patients. Richard Dylan."

"Dickie Dylan died? What'd he die of?" I snatched the chart from Lindy. I thought of Mr. Dylan knocking on the door of my empty house; of his looking up at me from his hospital bed as he vomited blood. I remembered the blast of disapproval, like heat from an oven door, that had hit me as I sat across from his family.

Lindy, chewing on a cinnamon bun, gave an elaborate shrug, as if she were putting an exclamation mark on her not caring.

There was nothing from the last few weeks in Mr. Dylan's chart. I went looking for Howard down his hall. "What happened to Dickie Dylan?" I said when he emerged from an exam room.

"He died."

"I heard he died. At home? What of?"

"He just died, Genie. He'd been having a little shortness of breath lately"—Howard must have regretted giving me that information the moment he uttered it, reading the dubiety in my gaze—"but nothing of consequence. He went to sleep and didn't wake up."

Progressive coronary artery disease, heart failure, recurrent pulmonary emboli, a repeat GI bleed—all these possible diagnoses filled my mind. Had Howard checked for them? Had Howard thought of them? "I saw he got a twenty-four-hour monitor last month," I said. "That didn't help you?"

Howard ignored the comment. "Not a bad way to go," he said. "I'd go like that."

"Did you get an autopsy?"

"Genie! He was seventy years old."

"That's not old."

"It was for him." Howard turned his back on me and reached for the chart beside his exam room door. "I think he had an excellent run, all things considered. Isn't he the one you tried to kill with heparin?"

Later, I sat slumped in my office gazing at the phone. What a balm Mickey had been to me. I'd never realized.

R ECORDS RELEASE HERE," Lindy said, waving a sheet of paper. "Jessica Crabbe. Wants her chart sent to some doc in West Virginia." It was the first week of March, the month for Jessica's follow-up office visit. I'd been hoping that, despite everything, she'd come back to me. I had almost thought she would.

"Oh, of course," I said. "West Virginia's where she lives." But my hands started shaking. Was I a topic of conversation at the Crabbe family table? Had Jessica told her mother how I dressed, the way I asked her questions in the office?

I taped and watched Mick's conference tournament games on TV. Mick was as still as ever, and the Warriors as overwhelming. "Your team seems to be peaking," one of the interviewers told Mick after the championship game.

"Not yet, I hope," Mick said. "We've still got the NCAA."

"The Warriors should be a real presence there. You're looking fit, by the way. Have you been working out with your team?"

Mick said, "I guess I'm eating less."

"I gotta get your diet," the interviewer said, patting his own round belly.

CLAUDIA'S MOUTH WENT SLACK when she opened the box. We were back in Toby's mother's living room, at a bridal shower three weeks before Claudia's wedding.

"Something blue," I said.

Toby's mother said, "Is it real?" Under the guise of planning for the shower, she had gone through Claudia's underwear drawer at her and Toby's apartment. "You wouldn't believe the things your daughter has!" she told me. "Why do they even bother with a honeymoon?"

"Cousin Ruth has a ring like that," said Toby's oldest sister.

"It's beautiful," Claudia said, looking up at me.

"Do you really think so?" I said, because when she'd snapped open the box she looked less delighted than stunned.

"Ruth's may be a little bigger," said Toby's aunt. "What is it, a sapphire?"

"Tanzanite," I said.

Another relative bent in. "Look at that, a cocktail ring!"

Claudia slipped the ring on, held up her hand. "I love it," she said. My ring made her engagement ring look tiny, which had not been my plan. I bent over and kissed the top of Claudia's head. A wedding in the groom's church, a handkerchief from sisters, earrings from Grandma—you could see Toby's family staking claim to her, but Claudia's right ring finger would stay mine.

·   ·   ·

M ARCH, that time of year again, and the doctors' lounge was filled with talk of matchups and seeding. Any miscellaneous group of men, I realized, had the comfort of sports. Women had nothing as easy to talk about. Work was always a loaded topic for women—who did, who didn't, how much, to what end—and the old female standards of recipes and gardening and children had fragmented into various strains of competition. Talking about your delicious pot roast could offend someone as much as your pants size or your daughter's SATs. But men had the comfort of a leveling, common topic, and they seemed to understand their own good fortune. March was the one time of year Howard stood beside the cath lab sinks and chatted with the male nurses.

"You rooting for Turkman again, Genie?" Raj asked in the doctors' lounge. "Or are you too busy with your daughter's wedding to care?"

"Oh, I care. Don't you think Turkman looks great this year?"

"Conference and tournament champions. I've got them in the NCAA for four rounds. I have them getting knocked out before they hit the Final Four. You should talk to Bilal," Raj nodded across the room. "He's got them going all the way."

Bilal Assadi was a neurologist I didn't really know. "I love Turkman," he said. "I love that crazy Corey Morgan." The three-point master who still had work to do on his free throws.

"And then there's Dickens," Raj said.

"And Flitt."

"And Kennilworth's back now."

"I like their coach too," Bilal said. "He's very"—he frowned, searching for the word—"sensible. I listen to his show every week."

Show? "Are you talking about Mick Crabbe?" I asked. "Which show?" Beyond his postgame interviews, I knew Mick was interviewed weekly by the college radio station, but we were miles beyond the radio range of Turkman.

"His show on WTKM. Every Saturday at five. He talks about his team, recent games, his . . ."

"How can you hear his show?" I interrupted. "Do you go to West Virginia on Saturdays?"

Bilal looked baffled. "I go on the Internet. I stream the station on my computer."

I had no idea that radio stations put broadcasts on the Internet. Bilal had to explain to me the concept and technology.

"Have you heard of this streaming?" I asked Claudia later on the phone.

"Screaming? Who's screaming? I'm not screaming." The last few weeks Claudia had been unremittingly jovial. I never asked her if she'd told Toby about her abortion; it wasn't my business to know.

"Streaming," I repeated. "Sending a radio broadcast live over the . . ."

Of course she'd heard of streaming. Everyone had.

"How come I hadn't?" I felt as if I were storming through the attic of my brain, picking up dusty items and hurling them out the windows.

"You're busy. You're not a computer person." Claudia's voice became even merrier. "You haven't had the need to stream!"

My face felt like a fist was thrusting around inside it.

"Claudia, Mick was streamed every Saturday and I didn't even know it! And now he won't do any more programs." I tried to breathe deeply but my chest wouldn't expand. "All those years and I missed hearing him," I whimpered. "Oh God. Oh God."

"I'll come over," Claudia said. "You hang up right this minute and I'll come over."

P AUL HENDRICKS had sick-sinus syndrome, a gradual slowing of his native heart rate; at some point in the future he would probably need a pacemaker. In the meantime, for monitoring purposes, he saw me every four months. At his last office visit, he reported that his wife of fifty-two years had died. At that time, he was still in the postdeath window when relatives changed their schedules; a son, I recalled, had brought him in. Now he was alone.

He's not going to make it, I thought, watching Paul Hendricks's laborious climb onto my exam table. The phrase "broken heart" swam into my mind.

"Are you eating?" I said, because he'd lost ten pounds. The grief diet, a social worker I knew called it.

"Sort of. I'm a Swansonian," he said, which confused me a moment, but then I got the wit in the phrase and looked to Mr. Hendricks for any hint of pleasure. None. "Old fellow told me that once," he said. "Now it's me."

The blotches on his shirt, his slightly sour smell—he was an old man, forgotten, even by himself. "Any dizzy spells or passing out?" I asked. "Any chest pain? Shortness of breath?" and as he shook his head he started crying, and then he was leaning forward precariously with his arms out, as if he were tossing himself from a cliff. I moved forward to catch him, and he threw his arms around me.

He was still half seated on the exam table, sobbing in my ear, his fingers clutching at my back like reptile claws. "Mr. Hendricks," I said, "I'm sorry." After an interval I tried to extricate myself, which seemed impossible without his toppling from the table. A lock of hair from his comb-over fell onto my shoulder.

This wouldn't happen to a male cardiologist, I thought.

"There, there." I patted his back. He cried for several minutes, then abruptly stopped, released me, and sat up.

"Did that help?" I asked.

He nodded, looking slightly dazed.

"I cry like that sometimes," I said, but Mr. Hendricks didn't seem to hear me, and I wondered if Claudia would have felt like me if she'd seen me break down, like some distant being moved and astonished at the passions of mankind. Pity, that was what I felt. "Do you want to come back in two weeks? Would that be good for you?" Mr. Hendricks nodded and slid down from the table. I stepped away so he wouldn't come after me, but instead he headed to the mirror over the sink and pulled a comb from his back pocket.

I should have let Claudia hold me. I should have kept crying until Claudia arrived, not gone to the bathroom and splashed cold water in my eyes, told myself to pull myself together. Crying in Claudia's arms would have sealed my daughter's adulthood. It would have been a gift beyond the ring.

BY THE MIDDLE OF MARCH, I was hardly sleeping. I had turned my bedside clock to face the wall so I couldn't see when I was awake. On call nights, I drove to the ER even when the patient did not sound acutely ill. Some nights I played winning Turkman tapes between one and three A.M., while I did yoga or Pilates on my bedroom floor. My patients were no longer telling me I looked great. One evening I boiled and ate an entire pound of spaghetti topped with Parmesan cheese and butter. Other evenings I didn't eat at all.

I had done it. I had destroyed, for no good reason, the central relationship of my life, and I would never see the man I loved again.

I knew I had to look decent for Claudia's wedding. I should look happy, or at least composed, for that one day. And I was happy—finally, truly—about Claudia's marriage. It was the rest of my life that scared me.

I arranged to watch Mick's games of the first NCAA weekend at Tessa and Herbie's. If Mick's team won both their games that weekend—Thursday and Saturday—they would play the weekend of the wedding, and I would find a way to deal with it, period. If they won both their games on Claudia's wedding weekend they'd stay alive to the following weekend and the Final Four.

If the Warriors could make it to Monday Night it would be a dream for Mick, a fitting cap to his career. Bilal the neurologist had predicted it. I wished I had that much faith. It seemed like something dangerous to even think of. When the notion crossed my mind, I used an old meditation mantra to drive it away. When Raj asked me if I wanted to join the betting pool I said, "Not this year."

"Wow," he said, shaking his head. "Weddings are hell, right?"

Herbie, Tessa's husband the dentist, was one of those people who always talked about their work as if it were a series of disasters. "I couldn't get your wife numb," he was telling someone on the phone as I arrived at his and Tessa's house. Herbie was bald, no taller than Tessa, and had a tendency to sweat. His hand made the phone receiver look enormous, but small hands were a plus for a dentist, Tessa said.

Tessa pointed me toward the den, where she reached into an ice chest to hand me a bottle of beer. An enormous TV screen was showing the game preceding Mick's game. Tessa and Herbie had a real den, with smoke in the air and dark walls and plaid recliners. Not only did Tessa smoke, but Herbie, in a gleeful spiting of the brochures in his office, was a connoisseur of cigars. Tessa nodded toward a chair, and I handed her a blank tape for recording. "I didn't tell Herbie you and Mick split up," Tessa said, and I nodded. "He doesn't know about Mick's PSA being up, either." She reached behind her neck and grabbed her hair in her left hand, draping the immense hank over her shoulder like a woman in an ad for shampoo. "I didn't want to upset him." Herbie had been having problems in his office—he suspected his longtime office manager was embezzling, and his best hygienist had had a miscarriage and was missing work—and I was touched that Tessa, protective wife that she was, worried that bad news about Mick would distress Herbie more. "Are you on call?" she asked.

"Howard's covering."

"Well, it's Thursday."

"How's Mick Crabbe these days, eh?" Herbie burst into the room, both tiny thumbs up. "Big Mick Crabbe?"

"I think he's reasonably big," Tessa said. "Isn't he, Genie?" I covered my eyes with my hands and shook my head.

Thank God I was at Tessa and Herbie's house. A game like this I couldn't take alone.

Turkman won. They won handily, making me anxious only a few times, and I made plans to come back Saturday an hour before their next game.

Mick looked happy, yes, but also distant, and even the post-game interviewer's malapropism ("Your team was just incredulous!") didn't seem to pierce the cloud of his thoughts. Maybe he's thinking about me, I thought. *Please, please, be thinking about me.* "Incredible," Mick said to the interviewer. "Yeah, our guys were good." He spat out a few more obligatory answers and turned away. Enjoy it, Mick, I thought, my hands going clammy. Enjoy it now.

"Beer?" Tessa said two nights later, handing me a bottle, and

I thought of that movie where Bill Murray gets stuck in time and wakes up each morning to the same Sonny and Cher song. I handed Tessa another blank tape, and moved my beeper and phone from my handbag to my pants pockets so I wouldn't have to stir from my chair.

It was a wonderful game. "I don't know how you can defend against this Turkman team," one of the commentators said. "They'll kill you in the paint and they'll kill you at the perimeter. It's almost like the ball's on their side."

"Dickens and Flitt," the commentator said. "Sounds like a moving company."

"Oh, they're moving things all right," his partner parried. "They're moving the ball."

"Maybe they'll get a better game next time," Herbie said after Turkman's win. "Mick doesn't want it too easy."

M. L. HOPKINS: WOKE UP IN A CHEVY

"They can win by fifty points," I said, slipping the phone from my pocket. "Fifty points would be perfect." Tonight they'd won by 32. Five nights to make it through until Mick's next game. I'll get Jeremy to write me a script for some sleepers, I thought, glad to have the excuse of Claudia's wedding.

I saw M.L. in the office on Wednesday, after she'd managed to detox herself using pills saved from old prescriptions. "I realized there's not much visual joy in drunkenness. I mean, you've got the occasional fabulous sunset"—M.L. bracketed these last two words with her fingers—"but there's nothing you can count on to be nourishing. You wake up and you're staring at stucco or some horrible upholstered chair."

I wondered what M.L. would think of the furniture in Tessa and Herbie's den. I sat down on my stool. "So you're quitting."

"I quit already. Four days."

Whatever drives a person to wellness, you have to take it as it comes. "Good for you," I said. "I can put you on Coumadin now? I don't have to worry about you forgetting to get your blood tests or falling down the stairs and bleeding in your head?"

"I'll be a good girl, I promise. I'm going to AA."

I smiled at her; I almost wanted to hug her. Her hair that day was done in merry spikes, its red tips freshly colored.

T HURSDAY, two days before Claudia's wedding, Mick's game was tied at the half, and it was two points in Turkman's favor with 9:16 left when Frederick Flitt, going for a pass from Tom Kennilworth, got hit by an opposing player, fell over the ball, and collided with the floor.

"Oh God!" I clapped my hands to my face.

The commentators were right on it. "O-o-h, that had to hurt!"

"That's a worrisome-looking injury, you hate to see an injury like that."

"That knee is going where a knee should not go."

"Here, we've got it on the replay: he goes up for the pass, there's Jacoby coming in on him, and Flitt is . . . Ouch."

"Maybe we can run that again, zoom in on it."

"There's Frederick Flitt's mother in the stands, she looks concerned. There's Coach Mick Crabbe, he looks concerned. He's staying out of the way of the medical people who are out there checking Flitt. There's Tom Kennilworth, he's concerned. Just a tremendous amount of concern here."

"I can't stand it," I said. "Turn it off."

"Hold on, hold on." Herbie set down his cigar and reached for the remote. "Let me mute it. Don't you want to see him get up?"

"What happened?" said Tessa, arriving in the den with a fresh bowl of chips.

"He's not going to get up," I said. "This'll kill Mick, kill him."

"It's only one knee," Herbie said. "These guys are macho. He'll get up."

But Frederick did not get up, and his spell on the floor became a commercial break, and when coverage resumed he was being loaded onto a stretcher and carried from the gym. In Tessa's family room, the three of us were as mute as the TV. There was a shot of Mickey standing with his mouth open, jowls slack. He looked like an old man in a nursing home, oblivious to his family at the door.

"Jesus," Tessa said, "and Mick's got to finish this game."

"Does Flitt have knee problems?" Herbie said. "I hadn't read that. Ask your buddy about that. Sometimes teams keep that stuff quiet."

"Genie and Mick aren't going to spend their time talking about some player's knees," Tessa snapped. "That's not what their time together is for."

Herbie snickered and I went red, and in an instant I was close to tears, thinking of Mick's smell, the slightly rough tips of his fingers. The screen showed his shoulders and the back of his head as he conferred with his assistant coaches.

"He'll put in Eggleston," I said quickly. "The guys'll really want to win it now." I swallowed, glanced toward Tessa (she was looking suggestively at Herbie), and perched myself on the edge of the sofa, half afraid and half eager to see more. Mick turned to face the court and his face was simply ferocious. His face said, *Frederick will be avenged*. His face said, *We are teaching that ball a lesson*. "Go ahead and put the sound on," I told Herbie.

W HEN I GOT HOME from Tessa and Herbie's, the red light on my answering machine was blinking. "Call me on my cell tomorrow between six and seven in the morning," Mick said. "If you can. I'll make sure I'm free. I . . . I'm thinking of you. I hope you're okay. Love you, cupcake."

Love you, cupcake. After all I'd done, he still loved me. I closed my eyes and warmth suffused through me, as if someone had switched on a heater in my soul.

"Where are you?" I said when I called. I'd been afraid to take a sleeping pill and risk missing the hour between six and seven. Instead, I'd barely slept, although Ginger, for the first time in weeks, had ensconced herself on my bed. In her own way, on her own schedule, she paid the rent.

"I'm in the hotel fitness center," Mick said. "No one's here."

"It was great," I said. "Unbelievable. I was screaming when Morgan made both free throws. I knew Chiswick would make that three-pointer, I could see it the second he shot, but I was holding my breath when they fouled Morgan."

"Me too. Did you see Frederick go down?"

"Oh, God, yeah. That was awful. Your other games seemed easy, but this one, this one . . ."

"At least Frederick got hurt while he was playing. He didn't crash a motorcycle or something. They kept him overnight at the hospital; I'll go see him right after I get off with you. Doc Kitchener says it's bad. He says Flitt's been playing with instability all season, can you believe that? Both knees."

"He never told you?"

"Nobody told me. And you couldn't tell. It makes me sick, sick. I mean, what do I do to point guards, Genie? I kill 'em, Genie. It's not right." His voice had gone high and curly.

"Oh, Frederick'll be fine," I said. "They've got great orthopedic procedures these days."

He made a slight noise.

"He'll be fine. It'll work out." I waited for him to agree but he said nothing. "How are you feeling?" I asked, suddenly anxious.

"I'm fine. I've got a doctor visit scheduled next week, but I can always postpone it if we . . ." He trailed off. If we win the regional. If we go next weekend to the Final Four. He would never say these things.

"You will, Mickey. I know you will. I can feel it." The moment the words were out I regretted them. A hex.

"Well, Frederick's our pillar. Without Frederick we might . . ."

I couldn't stand to hear him try to cover for me and my stupid wish, and my words rushed over his. "Claudia's getting married tomorrow, can you believe it? In Indiana. I drive over there in a couple hours. I'm talking to you from home; I actually took today off. Didn't realize I'd be celebrating *two* things today." Too much talk, I told myself. I sounded like a frantic TV hostess filling time.

"When tomorrow, can you . . . ?"

"Four in the afternoon. There's a dinner afterward in the church social hall. I should be out of there by eight at the latest. What's your game time? I can watch it from the hotel."

"It should be after eight."

"I can't wait, Mickey. I can't wait to see you and your team."

What I was saying was wrong. I didn't know what I should say, but I could tell by Mick's slight hesitations that he was disappointed. I heard myself go on. "We've got a rehearsal at five at the church today and then the rehearsal dinner. It's kind of a reversed wedding—I'm hosting the rehearsal dinner even though I'm the mother of the bride and Toby's family is doing the reception. Because it's in their town and in their church, which isn't what I would have wanted, but everyone in Toby's family has been married in the same place and . . ."

Mick interrupted. "Did you watch the game alone last night?"

"I went to Tessa's. I watched it with her and her husband."

"Good. I don't want to think of you watching it alone. Are you getting out some?"

"I get out plenty, Mick. I work. I'm not a recluse."

"I worry about you. I've got my team and my . . ." He faltered. "Don't watch alone tomorrow night, okay? Especially after Claudia's got herself married."

I made some kind of squeak.

"What?" Mick said, and when I couldn't answer right away he launched into a sermon about my goodness, what I had to offer, how I should start dating.

"Don't say that," I said. "It makes you seem too far away from me." Worse, it made him sound like he was dying.

"I am far," he said. "I'm in San Antonio."

Our city. Our imaginary city of our imaginary life, and there Mick really was. I should have let him stay the weekend that he showed up at my house. My whole world would be different if I had let him stay. My blood turned cold as ice but semiliquid, like one of those freezer bags you put on sprains. "I don't know, Mickey," I said. "I may just want to collapse in my hotel room and watch you guys."

"I told you," Mick barked, "don't watch it by yourself!" Like a grouchy old man, one grandchildren begged not to visit.

"Mick, I'm a grown-up. I'll be fine whatever happens."

"Why won't you listen to me? I worry about you!" Just eight hours before, he'd called me cupcake. I wanted to be a cupcake again. Then I realized that that was what he thought I was.

"I'll go watch it with Tessa and Herbie," I said, eager to reassure him. "They've got a room at the same hotel."

We said a few more things, but nothing else I'd remember.

A T THE REHEARSAL DINNER, I sat myself next to Alice, the black sheep of Toby's family. My brothers and their families weren't in yet. Alice's husband, the disliked dentist, couldn't make it, and I wondered if any of tonight's absences—Alice's husband, my brothers and their families, Claudia's stepbrother and stepsister by my ex and his wife—were statements about me. If so, I hated them for slighting Claudia. If so, I was really alone.

Alice did seem to inhabit a social stratum higher than her sisters', despite her unprepossessing yellow house. She wore a red satin jacket and black pants instead of a floral print dress, and she made a point of talking about colleges. "Claudia has lovely hair," she told me. Her husband's mother was in a nursing home, and hearing I was a doctor, Alice brought up end-of-life issues. She herself wanted a vial of morphine. Her husband had a gun. "He says most medical people have a plan," she said, looking pointedly at me.

Across from Alice and me at the long rectangular table sat my ex, Hank, and his wife, Sheryl. Sheryl wasn't attractive— she had crooked teeth and an enormous bottom—but she had a direct, frank way that was appealing. Much of her conversation involved the challenges of looking after Hank. She seemed to view him as an enormous restoration project that provided her regular, sometimes startling, satisfactions. She had gotten him out of jeans and T-shirts. She had found him vehicles for his retirement money and hobbies for his empty evenings. He was now certified in a special piano-teaching method, and students drove to him from over an hour away.

"What do you think of Hank's suit?" Sheryl asked me when Hank went to the restroom.

"Very natty."

Sheryl raised her eyebrows. "He didn't think he could wear green."

When Hank returned to the table I complimented him on his outfit, and he blushed and stammered in response. I was married to that man? I thought. Yet he'd always had a smiling passivity that people took as kindness.

"You're looking nice tonight too, Genie," Sheryl said, although I was sure I didn't. I'd put on a string of colored beads to draw attention from my worn face. "You must be thrilled about Claudia and Toby."

"I'm very happy," I said. "And did you hear Claudia's going to finish up her college this summer?"

"A woman has to look after herself," Hank said.

Sheryl nodded vigorously. "The woman is the looker-outer."

"Toby's a decent young man," Alice told me during dessert. "He used to stop by our house on occasion." She raised her eyebrows, as if his visits had been a secret. Alice left a few minutes later, before coffee. One of her children, the son in Baltimore, was calling home at nine.

"Now, who is she?" Sheryl asked once Alice left. "I swear, I need a flowchart for this family."

"Nice of you to talk to Alice," Toby's grandmother said reedily as our whole group walked to our cars.

"It's a little sad," one of the aunts said, "all her children far away."

I said, "She was very pleasant. We had a good visit."

Toby's mother said, "She didn't touch her dessert."

"Now, Kathy," Toby's father said to his wife, "that's not really your . . ."

"You know her and her diet!" A cousin.

"Boy," I said, "and I spent an extra dollar fifty on that nutball."

There was a silence, and Toby's mother eyed me briefly before she laughed. The other women laughed an instant later. Toby's father and I exchanged a rueful smile.

I could be my family's Alice, I realized. I could be the one everyone was scared of, the one whose choices weren't quite trusted or understood. "Of course, you only ever had *one* child," Myra, Rick's wife, mother of three, had said to me the previous

Thanksgiving. Even my brother Dean's nastiness, I realized, might mask wariness of my motives. Dealing with Genie, Dean might tell his harried wife, it's best to attack first.

"You can follow us to the B-and-B if you want," Sheryl said, tucking her hand under my ex-husband's upper arm.

But I was not staying at Harvest Haven like the rest of the out-of-town family. I was at the Holiday Inn. "Back problem," I explained to Sheryl. "The bed is more reliable." The television was more reliable, that was the point. Rick and Myra were arriving with their family later this evening at the B&B, while Dean was driving in from Chicago with his family tomorrow and only for the ceremony, because Dean's wife said there were only two places in the world worth leaving home to sleep in, a certain small hotel in Maui and the Four Seasons San Francisco. "My friends Tessa and Herbie come in tomorrow," I said to Sheryl, "and they're at the Holiday Inn too."

"Bad backs also, hunh?" Sheryl said knowingly, and I thought again how much I liked her.

"Maybe Alice can sit on the bride's side tomorrow," Toby's mother told me. "With you."

LATER THAT EVENING, my psychiatrist brother Rick and I were wedged together on a settee in the parlor of Harvest Haven, as his wife settled their children into bed upstairs. He had called me when they'd arrived, and I'd driven over from the Holiday Inn to greet them.

In the Harvest Haven parlor, once Sheryl had left to pick up her and Hank's son and daughter from the airport, I'd filled Rick in on the latest about me and Mick. "Why did I let myself get involved with him?" I asked in a whisper, not really meaning Rick to answer.

"Fear of intimacy?" Rick said, too loudly. "That's usually at least part of taking up with a married man."

I said, "I was very intimate with him."

Rick smiled in what might be pity. "That's what the lover always says." His face changed, and his voice became high and mocking. "My husband can't meet my needs. My husband can't *understand* me. For what it's worth," Rick went on, pulling his chin back and speaking in his doctor-on-the-radio voice, "here's a question I always ask my patients: What are you most afraid of?"

Mick's spark and dark, I thought. What drives a player and what he fears. And Rick thought he was original. "I'm afraid that Mick will die, of course," I said, appalled that Rick would make me voice this.

"What difference would his death make? You don't see him in person anyway."

"He called today. I talked to him this morning."

"But how long had it been?"

"Not forever."

"Oh, Genie."

I stood up and moved to Sheryl's former seat. "I don't like you as a psychiatrist," I said. "You're mean as a psychiatrist. So long as Mick doesn't die," I said, "I know he's there."

"*There*, where is *there*? In your mind?"

He really was mean. I wondered if there was trouble between him and Myra. *What about Myra,* he'd asked me earlier, *does she seem okay to you?* She seemed her usual. Stolid, unsmiling, kid-obsessed. "Upstairs now!" she said to her children at exactly ten, tapping the face of her watch. "And I want you each brushing your teeth for two full minutes!" The youngest had only eight teeth.

"It's ephemeral," Rick was saying now, "this relationship of yours. It's not the real work of making a life in the world with a partner and a family. It's a fantasy, it's a fairy tale, it's a fucking lie."

I glanced toward the door to the dining room, wondering if Patti the proprietress could hear us from the kitchen, or if Sheryl and the kids were about to burst through the front door. Rick turned his face from side to side as if he were stretching his neck. I should have asked him how he was, but I didn't think I had the strength to hear it. "Well," I said, standing up, "I should go. You must need some rest, after your long drive."

Rick's eyes rolled toward me, his mouth open. "You go, sure," he said. "You go."

To MY RELIEF, the bride's side in Toby's family's church did not at all look empty. My brothers and their families filled two pews. Rick's girls wore socks decorated with ribbons and jackets with shiny buttons; his son had on a bowtie. Dean and his wife looked like a couple in an ad for cognac, although their girls were dressed for a playground. In the front pew, I sat next to Sheryl and her two children by Hank, both of whom waved at me from the far side of their mother. I had on a silk suit in a shade of blue that clashed a bit with Sheryl's lavender dress. Tessa and Herbie and assorted friends of Claudia's from school and work filled the rows behind us. Howard was covering for me this weekend, so he couldn't make the trip to Indiana, and

I was disappointed in Jeremy and Sukie, who sent their regrets with an elaborate excuse. Alice was seated on Toby's side with a handsome man I took to be the dentist husband.

I was afraid I would cry. Not out of joy or relief or fear, but simply because my daughter's wedding would give me the opportunity to let go. But it would be wrong to cry about Mick here. The tears would be contaminating, red wine on a white tablecloth. No matter how much you scrubbed or what stain removers you tried, the tablecloth would never be the same.

I had seen Claudia in the brides' dressing room, I'd adjusted her veil and fiddled with her bra strap, I'd helped Detra, the maid of honor, whose barbed-wire tattoo on her upper arm was sure to start some conversations, get Claudia's train stretched out just so, and yet when I turned to watch my daughter come down the aisle, I was overwhelmed. Claudia looked different from anything I'd ever wanted to resemble (my own wedding gown had been severe, and I'd banned baby's breath as too fluffy). She looked exactly as she had dreamed of looking. She was, indeed, wearing her gown; her gown was not—in another of my mother's punishing phrases—wearing her. In the front of the church, the groom had appeared with his best man, and Claudia, on her father's arm, strained toward Toby, as if she were ready to make a break down the aisle. It felt like watching a lightning storm come in to see Claudia and Toby set their eyes upon each other, to feel, like a charge in the air, their headstrong faith that the two of them—despite Hank and me, despite Toby's clearly mismatched parents (his mother had had an allergy attack and was holding a hankie over her lower face)—would *do it right,* no matter the contradictory evidence around them. When Claudia passed my pew, she didn't even glance my way.

They may do it, I thought. They may make a real marriage. Something ordinary outside but voluptuous within—a shoebox lined with satin and scented with spices, a hobbyhorse with a wildly beating heart. That's what brought tears to my eyes, and it had nothing to do with Mickey. If I had to label them tears of anything, I'd say that they were tears of pride.

T ESSA OPENED THE DOOR to her hotel room. Behind her, Herbie was stationed in a chair directly in front of the TV, an unlit cigar jerking at the corner of his mouth. "You ready for the game?" Tessa said.

There had been nothing wrong with the reception, but nothing exciting about it, either—the sort of event whose attendees, asked about it later, would answer, "It was nice," in a vaguely challenging tone. Dean and his family were probably already back in Chicago. Rick and Myra, looking weary and walking apart, left the reception by six, trailed by their gloomy oldest, his bowtie askew. Claudia's bridesmaid, Detra, had offered to buy drinks for all Claudia's friends, and that group headed out stuffed into two cars. When I left, Hank and Sheryl were helping Toby's mother load her van. Toby's father nowhere in sight. "What a jewel!" Toby's mother said about my ex. "How'd you let him get away?"

"I called up LeeAnn from my office and asked if she could tape Mick's game," I said to Tessa.

"Oh, okay. Well, come on in. You can see Herbie has his pacifier."

My face, involuntarily, made a complicated twitch. I tried to calm myself. Breathe in two beats, breathe out four. "I can't watch it, Tessa. I'm going to that multiplex next door. I'll see two movies if I have to. I just want to walk out into the lobby and have it over."

On the television, the tournament theme music was playing. "You're not dragging me off to some movie," Herbie said, glancing at Tessa. "I'm staying here for the Battle of the Big Men." That was how Turkman's game had been billed; the opposing team also had a dominant center, Jared Winslow.

"I'll watch it on tape later," I said. "After I know how it ends."

"He'll do fine!" Herbie said. "Mick'll be fine!"

"I'll come with you," Tessa said, searching the floor for her shoes. "Just let me brush my teeth." I closed the door and waited outside the room. The empty hall narrowed in the distance, just as I imagined my future. "Men," Tessa mumbled as she closed the door behind me.

I knew she didn't mean this seriously. She loved Herbie, Herbie loved her, and both of them were excited to be in a hotel room. A hotel room, she said, made them feel like they were sneaking around. And as for Lady Godiva, she told me as we walked across the parking lot, well, Herbie adored it, he adored it!

Our first movie was a romantic comedy, and the second one was a thriller. In between, Tessa and I got drinks and used the bathroom. I don't remember those movies' names. I felt as if I'd swallowed a whole loaf of bread and it was swelling in my abdomen, until my heart and lungs were pressed up into my throat and I could hardly breathe. He isn't losing, I scolded myself. Stop being superstitious.

"Are you okay?" Tessa whispered.

"Nervous," I whispered back, and Tessa squeezed my elbow, and eventually the thriller ended in an embrace after gunfire, and Tessa and I emerged blinking into the lobby. We passed the kid collecting tickets. "You watch the Midwest final?" the kid called, speaking to a large bearded man across the lobby.

The big man was eating popcorn and walking, his eyes half closed and seemingly unfocused, and he moved with slow relentlessness in our direction. Finally he stopped a few feet from us, his middle eddying and wobbling, and it seemed to me he was the embodiment of grief. "Not much of a game," he said, inserting a kernel of popcorn into his pink slot of a mouth, and in that gruesome moment, I knew.

L eeANN's TAPE:
    I fast-forwarded through the first half, even the shots of Mickey, and I could see that things weren't right. There were flashes of Eluard being Eluard, but whole minutes when he wasn't, and Morgan was missing not only his free throws but his three-pointers as well, the shots he was supposed to rule. The usually cocky Kennilworth seemed timid, and Eggleston, filling in for Flitt, had the ball stripped from him two times in a row.

They weren't listening to the ball, I thought. They'd gone deaf.

"It's even more lopsided than the score," Mick said to the interviewer at halftime. "You better let me get to the locker room. We'll come back."

They didn't. In the final seconds, Eluard did manage to grab the ball away from Jared Winslow and run it down court alone, but somehow Eluard missed the basket, and he sank to his knees in what looked like despair as the horn blew to end the game. At this point Jared Winslow came to Eluard, bent over, put his hands on either side of Eluard's face, and spoke to him intently. Eluard stood and the two men embraced. That was it, the one mysterious and possibly redeeming moment, although even this was really Winslow's moment and not Eluard's.

There were people jumping up and down, Kennilworth with his head hanging, the coaches shaking hands. The camera flashed to Mick's family—Karn, who resembled a half-deflated blow-up figure, Jessica staring into space, Bobby and Eric slumped against each other not speaking. *What's wrong with you?* I felt like screaming to the cameraman, and a producer must have thought the same thing, because abruptly the scene changed and an interviewer was standing beside Mickey, his mike thrust in Mick's face. "We just didn't have it tonight," Mick said, "and they came out gunning."

This was supposed to be the Battle of the Big Men, but your center Eluard Dickens didn't . . . How much do you think the loss of your point guard Frederick . . . ? Any word on how Flitt . . . ?

Mick's eyes swung briefly as if he were looking for help. I'm erasing this tape, I thought. I never want to see this tape again. "The doctors are still evaluating him," Mickey said, glancing at someone offscreen, and he was already moving away as the scene flashed to another interviewer, this one standing with the winning coach.

Don't watch alone tomorrow night, okay? As if he'd known.

I had a tape of Claudia and Toby's wedding. That tape was a keeper.

C LAUDIA'S WEDDING, thank goodness, gave my patients and me something to discuss.

"What do you think of your new son-in-law?"

"Oh, she must have been gorgeous. You'll bring in the pictures, won't you?"

"You're all alone now, Dr. Toledo! Maybe you'll start dating?"

All through my office visits I was waiting for a knock on the door—"Dr. Toledo, there's a man on the phone for you." Each night I rushed into my house looking for the blinking red light on my answering machine, but the messages were only Tessa, or Claudia calling from her honeymoon, or perky computer voices promising free vacations. There were occasional hang-ups. Maybe the hang-ups were Mick, I thought. He was calling me at home during the day, working up the courage for a message. I wondered if he'd retire now, if he'd seen his doctors, if he had surgery or treatment scheduled. I wondered if he thought his season had been worth it. Even in the Turkman city paper, Mickey, after Turkman's loss, was given only an inch or so of column space, a couple of piddly quotes, but that was how the sports world worked. In a day the media forgot the losers and moved on to the next big matchup. What a cruel, impossible life Mick had chosen for himself. Thank God he loved it.

T HAT THURSDAY A PIECE OF MAIL arrived at my house, with a Turkman State Warriors seal on the envelope and a card inside fronted with a photograph of Mick on the court conversing with two players from his team of '98.

Dear Genie, I'm goeing to retire. Maybe we can meet for coffee somday. You can call me on my cell. Love, Mick

He couldn't spell, I realized. The errors I'd taken as jokes or typos on his e-mails were how he wrote.

W E MET IN MARIETTA AGAIN, on Saturday morning a week later. Monday Night was over, and Duke was again the national champion men's college basketball team. Raj had won his pool. I suggested Starbucks but Mick didn't believe in Starbucks—we met at a place that was basically a diner—and pulling my car in between two pickups I thought that this choice of Mick's was typical, that maybe if we were together we'd find each other irritating in a hundred unforeseen ways.

Once I'd spotted him, I didn't care where we were meeting.

He was already in a booth facing the door, stirring his coffee and looking out the window. He stood and we embraced, as much as we could in public, and I slid into the seat across from him.

"Thanks for coming," Mick said, and I hesitated to see if he meant this reference as a joke, but when his face didn't change I answered, "Oh, of course. It's wonderful to see you in person instead of on TV."

"You watched?"

"Every game. It was a great run. You should be really proud."

He nodded. "The guys did good."

"Are you having surgery?" I asked, shifting in my seat, nodding to the waitress that, yes, I wanted coffee.

"Not at this point." Mick shrugged. "No point to it, unless I get a blockage. The horse is out of the barn, Doc Leslie says."

I blinked, but I couldn't say I was totally surprised.

"I don't have pain. That's the weirdest thing, that's what everyone can't figure out. I don't feel too bad, really. Not at this point. Doc Leslie says that may change."

"Is it in your back?" Routinely, the first site of metastatic prostate cancer.

"All over. Back, ribs, leg bones." Mick rapped on his head with a fist. "Even in my thick skull."

"Jesus." My voice shook. *All over* did surprise me. "You really don't have pain? God, Mickey, I hope you don't ever get pain."

"If I do, Doc Leslie says she'll give me pain pills."

We looked at each other. "That's it for treatment?" I said. "You're sure?"

Mick shrugged. "I'm still getting the hormone shots. There's some chemo they could try, but I told Doc Leslie to call in hospice."

"Comfortably numb," I said, thinking of the morphine, feeling numb myself.

Mick said, "That's not bad."

"I watched every game," I said. "I taped them and I watch them over and over. You guys were amazing. It was really just . . . a *pleasure* to watch that team."

Mick smiled. "You hate for things to end like that, but the guys were tapped out. And without Frederick . . . They couldn't do one thing more. My retirement, they're announcing that Tuesday."

"I wondered about that. I hadn't seen it on the news."

"I told the guys. It was surprising, Kennilworth said it wouldn't be the same next year and I said, look, you'll be fine, you've got Eluard back as post man and Eggleston can handle point guard—he was nervous that last night, he wasn't the Eggleston I know—and you've still got Morgan and Chiswick, plus Brooks and Miller coming up, and Kennilworth says, no, it won't be the same without you." Mick looked at me with something like wonderment. "You could have knocked me over. Kennilworth said that. Kennilworth."

"It was all you," I said. "That team was all you."

Mick shook his head. "It was just a team that worked. We had our concept."

"You should see the tapes," I said. "You should see the way they look at you."

"I see the tapes. I spend hours with the tapes."

"But you see the team tapes. They don't show enough of you on them. The TV tapes show you." I leaned into the table, looked up into Mick's eyes. "You don't think enough of yourself." He didn't. But it was this simpleness, I saw suddenly, this plain as-is-ness, that made him such a comfort to me. He took what had been given him and accepted it. *Coaching basketball isn't that hard. . . . She's the designated worrier. . . . That's not bad.* "Did you tell them about your cancer?"

"I told Frederick. The other guys'll find out soon enough." Mick winced. "Frederick's got a tough road. They got in there, both knees, he's got this cleft in his meniscus that's probably congenital, and on top of that the right knee is torn up. They stitched up what they could, but . . ." He shook his head.

I took a sip of coffee. We were quiet for a moment, Mick looking away and out the window. "I remember when Dashona was dying," he said. "I stood in the hall outside his hospital room and said, 'God, take me instead.' Maybe God thought I meant it."

"Maybe you're sparing someone right now." This was hokum, of course, and I was relieved when Mick laughed.

"Don't I wish. No, I'm just your average cancer patient. It still surprises me, though. I kind of thought I'd get old." He shrugged. "I've had a lot longer than Dashona. I'll probably stay on for a month or two, help the new guy out."

Don't give up yet, I was thinking. Don't sink now. "Do you have anyone in mind?"

"It's not my decision. B.C. and the president asked me about it, but really they don't care. I'm history already, to them. That's okay, that's how teams work."

His bluntness was astonishing, but he had always been direct. I swallowed. "You were right. This was your year."

Mick smiled. "I loved the way that Winslow went to Eluard. That was one of the best things I've seen."

"What did Winslow say?"

Mick shook his head. "Eluard won't tell. That's another thing I love. Eluard was okay with losing, everyone was." He made a considering shrug with his mouth. "Whatever happens, Genie, I've had a lucky life."

"I know," I said. "Me too." I rubbed my left eyebrow, opened my fingers over my face, and rubbed the whole side of it, and as I finished this gesture I realized this was nothing I'd have done in front of Mick before. But now I had no self-consciousness; now Mick and I, seated in a diner, were stripped barer than we'd been in our hotel room. "I have this patient who has horrible coronary artery disease," I said. "Really diffuse stuff. He runs marathons. I don't know how he does it. He pops nitros the first five miles, and after that he feels okay. And he always says, 'If I die out there on the course somewhere, don't cry for me, Genie. I'm dying happy.'"

"Karn won't say the word 'death.' Just won't say it. After a while you live with someone like that, you start not wanting to say it too. Jessica was talking about some golf tournament with a sudden-death overtime and I thought Karn was going to have a stroke."

"It must get hard for you."

"It's a game. We all know what's happening. I like hearing you say it, though. Dying, death, dead. It's not something you can deny."

"I can't deny it. I work with it."

Mick was stroking the outside of his coffee cup. "Do you think my immune system's all right?"

I frowned. "What do you mean?" Usually when I heard a patient say the words "immune system," their worry was HIV. "I'm disease-free, I assure you."

Mick reddened. "Oh, no, no. It's just that you hear about people getting better with these cancers, and . . ."

"Some cancers are overwhelming, Mick. It's not your fault. And I don't think"—I hesitated, wanting to be truthful—"I'm not sure the treatment would have helped, honestly."

His mouth loosened then, and the area around his eyes relaxed, and when he smiled he looked like the old Mick. "Thanks," he said. "I needed that."

"My cardiologist opinion." I rolled my eyes at the presumptuousness of it.

"Of course. The best opinion." There was a moment of lightness between us, a glimmering soap bubble hovering in the air. Neither of us spoke. Mick dropped his gaze first. "I've talked to Marcus about it," he said. "Someday, if I need you, Marcus will call."

"Anytime," I said. Out of the corner of my eye, I saw our waitress approaching with the coffeepot. Mick glanced up, laid his hand over the top of the cup, and the waitress turned away. "If I came back to you now," Mick asked, lifting his hand like a magician, "could I stay?"

"Don't answer me," he said, before I had a chance to. "I don't want to know."

K ARN CALLED ME at the office. It was direct now. "I need to talk to her," Lindy said she'd said. "Now."

"I hear you saw him," Karn said when I got on the phone.

"Yes. We met for . . ."

"I don't care what you met for," Karn interrupted. "I don't care. I understand he told you?"

"About his cancer?"

"About his widely metastatic cancer," Karn said. "About his cancer that is eating through one hundred of his bones."

"He told me it was widely spread," I said, thinking it was probably not one hundred.

"Now there's a spot on his chest X-ray," Karn said. "Did he tell you about the spot on his X-ray? When did you see him, Saturday? He didn't have the report on Saturday."

"No," I said quietly.

"I canceled the cruise," Karn said. "We're not sitting through a hairy chest contest with Mick dying."

I made some sort of noise. Karn had said the word "dying"; to me, she had said the forbidden word.

"I can't stand it," Karn said. "It's like he won't try to fight. It's like he's walking into a big gigantic fire. What is wrong with his immune system? Everybody else gets cancer, their body tries to fight it off. It's like his body doesn't care!

"You find out who your friends are," Karn said. "You find out who only wants to talk about them, them, them." The president's wife, I thought. "Jessica said I should call you," Karn said. "Jessica said you sort of owe me."

I said nothing. "How am I supposed to get through this?" Karn said. "How? How?" And then she started wailing.

And so began the season of the phone calls. There were maybe twenty more. They came always—after that first call, when I gave her my home number—to my house in the late evening, just when I was getting in from work and Karn had Mickey down to bed and Jessica was upstairs with the toddler. I often listened as I ate my dinner, usually a low-cal frozen entrée I had microwaved. Ginger might be mewing at the other side of the table, asking to be fed herself. "It's me," Karn would say, and I would answer, "How's the patient? How are *you*?" After maybe a minute of information about Mick, Karn would launch into what might, more tightly focused and better constructed, be termed a soliloquy. There were minutes (long minutes) I could sit and chew, making an occasional "mmm" and closing my eyes at intervals and then, out of nowhere, there were questions—spoken urgently and followed by demanding pauses—that almost made me choke before I blurted out an answer.

"I went out in the ground cover out front and there are hardly any weeds. I can remember when there were hours of weeds. This weed I call snakeroot—for a year that was my front yard. It's like raising children. You spend all this time pulling up the weeds in them, and year after year, if you're doing your job right, the weeds die out. I mean, they're supposed to. What do you think, do you believe in Prozac?

". . . and when our kids got to be teenagers I thought, I'm not going to do what my dad did. He used to lock me in my bedroom. Didn't ever think of windows. I was on the first floor too. Rare night that someone wasn't out there, tapping on my glass. Oh, I know the tricks of teenage girls. That's why I used to talk to the school secretaries, find out who the good boys were. Drove Jessica crazy. It wasn't a *list,* it was just suggestions. Anyway, that's probably why she got pregnant, to spite me. I told her she didn't have to let him in her. I told her there were other things to do. Did you and Mick go in for . . . you know . . . other things?

"You wouldn't believe how he convinced me to marry him. We were watching some game on TV and they showed the coach's wife sitting there and he said, Wouldn't it be neat if that were you?

Well, I thought that was really something, but later on, let me tell you, it got hard. You don't know when they're going to show you. You could be yawning. You could be telling your kids to shut up. Did you see me on TV this year? Did I look normal?

"I taught him to write thank-you notes. His mother was decent enough, she had her good points, but the rest of them. . . . You'd be amazed at what he didn't know. Listen, I've been thinking, how can you tell if someone's dead?"

She'd never seen a person die, Karn said. Everyone she knew who'd passed had done it in the hospital, in private.

"They look different," I said. I was shaking dry food into Ginger's bowl. "If someone's really dead, you'll know. Someone in a coma can *look* dead, but you'll never mistake a dead person for a living one." I realized that this was not reassuring. "You check for a pulse," I said, "at the side of their neck. Or you can put your hand on their chest and feel for a heartbeat and breathing. You can even lay your head on their chest and listen."

Ginger's teeth were snapping on her food. Karn said, "That sort of scares me."

"I know, Karn," I said, sliding the bag of cat food back in the closet. "It scares everyone. Listen, you have hospice involved, right? If it gets to the point where you can't handle things at home, let Mick go to their inpatient unit."

"I want him home with me."

"Talk with him about it, Karn. Mick's realistic. Ask him what you should do if things get to be too much. Ask him soon."

In late June, as suddenly as they'd started, the phone calls stopped. As if Karn had gotten all she needed. As if I had atoned enough. Maybe one of Karn's sons—Eric, probably, the more proper one—had gotten wind of our conversations, said,

"Mother! What are you doing calling her?" Maybe Karn and the family had headed off on one last, long cruise (unlike Karn not to have mentioned it, but perhaps she was trying to be tactful). Maybe Karn didn't like me anymore. Or had no more use for me.

I found myself replaying our final conversation. Karn had asked me what to do if she had chest pain.

"You?" My throat had tightened. "You have chest pain?"

"No, but what if I did? I was thinking about that, if under the circumstances I would come see you."

"I hope not." And then, to forestall any damage, to explain: "I'm too far away from you to be your cardiologist, realistically."

"You're Jessica's doctor."

But I wasn't, not anymore. If Karn didn't realize this, then Jessica—to protect her mother? to make a statement to me?—had changed doctors on her own. "Listen, when Jessica got chest pain Mick kind of insisted I . . ." I trailed off, aware I'd just walked Karn past a vista she had never wanted to lay eyes on, a scene she must be sorry to have glimpsed. Karn's and my conversations, even those touching on sex, always looped back to Karn and Mick together, to—as I had come to think of it, not unbitterly—the Marital Unit. My comment made it clear that the Marital Unit was not Mick's only pairing.

"Mick insisted," Karn repeated dully. "Well, he knew you."

"He trusted me," I said.

That was Karn's last phone call. "I don't mind talking to her," I imagined Karn telling someone, "but she doesn't have the right to rub my nose in it.

"What is she, anyway?" Karn might say. "She's not his wife."

Normally I would have walked up the stairs to the third floor of the hospital, but the elevator doors were closing just as I passed and I slipped in, only to find myself alone with my gynecologist.

He backed himself to the far wall. "Hello, Genie," he said, not looking at me. "You feeling well?"

"I'm fine." I wouldn't get my Pap smears with him, I'd thought. I'd see the female gynecologist everyone raved about, although in my opinion she was simpery and wore too much makeup.

My gynecologist nodded pleasantly and fixed his eyes on the numbered lights above the door.

"It wasn't a real pineapple," I said, turning to face him. "It was a decorative wooden pineapple on a bedpost, and I was with my friend without any clothes on and I was standing on the bed doing the Golden Chicken—that's tai chi—and I fell over and that's how it happened. It wasn't anything perverse"—the gynecologist's eyes flicked toward me—"not at all. And now my friend's dying of prostate cancer and I don't see him, but I'm glad I had that night with him, I really am, that was maybe our best night ever. We talked."

The elevator stopped at 2, the maternity floor, and my gynecologist hesitated an instant before he took a step to leave. "I'm sorry," he said. I glanced up at his mild face and thin lips, and he looked, indeed, as if he understood, as if a gust of wind had blown away the doubts he had about me.

"I appreciate that," I said, and he left, the doors closing silently behind him.

. . .

I GOT THROUGH THE SUMMER. I played miniature golf with the newlyweds and took a cardiac arrythmia review course online. I ran four to five miles each evening after work. For two weeks I went with Helen, the recently widowed cath lab nurse, to a vacation cabin in Pennsylvania; over three weekends I stripped and restained my deck myself. I sometimes thought about Mick every minute—at a musical in Pennsylvania, I'd been startled to realize I hadn't thought of him through an entire song—and what kept me going was the certainty that Mick would ask to see me; he would summon me via Marcus, and I had only to wait for the day. That was how Helen-the-widow and I ended up fifty miles from Ohio and not, as Helen first suggested, by the sea: an old friend of mine was dying, I told her, and I didn't want to go too far away. It wouldn't be until after Mick's and my last meeting that I'd have to face being alone.

In the middle of August I got an emergency phone call. "Man or woman?" I asked Lindy, rushing toward my office.

"Woman," Lindy said. "That one who's called before."

There was a tribute dinner for Mick coming up, Karn said, and she was calling because if by any chance I got the Turkman paper I might see ads for tickets, and she wanted to be sure I didn't come.

It took me a moment to understand what she was saying. I took a breath. "How is he?"

"Oh, good as can be expected. He's on morphine around the clock now—capsules, they have—but he's awake a lot, he's home, he plays solitaire."

I sat down. "How are you?"

"The Prozac is fine, I love the Prozac, but I don't want you at the banquet." And then, in a stronger voice, "My children don't want you there."

The line about the children hurt. I had saved Jessica's life—put her at some risk doing it, true, but everything had worked out. Ten months before, Karn had thought I was a hero.

I said, "Is that what Mick wants?"

"It's not up to Mick." Karn's voice rose a notch. "This is a happy night for our whole family, and we don't need it tainted. I'm sure you understand our reasons."

I hadn't done a procedure as risky as Jessica's ever since. Probably never would again. There was no one else I wanted to prove myself to. The cardiologist who'd rushed in to open Jessica's artery seemed like a different, reckless person from the person I was now. Or perhaps I'd been a surer person, one who trusted, justifiably, in her own capabilities. Perhaps now I'd lost my nerve.

"I'm sorry to hear that," I said. "You've been very kind to me." This was not completely true: Karn had been exceptional in acknowledging me at all, in taking me as a confidante in certain personal matters, but Karn's phone calls had been for Karn's benefit, not mine. "I'd love to"—I tried to think of a proper phrase, as neutral and undemanding as possible—"clap eyes on him again, at least. At some point. You could be there too."

"I'm sure there will be banquet pictures in the paper," Karn said. "Or I can e-mail you a photo, if you want to give me your address."

"That's okay," I said, thinking of Mick's illness invaded by photographs, thinking of my e-mail invaded by Karn's name. "You don't have to."

"Better if you remember him like he was." Here, surprisingly, Karn's voice softened.

"Give him my best," I said. There was silence on the line, and I realized that for this message to be passed along Karn would require a payment. "I won't come to the banquet," I said, and Karn quickly—too quickly—said, "Good. Thank you." As if she were slapping her hands together, saying, *All right, that job's taken care of.*

I'll never see him again, I thought, the phone still clamped to my ear—and this was a heartbreaking concession, one Mick would never ask of me, but Mick no longer controlled his own life. It filled me with resentful grief when Karn, after no more than a brisk "Be good now," left me alone on the phone.

I TRIED COUNTING the tables for ten, which were round, but I lost track at close to fifty, and there were also long rectangular tables set up against the walls. Maroon-and-gold napkins. The room was cavernous, and I hoped the sound system was adequate. My escort Tabitha and I, both an hour early, had spotted each other in the lobby and waited together in the security line. Tabitha was friendly but nervous, especially before we got into the darker banquet hall and sat down. "Karn knows me," Tabitha said. "The kids know me. I used to babysit over there back when I was a teenager. We'll just sit here and blend in." I was wearing my maroon top with the front snaps and a black skirt and high-heeled black shoes, and even with no underwear I was feeling fairly blended, but Tabitha had on a top that exposed her upper breasts, and a hat with feathers. "If she looks this way when she comes in," Tabitha said, "I'll wave and you bend over like you dropped your napkin."

Tabitha actually had a map. A map and a walkie-talkie and a watch, timed to match Marcus's, propped up at the top of her place setting. "Don't worry, we've got this planned better than D-Day," she told me. No one else was seated yet at our table. "I'm going to go get us drinks," Tabitha said. "Can't you do with a drink?"

I never believed I'd make it to this day, to this place. Marcus's call finally came through. He reached me at home late one evening. His voice was deep and thrilling, a boyfriend's voice. "Mick wants you at his tribute," he said. It would be in three weeks, Thursday the 27th, at the Turkman Convention Center. "They were going to have it on campus but they've gotten too many reservations," Marcus said. "I have your ticket."

"Karn doesn't want me there," I said. "She phoned me not to come."

"We're hiding you. I've got you at a table out in East Jesus with my cousin, and at some point we'll make sure you and Mick can get together by yourselves. I take him to the bathroom, so this'll work out just fine."

Mick needed help to use the bathroom? I felt sick. I pictured a potty chair set up in the center of a room, Karn bustling around Mick with a roll of toilet paper in her hand. The indignity. The intimacy.

"He's in bed pretty much all the time," Marcus said. "He can't get up stairs. They've got a nice family room with a lot of windows—it's private, sticks out the back of the house—and Karn's got a hospital bed set up there in front of the TV. A lot of people'd like to see him, but Karn's not big on visitors. Kind of wants to keep him for herself. She lets me in. I get over there about every other day."

Marcus's call came during the first week of September, and then came September 11. I was in the cath lab. Helen heard what was going on but she kept it from me, between my second and third caths hustling me to the reading room and bringing me coffee and charts to sign and even the family of my patient, whom she counseled not to let me know. Helen managed to make my morning and my caths, two of which involved angioplasties and stenting, seem perfectly routine. I'm not sure, even now, why she did it. Something I'd said or done during our summer trip must have made me seem fragile. I don't know what it was.

Later that week, I was involved in a code in the CCU. It was a good code—that is, we wanted the patient to survive—and we got her back. The thing involved two doctors and three nurses and at least thirty minutes during which I doubt any one of us thought about the Twin Towers or the broken Pentagon or the plane crashed into the field in Pennsylvania. When it was done we stood around the nurses' station in a giddy communion, eyeing the monitors as if we hoped for someone else to work on, because that week it was a pleasure, truly, to lose ourselves together in something useful.

I hoped Mick was okay. I hoped Mick understood that his coaching really mattered.

It was a terrible time to be dying. People imagined war, strafings, forced conscription, poison gases overtaking grocery stores, men with rifles on top of buildings. People thought of grayness and soot and the smell of burning bodies. Sex at such a time would be resistance; dying had to feel like giving in. At home I never watched the news. I did my running and lifting and stretching and took long showers and fed Ginger and tried not to think about what Mick must be making of the situation. *What does my death matter next to these deaths? What will happen in my grandson's world? Who'll look after Karn and Genie if we're attacked?* It would be so easy—Mick's life now limited to one room—to put on videos, even the Three Stooges, instead of news. But this would require a willfulness and strength of character I doubted Karn had.

Toby was talking about quitting his job and moving to a remote cabin and living off the land. He told Claudia they should stop payment on their health insurance and put their extra cash into precious metals. He was researching weather patterns and average frost dates on the Internet, trying to find the best locations to grow food. In the middle of the night, he and Claudia clung together waiting for the dawn.

"Is the tribute still on?" I asked Marcus when he phoned the following week.

"Now more than ever," he said.

"Does Mick even know what's going on?"

Marcus made a despairing chuckle. "Karn has CNN on all the time."

The bitch. The idiot. The weakling. I pictured myself bursting into her house, grabbing her out of the family room, strangling her in her own foyer with my bare hands.

The people who eventually appeared at Tabitha's and my table, six men and two women, were all from the Turkman State English Department. I was dismayed to recognize, taking the seat next to me, the professor I'd seen on the TV news protesting Mick's salary. How dare a critic of Mick's come to a dinner in Mick's honor.

"We're not going to talk about anything serious," an older woman who sat directly across from me said. "Is that a deal, Preston?"

Preston, to Tabitha's left and a good twenty years younger than any of the other professors, nodded.

"What brings you here?" I asked the professor I'd seen on TV. Actually, the professor said, clearing his throat, their new department chair, a most interesting woman, had asked them to attend. Of course, she was seated nearer the front, at a table with the other department chairs. Still, it was good to get out, really. It was good to think about something other than tragedy.

I swallowed and said, "Your last chair went to Iowa, right?"

The man nodded.

"Lucky for us," said Preston, from the other side of Tabitha.

The older woman across the table gave a small gasp. I followed my gaze past her shoulder and turned to see Mickey twenty feet away from us in a wheelchair, being pushed by Eluard toward the raised head table. Mick was in his sports banquet best—a Turkman striped tie and a suit that now looked several sizes too big for him—and hanging from each side arm of his wheelchair was an American flag. I can't tell you how much those flags bothered me. As if Mick were no longer quite human but a thing to be used and festooned. As if Mick's goodness were something American, not his own. As if his death were communal, not personal. *That's it*, I thought, *I'm doing it.*

"What brings you here?" the professor next to me asked, his face turning from the sight of Mick, and I was glad to see the tactlessness of his "other than tragedy" comment belatedly hit him.

Tabitha answered for me. "She's a friend of mine. My cousin Marcus Masters is Coach Crabbe's best friend."

"Really," the professor said, and to someone's "Excuse me?" Tabitha repeated the information, and everyone around the table seemed to make a mental adjustment to the news that Mick's best friend must be a black man.

"Righteous!" Preston said, and the woman across from me shot him an exasperated glance.

The emcee was a sports broadcaster who'd flown in from Florida. Tabitha said he was a real character, but that night he read an introductory speech I doubted he'd written (". . . an honor and a consolation to come together at a time of national mourning, to celebrate the achievements of . . .") and ended by saying, "God bless America, and God bless Mick Crabbe."

A priest gave the invocation, a rather belligerent prayer.

"My cousin and Mickey were roommates at college," Tabitha said when the prayer ended, and that launched an onslaught of questions and comments, until the table was swapping room-mate anecdotes, Preston presenting himself, not surprisingly, as his roommate's worst nightmare, even describing what sounded like a bomb hoax before he caught himself and trailed off.

At some point during the salad course a waiter dropped a tray full of dishes and the vast room became suddenly silent, until a ripple of relief and understanding swept through the crowd.

We were halfway through the chicken when Tabitha's walkie-talkie squawked. "What's that?" Preston snapped, and as Tabitha turned her back to the table and spoke into the receiver the woman across the table smiled in a superior way.

"He's having chest pain," Tabitha said.

For an instant I thought he really was. "Excuse us," Tabitha said, leaning into the table, "but my friend here is a cardiologist, and Coach is right now having chest pain, and we want to get him through this celebration, so I'm going to have to take her with me to see him."

We left the table in a flurry of concern, and then I was following Tabitha through a side door and down a maze of halls, the map open in Tabitha's hand. In the distance a man of mighty size was beckoning, and when we reached him he opened a door.

"Dr. Toledo, I presume," Marcus said in his lovely voice, his round face glowing with concern. He looked like a man who couldn't possibly keep a secret, a secret-keeper's best disguise. He touched my shoulder, hurrying me along. "You go on in there. I'll try to give you two a full five minutes."

I stood in the room facing Mick ten feet away in his wheelchair as the door clicked shut behind me. A medium-sized windowless room, probably an ancillary banquet room, with blue-gray industrial carpeting and chairs and tables pushed against the walls. "Hi," I said.

"Hi."

I might not have recognized him, had he been hurried past me in a crowded mall. Astonishing how completely disease could change a person. His thick head of hair was exactly the same, but atop his wasted body it looked like a wig. "Thanks for asking me," I said.

"My only chance," he said. "I'm kind of a prisoner."

Now, I thought, and I swear it was those dreadful flags that gave me courage. "You're not a prisoner to me," I said, and I popped my snaps and unzipped and dropped my skirt and stood before him naked.

"That's pretty brazen," Mick said.

"I hope I'm not offending you."

"I don't know. Come closer and I'll decide." Mick's eyes flicked to my feet. "Nice shoes," he said, and I kicked one off and caught it in the air.

"Come here," he said, a goofy smile overtaking his face, and I had to drop my gaze to his outstretched arms, because his face was too excruciating to look at. If the room had been bigger, you could have said I ran to him. I put my hand on his shoulder and lowered myself onto his lap. It was scary, in a way, because for the first time in my life I seemed too big for him, and I knew he had disease in his bones. But I did sit, delicately at first and then letting myself relax onto him, and it was wonderful to feel his body, even if it was shockingly bony in places and caved-in and soft in its middle. When I got fully seated I adjusted my head on Mick's left shoulder, as close as we could get to our usual position. His buckle poked into my hip. "You're just the right size," Mick said. For a while he ran his hands over me, and neither of us spoke.

"It goes like that," he said, running a finger down my backbone. "I never knew."

"No one does." My eyes were closed and I was listening to his heartbeat. "So," I said, "I finally met Marcus."

Mick dropped his head and nuzzled me like a horse. "He's a great friend. He'll look after you when I'm gone."

"You're not going anywhere."

"Of course I am. Claudia happy being married?"

"She's fine. We're all doing fine." I lifted my head and looked into his eyes, as blue and as aching as ever. "I love my car," I said. "I'll always keep my car."

"Don't take it out when there's salt on the roads," Mick said. "Get the oil changed every two thousand miles."

I nodded. "I will. I have."

"Karn says she's called you."

"A few times."

"She's a good woman, Genie. I hope you two can work things out."

"We can do that." What else could I say?

"Good." Mick poked at my upper arm. "You feel like Eluard. You've lost your softness."

"I've been lifting weights."

"I thought your shoulders looked bigger." Mick cupped them in his hands. "You're becoming an Amazon. I'm glad. You can change a tire without me."

As if he'd ever been around to change my tires. I said, "Remember that accident I had with the pineapple?"

"Oh, gee." We both started giggling.

"I'm a basketball coach!" I said. *"I know when a vagina needs stitches!"*

"They called me Mr. Toledo in the emergency room, remember?"

A timid noise came from the door.

"We lived like kings," Mick said. "Kings. And we didn't even know it."

"Kings in the Marietta Marriott."

"You can have that kingdom anywhere. You can have that kingdom in the back seat of a car."

There was definitely someone knocking, and I felt a surge of fury at the interruption. I knew that part of me would always be, regarding Mick, ferocious and unrepentant, would understand that an illicit love affair could be the defining relationship of a life, would shout: I want that! even if *that* was imperfect, was selfish, was morally wrong.

"I've got to open it," said Marcus's muffled voice, and then there was the creaking of a door. I didn't care. That Marcus should see me naked seemed like the most trivial thing on earth. Mick and I were in the middle of a kiss. We didn't kiss enough, I was thinking, and neither of us wanted to stop, because a kiss was always beckoning the future, a kiss held the promise of something more. Still, Mick's lips were newly thin, uncushioned, and through them I could feel the divisions between his teeth. *There isn't any time for us!*

Marcus cleared his throat. "Dr. Toledo, you may want to put your clothes on. They're starting to ask about you, coach. Bobby says Karn's getting up to come searching." Bobby? Mick's son must be a coconspirator.

"Holy cow," Mick said, pushing at my legs, and Marcus slipped away out the door.

"Holy cow?" I chided. "Holy cow?"

Mick smiled, a gleam in his eye. "Thank you for coming."

"Oh, my pleasure."

"Come on, come on." The door was opened and closed again, and this time Marcus stayed inside. He bent over to pick up my shirt and skirt, one hand shading his eyes. "We don't want a scene. Dr. Toledo, you want to go back to your seat or go on home?"

I understood that in this building I'd need steering. "I'll go home."

"You'll miss the accolades," Mick said. "You'll miss how great I am."

"I can imagine." I zipped up my skirt, snapped my top, slipped my feet into my shoes. I bent over him, put my hands on each side of his face, gave him another kiss. Marcus held the door open as I walked to it, and when I turned to wave goodbye Mick was leaning forward the way he did during a game. He grinned, gave me his minimalist thumbs-up.

I followed Marcus through the twisting corridors, not rec-
ognizing a single thing from my trip in except for Tabitha, who
stood in an alcove waving and grinning, bobbing her befeathered
head. We reached the building lobby, and it startled me to see it
was still daylight, and confused me when, holding open the door
to outside, another woman was smiling and nodding, a woman
I recognized from somewhere—a nurse? an old patient?—but,
no, it was Elaine Johnson, the woman from ESPN, and in that
moment I was propelled into the parking lot and let go. "Thank
you, Marcus," I said, turning, and Marcus gave me a quick
salute. I bobbed through the sea of cars, the flags attached to
the window frames looking bizarrely festive, and I felt like a
singer borne across a mosh pit, uplifted by arms of collusion and
goodwill. *My God*, I realized, *people know. People wish us well.*
This thought was a consolation, this thought got me all the way
home. It was two or three evenings later that I collapsed, rolling
and sobbing, onto the cold tiles of my bathroom floor. Ginger
stood watching me from the door. She ended up licking the tears
off my face and arms, and that was the night we spent curled up
on my bath mat, covered by one of my towels.

A MONG THE THOUSANDS of people who died on September 11,
there had to have been some who left behind people like
me. The nonwidows and nonwidowers, survivors who were
not quoted in the paper, who might be whispered about and
pointed to, against whom brothers might be posted at funeral
home doors. People whose mere existence served to complicate
the rightful mourners' mourning. People who, despite this, had
to mourn too. People toward whom the dead indeed had had

feelings. I'm not saying we secret lovers were always right. But we were human, and we had our reasons.

"The tribute was fabulous," Karn said over the phone. "Even Leon Chiswick gave a speech, and Mick says he hardly talks. They had a bunch of Mick's old players, and all these coaches who talked about how much they respected him, and I wouldn't have expected this, the best speaker of all was Eluard's brother, what's his name? Evander. He used to be a druggie, but he's straightened out now."

I said the proper things. I was gracious.

"It was special," Karn said, her voice dropping, and I pictured her in her kitchen, or maybe the bedroom upstairs, somewhere Mick couldn't hear her, "and that's why I wanted to call you, because I should have let you come."

What answer could I have for this? Part of me was touched by Karn's kindness, part of me thought, "Good, she finally gets it," part of me, remembering Mick's hand on my naked back in the wheelchair, felt guilty, and part of me still wanted to strangle her. "Thank you for saying that," I managed, and Karn said, "Well, I meant it," and asked, almost beseechingly, if I minded if she called me again. "If something medical comes up," she said. "If there's something I don't understand."

O UR MONTHLY GROUP BUSINESS MEETING was held in Howard's office the first Tuesday in October after office hours. "Oh, good!" Howard said when I walked in that day. "Our monitor nihilist."

I sat down in the chair nearest the door. Howard distributed the September financial report and started talking. September had been a slow month—not, strictly speaking, our fault, but it showed the importance of maximizing each patient encounter.

JOHN BAREN: COUGHING UP YELLOW STUFF

I pulled my cellphone from my handbag and talked to Mr. Baren, then called in an antibiotic.

M. L. HOPKINS: BACK IN TOWN

"Oh!" I said, "that's good news!"—then looked up to see Jeremy and Howard eyeing me with irritation. "It's a patient of mine I haven't heard from since September eleventh," I said, dialing my phone. "She sometimes goes to New York on business." When M.L. answered I said three words: "Where were you?"

She'd been in Switzerland and she'd lost her passport.

"LeeAnn and I worried you could have been in the World Trade Center," I said, "because no one knew when you were coming back, and . . ."

Howard's voice was rising. "And Genie, particularly, is always forgetting to order them, so Lindy and I have devised a plan to . . ."

"Excuse me a sec," I said to M.L. "Lindy's a receptionist," I said to Howard, cupping my hand over the receiver.

Howard smiled in a patient way. "And all Genie has to do is put her diagnosis codes on the billing sheet, because Lindy will have a list of the codes that pay for monitoring, and if she spots one on the . . ."

"*Lindy's* going to order monitors on my patients?"

"Of course not. You'll be ordering the tests, by listing a bill-able diagnosis code."

"I'll make an appointment for next week," M.L. said. "It sounds like you're busy."

"I'm glad you're back safe and sound, M.L.," I said, and I hung up.

"M.L.?" Howard said. "Is she the one you asked me to unbill for her echo?"

That was back in July, before M.L. went overseas. "You weren't supposed to read that echo."

"It was a Wednesday echo," Howard said. "I'm the Wednes-day echo doc."

"Yes, but that one was supposed to come to me."

"What else aren't you billing her for, Dr. Toledo? Are you seeing her out of the goodness of your heart? Do you and she have a 'relationship'?" Howard knitted his eyebrows, tipped his head to one side. "Thursdays?" he said.

MELINDA ROTHMAN: HUSBAND TOM IS DEAD IN BED

Tom Rothman was my marathon-running patient with the used-pipe-cleaner coronary arteries. I reached for my phone.

"Couldn't this one wait?"

"It's a death."

Howard and Jeremy exchanged glances.

"Really," I said.

Jeremy said, "They'll probably still be dead in five minutes."

I called anyway. Mrs. Rothman picked up the phone. Her husband had said he felt tired and headed upstairs to lie down.

An hour later when she went upstairs to get a sweater, he was gone.

"Lawyers charge for phone calls," Howard said.

CLAUDIA HAD SET OUT a buffet in her and Toby's kitchen, and Toby's mother was the first one to dig in. It was a Sunday afternoon in early October. The tips of the leaves were turning orange and red and there was, that day, an almost turquoise sky. American flags were still up everywhere, but celebrity gossip and beauty tips were returning to newspapers and TV. Toby had stopped talking about water storage and precious metals and quitting his job.

"So this is fake meat?" Toby's mother said, peering at the patty on the serving fork.

"Basically," Toby said. "Don't worry, it tastes real."

Toby's mother plunked the fake meat onto her plate. "What's this green stuff?"

"Cole slaw with broccoli," Claudia said.

"Broccoli, I don't do broccoli." Toby's mother's hand fluttered above the dish. "Gas. What's on these vegetables?" she asked, moving down the table. "I see white specks. That's not garlic, is it?"

"For crying out loud, Kathy," said Toby's father.

Claudia said, "I spent a long time on this food. You should at least try it. It's good food."

I felt like clapping. The sensation was a surprise. I hadn't thought I'd feel, even for a moment, happiness again.

"I guess it's cardiologist food." Toby's mother glanced in my direction, spooning out a dab of cole slaw the size of a walnut. "We businesspeople aren't this healthy."

"This is food Toby likes," Claudia said. "He's a businessperson!" I saw Claudia look toward her husband, as Toby's mother busied herself with condiments, her back turned elaborately away. Toby lifted two fingers and blew across them, winking at his wife.

KARN SAID, "Our biggest problem with the morphine is the constipation. My God, do we need a bomb?"

Karn said, "Doc Leslie said three to six months, and it's been seven months!"

And: "You don't think I'm selfish, do you? He gets worn out even watching a TV show. I can't have every coach in Division One trooping in to see him!"

And: "Okay, you tell me. Do we really have to worry about anthrax?"

In the middle of October, Karn asked to meet me for coffee. Saturday would work, between two and three. The boys would be in and could look after Mick. Jessica alone with him didn't work because she wouldn't take him to the bathroom. Could I drive to Turkman and meet her? "It would mean a lot to me," Karn said.

We sat at a painted wrought-iron table in a coffee shop tucked into the corner of an antique store. Karn's face was lined and there were bags under her eyes; her hair was flat on the right side, as if it hadn't yet recovered from being slept on.

"I've been dealing and dealing with this, I'm dealing every day, and when those planes hit I thought, this is it, I'm not going to let this thing fester." Karn shook her head, not meeting my eyes. "I prayed about it. I asked the Lord what to do and He said Father DeMarco. And I talked to Father DeMarco and he said, Karn, you've got to forgive. Now, I've done that to Mickey, and he knows. So what I want now is to do it to you." Her eyes, full of challenge, met mine.

I reached for my mug, blue with pink flowers. "Forgive me?" I envisaged a ritual of some sort, a priest in black and beads of water.

"It's like Father DeMarco says, forgiveness is an act of . . ."

"Love," I interrupted, wanting this over with. People sprayed that word around like room deodorizer, a spritz here, a spritz there, how can anyone object and doesn't it smell nice?

Karn gave a tiny shake of her head.

"God," I tried again—another word used for deodorizing purposes.

"Imagination," Karn said, looking straight at me and raising her eyebrows. "Forgiveness is an act of imagination." She smiled at my obvious surprise. "My friend's a Jesuit, he doesn't say what you expect."

No, this was not what I expected. The high-end, brand-name priest, yes, but not the priest's concept. I tried to take it in as Karn kept talking. "See? When I forgave Mick I had to imagine what he was thinking, that he had his needs I didn't meet—we didn't talk enough, we were never together—and then if I'm forgiving you I have to think about how you felt, and honestly, there you were all alone, this all-alone lonely woman, and he's this powerful man who's willing to take his time for you once a week, for a couple hours tops, and maybe you thought that was all you deserved, and . . ."

Thank God there was no one else around to hear her. A

sex-starved man, a lonely woman—I gave a shiver at the paltri-
ness of motivation Karn had cooked up for us. "But we were
friends too"—*were*, how did that pop out of me?—"we com-
municated, we didn't just . . ." But how could I force this issue,
with Mick dying and his wife in front of me, insisting that she
understood? "But he was a married man," I admitted, "and I can
see now that we did wrong to you."

We did wrong to you. You couldn't acknowledge blame more
baldly than that. I could hear my words drop into Karn's memory bank, plinking like golden coins.

Karn wasn't the smartest woman. She wasn't subtle. I thought
of Mick's face lighting up as I walked through the hotel room
door. *You can have that kingdom anywhere. You can have that kingdom
in the . . .* I could have run into a wife who could imagine such
a thing, who could see the situation in all its glorious, painful
ambiguity—but Karn was not that woman, and I had Karn.

Just as well. There were details a forgiver should never know.

"There's something else I wanted to talk with you about,"
Karn said. "I've got him in the family room and we have that
big TV, but even now all that's on is anthrax and the hunt for
Osama bin Laden and it's not good to watch that stuff all day,
you know? It's depressing."

"It is," I said, relieved.

"Didn't you tape his games last year? Mick said you taped
his games from your TV. I thought maybe you could tape your
tapes, and I'll play them for Mick."

"I'd be happy to. I'd love to."

Karn gave me a closed-mouth smile and nodded eagerly, and
for a second—with her wayward hair, her lit-up eyes—I could
see her as a little girl. She looked a bit like Claudia, that same

sweetness. "I'm lucky you're Mick's wife," I said, to my surprise. But that wasn't enough. "Mick is lucky. You're a good woman."

"I try to be. Oh, honey," Karn said, "I'm lucky you were Mick's girlfriend." Karn's face knotted, as if she couldn't believe she'd said this, but an instant later she was beaming.

S WEETIE," Karn said, smoothing the hair back from Mick's forehead, "your friend Genie's here." A farewell visit to the hospice. The furniture was Danish modern. The sliding glass door opened onto a patio with a bird feeder. A pianist in the lobby was playing Broadway tunes. Karn waved me closer. "You can talk to him," she said. "Doc Leslie says he can hear us."

I felt like I was moving in a dream, that I was maneuvering from place to place without my feet or legs. Here I was, part of Mick's forbidden world, and even though there were moments when Mick's and my world seemed like the real one, in the end the social world reasserted itself, a great columned building gleaming in the sun. But at this moment, in this room, Mick's worlds were being brought together, and it was amazing—staggering, really—that Karn should permit this, that she should bang her gavel and peer out to the distant, darker corner of the room. Simple human recognition. Something most women in Karn's position would never have the guts to give. "Thank you," I said, looking at Karn, but Karn's eyes slid away, as if the very surface of my face were treacherous footing. She hadn't called me in the two weeks since our meeting in the coffee shop. Instead Bobby had phoned on her behalf, summoning me here.

"Mick?" I said, and in my imagination his eyelids fluttered, then opened, and I sensed Karn beside me shrinking like someone hit with a movie raygun, but then Mick's eyes were on me, and I forgot about Karn. "Mickey," I said, laying my hands on both sides of his face—Winslow's gesture with Eluard—"Mickey my love." He said nothing, didn't move his lips, but lifted up—laboriously, painfully—his right hand to touch mine. We looked at each other for maybe three seconds, the length of a held breath, and then Mick's eyes lost their touch on my face and his hand loosened and his eyelids closed. Goodbye. That was the way I'd imagined it.

Instead at the word "Mick," his eyes stayed closed. Instead I took his fingers, cool and mottled. "Mick? Mick?"

"He was awake last night," Karn said. She looked around to her daughter and sons for confirmation. Eric and Jessica were huddled sullenly in the corner, but Bobby, beside his mother, was looking at me eagerly, as if I were a prize fish that he'd landed.

"He talked to us last night," Bobby said. "We asked him if he wanted to see you and he nodded."

Mick never responded. Other people might say he had, but I was a doctor and I didn't imagine things. I didn't stay long. "Thank you," I said, hugging Karn at the door.

I suspect that, to people attending the funeral, the remarkable moment was when they first saw Karn and me together, when they looked out at the limousine or glanced up the aisle or craned their heads from their spot in the condolence line. For me, the surprise was at the door of Mick's room at hospice, when Karn and I embraced.

Odd that Karn had asked me for the television tapes to Mickey's games. The athletic director could have gotten her those tapes, or the Turkman TV station, or Frederick Flitt's parents, or any number of local fans. She really didn't need those tapes from me. Her request for them had been a sort of gift, a way she could involve me in Mick's care.

People have a hard time describing their chest pain. It aches, it hurts, it's heavy, it's pressure, I can't breathe right, it's like indigestion, it's like I'm scared about something, I can't describe it but I know that it's not right. So many descriptions converging on one cause, a lack of circulation to a section of the heart. You look at a cow's heart (structurally almost identical to a human's) and the arteries look like rivers seen from the air. You can take out your scalpel and cut into the cow heart and discover its grain and crossgrain; you recognize that a heart is nothing, in its essence, but a chambered hunk of meat. Yet it's the motor of our existence, the thing that we can't live without, and many of its aches are warnings that it's dying.

I've never had chest pain, not a twinge. I often wonder, listening to my patients, what heart pain would feel like for me, if my warnings (if I ever get them) will be heavy or ones I barely feel. I don't know. I do know that for months before I visited Mick at hospice I was constricted and tense, I couldn't fill my lungs deeply, I felt like something deep in me was wrong.

There's a cath lab moment, a gorgeous moment, when the dye squirts down a newly opened vessel and what has been a thread is now the fatness of a pencil. Such joy in that opening, a sense of cure, of hope. I felt—Karn's arms around me, the tapes on my mind—as if I were experiencing that feeling in my own body, that Karn had opened something up for me.

I can't say that everything after was easy, but nothing was terribly hard.

H ɪ, Genie!" The driver held the back door of the limousine open and Karn flapped her fingers in a wave—a gesture she had probably used since high school.

I was standing in front of another Marriott, this one only blocks from Turkman State. It was the second Saturday in November, a time of year when Mick would say that things were just beginning. It was raw and windy and the trees were nearly bare, a day when the warmest place in town might be an arena packed with people watching basketball.

"Hi." I climbed into the car. There were empty seats facing our seats; the window between us and the driver was closed. "Thank you for doing this. For having me, I mean."

"My pleasure," said Karn, and she laughed. Was she drunk? Tranquilized? I eyed her warily. No. Karn was scared too.

"She wants you two to be obvious," Bobby had said on the phone. "Have you heard of François Mitterrand? He was the

president of France and he was married and his mistress came
to the funeral along with his wife. Mom read about that somewhere and that's all she talks about."

"It'll be fine," I said to Karn now. "Mick had so many people
who loved him."

Karn was wringing her hands, looking out the window as
the car left the parking lot, and abruptly her wringing seemed to
crescendo, and I thought that I had said the wrong thing, that it
wasn't my right to use the words "love" and "Mick" in the same
sentence. "All his old players, his fans . . ." I said. I felt Karn's
quick glance my way, although I was slow to turn to meet it.

"I used the same florist," Karn said. "I mean, if people said
they were sending flowers I suggested my florist." She gave me a
coy glance. "It's nice when things coordinate, you know?"

We were both in black suits. Mine was trim and conserva-
tive, Karn's shiny and flowing and done in a knit fabric, with a
long jacket and a lapel trim of lavender ribbon.

"I'm trying to be very French about this," Karn said, her
hands still busy in her lap. "I break down, I get angry—I think
French, French, French. I wish I'd taken French in high school.
Bobby told you about Madame Mitterrand?"

I nodded.

"I know people thought, Oh, that's just how the French do
things, but she's human. And she must be a woman of great"—I
looked toward her, waiting for the word—"imagination."

The Jesuit, I thought.

"It was brave of you to invite me."

Karn nodded. "I know. I talked to Father DeMarco about
it. He's big on outward and visible signs. 'I'll bring her in the
limo with me,' I said, and he liked that. I might not be this nice

without those planes. Those planes hit, it softens you." Then, before I had a chance to respond, "Hold my hand."

Brave of me too, I thought, reaching toward Karn. Her hand was clammy and quivering, while my own hand felt warm, calm, strong—which surprised me; I would have thought it would be the other way around. "Your hand's cozy," Karn said almost wistfully, and I wished I could command my own hand to cool down. "It's okay," Karn said, as if reading my thoughts. "You make me feel better, you really do."

"You make me feel better too." We smiled shyly at each other, rode in silence several minutes. What do you think about, riding in the back of a limo on your way to your lover's funeral, holding hands with his wife? Everything and nothing. The wonderful strangeness of life.

"It was the sex," I said. "Ninety percent of the time." *Say something simple. Even if it's not true.*

"I thought so," Karn said. "I knew so." My gift to her, I thought at first, my payment. But then I realized that the statement gave me protection: in saying it, I'd found a way for Mick and me to keep our secrets.

"It's a weird thing," said Karn, her hand still tight on mine, "but I think that between the two of us we knew Mick."

"He couldn't spell, could he?"

"Terrible!" Karn snorted. "I think he was dyslexic."

We were close to the church, and we halted behind a line of cars backed up at a corner.

"We had a wonderful few months at the end," Karn said. "He thanked and thanked me." This hurt me—I had told myself that Mick spent his last few months with Karn as an atonement, but maybe it was something more—and Karn must have seen my surprise, because she looked away quickly and said, "He loved those tapes you sent."

"I'm glad."

Karn gave me a small smile. "People are going to stare at us." Her hand was warming up, while mine seemed to be getting colder.

"I couldn't have done it," I said. "Cared for him in a family room for months."

Karn shot me a quick appraising glance, gave my hand an almost painful squeeze. "You could have," she said.

"I don't know."

He'd be proud of us, I thought. I almost said it, but we were moving, turning into the church driveway, and Karn pulled her hand away to clutch her handbag. "Let me know if you need tissues," Karn said. The people standing on the asphalt stepped aside to let us through. Karn's hands were starting to shake again. "French," she murmured. "French, French, French."

The crowd was so thick I could barely see the church entrance. "Just follow me," Karn said, waiting for the driver to open her door.

Once I was behind Karn, it was easy. This was a funeral, this was theater, and here I was brought in for my supporting role. Karn was the gracious heroine, and simply moving up the steps she performed well. *Mick knew how to pick 'em*, I thought, and I wondered if he'd coached her, if he'd had her lie skin to skin on his hospital bed and said, "Genie's a good woman," and "Karn, you're my number-one seed." But maybe that was making too much of Mickey. Maybe Karn was simply a woman who'd tired of loss, who'd decided "blessed are the peacemakers" could be personal.

Marcus was holding open one of the church's big wooden doors. When he caught sight of Karn and me he dropped his head and gave a little smile, as if the sight of us together were some kind of happy proof, as if he were saying to himself, about Mick: *That devil pulled it off.*

In the receiving line in the church narthex after the service, Karn pulled me between herself and Bobby, with Jessica on Karn's other side. Karn had mascara running down her cheeks, but the service had made her calmer. "She was a special friend to Mickey," Karn said to the first person to offer condolences, nodding toward me in an encouraging, almost instructive, way, and the elderly woman glanced between the two of us before reaching for my hand.

"Are you a coach?" the elderly woman asked me. "Are women coaching basketball now?"

I shook my head and Karn said, "She's a doctor." The woman looked puzzled and Karn added, "A cardiologist!" and the woman smiled as if this explained things and moved down the line. There were several more people who passed in similar confusion, and then I was faced with a woman who looked like a younger, prettier version of Karn, and Karn was saying her usual, "This is Dr. Genie Toledo, who . . ." when she stopped herself and said, "What the heck. This was Mickey's girlfriend."

"Mother!" Jessica said. Karn raised a hand to shush her.

The Karn look-alike's eyes widened. "You're incredible," she said to Karn. "You're Mother Teresa."

"Not exactly," said Karn, and she and I both started giggling. I touched Karn's upper arm, the slippery warmth of the knit fabric.

"No," said the blond woman to Karn, "you are. I'm spreading it around"—and it must have been spread, because in a few moments I found myself with Mick's three sisters in a ragged spur off the main line, where most people didn't greet me, although Tom Kennilworth and his girlfriend both gave me a hug. There were some sports celebrities at the service whom Mick's sisters misidentified in loud voices, and at one point a storied coach, a coach from Monday Night, moved past us in a nimbus of hushed voices. Marcus was part of that nimbus, looking gawky and star-struck, as if he'd been transformed into a teenager. "A nice guy," the Big Coach was saying, "a solid coach."

I felt myself blanch. Barely a step above ho-hum. ". . . A lucky year and that guy," the Big Coach was saying, nodding in the direction of what I found to be, swiveling my head, Frederick, and then someone was in front of me with his hand out, a slight dark-haired man in a clerical collar. "My condolences," he said. "I'm Father DeMarco."

"The Jesuit!" I reached for his hand.

"Thank you for coming," the priest said, in his eyes the mild-est of assessments.

"Oh," I said without thinking, "my pleasure."

Behind me the Big Coach had gotten to Karn, and to my relief I heard him use words like "great" and "battler" and "vision." I half turned to better hear him and spotted Marcus, his eyes fixed and his face taut, blinking fast.

At this point Mick's sisters broke away from me in a flurry of excitement, having spotted a man they believed to be Michael Jordan.

When Karn left in the limo for the graveside she took her children with her but forgot me, and I had to get a ride with Marcus. Karn's apologies at the graveside, as I'd expected, were profuse. But her leaving without me, under the circumstances, was a minor slight, and I didn't hold it against her.

I WALKED INTO JEREMY'S OFFICE to check about call coverage for the weekend and surprised him at the window. He was holding a film in the air, peering at one of the nuclear heart scans. I knew what he was doing: he'd gotten an unexpected report from Howard on one of his patients, and he was checking the reading himself. "Jeremy?" I said, and he put the film hurriedly down.

I looked at Jeremy's desk and the film he'd slipped under a pile of charts. "Why don't we fire him?"

"Howard?" Jeremy laughed awkwardly. "He's our partner."

"He's a lousy doctor. We only hired him because we were desperate for weekend coverage and we couldn't get anyone better. So why are we keeping him?"

Jeremy stared. "Look at what he does for us! Look at his business acumen!" Taking in my face, Jeremy changed his focus. "We can't get rid of him. He'd be all over us with lawsuits. I'm not at the age for changes, Genie." His voice gained strength, as if he'd come up with an unassailable argument. "I want to finish out my practice years in peace. I think you'd want that too." College friends of Sukie's had been at Mick's funeral. *I didn't know you knew him,* Jeremy had said. *And I guess you knew him well.*

"He's a menace."

Jeremy gave an equivocating shrug of his eyebrows and tried without success to hide a smile. "He got you ordering monitors, that's for sure."

"He's incompetent," I said.

"That's a little strong."

"It's like we're harboring a virus. I don't trust his thalliums at all."

"Talk to him! Ask him to take another course. Take the nuclear course yourself."

"Do you trust his caths?"

Jeremy's posture shifted uncomfortably. "I'm not sure I want him in there doing peripheral angios"—the new revenue stream Howard was promoting—"but his diagnostic caths are fine." His diagnostic caths, not his angioplasties or stents: there was a lot in what Jeremy didn't say.

"Why can't we go back to Lenny reading our heart scans?"

"Come on." For the first time Jeremy's voice took on urgency. "Nuclear is a gold mine for us."

Jeremy and I had been friends for over twenty years, partners for almost sixteen. "So that's it," I said. "Proficiency and experience don't matter. Loyalty doesn't matter. Giving the best care to our patients doesn't matter. Only money matters." I turned away. "I don't have to be part of this."

Jeremy was already protesting, following me out his door and down the hall. "Genie, Howard and I aren't your enemies. We're your partners." I ignored him. I walked down my own hall and into my office and closed the door.

At Mick's funeral, the most moving eulogy had come from Frederick Flitt, who followed the Turkman State president and the athletic director. The Turkman president had equated his own struggles with chemical imbalance to Mick's battle with cancer, and the athletic director had envisioned Mick and Dashona Lykins meeting up to start a basketball team in heaven.

Frederick's address was much briefer, although he took, because of his leg brace, considerably more time to reach the pulpit. There was space for the congregation to ponder, with each footstep, the things he had recently lost. His quickness, his athletic career, his dreams for the future, his coach. From the pulpit, Frederick said he hated to think that Mick had put off treating his cancer so he could spend the season with his players. "I asked him about it, and he said our team was worth it," Frederick said. "I hope it was worth it. It was worth it to me."

I wanted to be part of something worth it. I hated the way I acted with Howard and Jeremy—snide, superior, angry. I should quit and set up my own practice, lease the empty office space upstairs. An outward and visible sign: I pictured my own name, alone, on a hall door.

I felt, again, Mick's hands assessing my shoulders. *Good, you can change a tire without me.* He'd be proud of me. He'd admire my guts, my caring, he'd tell me: You get 'em, cupcake. But he was such a man of connections and accommodations—such a team player, in a way—that there was part of my motivation he might not honestly understand. *I'm out of here, Mick. I'm cutting my losses. I'm gone.*

I could hire a receptionist I trusted (Claudia?), bring LeeAnn with me as my nurse, contract with Lenny to read my scans. Maybe Helen, who was always saying she'd had enough of the cath lab, could join me as a nurse practitioner. M.L. could design my decor. I realized in astonishment that Mick would know exactly what I was doing: I was assembling a team.

Martha Moody is the author of the national bestseller *Best Friends* and *The Office of Desire*. A practicing physician, she lives in Ohio with her family.